MURDER

in the SENTIER

MURDER
in the SENTIER

Cara Black

Published by
Soho Press
853 Broadway
New York, NY 10003

Library of Congress Cataloging-in-Publication Data
Black, Cara, 1951–
Murder in the Sentier / Cara Black.
p. cm.
ISBN 1-56947-278-5 (alk. paper)
1. Leduc, Aimee (Fictitious character)—Fiction. 2. Women private
investigators—France—Paris—Fiction. 3. Sentier (Paris, France)—
Fiction. 4. Computer security—Fiction. 5. Paris (France)—Fiction.
6. Terrorists—Fiction. I. Title.
PS3552.L297 M84 2002
813'.54—dc21
2002017566

Printed in the United States

10 9 8 7 6 5 4 3 2 1

Dedicated to the 'real' Romain, Nina, my father
and all the ghosts, past and present.

Every capitalist has a terrorist in the family.

—Anarchist interviewed by Jean-Paul Sartre
in *Libération*, a newspaper

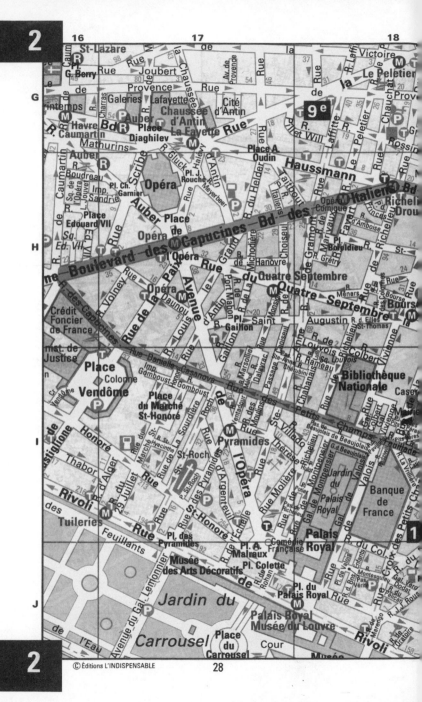

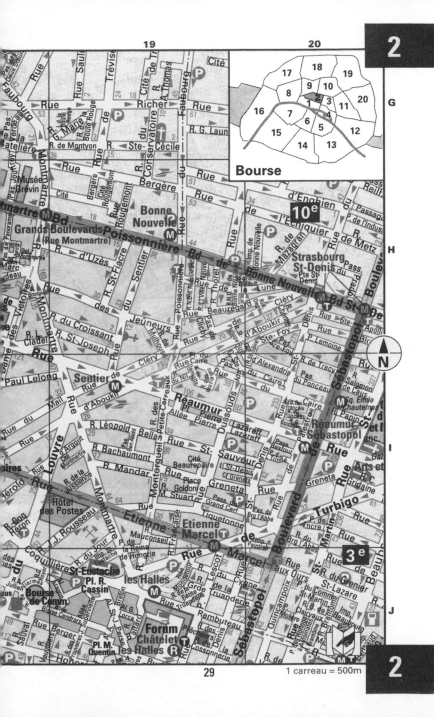

1 carreau = 500m

PARIS

LATE JULY, 1994

SATURDAY

AIMÉE LEDUC OPENED THE tall windows of her apartment overlooking the Seine, which bordered the tree-lined quai. She inhaled the scent of flowering lime. Despite the humidity she was glad to be home.

She knew it was time to let the past go. The hard part was doing it.

She sank into the Louis XV sofa, ruffled her short, spiky hair, and reached for her laptop. Time to concentrate on Leduc Detective's computer security contracts. Rent loomed. So did other bills.

Her phone rang. "*Allô?*" she answered irritably.

"Aimée Leduc?" a woman's voice asked.

"Who is it?"

A pause. "Daughter of Jean-Claude and Sydney Leduc?"

Aimée lost her grip on the phone. No one had referred to her that way in years. She recovered and put the phone to her ear again.

"You were looking for information about your father?" the woman's heavily German-accented voice asked.

Had word of her inquiries reached the right person . . . at last?

"You knew him?"

A long pause. Hope fluttered in Aimée's chest. In the silence, she heard the whine of a passing motor scooter from the quai.

"*Nein*, I knew your mother."

Her mother? "Sydney Leduc?"

"Her name was different," the voice went on. "But she talked about you."

The last time Aimée had seen her mother, she'd been wearing

an old silk kimono, standing at the stove and heating milk. Her
long hair, knotted and held in place by a worn pencil, escaped
down her neck. Rain splattered against their courtyard windows,
steamy from the heat. The Mozart piano concerto theme from
the film *Elvira Madigan* played on the kitchen radio. "Don't forget your raincoat," her mother had said, then "Crap," under her
breath, as the milk foamed and overflowed. Those were the last
words eight-year-old Aimée remembered her speaking.

Her mother left the apartment that day, while Aimée was at
school, and never returned.

"Do you know where my mother is?"

"Maybe we should meet and talk," the voice said.

"Yes, certainly," she said.

Then doubt hit her. Could this woman be an Internet crawler,
one who searched the personals and got innocent people's hopes
up? Someone with a sick idea of fun? "Excuse my caution," Aimée said. "But first I need to know . . ."

"That I'm for real?" the voice interrupted her. "I spent time
with your mother. You have a fish-shaped birthmark on your left
thigh, do you not?"

Aimée's hand instinctively went to her thigh. It was true.

"When can we meet?" Aimée asked.

"May I come over?"

Aimée paused, wary. "We could meet at a café . . ."

The voice interrupted again. "I'm leaving Paris tonight. You
live at 7, Quai d'Anjou on L'Ile Saint Louis, yes? I'll be there
soon."

"First, tell me how you knew my mother."

A car door slammed in the background.

"We were cell mates."

Cell mates? Her mother in prison? Her father never spoke of
her mother after she left, nor had her grandparents. Now her
curiosity was mixed with fear.

She looked over to her writing desk. Her answering machine

blinked red, filled with messages. She hit the play button. The first message came from René, her partner in the Leduc Detective agency.

"It's a go!" he shouted. "I'm about to ink our security systems contract with Media 9! I need to convince them to give us a retainer."

Finally! Her relief was cut short by the sound of the buzzer.

Miles Davis, her bichon frise puppy, growled as Aimée answered the door. The tall, bony woman at the entrance stared at her. Her brown shoulder-length hair was flecked with gray, and she wore brown pants and a jacket. A nondescript appearance. However, the Danish clogs provided an ambiguous clue: bad feet, or an artist.

"You are Aimée Leduc?" The woman's eyes, wide set and gray, sized her up.

"Yes."

"*Ja*, the resemblance is clear."

"Who are you?" Aimée asked, the words catching in her throat.

"Jutta Hald," she said, hefting her bag higher on her shoulder. "Give me five minutes, then decide if you believe me."

Aimée hesitated, then showed her down the hall into the old wood-paneled dining room.

"Going somewhere?" Jutta Hald pointed to Aimée's scattered luggage on the floor.

"How did you say you knew my mother?" Aimée asked, motioning for her to sit.

Jutta Hald sank into the couch. Outside Aimée's window, pinpricks of light reflected from windows on the riverbank opposite. Heat still hung like a damp blanket over the rippling Seine.

"Frésnes, prisoner number 6509," she said. "We shared a cell in 1976 and 1977."

Aimée gripped Miles Davis tight. "What had she done?"

"High crimes against the state. Terrorism."

Terrorism.... Her heart sank.

"Aren't you going to offer me coffee, something to drink?" Jutta Hald asked, glancing around the apartment. She emitted a faint vinegary odor.

"But that was years ago," Aimée said. Suspicion fought with her longing to know about her mother. "Maybe you should get to the point."

Jutta Hald's lips tightened. She unbuckled a brown leather bag, a ragged remnant from the seventies by the look of it.

"You're in your early thirties, right?"

"Close enough," Aimée said. "Look, I need to see some proof that you really knew my mother and that you're telling the truth."

"She wrote things. Lots of them," Jutta Hald said, pulling out an envelope. "The guard confiscated this during a lockdown. Take a look." Jutta Hald set the envelope on Aimée's marble-topped claw-footed table. She took out a package of unfiltered Turkish cigarettes, lit one.

The short hairs on Aimée's neck bristled as she reached for the envelope. "How did you get this?" Aimée asked.

"You don't know much about prison, do you?" Jutta Hald replied, taking a drag.

The yellowish creased envelope with FRÉSNES PRISON stamped on it seemed to glow in the afternoon light. Aimée reached for it, trying to control the trembling of her hands. What if the mother who deserted her really had been a convicted terrorist?

Her heart hammered. And what if it wasn't true?

Aimée expected something weighty with answers, reasons, and excuses. But the envelope felt curiously light as she held it suspended aloft in the rays of the sun.

For a moment, the face of her mother appeared to her. The carmine red lips and eyes crinkling in laughter. The warmth of her large hands, the faint smell of lilies of the valley—*muguets*—clinging to her clothes.

Aimée didn't want to open the envelope. She wanted to keep her mother hovering in the ether, between reality and her little girl's fantasy.

Slowly, she opened the envelope.

Inside lay a once-glossy sheet torn from a fashion magazine. Wrinkled and worn. She unfolded the paper carefully.

A washing-machine advertisement covered one side. On the other, a mother, sweater draped around her shoulders with sleeves knotted, strolled hand in hand with a child in the Palais Royal garden. The caption read, "Arpége for the active woman—for every part of her life!"

Under the caption was written in ballpoint pen: "Like Amy, like us . . . she loved that sandbox."

Below that, Aimée saw skillful cartoons of a pudgy mouse with long whiskers bordering the bottom of the page.

A dagger went through her heart. Her "Emil," her stuffed mouse! The ragged little *doudou* she had hugged to sleep every night. For years. How would anyone know this but her mother?

Aimée emptied the envelope. That was all. She looked at the envelope again. The name B. de Chambly written in pencil was visible in the lower right-hand corner.

"What's this?"

"Her name," Jutta Hald said.

"What does 'B.' stand for?"

"I forget," Jutta Hald said.

Not only her language but everything about Jutta Hald seemed stilted, forced.

"Tell me about her," Aimée said. She pulled Miles Davis closer.

"I was transferred. Later, I heard she'd been released."

"Released and then?"

"The trail leads to you." Jutta Hald crossed her spindly legs.

"Trail?"

Jutta Hald looked around again, surveying the faded eighteenth-century murals on the twenty-foot ceilings.

"How do you keep this place clean?" She didn't wait for an answer, but wiped her palm on the table. "You don't."

Not only was the woman rude, she'd come for something and Aimée didn't know what. Shouldn't it be the other way around, wasn't *she* supposed to give information to Aimée?

"You've lived here a long time, haven't you?"

She didn't like the woman's manner or anything about her.

"Instead of offering me information," Aimée said, "you seem to want something, Madame Hald. What is it?"

The woman's pale face cracked into a huge and disconcerting smile. She wet her fingers, tamped the cigarette out between them, and put the stub in her pocket. "No one's called me Madame Hald in years." Jutta Hald shook her head, still smiling.

For a moment Aimée thought she looked human. "Tell me about her," she repeated.

"I'm a little short of cash right now."

"Maybe you just found this piece of paper, just heard some stories. . . ."

"She was released in 1977; she must have come back here or gone to the cemetery."

Aimée had been in the *lycée* then. No, she'd been an exchange student in New York! Aimée grasped the table edge and took a deep breath. This woman spoke in riddles.

"What are you talking about?"

Jutta Hald looked down. Aimée wondered if she was assessing the carpet's price. "What do you want?" she demanded.

"You saw the proof," Jutta Hald said. "Fifty thousand francs."

Fifty thousand francs! That was office rent for six months!

"What do I get for it?"

"I have more things," Jutta said. "Her things."

"Things like her photo? Or a location where I can find her?" Aimée asked, hoping she didn't sound as desperate as she felt.

"Drawings," she said. "There's an anklet chain, an address book."

"*Her* address book?"

"Lots of foreign addresses in it," Jutta said, taking a deep breath. "*Aah*, free air, like I remember. So sweet after twenty years."

"But I don't have that kind of money."

In theory she did, but Leduc Detective's assets consisted of a bloated file of accounts receivable that René was trying to collect. He'd had little success with their big corporate clients, who took several months to pay up.

"I'm sure you can find it, if you want to," Jutta Hald said, jotting something in her notebook, then snapping it shut. "I came straight from prison, just to see you." She looked out the French doors that stretched from the floor to the ceiling. Then she picked up her bag and took another look around the room.

"You know," Jutta Hald said, "a little dusting and cleaning would improve this place."

Aimée bit back her reply.

"Guess you're not interested. I'm leaving."

Aimée hesitated. "*Non. . . .*" She didn't want the woman to leave. She had an urge to entreat Jutta Hald to stay, to ask what her mother had said about her.

Jutta Hald's eyes darted around the apartment. Her long fingers pinched and worried the leather bag handle.

Her fidgeting made Aimée uneasy.

"Think about it," Jutta Hald said. "Maybe when your mother came back to your apartment . . . she left something?"

Wouldn't her father have told her? Could her mother have come and gone without wanting to see Aimée, her daughter?

"This should convince you," Jutta said, pulling out a small bound notebook from her bag. Aimée saw a faded blue cover lettered in fine script: *Stories of Emil's Life: a Royal Mouse in the Louvre.*

Her heart caught.

"I believe she wrote this for you."

Something cracked inside Aimée. And those long-ago afternoons flowed back to her, afternoons spent together making up Emil's story, writing down lists of foods he ate, games he played, and pretending he slept in a matchbox.

"Look," Jutta Hald said, thrusting the notebook into her moist palms.

Aimée's hands shook as she grasped the musty cover. Afraid to drop it, she stopped, took a breath, then slowly opened the book.

The first page read, "For Amy."

"How did you get this?"

"No questions."

For a moment, Aimée was a little girl again, on her tiptoes tugging her *maman*'s skirt, trying to see what she drew. Always out of reach.

With her forefinger and thumb she gingerly turned the first page and read: "Chapter One—How Emil Came to Be Born on King Henri's Throne."

"You've seen my proof," Jutta Hald said. "Now admit it, she owes me my share."

"Share . . . what do you mean?"

Jutta Hald's lip curled. To Aimée's horror, she grabbed the book back.

"Wait, please," Aimée said. "I'll get the money. Please, be fair."

"Life's not fair . . . then you die," Jutta Hald said. "Think back. Didn't your mother ever send you presents, little boxes or keys . . . maybe drawings?"

"If she did," Aimée paused, saddened, "I never saw them." She knew her father would have destroyed them, just as he had destroyed everything else that had to do with her mother.

Jutta dabbed a slight sheen of perspiration from her forehead with a handkerchief. "Pills," she said. "Awful ones, they make me pee all the time." She shook her head. "Where's your bathroom?"

Aimée showed her. She took a long time before emerging.

"Tell me about my mother," Aimée asked once more. "About the terrorism."

"Now you're speaking with negotiation in mind, *ja?* We can share."

"*D'accord,*" Aimée said. Let Jutta Hald think what she wanted.

"She was a courier," Jutta Hald said.

"A courier?"

"That's the polite term," Jutta Hald said. "A drug mule describes it better."

"My mother, involved with drugs?" Aimée tried to keep her surprise in check. "From where and to whom?"

"Mostly Morocco," Jutta said, then shrugged. "Some hashish connection. But I knew her before we were sent to prison."

"How did you know her?" Aimée asked.

"Back then we were all part of a loose network," said Jutta Hald. "Rumor was her group shifted weapons, set up safe houses and printing presses for the Haader-Rofmein gang."

Aimée leaned against the wall. It was as if Jutta Hald had struck her. Over the years, she'd imagined various scenarios. But never a mother in league with the notorious seventies Haader-Rofmein radicals, who kidnapped people, bombed jails, and robbed banks.

Were her mother's terrorist activities connected to the bomb that had killed her father? Her hands shook. But that had happened much later. "This connects to my father, doesn't it? That's how you found me."

"Enough questions," Jutta Hald's voice trailed off. "You don't seem interested in buying the address book." A look of fleeting remorse crossed the woman's face. She dropped her gaze, unable to meet Aimée's eyes.

"One day after school I found a note from my mother taped to the door telling me to stay with our neighbor," Aimée told her. "That's the last I heard from her. If the address book will help me find her, I'll get the money. But I need some time."

"You have until tonight," Jutta Hald said. "Then I'm gone."

"But . . ."

"I'm leaving the country," Jutta Hald said, checking her watch. She rose and headed for the hall. "I'll contact you later. Have you a cell phone?"

Aimée gave her the number. The door slammed behind her.

Aimée sighed. Her checking account held less than a quarter of what Jutta Hald wanted. Leduc Detective had even less.

She ran to the French doors, flung them open, and leaned over the metal railing. The quai before her was empty.

Further up the street Jutta Hald emerged from beneath an over-hang, walking with a brisk step. Aimée called out to her. But the incessant beep of a van backing up drowned out her words. At the end of the quai, Jutta Hald stopped. She turned and looked up at Aimée, gave her a half-smile, then disappeared from view.

Aimée pulled on her denim jacket. She was dying for a cigarette and rifled through her pocket for Nicorette gum. But all she came up with was a software encryption manual and a travel-size flacon of Citron Vert. She'd stopped smoking last week. Again.

The longing to see her mother, that bottomless desire dormant for years, had returned. Even if she was dead, just to know where she'd been buried. Constant and nagging, it was like a piece of gravel in her shoe.

Aimée's worn Vuitton leather wallet held fifty francs. Enough for a taxi to the office of René's friend, Michel. She'd ask him for a loan.

She found a cab on Pont Marie and bummed a nonfiltered Gauloise from the driver. As they sped along the quai, she inhaled the harsh, woody tobacco, enjoying the jolt.

Michel had a cash-flow problem unlike most people's. He had too much. His fashion-house backers were cyber entrepreneurs in the Sentier, the district had been dubbed "Siliconsentier" by the press. But she and René were leery of the New Economy and of software start-ups, so they'd kept to corporate security.

Space came cheap in the Sentier, the hub of the wholesale rag trade and of the flesh trade. In the entire Sentier, green space scarcely existed. Six trees in Place du Caire, a spreading plane tree in square Bidault, and several struggling saplings in the Place Ste-Foy were the most notable exceptions.

The driver let her off on crowded rue Saint Denis, the medieval route to the royal tombs. Traffic had ground to a standstill. The knock of a stalled diesel truck and its exhaust fumes permeated the narrow street.

Dilapidated *hôtel particuliers*, once home to the Marquise de Pompadour, Josephine Bonaparte, and Madame du Barry, had been turned into fabric warehouses. Hookers kept the rent down in the old stomping grounds of Irma la Douce. But that was what attracted the start-ups. Urban decay with a new meaning, Aimée thought.

A dense haze of heat flickered in the late summer afternoon, lit by the still shining sun. She found Michel's place on rue du Sentier between Paris Hydro, a plumbing shop, and Tissus Arnaud, a fabric store. A welcome chill radiated from the limestone. Inside the seventeenth-century *hôtel particulier*, across from Mozart's former residence, Aimée rubbed the goose bumps on her arms.

The smell of sawdust and mold rose from the floor. Watermarked walls supported a high ceiling whose paint was peeling in the cavernous foyer.

The tall door stood ajar. Peering inside, she saw expensive state-of-the-art computer monitors on makeshift shelves. Cartons labeled *tissus en gros* were piled against the window. Remnants of antique industrial sewing machines for punching holes in leather sat by rusted metal clothing racks.

Michel Mamou was reaching high above him for the old gas line on the wall. He balanced on a sawhorse straddled over a three-legged table and a bench. His head just missed the old hanging light fixture.

"*Ça va*, Michel?" she asked.

"After I cap the gas, I'll feel happy," Michel grinned.

"Michel, I need a favor."

Michel's black-framed glasses under his wool cap pulled low didn't hide his pink eyes. Or his white eyelashes.

Michel often boasted he was the only albino Jew in Paris. Maybe that was why his family gave him free rein rather than insisting on his working in the wholesale clothing business.

He and her partner, René, a dwarf and a computer genius, had formed an unholy alliance at the Sorbonne, the albino and the dwarf, or "the freak brothers," as some had called them.

"What do you need?"

Before she could answer, he leaned back on the sawhorse. "Stop me if I've told you this one," he said, grinning. "*Écoute*, here in the Sentier, a wholesaler pays for his child's studies. First, the son spends three years in law. Then he studies business for three years at the fancy Hautes Études Commerciales. After that he obtains an M.B.A. from Harvard. Then he wants to study Japanese. But the father says, 'Listen, my boy. I paid all those years for your studies, but God says you finally have to choose your career: either clothing for men or clothing for women.'"

Michel slapped his thighs and roared. Aimée returned a thin smile as she checked the terminal ports on a nearby computer.

"Just like my uncle Nessim!" said Michel. "Too cheap to fix this place up but he lets me use it. I design upstairs. They figure they'll make money on me. If my designs never sell, his brilliant son says he can claim it as a tax write-off, a property value loss!"

Michel had placed high in the *Concours de Haute Couture*, the prestigious fashion competition organized by the Ministry of Culture. His talent hadn't gone unnoticed. He'd turned down an offer from a couture house in order to be his own boss.

"The ministry's sponsoring our couture showing in the Palais Royal," he said. "And my uncle's fronting the money but I need you and René to help me with my computer system."

"Michel, I doubt that there's any juice for the cables and fiber optic hookups," Aimée said, gesturing to the dusty fuse box.

"*Pas grave,*" he said. "With the Bourse nearby and Reuters news service in the *hôtel particulier* across the street, we've got plenty of available power."

But what about the rats who might gnaw through the cables, Aimée thought.

"Michel, about that favor . . ."

"I call it *couture contre couture*, couture in reverse," he said. "Rollerblading assistants, with laptops strapped to their chests, accompany the models to the clients and take orders and measurements. We do it all at once."

So that's why he needed the computers.

"Michel, I need to borrow fifty thousand francs."

But she spoke to Michel's denim-covered hindquarters. He was on his knees digging for a power source.

She got down on her knees and pulled Michel's arm.

"I need a personal loan. I'll pay you back."

Michel waved his pale arm. "OK, but better to funnel it through the business."

"What do you mean?"

"My uncle's company finances us."

"I thought your Siliconsentier friends helped you."

"My uncle made me a better offer." He grinned. "We could really use your expertise."

An alarm bell sounded in her head. The Sentier was notorious for under-the-table, cash-only deals. No receipts, a little payoff here and there. *Voilà!* No taxes. Was it wise for Leduc Detective to get involved with a project based on dodgy money? Did they have a choice?

"Let me discuss this with René," she said. "But I'm in a jam, Michel, I need fifty thousand francs right now."

"*Tiens*, come upstairs," Michel said. He'd crawled to the end of the room, where a scrollwork metal sconce hung above him by a frayed cord.

She followed him up the wide marble stairs, with deep grooves worn in the center. The banister snaked, coiling tighter as they mounted, like a serpent about to strike upward.

On the black-and-white-tiled landing, several bicycles leaned against the ornate wrought-iron railing of vine tendrils twined with grape clusters.

Aimée's cell phone rang. "Ready to offer me a drink yet?" said Jutta Hald in a dry voice.

Aimée's heart hammered. She didn't have the money yet.

"Paris is full of cafés, Jutta," she said. "There's probably one in front of you right now. I'm trying to get the money."

In the background, Aimée heard the *hee-haw* of a siren.

"There's something you should know about your mother . . ." The rest of Jutta Hald's words were swallowed by the blare of sirens.

"What should I know?" Aimée shouted.

When the noise receded, ". . . Tour Jean-Sans-Peur in twenty minutes" was all she heard.

"You know where she is?"

Pause. Aimée heard Jutta Hald draw in a deep breath.

"Twenty minutes. Bring the money," Jutta Hald said.

"But I must know . . . ," Aimée said.

But Jutta Hald had hung up.

This was the first chance in years to find out about her

mother! Despite her misgivings, she decided to talk with René and, clutching Michel's check made out for fifty thousand francs, she shouldered her backpack.

Out on the narrow street, pangs of longing hit her. For years, deep down, she'd feared her mother was dead. Yet she couldn't ignore the tissue-thin shred of hope Jutta Hald offered, at a price.

She cashed the check at Banque Nationale de Paris on the corner. As she turned into the Montorgueil, the tiled pedestrian walkway lined with upscale *boucheries*, more memories of her mother, with a pencil tucked behind her ear, floated back to her. She was always drawing, scribbling on anything—*brasserie* paper napkins, envelopes, the gas meter rate book. All of it had been burned by her father, except for the cardboard box from her fric-frac bicycle lock that had been bordered with doodles by her mother. Aimée had ceased using the awkward lock, insisted on by her father, after her training wheels came off.

Aimée passed a shoe shop and small *parfumerie* before she reached the fifteenth-century tower abutting what once was part of the old wall of Paris. Medieval dwellers had thrown garbage over the walls. After the population doubled, the next king constructed a new rampart and the centuries-old refuse was paved over. The ground rose higher and higher, hence the hills and buckling streets of the Sentier.

The tower, a four-story narrow rectangle of butterscotch stone with a tiled turreted roof, had been partially restored. She remembered it from a field trip in grade school. Some duke or marquis once hid there. There were so many, she got them mixed up.

The iron grillwork gate scraped as she opened it. Before her stood a leafy plane tree in the fenced stone courtyard sheltered from the busy street. Shadows from the leaves filigreed the stones. Late afternoon quiet hung in the air. On her right, an L-shaped *école maternelle* faced the tower.

No students. No Jutta Hald. Only darkening rain clouds and a crackle of hot wind.

According to the sign, tower tours were suspended until further restoration. "Welcome to the only remaining fortified feudal tower surviving in Paris," read the inscription. "Here, Jean-Sans-Peur, the Duc de Bourgogne, built a refuge following his assassination of Louis d'Orleans in the Hundred Years' War."

Tools, sandblasting equipment, and a small cement mixer sat under the tree. Work, she figured, had ended for the day.

Aimée cursed under her breath when her shoe caught between the stones. She turned it sideways. The heel of her Prada sandal, a flea-market find, emerged scratched and covered with grit. She scraped it over the iron *décrottoir* sunk in the stones. Mud-filled streets had been a part of medieval life.

Inside the tower, rays of light slanted in from windows and doors. So many windows. It seemed odd for a medieval structure built for defense, nestled against the old fortified wall. On her right stood a pile of rebar scraps.

Still no Jutta. She mounted the spiral staircase.

Cold air rose up from the stone. She rubbed her arms and looked up. Exquisite carved vaulting, a design of entwined branches with oak and hawthorn leaves and hop vines, wound above her. The circular staircase and open landings were islanded aloft. Shiny black birds perched in the turret. Their sharp cawing grated in Aimée's ears.

Was Jutta Hald playing games, screwing with her mind? She seemed to think that Aimée was hiding something, had some secret.

Footsteps shuffled below in the courtyard. Aimée peered through the window illuminating what had once been the small chapel. Carved ravens with two figures on a ribbed band supported the ancient ducal crest.

The damn birds had been around even then.

Aimée shifted her feet on the uneven stone. Below, a group of tourists stood in the courtyard.

The noise of churning gravel came from outside as she descended. Perhaps the workmen were starting another shift after all, she figured.

She moved into the pale Camembert-colored light ruminating . . . afraid Jutta Hald's words about her mother were true. And afraid this was connected to her father's death in some way.

But where was Jutta?

Outside, a trio of Portuguese-speaking tourists wandered and consulted maps on the far side of the courtyard. A workman in blue overalls shoveled sand in the rear. A shovel stood up in the sand pile. And Jutta Hald sat, huddled on a green bench next to the wall, her back to Aimée.

Odd, Aimée thought. She hadn't been there before.

"Ça va . . . Jutta?" she asked, sitting down next to her.

Jutta Hald, leaning against the grimy stone wall, said nothing. She smelled of warm hair tinged by the singular vinegary odor she emitted.

Aimée looked closer. Jutta Hald's eyes were wide with surprise. "Don't you hear me?"

No response. What was wrong with her?

She grabbed Jutta Hald's arm, started to shake her. But the woman's head slumped over, revealing pink gristle and congealed reddish matter sliding down the stone wall. The rest of her brain was still visible in the back of her skull, the part that hadn't been blown off.

Aimée reared back, unable to speak. She struggled to breathe. Blood from a black hole seeped through Jutta Hald's matted hair.

Jutta Hald had been shot at close range. Scarcely a minute ago.

Aimée looked up. She heard a burst of laughter from the tourists, the scrape of the iron gate in the courtyard, and crows cawing in the turrets.

No one had noticed.

Aimée had heard nothing. Neither had anyone else.

Was the killer still here?

She froze.

Jutta Hald's hands were empty. Her purse and the book she had showed Aimée were gone.

Aimée noticed the pill bottle Jutta must have meant to open, lying on her lap. She carefully picked it up and slipped it into her backpack.

"*Veja, veja!*" one of the tourists shouted. A woman screamed and pointed.

At Aimée and Jutta Hald.

The workman . . . where was the workman? Aimée looked around. Gone. She heard more shouting in Portuguese.

Quickly she approached one of the tourists, a woman with frizzy black hair, who backed away.

"Where did the workman go?"

Wide-eyed looks of fear greeted her. Aimée pantomimed shoveling.

A salvo of Portuguese rushed toward her. *Policia* was all she understood. She tried not to look at Jutta Hald's slumped corpse while she punched in 17 for SAMU—the *Service d'Assistance Médicale Urgente*—on her cell phone.

The Portuguese woman made for the gate. Aimée followed, scrutinizing rue Etienne Marcel, the street she faced.

"I'm reporting a murder," she said into the phone. "The shooter could be posing as a tourist or a workman."

"Address and victim?" the dispatcher asked.

Twenty meters away the Portuguese woman had found a *flic*. She was pointing at Aimée.

"Tour Jean-Sans-Peur on rue Etienne Marcel," she said. "A released prisoner from Frésnes, Jutta Hald."

The *flic* began walking toward her.

"Your name?" the dispatcher asked.

The *flic*'s pace increased.

"Call me a concerned citizen," she said, clicked off, and ran around the corner.

Saturday Afternoon

INSIDE THE OIL-PUDDLED GARAGE in a Paris suburb, Stefan adjusted his hearing aid to listen to the radio. "Former seventies radical" had caught his attention as he bent over a Mercedes SL 320 engine. "Jutta Hald, just released today after a twenty-year prison term, was found murdered . . ."

Stefan went cold. He dropped his wrench and leaned against the engine hood. His jaw worked but nothing came out.

The radio report continued. A police inspector interviewed by the reporter described the homicide location and a woman running from the scene.

The sound faded. Buzzed. Stefan fiddled with his hearing aid. *Scheisser . . .* only a low buzz. His bad hearing was the reward of his life of crime.

And then the news bulletin ended.

Stefan glanced nervously at the mechanic working across the garage. But the man in the greasy jumpsuit hadn't lifted his head from the engine hood he was working on.

Jutta Hald killed . . . on the day she got out of prison! Who was left who could have gotten to her?

Stefan straightened up. He recalled those days, back in 1972.

He saw the faces frozen with shock as his Red Army gang burst into the bank yelling, "Hands up, we're relieving you of your capitalist gains. . . . Long live the PROLETARIAT!"

Forget the ideology. The power had thrilled him.

He'd hated the nightly meetings, typing communiqués and discussing manifestos on *organized armed resistance* and *spreading the class struggle*.

But robbing banks had been fun. It was all spoiled when they had decided to aim higher, when they'd become too greedy. Yet it was their mistake. The biggest one.

So for twenty years Stefan had been underground. His Red Army group scattered: Jutta imprisoned, Marcus and Ingrid shot in the head; Ulrike had strangled herself with bedsheets in her cell. Beate and Jules had vanished. Mercenaries in Angola, last he'd heard.

Now Jutta was dead.

He stared down at his callused grease-stained fingers. Lucky thing he'd been good at fixing engines.

"*Alors!*" said Anton, the barrel-chested owner, waving a socket wrench in his face. "Come back to earth, a carburetor's waiting."

Stefan nodded and leaned over the gleaming engine.

Anton kept him despite Stefan's "dreamy fits," as he called them. Because if Stefan knew one thing, it was Mercedes engines.

He'd repair a thrown rod and make it smooth as lambskin, get a grinding gearbox purring in no time. If Anton suspected shadows in his workman's past, he ignored them. Ignored them in favor of the forty percent markup he made on Stefan's installation of Bulgarian-made parts stamped MADE IN GERMANY.

"Fits like a woman's stocking," Anton said loudly. He shouted at Stefan as if he were half-witted, not just partly deaf.

Stefan slid in the fuel injector, the socket wrench ratcheting with a grating noise side to side. Suddenly, his co-worker's air gun shot lug nuts onto the tires on the huge Mercedes truck opposite.

Like bullets.

Stefan jumped. He always did. He couldn't help it.

"This little lady could use some oil, then *voilà*," Anton said. "You know how to write the invoice, eh, Pascal?" His eyes narrowed.

Stefan nodded. He hated the name Pascal.

But he had to make do. Twenty years of making do, with his

glasses, dyed hair, and the hearing aid. He'd lost a lot of his hearing in the explosion. His hair grayed naturally now and he didn't need to retouch his sideburns and mustache every month.

Outside the garage, the *boulangerie*'s metal awning rolled down, slat by slat. In the square, Stefan saw the orange-red of the traffic light flicker in the twilight. Everyone was going home. Home to someone.

Stefan's mind rewound as he put his tools away.

After the robbery and kidnapping, the gang had regrouped at their safe house in the woods.

But safe it wasn't. Some maggot had informed on them.

Stefan had been in the back barn, repainting the car, when smoke, screams, and loud thuds reached him. The *flics* were fire-bombing the old farmhouse. He ran from the burning barn through the woods, as rippling gunfire tore the alder tree trunks behind him. He ran for miles without stopping, his body scratched and torn when he emerged.

He was panting and exhausted when he came out of the underbrush and crossed over the highway, running from the sirens. A rusted-out Opel 127's wheels were askew, its right front tire stuck in the ditch. Stefan helped the plaid-jacketed old hunter, who was grinding his wheels, to get out of the mud. He helped him push the car onto dry ground, then asked for a lift. Glad for the help, the hunter happily obliged and even shared his black bread and wurst.

Then the bulletin concerning the shoot-out had come over the radio. Stefan had never forgotten the hunter's face when he realized Stefan's identity. The man tried to hide his reaction but his shaking hands on the steering wheel gave him away. He pulled over onto an Autobahn emergency turnout and got out, saying he felt sick.

But in the rearview mirror, Stefan saw the old man stumble and run toward the Autobahn, waving his arms frantically for help. Terror-stricken and confused, he plunged headlong into oncoming traffic, speeding vans, and whizzing cars. His body was batted like a marble in a foosball game as vehicles tried to brake, screeching and swerving. Stefan grabbed the Opel's wheel, pumped the accelerator, and took off. The last image he had was of the man's body lying in the road like a rag doll as cars piled up.

Near Frankfurt, Stefan careened the car off the highway into rocky brush. But not before he took the old man's wallet, scraped the serial numbers off the chassis, and buried the license plates under a pine tree. Then he hiked to the train station.

The police would think he'd escaped. Now he'd be on the run for the rest of his life even though his joining the Haader-Rofmein gang was only a fluke.

No. Face it. He'd joined to impress the long-haired girl who'd ignored him, chanting, "Death to imperialist tendencies" when he bought her a beer. He would have done anything for her. He'd ended up driving the getaway car on the fateful day.

Stefan shook the memories aside as he walked home.

Several years ago, he'd begun therapy in Poissy, not far from his village. Why not? Everyone had secrets. His weighed heavy. Especially the old hunter, who hadn't had a proper funeral, and Beate and Ulrike. He still wished he'd helped them instead of running.

In 1989, he'd verged on confession—there were rumors of an amnesty. But the Wall came down. The Stasi files appeared. Nasty East German files, sure to convict him. He kept silent.

Now there was no hope of presidential pardon or amnesty. He came to the conclusion that Jutta was looking for the rest of the Laborde stash they'd stolen: the bonds, the paintings, and more. She'd known where some of it was hidden. He'd have to get to it before her killer did.

"TATOUAGE," FLASHED THE ORANGE-PINK neon sign around the corner from the tower on rue Tiquetonne. The area was full of apartments and shops, combed by narrow alleys, and courtyards. Sirens wailed in the distance. From a doorway, Aimée saw the *flic* round the corner, then stop and question a woman with shopping bags. Quickly, Aimée slipped inside the tattoo parlor.

The dust-laden velvet curtains had known better days. Muggy air, tinged by sweat and old wine, clung in the corners. An insistent, low whir competed with a Gypsy Kings tape.

In the large room, a woman in a violet smock, her back to Aimée, filled jars with varying shades of makeup. Aimée stepped into a long curtained cubicle.

Seated before the mirror, a tanned, topless woman fanned herself with a *Paris Match* magazine. From the edge of her left shoulder to the top of her spine, an intricate lizard design was etched in green-blue. Fine droplets of blood beaded the edges. Hunched behind her, a man with a whirring instrument stared intently at her back.

Aimée winced. The price of adornment was minimal to some. Not to her.

A muscular man in a tight white T-shirt ducked inside. Tattoos covered his arms: His bald head shone under the reddish heat lamps. He smiled at Aimée, revealing a row of gold-capped teeth.

"Have you chosen?" He pointed to a seat like a dentist's chair, hard and metallic.

"Chosen?" she said, edging back toward the curtain.

"Your design," he said, pointing to the walls lined with photos of tattoos.

The coppery smell of blood made her uneasy.

Outside the curtain, she heard the *flic* questioning the makeup artist in the next room. No way could she go out there now.

The tattooist tapped his fingers on a Formica table lined with instruments.

"So, what would you like?"

Nothing, she wanted to say.

"Try the old Pigalle gangster designs," he said. "A rooster symbolizing hope, the butterfly with a knife dripping blood for *joie de vivre.* . . ."

"Like hers," she whispered, pointing to the tanned, topless woman.

She pulled up her shirt and put her finger midback to the left of her spine. "Here. I don't want to look."

"Aah, a Marquesan lizard," he said. "The symbol of change. With the sacred tortoise inside?"

"*Oui*, delicate and *trés petit.*"

The man's smiled faded. His lips pursed. "That motif doesn't work in less than a six-millimeter format."

Footsteps approached.

"Go ahead." She nodded, then put her head down. She covered her face with a towel and pulled a sheet over her leather skirt, praying it would be over quick. And that the *flic* would leave.

"I trained with Rataru in Tahiti," he said, as if Aimée would know. "Of course, he's the master of the Marquesas."

Not only would it hurt, René would never let her forget this.

He swabbed her back with alcohol. Cold and tingling. He rubbed his hands, probably in glee.

"*Tout va bien*, Nico?"

So the tattooist was Nico.

"No complaints, Lieutenant Mercier," he said.

From the direction of the conversation, she figured the *flic* stood a meter away. Keep going, she thought, don't stop.

"Any news for me . . . anybody run in here?"

Aimée's heart hammered. Something clattered in the metal tray by her ear. If she bolted, she'd send the tattoo machine flying but she wouldn't make it to the door.

"We sent runners for coffee," Nico said, "but they're not back yet."

So Lieutenant Mercier was the friendly type, taking the pulse of his *quartier*. Maybe he contacted his informers here. Or he was on the take. Or looking for her.

The tattoo needle ripped her flesh like a fine-toothed hacksaw. Twenty tears to the minute, searing and precise, the needle punched tiny holes in her skin. She blinked away tears, gritting her teeth, praying it would end soon.

After what seemed like forever, Aimée heard Mercier move away. A long while later the tattoo artist switched off his torture machine.

Aimée got up slowly and reached for her wallet. "In case service isn't included," she said, slipping him an extra hundred-franc note.

"Like a complimentary makeover?" a woman's voice asked. "You'll love it."

Aimée turned and saw a petite smiling woman standing near the chair. Beyond the curtain, another *flic* had joined Mercier.

"Seems it's time for me to get a new image," Aimée said, her mouth compressed.

"Speed bump . . . like it?" the makeup artist asked, as she traced the arch in Aimée's brow using a tapered makeup brush. "It does wonders for those lines."

Aimée's shoulders tightened in pain. The tattoo hurt. In the outer room, Mercier's voice competed with the whirring of the tattoo needle.

"Try this too," the woman said, holding out swabs of glittery peach powder. "This brightens up your skin tone and makes you glow. Positively glow." She brushed a velvety sheen over Aimée's arms, shoulders, and neck. "I'm writing a book," she said, talking nonstop, "called *How to Look Like a Goddess When You Feel like a Dog*. Full of useful hints for fast-living people who have to look good at airports even in times of excess or trauma." The woman grinned. "You know, big sunglasses, fur collars to make you appear frail and exotic, that sort of thing."

By the time Aimée got out of the *tatouage* parlor, her back ached and she positively glowed. The *flics* were gone and she'd signed up for a copy of the book.

Aimée's uneasiness followed her all the way home. She shuddered, thinking of Jutta Hald. Pathetic, desperate Jutta. As greedy and evasive as she'd been, Jutta didn't deserve to have her brains splattered on a stone wall. No one did. After twenty years of prison, she'd paid her dues.

Part of Aimée wanted to forget she'd ever met Jutta. Another part of her said Jutta's killer might be able to lead to her mother.

From her backpack she pulled out Jutta's pill bottle. Inside was a balled-up sketch of the tower along with a torn magazine photo. In it, a salt-and-pepper-haired man was holding an award. The caption read "Romain Figeac."

She recognized the name. Romain Figeac, the *monstre sacré*, Prix Goncourt–winning author, and sixties radical. In the seventies he'd been the *ruine du jour* and in the eighties, *passé*. Now the old man was still a bleeding liberal, according to his own autobiography. Or was that his wife, an actress . . . she couldn't remember.

She ran her fingers over the smooth blue tiles on the basin counter. Was what Jutta Hald told her the truth . . . any of it? Aimée wondered if the address book Jutta had waved by her had really been her mother's.

She turned on the tap and stuck her head under the cold water. Squeezing her lavender soap, she washed the tattoo parlor smell out of her hair, then shook her wet locks like a dog. But it didn't clear her head. Her mind was spinning.

Jutta Hald's words kept coming back. She had asked if Aimée's mother had sent her something. And then Aimée realized a bathroom drawer had been left half open, her towels hastily folded, and the medicine cabinet ajar. Nothing was missing but what had Jutta been searching for?

Then the realization hit her. Someone had *killed* Jutta. She could be next!

Nothing made sense, yet it connected to her mother.

Since the day her mother left, Aimée had been desperate to know what happened to her. Now she had a chance to find out. Slim at best. But more than before. She had to pursue it.

She went to the kitchen and plugged in the small refrigerator. It was empty and emitted the hiss of slow-leaking Freon. She filled Miles Davis's chipped Limoges bowl with steak tartare left from the train trip. He sniffed, then cocked his head as if to say, *"What's this?"*

"Sorry, furball," she said. "I'll pop into the *charcuterie* later."

Her seventeenth-century apartment needed an overhaul: central heating instead of feeble steam radiators for bone-chilling winters; plumbing more current than the nineteenth century; enough juice to keep a chandelier, computer, fax, scanner, DSL line, and hair dryer on concurrently; and access to her basement *cave* for storage. Too bad the *cave* had been declared a historical treasure because it had provided an underground escape route to the Seine for nobility during the Revolution, and had been closed for repairs. Closed for as long as she could remember.

She kept buying lottery tickets. Someday, she told herself, *Architectural Digest* would visit. But maybe not in her lifetime.

She remembered her mother calling her *Aa-mee* in a flat American monotone, unlike her father's French *A-yemay*, his syllables dipping at the beginning. Had he refused to speak of her mother, because of shame that he, a *flic*, had a wife in prison?

Aimée consulted the Minitel. No listing for Romain Figeac. She tried his publisher, Tallimard.

"Can you help me reach Romain Figeac?"

"*Tiens*, this is a joke, right?" the receptionist said.

Taken aback, Aimée paused. "If you can't give his number, his address . . . ?"

"Such bad taste," the receptionist interrupted.

"Look I need to talk with him," said Aimée.

"Don't you know?" the receptionist said.

"Enlighten me."

"His funeral was yesterday."

SUNDAY

AIMÉE SURVEYED THE MIRRORED Café d'Or on busy rue d'Aboukir and tapped her chipped red nails. A fly landed on the sugar bowl tongs and she shooed it from the counter. Few patrons were inside on this sun-filled day, most sat under the awning on the *terrasse*. Shadows from the few clipped the trees on Place du Caire dappled the sidewalk.

Christian Figeac, the deceased author's son, was twenty minutes late to the café he'd chosen for their meeting. She'd contacted him via his father's publisher, saying it was a police matter. After her bike ride from the office, she'd ordered an espresso. And waited.

A tall man with stringy sandy hair entered. He was in his late twenties, a few years younger than she was. He wore a synthetic leather jacket, silver and tight, over a black shirt. His deep gray eyes sought her, nailed her, and she knew it was him.

"Christian Figeac," he said simply and shook her hand. His palms were moist and warm. He looked around, warily then said, "Let's sit down over there." He pointed toward an old-fashioned leather banquette.

"For meeting me, *merci*," she said, bringing her espresso with her. "I apologize for the bad timing. . . ."

"I only agreed because you can help me," he said.

Help him?

"Your father might have known my mother," she said. "That's why . . ."

"He knew lots of people," Christian Figeac interrupted, apparently uninterested.

"Ever heard of Sydney Leduc or a woman named de Chambly?" She remembered the name B. de Chambly from the Frésnes Prison envelope.

Christian Figeac shook his head. He rubbed his nose with his sleeve.

"What about Jutta Hald?" Aimée asked. "Did she call or visit you?"

He waved his hand dismissively. A nervous twitch shook his jaw every so often. "Listen, I can't go in there anymore."

"Go in where?" She felt sorry for him but so far this conversation was going nowhere.

He pulled out a thick cigar, Cuban by the look of it, and proceeded to light the end. But his hands shook, a steady tremor.

"It's Papa's atelier, you see," he said, his eyes boring into hers. "Can't seem to sell it. The realtor told me to spruce it up, you know, the vanilla treatment. But this is the 2nd arrondissement on the tony Right Bank. The place should sell itself."

"I'm sure you're right," she said. "Now, I'm sorry to keep bringing this back to Jutta Hald, but I think she was looking for your father."

"Now she can find him under the earth with the worms."

He sounded bitter. And clueless.

"It's the ghosts, you see," he leaned forward, a stricken look on his face. "They won't let me."

Maybe he was insane. A dead end.

She found a ten-franc piece and slapped it onto the table.

"Look," Aimée said, opening her backpack, "you're going through a hard time. I wish you the best, but . . ."

"Wait, please." He grabbed her arm. Perspiration beaded his upper lip. She hadn't seen him order but a white-aproned waiter appeared with an espresso, set it on the table for Figeac, and whisked her ten francs away.

"I'll think about those names you mentioned. What were they again? Signe? And who?"

"*Tiens*, I've got to go," she said, trying to slide off the leather banquette. But her leather skirt stuck to the seat, making a sucking noise and riding up her thighs.

"Hear me out." He grabbed her arm again and wouldn't let go. His cigar smoke got in her face.

She kept her tone civil. "I came here to find out if there was some connection between your father, Jutta Hald, and my mother—"

"Papa committed suicide last week," he interrupted. "It was ten years to the day since my mother did the same thing." He puffed on his cigar.

Now the story came back to Aimée. In the seventies, his mother, an American actress, was rumored to be carrying a French terrorist's baby. She miscarried and had a breakdown. Her career was over. Several years later, on the anniversary of the miscarriage, her body was found in her car in the Bois de Vincennes. Too many pills.

"Papa wanted to clear her name," Christian Figeac said. "Reveal how Interpol targeted her."

"Hadn't he done that before?" Aimée remembered him being interviewed on television, delivering a tirade against the "establishment." He had distinctive blue eyes and a long face. A potent cocktail of literary talent and liberal political blunders.

"Papa said there were documents," he said. "I think he was working on something to do with that. The research had been his reason for living. After that he took his life."

"Are you sure the book was about Interpol . . . not about the terrorists?" What if he'd been researching Haader-Rofmein, something dealing with Jutta, or with her mother? She leaned forward, interested. "Did he mention the Haader-Rofmein gang?"

"Haader-Rofmein? Maybe, I'm not sure. He'd had a dry spell," Christian Figeac said, looking down. He knocked cigar ash into the Ricard ashtray. The ashes missed and particles floated onto his pants. "And then I heard him working."

"Working on what?"

"He never talked about what he wrote. Taboo. A jinx, he said."

Aimée thought she could see sadness in Christian Figeac's eyes. And a kind of defeat. Had he felt sidelined, growing up in the shadow of famous parents who'd been obsessed by the unborn child? Aimée felt sorry for this man.

"Why would your father take his life now?"

Instead of answering her, Christian Figeac shrugged. "Late at night," he said, his long lashes fluttering, "the time Papa used to work in the breakfast room, I think I can still hear him pounding on typewriter keys. Strange, because he wrote everything in long-hand first. I open the door and it's empty, of course, but it's like he's trying to tell me something."

"Rational consideration would preclude that, Monsieur Figeac," she said.

Christian Figeac was delusional but maybe she could turn it to her advantage. Find the link to her mother, figure out what Jutta Hald had really wanted. "If you're the literary executor for your father's estate," she said, "may I go through his papers?"

Christian Figeac pulled a crumpled paper from his jacket pocket and smoothed it out on the marble-topped café table.

"How much?" he asked, writing her name on the check.

"For what? My field is computer security, data recovery for firms and corporations."

"Someone's stalking me," he said, his eyes huge. "Twenty thousand do for a retainer?"

"A retainer for what?"

"Find out who's stalking me."

That got her attention. She leaned back against the banquette. If she took his check maybe she could pay the rent as well as find out about her mother.

Outside the café window, a Pakistani man with a pushcart full of cloth rolled his eyes at a burly man making deliveries whose truck blocked the street.

"I'll take the job on the condition that I can have access to your father's papers," she said. "They may contain information about my mother or Jutta Hald."

"*Tant pis* but I've never heard of them."

"Think back. Didn't an older woman, Jutta Hald, come to your . . . ?"

"But it's so like something my father would do," he interrupted. "I've even heard their noises."

"Noises?" Aimée felt like standing up. "Is that why you think someone's stalking you?"

"The funny thing was, when I checked in the morning, the room had been disturbed. Discreetly, but I could tell."

"How's that?"

"The dust, of course." he stared at Aimée. "Footprints in the dust."

AIMÉE AND Christian Figeac reached the door of 107, rue de Cléry, a block away. The building occupied the corner of the narrow street where it met rue des Petits Carreaux. The inner courtyard, with ivy-covered facades and deep balconies, seemed like another world, an oasis far removed from the hookers on Saint Denis, from the Metro and the bus exhaust.

Inside the tall-ceilinged apartment, once an industrial workshop she figured, stood a few rattan café-style chairs. Apart from the formal dining room, with its long table, the place had few furnishings. In the front of the atelier were huge period windows encased in dark green iron, overlooking the rooftops across the narrow street.

Christian Figeac's face was a mask, yet anxiety emanated from him.

"Something wrong?" Aimée asked.

He tore out of the room and rushed down the hallway.

Aimée followed.

"Idrissa, Idrissa, I'm back," he shouted.

By the time she'd caught up with him, he was leaning against the wall of the dark-timbered kitchen.

"Weren't you going to show me . . ."

"She's gone," he interrupted.

"Who's gone?" Aimée asked, looking around. A blue iron La Cornue stove filled a third of the kitchen.

"My girlfriend, Idrissa. Idrissa Diaffa," he said. "Her bags, her things, her prints gone from the walls."

Piles of dishes, encrusted with dried food, filled the porcelain sink. A pot of turmeric-peanutty-smelling stew sat on the cooktop.

"I'm sorry, but we really need to continue talking about your father's work."

"After I sold the apartment, we were going to invest in Gouée, that island in Senegal," he said, his tone wistful. "She's from there."

Then he sniffled and his head drooped. Like a beaten dog, Aimée thought. He wiped his runny nose with his jacket sleeve.

"Anyway, I must get rid of this museum," Christian Figeac said. "Sell it."

He seemed to gather himself together. Had this happened before, she wondered, or was he used to being abandoned? Aimée noticed a dark wood-paneled room off to the right. The room was sealed—protected from trespassers—with glass. Women's clothes were strewn on the bed, leopard jumpsuits and fringed vests. He followed her gaze.

"That was my mother's room. *Le Palais de Nostalgie*, I call it, like a shrine. Papa wouldn't let it be touched."

The ghoul factor, she thought. Someone would want this apartment just for that . . . not to mention the location.

She noticed the scuffed woodwork and cobwebbed corners.

"Do you live here?"

"Most of the time," he said, scratching his arm. He kept his jacket on in the musty apartment. "But I haven't been back since I heard the typewriter."

"The typewriter?"

"Papa had a typewriter."

What was this about? He knew his father was dead. It was hot and sticky and she felt cranky.

"Why don't you show me your father's room, tell me about his work," she said, keeping her voice level.

"There's nothing to see," he said. "Take my word for it."

Christian seemed intent on being contradictory. Something sad clung to him, like a shroud.

"Sorry, all this must be difficult," she said. "And I understand it's painful but I can't help if you don't let me see it."

"The room hasn't been cleaned." He stood, hesitant.

"No problem." Even better, but she didn't say it.

In the front hallway, Christian Figeac took a ring of old-fashioned keys from a hook. He tried several before one grated in the lock, which opened with a loud click that echoed in the parquet-floored entrance.

The twenty-foot double doors swung back to reveal a rectangular breakfast room, spacious and light due to floor-to-ceiling windows.

"Doesn't look used much."

"I haven't stepped inside since . . ." He paused. "The cleaners should be here soon."

"Maybe your girlfriend . . ."

"Never," he said. "She didn't like rooms where spirits linger."

"Lingering spirits?"

"That's why I curse him," Christian Figeac said. His voice had slowed. "We told the newspapers Papa took his life in bed. But he shot himself here." He pointed to the long panel of a desk, in the middle of the room. Chocolate-looking smudges covered the wallpaper behind the chair.

Poor Christian Figeac. Why would a father let his son discover that?

"Right at his desk," he said. "Couldn't be bothered to do it in the park. Left his brains on the wall for me to find."

Like Jutta Hald.

"Did he leave a suicide note?

"Just 'Goodbye' and a Mallarmé poem on the typewriter. One my mother loved."

Every poem has an unwritten line. In this case, Aimée thought, a tragic one.

She thought again of Jutta Hald.

"Sorry to ask, but was he holding the gun?" It would have had to be a large caliber for a bullet to cause splatter like that.

"I think so . . . no, it had fallen onto the floor."

"It fell on the floor?" she said. Something didn't add up.

"The room was dark, Papa was slumped over."

Had shock confused Christian Figeac?

"Over his desk?"

Christian Figeac's face contorted. "Maybe it fell when I tried to pull him up."

The desk and chair were in the middle of the room, the wall a few feet away. "Was it a handgun?"

He nodded, adding, "Papa drank, a lot. We wiped up most of the whiskey."

And the evidence of foul play if any had existed.

"Were the *flics* suspicious?"

"They weren't involved. It was a suicide. Papa always said true writers die for their art."

"How's that?"

"Molière, for example—he died in his chair onstage at the Comédie-Française."

She walked past the desk. "Where was the manuscript he was working on and his research notes?"

Figeac's eyes welled with tears. "Idrissa said there were things in boxes. I don't know."

He sniffled, rubbing his dirty sleeve across his eyes.

Aimée bent, then stopped. Footprints trailed across the dust.

Either someone had walked backward in his own footsteps, or he had floated up to the ceiling. She wasn't so certain it hadn't been the latter. Stale dead air filled the space. The calendar on the wall was opened to July. . . .

"Where's the gun now?" she asked.

Christian Figeac looked stricken, as if his memory had blanked. "So much happened at once . . ." he trailed off.

"What kind of gun was it?"

"Papa's prized possession was a fancy-handled one, a gift from Hemingway, his favorite author. They drank in the Ritz bar after the war. He kept it over there."

Aimée looked. A plaque beneath empty glass read .25-CALIBER DESIGNED BY TOCHER FOR HEMINGWAY. The outline where a small pistol had rested was visible against the yellowed background.

"The autopsy results?"

"No *flics*, no autopsy. Our family's tired of public circuses."

She knew, in cases of suicide, families had the right to refuse an autopsy and insist on immediate burial. The police would be happy to declare it a suicide if the corpse was that of an old geezer who drank. Even more so if he'd left a note. Or if he was a depressed writer suffering from writer's block.

But Romain Figeac, according to his son, didn't fit the latter category. And the wall smudges bothered her.

Still, she was here to find out about her mother. And Christian Figeac wasn't asking her to investigate his father's death. Just his ghosts.

"Papa's big fear was when he died someone would take photos and sell them." He looked away. "Like they did of my mother."

Not only bad taste, Aimée thought, but sick.

"Where would your father have kept his files?"

No answer.

Aimée turned around.

Christian Figeac had disappeared.

Aimée walked toward the kitchen. She wanted to go through Romain Figeac's papers, search for connections to her mother, Jutta, or Haader-Rofmein. The similarity of Jutta's and Figeac's deaths was inescapable.

"Monsieur Figeac?"

No answer.

She edged down the hall, peering into the dining room. The Prix Goncourt plaque, tarnished, and a *médaille d'honneur* sat in a dusty glass case. A framed yellowed newspaper clipping about his mother's Cannes Film Festival nomination occupied one wall.

She agreed with Christian Figeac—the place felt like a museum. A *frisson* of apprehension went through her. For a split second she wondered if he would follow the route of his parents . . . with his girlfriend gone, in a bout of panic, he might be capable of it. She would be the only witness.

Maybe the aura of these strong personalities was getting to her. She brushed the thought aside and stepped into the high-ceilinged room.

Piles of heavy metal CDs along with those of the Senegalese singer Youssou D'Nour cluttered a heavy-legged Spanish-style table. Bank statements, along with letters headed by a Tallimard Presse logo, were scattered among the CDs.

Water flushed in the background. Christian Figeac emerged from a floral-stenciled door in the hallway, his pupils dilated, his face flushed.

Aimée shook her head. Dealing with druggies spelled trouble.

"Does your father's editor know what you're doing?"

"He's welcome to," Christian Figeac said, craning his neck

forward like an awkward bird. He spread his arms expansively. Now he exuded an aura of confidence.

"You know what I mean," Aimée said. The man was a mess. "Getting your courage from a needle?"

"Xanax," he said. "I'm working on my equilibrium."

Great.

Maybe she'd given him too much credence. His hallucinations probably came from dope, and his girlfriend had wised up.

Aimée felt something crackle under her sandaled foot. A bright yellow feather. She picked it up. The sharp quill was beaded, a broken bit of mirror tied to it.

"What's this?"

"Some *ju-ju* crap from Senegal," Christian Figeac said, sighing. "I told Idrissa to stop it. She gets it from her *kora* player, Ousmane. He's so superstitious."

Aimée turned it over. What looked like dried, crusted blood coated the feathers. Gingerly, she set it on a chair.

She decided she'd better leave the dead air of the apartment, the *ju-ju*, and Christian Figeac.

The doorbell rang.

"Idrissa?" he asked, lurching toward the door.

Aimée couldn't see the look on his face, but his shoulders stiffened. A cool breeze entered from the hall, smelling of wax wood polish.

"Monsieur Christian Figeac, son of Romain Figeac?" she heard from the hallway.

He nodded, bracing himself against the doorjamb.

And then she heard the metal clink . . . something so familiar it was like slicing bread. The sound of handcuffs. Like the pair her father had.

"We'd like you to answer some questions," a voice said. "It's regarding your father's account at the Crédit Industriel et Commercial in Place des Victoires."

"But I'm busy right now."

"Down at the Commissariat."

Aimée walked up and stood by the door. She recognized the *flic*, Loïc Bellan.

She froze.

Bellan had been one of the new breed before her father retired, recruited to combat corruption.

Her feet felt rooted to the ground. She wanted to hide but she was stuck. A sitting duck. Running away from a murder scene wasn't looked on with favor. What if the police had circulated her description in connection with Jutta Hald's murder? But would Bellan put it together?

"Monsieur Figeac, we'd like you to cooperate with us," Bellan said, taking her in with a quick glance.

"You've made a mistake." Christian Figeac shook his head dismissively. "My father had no account there."

Bellan nodded. He'd changed. His dark hair had grayed, his once thin frame had settled into a stocky middle age. If he recognized her, he didn't let on. But *flics* were trained for that, she knew. Let a perp sweat, then play with him. Like a cat with a mouse.

"We'll just have a talk and clear all this up," Bellan said. "After you, Monsieur Figeac."

He lunged past Bellan. Too bad he tripped over the *flic*'s foot and landed hard on the floor. Scuffling and kicking sounds came from the landing, then a metallic snap as the cuffs closed.

"If you haven't charged Monsieur Figeac, you need an *interpellation* to demand his attendance," Aimée said, stepping forward reluctantly. "The handcuffs are unnecessary. In fact, illegal."

"We'll leave the niceties to the police *judiciaire*, eh, Mademoiselle Leduc?" Bellan said. He nodded to his partner, another *flic* with a long, sallow face who stood in the foyer.

Her heart thumped in her chest. Bellan didn't miss a trick; he had recognized her. But if he had found evidence of a crime he would have searched the premises.

"Monsieur Figeac and I know each other . . ." Bellan let his words dangle in the air. "Let's say, quite well. I really wouldn't want to charge him with possession of illegal substances." Bellan smiled. "But I could."

Christian Figeac's jacket sleeve had ripped. Aimée saw needle tracks on his wrists. Purplish brown and old.

"Call this number," Christian Figeac said, his manacled fingers fishing a card from his front pants pocket. "Tell him to meet me at the Commissariat. I'll be out in an hour."

The card read, "Etienne Mabry, 28 Boulevard de Sébastopol." There was also an office in the Bourse, the Paris stock exchange.

"He's your attorney?" she said.

"My financial advisor on stocks."

On the stairs, two older women paused, speaking in a Slavic dialect. Mops and buckets were in their hands. "Agence Immobilière sent us. The agent wants the apartment cleaned for a showing."

Downstairs, the *flics* took Figeac to a waiting Peugeot. Aimée didn't know whether to be relieved that Bellan hadn't asked her to accompany him, or suspicious.

Bellan drove away without so much as another glance. As soon as the car turned the corner, she ran back to Christian Figeac's apartment.

READY FOR THE DRIVE into Paris, Stefan eased the old Mercedes onto the *périphérique*. He adjusted the headphone for his left ear. His only good ear. The one able to hear subtly differing tones and low frequencies.

The opening strains of Pink Floyd's "Dark Side of the Moon" rippled over him. The notes calmed him, transported him back to the commune. To the crisp autumn day when the Pink Floyd record played continuously like a theme song. Back to the day Ulrike tore the joint from his hand and shoved a Mauser in it.

"Time for you to join the Revolution," she'd said, throwing an ammo clip onto the sheets next to a long-haired girl. "Not sleep with it."

It was either that or leave the commune. Time to go the *distanz*. The long-haired girl, his Maoist tutor, not only smelled of vanilla, her kisses tasted of it. And he'd grown comfortable there.

Ulrike's eyes, dark and flat, were hidden behind the sun glasses she always wore. To conceal her intellect, he realized. Or the fact that she'd cofounded and edited the radical German paper *Dïe social*. She gave no hint of her astute dissection of current politics. Or her influence on them.

Mousy and awkward, at times painfully shy when in front of the group, Ulrike, with her distinctive patchouli fragrance, kept her distance from Ingrid and Marcus, the rock star revolutionaries.

Yet Ulrike needed their in-your-face terrorist pranks and brazen lifestyle to publicize the Revolution. They needed her brains and media prominence for credibility. Molding urban guerrillas to fight the Revolution was the only thing they agreed on.

The endless ideological conflicts, studying Marx and Mao, bickering over who slept with whom, Marcus's ranting if he couldn't get his drugs, Jutta's sullenness, all drained Ulrike. Stefan sensed that right away.

He looked up to her. She'd cultivated him after a demonstration in Colmar. "You have potential," she'd said. "The Revolution needs people like you." He was eighteen, she twenty-eight, a mother of twins, who'd given up her children and life for the cause. Like Ingrid. But Ingrid was different, stone cold and calculating.

"Go downstairs, Stefan, help pack the van," she'd said that day. "We're going to visit our brothers."

"Brothers?" he'd asked as he struggled into his faded, patched jeans. The glamour was fading from his Revolution.

"Action-Réaction," she said. "Our French brothers and sisters."

Stefan shrugged. He had a hard time keeping up with the various radicals.

"Ever been to Paris?"

Stefan shook his head.

Her mouth crinkled in a small smile. "Join the Red Army and see the world."

Stefan remembered their 1972 Paris visit, full of endless espresso, Moroccan hashish, and sleeping on the floor in an intellectual writer's fancy apartment. What a contrast, he'd thought, to nearby rue Saint Denis, where every kind of hooker waited in the crumbling doorways.

They had been hosted by the writer's wife, an American actress and Revolutionary wanna-be. She supplied them with wine and champagne, played with their guns, and popped pills.

Her young child, his overalls dirty and torn, followed her

around. She'd pay attention to him sometimes, blowing hashish smoke in his face to keep him quiet. Stefan remembered Ulrike's stricken look at this. But Ulrike kept quiet. The actress wrote big checks for their cause, found them a safe house, and slept with some of them.

Action-Réaction's organization proved loose. But they were passionate and had a certain Gallic flair. Dogma's for the *boche*, they'd said, discussion and dialectic for us.

Stefan liked that.

He'd also liked Beate, a long-haired American hanger-on. Like Ulrike, she showed a certain *élan* and she understood his halting French. Or seemed to. He liked their midnight talks over *vin rouge*, sharing dreams under the chandeliers. Subversion with style.

He'd met leftist students in Action-Réaction. Ones who kick-started the cause through terrorism, but a decade later were the main force behind the Green Party. He'd even recognized a Mao-ist years later on the news; he'd toned down, bought a suit, and joined the ministry.

But he'd never told Beate, or Ulrike, the plans Marcus outlined for him.

"How about a drink?" Marcus had asked him one afternoon.

They'd gone to a nearby café where cart pullers stood drinking *panaché*, beer laced with lemonade.

"Here's your urban guerrilla future," he'd said, introducing him to a *mec* standing at the bar. "Meet Jules."

Jules smelled of Gitanes. His shaggy hair in a stylish cut hit his shoulders. A Che Guevara T-shirt peeked from under his slim-fitting jacket. Another French *intello*, in expensive clothes, flirting with revolution.

"Marcus spoke of you." Jules shook his hand, then pulled him close. "I like you already."

The radioactive look in Jules's eyes nailed him. Restless and lethal.

"We're doing something big," Jules said, dinging his glass with his finger. The insistent *ping* echoed in the quiet café. "Every piece needs orchestration, fine-tuning. No detail is too small." Jules signaled to the barman wiping the zinc counter. *"Encore."* He turned to Stefan. "And you're the linchpin."

The bewilderment on Stefan's face and a warning look from Marcus made Jules simplify.

"I hear you're good with engines. You'll drive the getaway car." He winked and raised his cloudy amber glass. *"Salut."*

Now, as he drove into Paris, Stefan realized he'd guessed wrong. Jules was an *arnaqueur*, a con man, using the cause for his own purposes. But, Stefan reasoned, hadn't they all . . . in one way or another?

Paris had changed over the years, he thought, but it still made him nervous. He shuddered, easing the old Mercedes into the parking spot. Time for his quarterly visit. Time to pick up some goodies. The older he got, the more careful he grew. No big amounts to attract attention. Just a little at a time.

He adjusted his Basque beret, donned dark glasses and a brown raincoat. Outside the car, he walked fast, his hands swinging by his sides.

For all he knew, some off-duty *flic* might recognize him from the old Interpol wanted list. Now they called it Europol. Same thing. He was still wanted. They all were. Small chance after all this time, but the fear jelled his bone marrow some nights.

He bought a mixed floral bouquet. Like always. Inside the cemetery gate, he took a deep breath. Not to worry, he told himself, patting the tools inside his pocket. This wouldn't take long.

Flowering plane trees swayed in the weak breeze. Distant traffic and shouts of children in the nearby playground hummed in his good ear.

He walked down the path to the mausoleum, pulled the grill gate open.

The coffin was there. He raised the lid. It was empty.
He stood stock-still. Shock waves hit his heart.
Where?
He collapsed onto the sandy gravel.
Who? Had Jules taken it?

Sunday Afternoon

AIMÉE KNOCKED ON THE Figeac apartment door. The Polish cleaning woman who answered surveyed her with narrowed eyes. She had a weathered face with high cheekbones and was wearing a short blue skirt and rolled-down ankle socks with sandals. Radio talk blared in the background.

"*Pardon*," Aimée said. "You remember me, eh? I've come to gather the owner's things."

The woman leaned on her mop, tucking wisps of hair back under her scarf. "The *immobiliére* doesn't want people in here," the woman said, shaking her head.

"*Bien sûr*, the agent's right," Aimée said, thinking fast. "But he forgot his *carte d'identité*."

"We're not supposed to . . . something to do with insurance," the woman said, shaking her head.

"Only take a moment." Aimée smiled, hoping she sounded more authoritative than she felt. She edged her foot in the doorway.

"Tanya!" the other cleaning woman shouted from inside. The rest of the words were in Polish.

"Go ahead," Aimée said, "I'll just pop into the study, then leave."

The woman looked at her wristwatch, hesitating.

"We're running behind," she said. "Got two more places to clean today."

"I'll make it quick," Aimée said, stepping inside. "For your help, *merci*."

The woman moved back reluctantly.

Thank God they hadn't started in Romain Figeac's writing room yet.

Aimée walked into the tall-windowed room, closed the door, and locked it with the key Christian had used. Pulling on latex gloves from her backpack, she found her Swiss Army knife and surveyed the room.

No bookshelves lined with books. No photos. No announcements tacked on the wall. Not even old mail or torn envelopes. Just a *secrétaire*, with cabriole legs, in the middle of the room. The room's stillness and stale air bothered her. But she knew people had shot themselves with a .25 and lived. It didn't add up.

She opened the desk's only drawer. Full of off-white, thick vellum paper.

Blank.

On the desktop lay a wooden pen and an assortment of nibs by a bottle of *bleu des mers du sud* Waterman ink. The typewriter, a shiny red Olivetti, was a classic. Under it was tucked a sheet of paper, a reference sheet, on which appeared a series of page numbers and typographical error symbols. A copy editor's comments, she imagined.

She looked closer. Under the Tallimard logo, a line read, "From the desk of Alain Vigot, *éditeur*." In the bottom right-hand corner, she saw "agit888 . . . Frésnes," written in blue ink, running off the paper.

Frésnes was the prison where Jutta said her mother had been held!

She didn't know its significance but she folded the paper and stuck it in her backpack.

If Romain Figeac wrote in ink, then transcribed it on the typewriter, where were the boxes of his work—as well as newspaper clippings, photos, or research notes? Where would Idrissa have put them?

She got on her hands and knees and went over the sloping wood floor looking for a floor safe.

Nothing but dust and cracks in the honey-colored parquet.

The floor creaked every time she moved. No wonder Christian Figeac heard noises. Or thought he did.

Dust motes flickered in the fading light slanting through the windows. She knew she was missing something. What, she didn't know.

She sat in the desk chair, an old leather one. Then put her head down on the desk. She measured from that point to the red-brown bloodstain smudged on the wallpaper. At least a meter and a half.

She knelt. With her Swiss Army knife she cut away a long rectangle of the bloodstained floral wallpaper from the recess bordering the door frame. She peeled it down to the baseboard. Another layer of smudged wallpaper, older and with a faded blue striped pattern, emerged. The bloodstain was fainter.

She cut into the faded stripes, peeled off a section, and found an older layer with dense clusters of roses. Quaint, turn of the century.

Dark red blood splatters had even soaked into this old-fashioned rose wallpaper. Not only gruesome, she thought, but odd.

Carefully, she pulled the wallpaper down to the baseboard and pried loose the edge.

A dark red congealed clump had seeped down. She sat back; she really didn't want to do this. Jutta Hald's face flashed before her.

A faint metallic odor came from the dried, encrusted blood. She scraped up a sample, took a glue stick from her bag, and rubbed it over the wallpaper. She pasted each layer, except for the old-fashioned roses, back on and smoothed them over.

Still on her knees, she checked the creaking parquet floor. At the tall window, the rooftops of the Sentier spread before her, squat chimneys, impossibly angled rooflines, and bricked-up windows opposite.

Doubtful if anyone could see in.

She traced her gloved fingers over the cold glass windowpanes. Felt in the grooves where glass was framed by metal. Something hard was stuck between the glass and metal.

She wedged it out, fingered it.

A small ivory bone fragment.

She turned the fragment over in her palm. Curved and with jagged lines, like a river seen from space.

She felt around more. Near where the metal joined the floor was another bone bit.

Apprehension came over her. What gun had sufficient force to scatter bone this far?

She'd come here looking for clues about her mother. And they were here somewhere. But if Romain Figeac was a suicide, she was his onetime neighbor Madame du Barry.

The door rattled as the knob turned.

"Mademoiselle, we have to clean in here!"

Aimée scanned the room again, wondering where the writer's files could be kept.

"Open up at once or I'm calling the agent!"

She slipped the bone fragments, the wallpaper sample, and then her gloves into a Baggie. Time to get out of here.

The cleaning woman shook her fist, but Aimée was out the door and bidding her *adieu* before she could do anything else.

"SO YOU'VE joined the big boys now, eh, Serge? Working on a Sunday?" Aimée said, dumping the Baggie on the Institut Medico-Legal's stainless steel counter. "Congratulations!"

Serge Leaud, with his rosy cheeks and trimmed beard, appeared too dapper to be a pathologist. He looked up from his microscope. "At least I don't have to run from Belleville to Quai des Orfèvres! They saddled me with the blood inquiries."

From Leaud's window, distant pinpricks of light could be seen twinkling on the quai. The muffled clatter of the Metro as it crossed Pont d'Austerlitz reached them in the white-tiled lab. Arctic air-conditioning brought goose bumps to Aimée's arms.

"Seems I'll never live down that Luminol case in the Marais," he said.

"You're a world authority on Luminol now . . . why would you want to?" she asked, gesturing around the lab. The high-powered microscopes and microtomes for tissue sectioning were impressive.

"I'd like to see my twins once in a while. My wife says they've forgotten how to say Papa." He grinned, setting down long-handled tweezers. "But something tells me this isn't a social call."

Aimée was about to reply when a posse strode into the adjoining waiting room, three big-shouldered men in black suits.

Aimée grabbed a physician's lab coat, slipped it on, and set the Baggie on a glass specimen tray. "I need your help, Serge."

The men burst through the lab doors. Only Renseignements Generaux, an intelligence-gathering arm of the Interior Ministry linked to the police, entered the morgue's lab like that.

"Gentlemen, we're wrapping up a minor detail before I finish your report. . . ."

"We'll wait, Dr. Leaud," interrupted the biggest one. He had a headful of curly red hair and thick lips parted in a smile. "No pressure, you understand, of course. Our report goes to the Quai des Orfèvres." His grin widened and he glanced pointedly at his wristwatch. "Within the hour, you understand. Priorities. But don't rush on our account."

Priorities my *derrière*, Aimée thought. Leave it to the RG to act as if the rest of the law enforcement world didn't exist.

"Dr. Leaud, this detail puzzles me," she said, sticking the glass tray in front of Serge, sliding the specimen from his microscope and ignoring his look of surprise. "These lines. Those striations. Visible more closely under magnification, I suppose."

One of the RG men cleared his throat. Another tapped his blunt fingers on the windowsill.

She emptied the Baggie onto a fresh petri dish, slipped it under the microscope. "Quick and dirty, doctor, then I'll leave you to these gentlemen."

"No need for magnification to see the beveling," Serge said. "It's obvious. But to see the powder residue, it's useful."

She smiled at the biggest man. "Forgive me, but Dr. Leaud's extensive background in forensic pathology saves so much time."

Serge Leaud put his eye to the lens, whether to keep from laughing or to hide his trepidation, she wasn't sure.

"Interesting," he said slowly. "Give me a brief description of the recovery scene."

She did, mentioning the suicide and caliber of the gun.

"Nice fragment of occipital bone," he said a minute later.

A part of the skull, she remembered that much from her year of premed at the Ecole des Médicines.

"Those lines are part of the lambdoidal suture," Serge Leaud said.

"Lambdoidal suture?"

"The union between the bones of the cranium, on the side of the skull," he said. "What's this?" He pointed to the other items.

"A wallpaper sample I obtained," she said. "From a wall a meter and a half away from the victim."

Serge Leaud turned a knob and adjusted the microscope light. He studied a portion of the sample. "There's the blood mist from the blast. Distinctive spatter and darker stain. Heavier particles follow."

He looked up at her. "Did you say this was a suicide with a .25 that perforated the skull?"

Aimée nodded.

"You're telling me a .25-caliber perforated the skull and sent tissue spattering against the wall?"

Aimée shrugged, watching his eyebrows knit.

"Sounds like a contradiction, eh, Dr. Leaud?" the red-haired RG man said. His feet beat a rhythm on the linoleum floor. "More like a .357 or a .44."

Mentally, she agreed.

"*Attends*," Serge said. "There's internal beveling on the bone."

"Internal beveling?"

She noticed the RG men had stopped looking bored. Interest flickered in their eyes.

"As the bullet enters the skull it causes a wider fracture on the inside, beveling it," Leaud said. "There's a very clear demonstration right here. You can see it with the naked eye." He pointed to a curved line. "But that's not all."

More from that small bone fragment?

"Look at those traces of soot—gunpowder residue deposited on bone," he said, "right there. That helps with the range of firing. Of course, I can't say exactly without further tests but it was close range."

"How close?"

"Within centimeters, I would say."

Like Jutta Hald.

"Anything you can be sure of?"

"If a .25 did this, then it will snow tiny white chocolate nonpareils on Noël," Serge Leaud said, pouring the bits back into the Baggie for her. "My twins would like that."

Aimée could hear the RG men laughing as she hung up the lab coat. Serge's quick and dirty analysis confirmed her suspicions. She beckoned to him on her way out. He excused himself and met her in the tiled hallway.

"You know, Aimée, I'll have to write this up," he said in a low voice. "It's procedure with suspicious findings. I'll need more details."

Good, she wanted Serge to make a report, to spur the police to investigate Figeac's death.

"Serge, request the autopsy findings on Jutta Hald, a woman

murdered at Tour Jean-Sans-Peur. You should see a match with
the bone beveling and gunpowder soot. If the same gun didn't
do it, I'll make it snow nonpareils in your twins' room. That's a
promise."

Outside the morgue, couples strolled along the quai, outlined
against the fading dusk. Aimée stared at a *bateau-mouche* on the
rippling Seine, black and thick like pudding, wondering what
these deaths had to do with her mother.

From Place Mazas, she took Pont Morland past the swaying
péniches moored in the canal facing the Bastille. Colored laundry
hung from clotheslines, tricycles and pots of geraniums stood on
the barge decks. A lone fisherman sat with a camp lantern, his
legs dangling over the stone.

Muggy heat still hugged the narrow streets. Not a breath of
air stirred. All the way to her apartment, a bridge away on the
Ile St. Louis, her uneasiness mounted.

She tried to telephone Etienne Mabry, without success, so she
took Miles Davis for a walk, grabbing a baguette and pâté before
the shops closed. After sharing the pâté with the puppy, she
cracked open her tall windows, rested her feet on the top of the
balcony grillwork, the Seine visible through her toes, and got to
work on her laptop. Miles Davis curled up next to her.

Once online, her fingers flew over the keyboard. Within
minutes, she found Haader-Rofmein, the seventies terrorists' site.
A Web page with photos of young people circled around a
hookah. Her cousin Sebastian had a hippie coat like that from
Istanbul, she remembered. Probably still in his closet.

Aimée leaned over, and clicked to the next Web page.

She saw long-haired men and women clutching Mausers and
Russian bazookas. They stood by a cinder-block building. Distant
targets showed in what appeared to be desert bleakness. Some
wore El Fateh headgear and army fatigues. None looked much
over twenty.

Aimée combed her nails through her hair. Some of the members had died in shoot-outs. The leaders, the rock-star types, had hung themselves in prison but, according to the site, controversy still surrounded the supposed suicides since there was only the warden's word for it.

She saw the name J. Hald on the once-active list in a sidebar. What had her role been, besides the young and dumb part?

She hacked into a German court records site. According to what she could understand from the West German trial transcripts, Jutta had been charged with multiple counts: arson, armed robbery, stolen vehicles. A heavy-duty powder puff!

Reading further, she saw Jutta's indictment in France was for complicity in a bank heist and murder. For that, she'd gotten twenty years.

Aimée stood up, stretched, and picked up Miles Davis.

But still no answer as to why Jutta had said her mother owed her!

MONDAY

AIMÉE WOKE UP KNOWING she had to contact Etienne Mabry and find Christian Figeac's girlfriend, Idrissa.

On the Minitel she found two clubs with Senegalese music, one in Montmartre and the other, Club Exe, in the Sentier. The one in Montmartre had never heard of Idrissa.

"Idrissa Diaffa who sings with Ousmane?" asked a woman with high-pitched voice at Club Exe.

"Yes, where can I find her?"

"She quit."

Perfect.

"Her boyfriend, Christian, is in jail," Aimée said. "Please, I need to find her."

"I'd like to help you," the woman said, "but I'm just a part-time cashier. Sorry."

Aimée was about to hang up. "What about her friends . . . who was she close to at the club?"

"*Bien sûr*, everyone liked Idrissa," the woman said. "But she hung out with Mala, the dishwasher, another student."

"Where can I find Mala?"

"Around the corner."

"Where's that?"

"Rue Jeûneurs. Number 7. And could you tell her she's needed for a double shift today?"

Aimée thanked her. At least she had something to go on.

She took the Metro into the Sentier, climbing the stairs to emerge into the heat.

Dark windows, like dead eyes, stared from above the wide marble steps of 7, rue Jeûneurs. The ancient building, once a clothier's, as evidenced by the faded *drapier* sign, was typical of the Sentier district. Filigreed metal balconies, limestone walls in need of steam cleaning, and the cobbled courtyard exuded a forlorn charm.

On the left was a faded concierge sign, lights glowing behind lace curtains covering the glass door.

Aimée knocked.

"*Bonsoir*," said a man, poking his long face out. He worked his horselike teeth, chewing a piece of bread. The smell of frying onions clung to him.

Few buildings in the Sentier would have concierges, she imagined. From inside the *logement* came the sound of a piano scale being practiced, the same note missed each time.

"Monsieur, can you direct me to Mala's apartment?"

The concierge scratched his neck. "She didn't leave word to expect anyone," he said, his syllables rolled in a Spanish accent.

"This concerns—"

"*Tiens*, I don't pry into tenants' lives," he interrupted.

He must be an unusual concierge.

"What floor, Monsieur?"

He shook his head.

"Who might you be, Mademoiselle?"

A brown baguette crumb had lodged in his mustache. Aimée wanted to brush it off.

"Aimée Leduc," she said.

"Got an appointment?"

"Sorry to disturb your meal, Monsieur," she said with a smile, "but they need Mala to work a double shift today at Club Exe. Her phone's off the hook. I'd appreciate your help."

The crumb rode up and down as the man chewed. He debated for a long moment.

"Left rear staircase, third floor, door on the left."

She felt him watch her as she crossed the courtyard.

Seventeenth century, by the look of it. Like her building. However, much of the rear courtyard and first floor of this *hôtel particulier* had been hacked into warehouses, divvied up among small manufacturers over the centuries. She heard the whine of sewing machines.

After a steep climb, she reached the dark green door. One other massive door kept it company on the black-and-white-diamond-patterned landing. Dirt filmed the single small circular window.

She knocked several times. No answer. She tried the other door. A small bronze nameplate with *click.mango* was affixed to the grime-patinaed wall.

An Internet company here? Frustrated at finding neither Mala nor Idrissa, Aimée leaned against the wall and thought.

She looked up to see a lean, caramel-skinned young woman coming up the stairs. She was in her early twenties with a boyish figure, and she wore a red, yellow, and green Rasta cap from which an errant braid escaped, a tank top, and army fatigue pants.

"*Bonjour*, do you know where I can find Idrissa Diaffa?"

The woman's eyes narrowed. "But I don't know you," she said with a lilting West African accent.

"I'm Aimée Leduc," she said. "Christian Figeac's in jail. You were his girlfriend, right? Could we talk?"

Idrissa's almond-shaped eyes darted around the landing. She shifted in her sandals.

"May I come in?"

Idrissa didn't move. In the dark, cool hallway, she seemed ready to bolt down the stairs.

"I'm sorry, it's not my place," Idrissa said. "And I'm in a hurry."

"Christian's in trouble," Aimée said.

Idrissa sighed. "Always him and his big ideas!"

"Last time I saw him he was being taken to the Commissariat for questioning."

Idrissa waved her hand as if that were old news. Odd.

Jumbles of red and yellow beads clacked on her wrist. Aimée caught a whiff of coconut oil.

"Matter of fact, I'm trying to reach his financial advisor to spring him from the Commissariat," Aimée said.

"Christian calls me his girlfriend but . . . it's just the friend part now," Idrissa said. "I won't go to the apartment, *vous comprenez?*"

Idrissa's speech didn't match her looks. Most young women in the *quartier* would have used the familiar *tu* form of address, not the formal *vous*. Was she a Sorbonne student? A heavy denim bag hung from her shoulder, weighing down her slim frame.

"Christian can't find some boxes of his father's work," Aimée said. "He thought you might know where they are."

"Accusing me of stealing?"

Why hadn't she worded it another way? She'd put Idrissa on the defensive! As René often told her, tact wasn't her strongest suit. "Actually," Aimée said, trying for an ingratiating smile, "Christian's being generous, trying to help me find his father's research on terrorism," she said. "My mother was involved."

Idrissa shrugged. "My music only earns half the rent," she said, her accent thickened. "So I typed, transcribed for his father."

Aimée took a step forward. "For Christian's father's book?"

Idrissa nodded.

"How interesting," Aimée said. "Were they his memoirs or, perhaps, stories about people involved in the radical movements?"

"I didn't pay attention," Idrissa said. Her gaze didn't meet Aimée's.

"Did he mention the Haader-Rofmein gang?"

"Nothing made much sense to me," Idrissa said. "It seemed jumbled."

"Jumbled . . . how do you mean?"

Idrissa shrugged. "He rambled, talking about the past one minute, then he'd zoom to the present."

"So would you take dictation, or did he give you tapes to transcribe?"

Idrissa shifted against the wall. "What does it matter?"

"Do you have any of those tapes?"   •

"Look, it was only a job. I gave them back," she said. "The boxes, too!" Idrissa looked at her Swatch watch. "I'm late."

"Christian is so upset. He doesn't know why his father committed suicide," Aimée said, edging toward her.

Idrissa winced. "Excuse me," she said, opening the door, "I've got to go."

Aimée wanted her to talk. But Idrissa shut the door in her face.

As she passed by the concierge's place, the piano scales climbed in an agonizing march.

Monday Noon

AIMÉE RANG COMMISSAIRE MORBIER, her father's old colleague, at the Commissariat.

"He's not here," said a bored receptionist. "Gone."

She knew he would qualify for retirement soon. But it wouldn't be like him to leave without telling her.

"Can I reach him somewhere else?"

"Who's this?"

"Aimée Leduc, his goddaughter."

She waited while the receptionist checked.

"As it happens, Mademoiselle Leduc, we refer his calls to the *préfecture* at the Quai des Orfèvres on Mondays."

"Quai des Orfèvres?" That Morbier would be at police head-quarters on Ile de la Cité took Aimée aback.

"He's in charge of a unit there," the receptionist said.

"Since when?"

But the receptionist had already patched her through. Several clicks, then a sustained buzz, and then the phone was picked up. "Groupe R," came Morbier's voice on the line.

What was Morbier doing in the special branch? "Got a new job?"

"Temporary assignment, Leduc," Morbier said, his voice gruff.

In the background she heard the murmur of voices, the noise of an ancient Teletype, still in use in this age of computers, echoing off stone walls.

"Weren't you going to tell me, Morbier?" She didn't wait for an answer. "Clue me in on the *secrets d'état*."

A slight pause. "I've got another call," Morbier said.

He seemed bent on stonewalling her. His hand muffled the

receiver. She heard indistinct conversation, then recognized his hacking cough. Almost a two-pack-a-day man.

"Leduc, I'm busy."

"Everyone in Paris either works frantically or collects *le dole*," she said. "So what else is new?"

He put his hand over the receiver again.

"Let's meet for lunch and you can tell me all about your new job," she said.

"Things seem tight. . . ."

"I think you'll be interested in what I have to say," she said. "I'm in the Sentier, but you name the place."

"MAKE IT good, Leduc," Morbier said over the dog-eared menu. "I don't have much time."

Outside, hookers plied their trade by the open *brasserie* window.

"Does murder qualify?"

"Important things first. We order."

A true Gallic response. His mismatched socks—one tan, the other brown—his suspenders, and wrinkled jacket were as usual but he seemed different.

"Order the *formule*," Morbier said. He didn't look up but pointed to the blackboard, where "59 francs" had been chalked. "Cart-pusher's special, but worth it."

A promising scent of garlic and rosemary wafted from the black hole of a kitchen.

"The chef's from Marseilles," he said. "His son's on parole."

Aimée hated that. It meant no bill and general toadying-up from the poor staff. They ordered the *formule* from a gap-toothed young woman, who wore an apron over her jeans.

The *brasserie* bustled with a late lunch crowd: auto mechanics, white-haired ladies with full shopping bags from the outdoor *marché* at their feet, African security guards nursing *bières*, and stockbrokers from the nearby Bourse.

"*Tant pis*, my Marie's teething," Aimée overheard a tinsel-wigged hooker say to her sidewalk mate. Her mate, a middle-aged woman, adjusted an orange latex miniskirt, her eyes never leaving the passersby. "My sitter's complaining," the woman continued, "*alors*, that's all the sitter ever does, that one!"

Why had Morbier chosen this place?

"Jean Jaurès was stabbed at that table, Leduc," Morbier said. "The bloodstains are still there."

Aimée looked over. A dark brown ghoulish stain, shaped like a butterfly, spread over the old table.

"As always, Morbier, you pick the scenic and informative." She set the menu down. "Food any good?"

Was this her socialist lesson for the day? When she was in grade school, he'd insisted she read the transcript of Julius and Ethel Rosenberg's trial, even quizzed her about it.

From the next table came the tang of a Gauloise. The acrid smoke teased her. Too bad she'd quit. The second time this week.

And then it hit her.

"You quit smoking, Morbier?"

He pointed to the patch on his arm.

"I'm full of surprises today, eh, Leduc?"

The waitress set two bowls of Provençal *soupe au pistou* in front of them, swirls of basil *crème* in the center.

"My visit to Berlin generated some interest."

"And you're proud of that, Leduc?"

"I wouldn't say that." She took a big swig of the rosé, light and with a peachlike aroma.

Not bad. She took another.

"Tell me about this murder while I eat," Morbier said.

She told him about Jutta Hald. "She said she'd been in prison with my mother and would give me her things, but she needed money," Aimée said. "Later she called to say there was something I should know about my mother, but I got to the meeting too late. Jutta's brains were all over the tower wall." She watched Morbier run the napkin across his mouth, then snap toothpicks between his splayed fingers.

"Doesn't sound pretty."

She told him about Jutta's photo of Romain Figeac, Christian's behavior, and the blood-smudged wall. "Figeac didn't commit suicide, Morbier, he was murdered."

"And you can prove that?"

"Serge at the morgue concurs," she said, hoping Morbier wouldn't check up on her stretch of the truth. "Both Figeac and Jutta Hald were killed by high-caliber gun blasts. Serge has the evidence Baggie for testing but I know it's the same gun."

"What do you want from me?" Morbier sighed.

"I know it's related to my mother."

"Leduc, I can't help you anymore."

"*Attention, c'est chaud,*" the waitress interrupted, wedging two heaping plates of grilled *rougets*, the brilliant red fish skin still crackling, in front of them. Thyme and olive oil aromas filled the air.

She felt sure the Berlin trip, to investigate clues to her father's death, from which she'd just returned had kick-started Jutta's effort to contact her. She pulled out the paper she'd taken from Romain Figeac's desk.

"Figeac wrote 'agit888' and 'Frésnes,' the prison where Jutta and my mother were held," she said. "Know anything about it?"

His eyebrows knit in concentration. "How old are you?"

He should know. She'd been nine when he and her father assembled her bike over a bottle of wine on a long-ago Christmas Eve. She'd watched from behind a door. The bike had always wobbled.

"You know a woman never reveals her age."

"Will you let me eat in peace?"

She nodded.

Morbier tucked his napkin into his collar, spreading it over his suspenders. "All I know, which isn't much, is that sometime in the early eighties a number of RAD members—"

"RAD?" Aimée interrupted.

"The Red Army Division," he said. "Some German fugitive terrorists wanted to leave the underground. They were given a chance to lead new lives in East Germany, under different names.

"So by Red Army Division," she said, dipping her bread in the sauce, and keeping her hand steady with effort, "you mean the seventies Haader-Rofmein gang who blew up banks and kidnapped people?"

"The newspapers called them that." Morbier took a long sip of rosé. He raised his thick eyebrows. "They called themselves the RAD. Their French counterparts were Action-Réaction."

This fit what Jutta had told her.

"This came out in the late eighties when some ex-terrorists living in East Germany were arrested. Then the Wall came down."

"What's the connection to agit888?"

"Thank Jean-Paul Sartre for that," Morbier said, attacking the *rouget* with gusto.

"Sartre?"

"The Marxist fool interviewed Haader in his cell," he said. "And gave that infamous press conference about terrorists. For that the Ministry of Interior kept Sartre under surveillance until he died." Morbier made a moué of distaste. "Your tax francs at work."

"Sounds convoluted to me."

"Agit888 is what they called the Sartre surveillance squad."

Aimée thought old Sartre would have been secretly pleased. An existential thorn in the establishment's side until the end.

"What happened to the RAD gang?"

"Most of them testified against their former comrades and received fairly mild sentences."

"What about . . . ?"

"Some did time in Frésnes. Most are free by now, I imagine."

Aimée paused. Jutta Hald's visit—the timing of it—right after her release, was significant. She took a deep breath. "Was my mother one of them?"

Morbier's fork stopped midair. He didn't look at her.

"I asked you a question, Morbier," she said, trying to keep her voice calm.

"Some things in life should stay buried," he said.

Her appetite disappeared. "I just want to know if she's alive."

"Rumors circulated," he said.

"What kind of rumors?"

"A *moucharde*, a stoolie," he said. "That she played both sides."

"A stoolie?" She gripped the table edge. Hard. "For who?"

"The Sorbonne riots in '68 threw everyone into turmoil," he said. "Crazy times."

"What do you mean?"

"She put her nose into places it didn't belong."

Morbier got the waitress's attention and pointed to his empty glass.

"I asked your father once, but he avoided the topic."

"But . . ."

"*C'est fini*, Leduc," Morbier said.

Aimée's heart sank.

Her father had refused to discuss it with her, too. The whole family had.

She didn't know what to think or how to figure out what her mother had or hadn't done.

"You knew my mother, didn't you, Morbier?"

He shrugged. "Not well."

"What was she like?" Sadly, she realized she'd used the past tense.

"A handful. Like you," he said.

The lunchtime rush had subsided. Shouts and horns sounded from the street.

Here she was sitting with a man who knew her mother and father, but wouldn't talk about them. Why couldn't he cooperate?

"Jutta Hald's gone," Morbier said after a long pause. "Those radicals have a death wish, always did." He swirled the wine, sniffed his glass. "Take my advice, eh—move on."

Aimée remembered that the only good thing to do with advice, as Oscar Wilde pointed out, was to pass it on to someone else.

She managed a thin smile. "I'll try."

"*Tiens*, say it like you mean it, Leduc," Morbier said.

"Just make one inquiry about Jutta Hald, that's all I ask."

Morbier leaned back in the chair, shaking his head. His thick salt-and-pepper head of hair could use a wash, Aimée thought. He looked like he'd been up all night.

"You're well acquainted with the French legal system, Leduc."

"But there's a lot I don't know."

"There's a rule stating that for 150 years no one can look at a prisoner's dossier," he said. His thick eyebrows crinkled, tenting his eyes. "Just to be clear, that's 150 years from date of birth. I can't find out anything about your mother, even if I wanted to."

"But, Morbier, if you're working a case and need the info . . ."

"My hands are tied," he said. "This is to protect the prisoner."

She tried to hide her disappointment.

If she couldn't see the file on her mother, the trail ended.

"Any idea how to get around this rule?" she asked.

Morbier shrugged, a typical Gallic shrug. "You're friends with higher-ups. Complain to the ministry."

At least two ministers in the Ministry of Interior weren't happy with her after the incidents in Belleville, although Martine, the sister-in-law of one, remained her best friend.

She thought about Frésnes, the old brick prison on the outskirts of Paris where Jutta had been held. Unheated and the worst in the system. She remembered something. "No cell holds just two," she said. "They usually cram in three or four prisoners. . . say Jutta and my mother—"

"Wasn't that years ago?" Morbier interrupted.

She nodded. The words caught in her throat. She made herself go on, leaning forward, her eyes locked on Morbier's. "But Jutta was just released, it should be easy to find out whom she roomed with."

Morbier frowned. "Her last cell mate might not be the same person."

"True." Morbier had a point. "But if Jutta was excited about getting out, she could have talked to a cell mate about the past, discussed her plans. She told me she came straight from prison to my apartment."

She knew Frésnes also held the CNO, the Centre National d'Observation, for prisoners who required physical and psychiatric evaluations when up for parole. Or those under surveillance for undesirable behavior.

The CNO assessments could take up to six weeks. All the prisoners hated them, but several times in their prison life they had to endure them. Some more often than others. Prisoners in this transit loop were much easier to track down than others in the penal system.

"Morbier, do me a favor," she said. "Discover who shared Jutta's cell in Frésnes before her release. Maybe she can help me to find out about my mother."

"You're chasing pipe dreams, Leduc." Morbier expelled a quick breath. "Wasting your time."

From the table behind them, several patrons sat smoking and drinking espresso. Such a perfect end to a meal! She could almost taste the tobacco, feel the jolt in her lungs. Instead of turning around and begging for a cigarette, she popped some Nicorette gum and forced herself to continue.

"A lot of retired *flics* sit on the parole board," she said, chewing fast. "Can't you make a phone call or two?"

"Favors cost," he said. "If I start nosing around Frésnes, they expect their backs scratched. On my turf."

Now she was stroking his fur the right way. He always wanted a favor in return and would bargain until he got it. Being his goddaughter gave her no exemption.

"But you do it so well, Morbier," she said, "and you always come out on top."

Morbier reached into his pocket, found an empty packet of cigarettes, and crumpled the cellophane on the table. He reached again, pulling out a half-full packet.

"You quit, remember?"

He nodded, threw the packet on the table, and picked up another toothpick. A glimmer of a smile passed over his face.

"Include yourself, Leduc," he said. "At payback time."

Morbier ran true to form. Nothing came free.

"I'll make some calls, but no promises," he said, hitching up his suspenders.

He'd lost weight. A lot.

"You've slimmed down," she said. "Gone for your annual checkup, Morbier?"

"I'll ignore the last part and take that as a compliment."

She doubted but asked anyway. "On a diet?"

"Grapefruit, seaweed, and raisin capsules!" he said. "Drains the toxins, fatty lipids, eliminates cellulite buildup."

Morbier . . . talking about cellulite?

"You might try it," he said.

She'd struggled with the zipper in her leather skirt that morning.

"My new concierge, Madame Guegnon, told me. She buys them in bulk at the Carrefour."

Before she could recover he stood up. "I must get the train tickets; I'm taking Marc to Brittany for *les vacances*."

A doting grandfather? Morbier certainly was full of surprises.

Guilt flooded her. Morbier's daughter, Samia, a young half-Algerian prostitute, had been killed by the underground before Aimée could protect her. The image of Samia's eyes open to the rain in the Belleville alley, the red bullet hole in her peach-colored twinset, flashed before her.

Marc, her honey-faced son, attended Catholic boarding school and had made his first Communion under the proud eyes of his grandfather, Morbier.

Her face reddened. Determined, she pushed her guilt aside. "I'll keep my cell phone on," she said. "You know the number."

BACK IN the Leduc Detective office she tried Etienne Mabry again.

Still no answer. And none at Christian Figeac's apartment. Worried, she wondered if he was still in custody.

She looked up from her computer terminal as René entered, wearing a tailored straw-colored linen suit, wiping perspiration from his large forehead.

"Diuretics!" he said. "The humidity's equal to the temperature and the doctor prescribed diuretics!" He unbuttoned the linen jacket, tailored to his four-foot height. "I need another glass of Evian!"

She passed him bottled water and one of the Baccarat tumblers, the only glasses they had left from her grandfather's time.

"I heard you borrowed money from Michel. But I've learned that his uncle Nessim needs extra laundry service," he said, rolling his eyes. "We need to play it safe."

"What do you mean?"

"Nessim's wholesale fabric business needs outlets besides the Deauville casinos in which to launder money." René shrugged. "And Michel's couture is one of them."

"But I want to help Michel."

"So do I," he said. "A lot of questionable bankruptcies are

declared in the Sentier. I wouldn't want Michel to be a victim of his uncle. We should see what security his computer system needs."

René pushed up his shirtsleeves. "The Société Générale's account is overdue. They owe us but the manager keeps stalling me."

Insurance companies were the worst when it came to paying for contracted services.

"It takes two weeks to authorize issuance of a check." René tugged on his goatee, something he did when worried. He mounted his orthopedic chair and swiveled to face his computer screen.

She gathered up papers and stuffed them in her black leather backpack.

"In the meantime, rent's due," René said, looking at the pile of bills on her desk. "What's our Media 9 contract status?"

"Pending," she said, pointing to the thick folder labeled MEDIA 9 on his desk.

"*Attends*, let me look at Nessim's business structure," he said.

"There's tons of legalese. I'll have to decipher it after I return."

"Return?" He peered at the dated Post-Its on the pile. "This was due yesterday."

She paused, feeling guilty. "*Désolée*, René, but these things . . ."

He tugged his goatee. "It's more than that, about your father, Aimée. All that time poking around government departments, then the trip to Berlin. I thought you'd pick up the slack when you returned. Now, this new wild goose chase . . ."

"René, I know I need to be here more, helping you out."

Remorse assailed her. But she couldn't postpone investigating this lead to her mother.

She stood up, paced to their office window overlooking rue du Louvre. Below, leafy lime trees shifted in an arid breeze, throwing shadows over a roadwork crew. Her hands shook. She didn't want René to see.

But he did. "What's wrong?"

Aimée hesitated. "It's worse than bad." She told him about Jutta Hald, her suspicions concerning Romain Figeac's suicide, and her mother. "I can't stop now, René. This woman was murdered almost in front of me. And there's news about my mother. After all these years, I have a chance to find out what happened to her."

"I know, but . . ." He looked away. "But you borrowed money from Michel and *we* need it!"

"Yes, of course we do," she said, conflicted. With Jutta gone she might as well use the money, think of it as a temporary business loan. "And we'll use it for the business. We'll survive, we always do." She pulled out all but five thousand francs of the fifty she'd borrowed from Michel. "Here, this should help." She stuffed her laptop in her bag, then made for the door. But she had to make him understand. She turned around. "René, you know I have given everything I have to the business. But for once, this has to come first."

René's eyes flashed. "Dot-coms court me, Aimée," he said. "All the time. Offering me nice sign-up packages, stock options. The works."

Shocked, she sat down. She'd had no idea. She felt stupid. Of course they would, but she'd been too distracted to notice.

"What are you saying, René?"

He opened his mouth to speak, then shut it, his goatee quivering. He slid down from his orthopedic chair, grabbed his jacket, and walked out the office door. She'd never seen him so upset.

"René!"

No answer. She ran into the hallway after him. The wire-cage lift rumbled and creaked below her. She ran down the spiral steps, her high-heeled sandals clattering, meeting René as he opened the curlicue-work metal door.

"Look, René," she said. "We're in this together, I need you.

Please understand. . . ." She wasn't prepared to tell him she simply couldn't focus on anything else.

"Friends honor commitments, it's that simple." René snorted. "Your mind's been somewhere else."

So he'd noticed.

She was obsessed: her mother, Jutta, the terrorists. Yet, René had always been there for her, time and again in the past. She knew she was jeopardizing their relationship.

She hung her head. "You're right. I'm sorry." She rocked on her heels. "I'll catch up. I promise. Forgive me, partner?"

His green eyes fluttered and he dusted invisible lint from his trousers. "Writing code all day bores *me* but I like to pay the rent and eat out once in a while."

"We've got receivables. Like you said, people owe us! I've sent them warnings, next step is the collection agency. They cough up when they get that red-bordered notice."

She took a deep breath. "Hungry?"

René gazed at the sushi bar opposite them on rue du Louvre. "Are you buying?"

She nodded.

"Later," he said, looking at his pocket watch. "I have to meet our bank manager about a loan."

"A loan?"

"To tide us over until we get paid."

René was smart. Now she should make a dent in the pile of work on her desk. Upstairs, she filled Miles Davis's water bowl, then tried Etienne Mabry's number again. Still no answer.

The door opened. "I forgot my briefcase," René said, looking pointedly at the papers on her desk.

Aimée returned the look as she stuck her detailed Paris Plan into her leather backpack.

"Going someplace again?

"I have to find Etienne Mabry so Christian Figeac can get out of jail."

TUCKED DOWN BELOW street level, in the hollow of a quarry, the cemetery was a tangle of trees and pompous mausoleums. Stefan blinked as crunching noises sounded behind him. He balled his hand into a fist. Turned around.

But it was just the grave digger shoveling shiny white stones into a wheelbarrow. Near the Virgin Mary marble statue, a squirrel nibbled an old furred chestnut.

Stefan pulled himself up.

Fear curdled his thoughts.

Would he be killed next?

Except for an old bag, the coffin, lined with dirty cobwebs, lay empty.

Jutta had taken the Laborde stash and all the bonds. She'd demolished him.

But whoever killed her would have them . . . wouldn't they?

Thoughts crowded his mind. Had Jutta joined forces with some new terrorist fanatics, planning to strike again? Had she blabbed to someone in prison? Or had one of the gang survived and followed her?

Stefan went rigid with terror. As he rubbed the gray stubble on his chin, his mind spun. Everything ruined, his future gone. Greedy Jutta. He remembered. She hadn't changed.

Despair hit him as he crouched among the gravestones. A bird's molted gray feathers lay clumped by his elbow. *Still on the run. Still wanted after twenty years, and now he had no money.*

He hadn't supported himself with his mechanic's pay . . . he'd only done this work because he loved Mercedes engines. Now he couldn't go back to the garage.

That was the one rule branded into him by the Palestinians about going underground: If anyone makes a mistake, assume your cover is blown. Nine times out of ten, it was. Play it safe. Never go back to your old identity. The police might be waiting.

He'd have to disappear. Once more. Over and over again.

Paris had more than two hundred banks listed in the phone book—triple that, if one counted the branches of the main ones. With the old hunter's ID, Stefan had opened accounts in many of them over the years. Always in Paris. Never in the country-side—people remembered there. Paris made him nervous but at least he could stay anonymous. Each account held the minimum balance. He maintained them only to enable him to cash the bonds and send his mother money.

He'd waited years before he'd begun cashing the old bonds. Until he figured even if they were numbered and so eventually traceable by Europol, they weren't high on any priority list. He'd cash them in every few months in a different arrondissement taking care not to follow a pattern. He supplemented this money with his poker winnings, though lately he'd been losing to Anton and others in the garage. A lot.

He picked up a stone, trying to ignore the tremor in his hand. Briefly, he thought of the room he'd lived in for the past seven years. It was sparsely furnished, utilitarian. The reference books on Mercedes engines were the only things he'd miss. He kept nothing in his apartment. He remembered how thorough the Stasi were . . . the Stasi didn't exist now but the French equivalent, the DST*, did. And somewhere, so did the *flic* who nursed a special grudge against the members of the gang.

He thought of his Mercedes, parked a few blocks over, realizing he'd need to change the license plates. His palms, thick with encrusted grease, the curse of a mechanic, traveled over the rough bark of a plane tree.

Direction de Surveillance du Territoire

The headstone opposite read "Alphonsine Plessis," better known as Dumas's *La Dame aux Camélias*. Dumas's account of his doomed love affair with this courtesan was the one book Stefan remembered from the university. And here lay the courtesan, once the object of a man's love, now only dust under dried flowers.

He thought of Ulrike's, Marcus's, and Ingrid's graves: they'd been buried three times deeper than usual, for security. He'd only glimpsed the pictures from *Ici Paris*, the sensational tabloid weekly that had published the forbidden funeral photos, showing Ulrike's El Fateh scarf draped over her casket.

She had remained defiant to the end.

Stefan remembered that scarf, the red-and-white one given to her by a rifle instructor in the South Yemen camp. She liked to protect her black hair from the sand and biting wind, wear her dark glasses, and pose for photos with the Uzi. It was her only vanity . . . had it made her feel authentic?

Stefan had liked the training camp in Yemen, put up with the military-like dormitories, daily shooting practice, and spicy Middle Eastern food. Didn't even mind Marcus. Or his political diatribes and earnest protestations of brotherhood to the PLO and South Yemeni secret service over the campfires.

He remembered the Persian Gulf, a black spot in the distance, and how the wind howled over the desert at night. Like baying wolves. The strange, savage beauty called to him. Stefan never knew so many stars existed, studding the universe. Every night he sat back in the Jeep, staring transfixed into the navy blue night, thousands upon thousands of glimmering pinpricks webbing the sky as if with diamond dust.

Nice *mecs*, the PLO, he'd thought. They'd put up with his group, didn't ogle the women too much. The real difference was their seriousness, their purpose. Struggle was reality for these desert men.

The more Stefan saw, the more he realized how they—a

scruffy, spoiled bunch of Germans spouting revolution, robbing banks, and stealing BMWs—mocked their hosts' real struggle.

Yet when he tried to talk to Ulrike about it, she waved him off. "We learn by doing, striking back in our own way. Otherwise the system wins," she'd said.

But the system had won. Events had proved her right.

The Yemen plane tickets were courtesy of the East German Secret Police, the Stasi. The Stasi had wined and dined the Haader-Rofmein gang as a sort of twisted revenge on West Germany. But that was all before the Wall came down. The Stasi had posed the PLO, portraying them as civilized savages with guns, in the perfect photo opportunity. Everyone was being used . . . all of them. Stefan had realized the whole thing was to further the East Germans' political agenda.

Right after that, the PLO had kicked them out.

Upon their return they'd been sheltered at the Stasi training camps near Berlin, Star I and Star II, where their cadres learned the use of explosives and various weapons: 9mm Heckler & Koch submachine gun, the G-3 automatic rifle, .357 Smith & Wesson, the AK-47 Kalashnikov rifle, and the Soviet RPG-7 antitank rocket weapon. Experts on explosives demonstrated bomb-triggering devices consisting of battery-fed photoelectric beams that could be employed against moving objects—interruption of the beam would detonate the bomb. A technique they used often.

The Stasi later helped the terrorists "retire" in East Germany. But Jutta had been imprisoned in France. Had ex-Stasi members still watched her? Or had she been killed by that rabid *flic* who'd wanted them all dead and gone long ago? Teynard, the *flic* who'd planted the informer.

Now Stefan had to escape. He scanned the cemetery. If someone had gotten to Jutta, they could get to him.

Anxiously, he paced under the tree, ignoring the crunch of

the grave digger's shovel. There had been only four of them who knew of this place.

Now there were three. He had to leave, get away. What if the killer was one of them?

Stefan pulled his beret low, edged among the headstones. He surveyed the cemetery. Besides the grave digger, there was only an old lady, bent and black-clad, who swept the path.

He knew who he had to see.

AIMÉE WANTED to concentrate on finding the link between Figeac and her mother. Yet when she thought of Christian sitting in a Commissariat cell, she felt guilty.

At least she'd found out from Idrissa that Romain Figeac had made tapes. If she got Christian out he could help her find them.

The other address for Etienne Mabry, besides his apartment, was at the Bourse, the stock market. As she walked through the Sentier the whir of sewing machines escaped from windows above her. On the corner stood a Pakistani man. The jackets draped from his arm caught her eye. *"La jaquette à la mode!"* he propositioned all passersby. For a hundred francs she walked away with a linen shirt and jacket, their labels ripped out, probably designer seconds from the sweatshop above her. As a truck pulled up, the man swiftly folded the goods under his long coat and slinked around the corner.

A block away, she entered a deserted courtyard, set down her backpack, and got to work. She stood on the cobbles, reapplying her Chanel-red lipstick in a window. Looking in a tall truck's side-view mirror, she reapplied mascara. She flattened her spiky hair with gel, then slid into the heels she carried, along with a new cryptography manual, calcium biscuits for Miles Davis, and black silk underwear crushed at the bottom of her bag.

One never knew.

Agence France-Presse loomed beyond the Bourse's forest of columns. Good thing her Beretta rested in her office drawer, she thought, as she saw the metal sensors of the Greek temple-like Bourse, the former Hôtel Bronignart.

Nearby stood an artists' squat, in a Haussmann-era building, the whole six floors covered with fluorescent graffiti. It was an unexpected bright spot in the middle of the financial district.

Aimée paused in the central enclosure of the Bourse. A speckled gray pigeon had flown inside. Disoriented, it pecked at the *tommettes*, the hexagonal red clay floor tiles. She knew how it felt, away from familiar ground and looking for crumbs.

Kind of like now.

Several men passed in formal evening attire. She wished she was wearing something more dressy than the crisp linen jacket over her jeans.

More business and efficiency exuded from the antenna-topped Agence France Presse opposite, she thought, than from the deserted wide marble corridors of the Bourse. Rounding a corner, she strode toward the trading hall.

"Trading has ended for the day, Mademoiselle," said a plainclothes guard wearing a headset. His massive shoulders barred her way. "No unauthorized visitors. Do you have an appointment?"

"But of course," she said, trying to scan the trader directory behind him for Mabry's name. She had to make sure he was listed and where he could be found.

Before she could think of what to say next, the guard smiled broadly.

"Another convert baptized," he said.

"Baptized?"

His massive hand pointed to the yellow-green splotch on her shoulder. Big and spreading.

"You must be special," he winked. "Our winged friends don't bestow this honor on everyone."

Great. Just what I need, she thought. No way in and bird poop on my suit.

On his desk, a halogen lamp beam focused on the visitors' log. Too bad she hadn't mastered reading upside down.

"Happen to have a tissue?"

He pulled a Wet Wipe from his desk.

"Try this."

"*Merci.*" She spotted an Evian bottle on the floor. "Mind if I use a bit of this, too?"

"Be my guest," he said with a gesture. Quickly, she rubbed at her linen jacket.

"He's following me," she said. "Look!"

As the guard turned, Aimée bent over the tenants' register. She scanned the entries and found the name Etienne Mabry.

"Who?"

She grinned, pointing to the pigeon who'd waddled into view.

"If you don't watch out, you're next," she said. "Please, tell Etienne Mabry I'm en route and I apologize for arriving late."

SHE DIDN'T know what to expect upstairs. The oddly narrow marble staircase echoed to the click of her heels. But by the time she arrived she'd dug in her bag, looped a silk scarf around her neck, and attached chunky silver earrings.

The placard on the landing read, "Mabry—YI Burobourse *ré-ception, salle A '2ième étage.*"

The small room didn't hold more than fifteeen people. All men. And as much ethnic variety as *béchamel* sauce. Fat binders and business prospectuses sat on the Directoire table. A few of the men, tanned and distinguished, could have stepped out of an Armani commercial.

"I'm looking for Monsieur Mabry," she said to one with a flute of champagne in his hand. "Can you point him out to me?"

"*Désolé,* Mademoiselle," he said.

But another man appeared at her elbow. Tanned, with graying hair, he leaned forward conspiratorially. "You and me both."

She looked up, surprised to be at the receiving end of a major charm offensive. She didn't mind too much. He wasn't hard on the eyes. At all. She'd had an affair with an older man in her neighborhood who walked his dog when she did. An aristo with old money and *de la* before his last name. He'd offered her a life of *luxe, calme, et volupté* . . . but she'd refused. She was her own mistress. No one else's.

"Let me know when you find him."

"And why should I?"

"I'm his uncle," he said. "Jean Buisson."

"Aimée Leduc," she said. As she turned, he clasped her elbow. "But if we don't find him, come to the reception with me." He nodded toward the room opposite, where tuxedoed men clustered in the doorway.

"Why should I do that?"

"The champagne's better!"

She smiled. He had a point.

Aimée slipped past the throng of men in black suits. She questioned several, getting quizzical looks in response. Above her hung a *fin de siécle* chandelier, its crystal swags catching the light. Had Christian gotten word to Mabry somehow? Had he already gone to retrieve Christian from the hands of the police?

Better move on, she thought. Try the champagne, then disappear. As she left the salon and walked down the hallway, she noticed a door to another room and peeked inside. A group of teenagers, mostly girls with a mélange of skin tones, perched by a computer terminal. A slim man in his early thirties leaned over it, pointing to items on the screen.

"Monsieur Mabry, the shares in networking and opticals indicate high risks," said a girl. Her light chocolate skin was like Idrissa's, Aimée thought.

"Mademoiselle Scalbert, can you support your view?" he said. "I think you're on the right track but tell us why."

Aimée slipped inside just as he looked up.

Mabry pulled his longish red-brown hair behind his ears. The man was a hunk, no getting around it; all six feet of him, in his pinstriped suit.

"Lost your way, Mademoiselle?" he asked, his voice dense as

crème fraîche. His large, smoke-colored eyes crinkled in amusement, then his lips curled in a smile.

He had a wonderful smile.

It reminded her of Yves, her former boyfriend, a Middle East correspondent. Etienne Mabry's lips curled the same way.

She and Yves had an on-again, off-again relationship, a disaster that had ended the year before on a corner in the old part of Cairo, sun-baked pyramids and buzzing flies for a backdrop.

"Sorry to disturb you," she said, wishing she could fuse with a nearby pillar and just watch him. "I'll wait until you're finished."

Etienne Mabry glanced at his watch and shook his head.

"We're running into overtime again," he said. "At our next Young Investors' meeting, we'll tackle Mademoiselle Scalbert's argument as to what constitutes excessive risk and what's smart."

The Young Investors gathered their things. Some cast long looks at Aimée as they left. Mabry spoke to a student and then pulled on his jacket. "How can I help you?" he said, as he reached the door.

"Aimée Leduc," she said, handing him her card. "Your uncle's looking for you, too."

He set down his worn brown leather briefcase. "Leduc Detective?" he asked, reading her card. "Is there some problem?"

"Christian Figeac's been taken in for questioning," she said. "He wants you to bail him out."

Etienne Mabry's brow creased with concern. "Not again."

So this wouldn't be the first time Mabry had rescued Christian from jail.

"I've been trying to reach you for some time," she said.

He patted the breast pocket of his fine-checked blue shirt. He even wore a red tie *de rigueur* for a businessman. "My fault . . . I forgot my phone. So sorry to make you come here to find me! I sponsor the Young Investors from the local *lycée*, the high school where my partner and I volunteer."

To her relief she realized he wasn't her bad-boy type.

"What happened to Christian?" he asked.

"The *flics* took him to the Commissariat," Aimée said. "Something to do with the Crédit Bank."

Etienne Mabry looked puzzled.

"Which Commissariat?" he asked, turning to lock the door.

"Nearby, the SPQ* on rue d'Amboise," she said. "I'm sure this isn't news to you but he seems to have . . ." She paused on the stairs.

Mabry watched her intently, waiting. He didn't help her finish her sentence. He guided her downstairs with his warm hand under her elbow, and she detected a faint smell of citrus in his cologne.

". . . substance abuse problems," she finished.

"Chronic ones," Mabry said, his brow still furrowed, as they arrived outside. "Why are you involved, if you don't mind my asking?"

"Something in the past involving his father and my mother." She winced. Had she said that out loud?

"Crédit Industriel et Commercial, you said?"

She nodded.

"Odd, both Figeacs banked with Barclays."

He pulled out a helmet and mounted the black-and-chrome Harley-Davidson parked on the cobblestones in front of them.

Maybe there was *some* bad boy in him after all.

AIMÉE WAS puzzled. As she walked toward her office, she tried to make sense of Mabry's comment about Christian's bank account.

She wondered why Romain Figeac lived in the Sentier amid garment sweatshops, fabric wholesalers, and working girls: the rag and shag trade. It wasn't fashionable or arty like the Left

---

Service de Police du Quartier.

Bank, though she vaguely remembered that Balzac had set dramas in the Sentier and Zola had been born there. Had Romain Figeac been an antihero, opposed to the literary establishment?

She leaned against a column and pulled out her cell phone. She punched in the private number for Martine, her friend from the *lycée* and current editor at *Madame Figaro*, the watered-down right-wing women's magazine.

"*Allô, cheri?*" breathed Martine after the first ring.

"Not even close," said Aimée. "Should I call back?"

"Just wishful thinking, Aimée," Martine said. "Jérôme's taken his kid *en vacances*. Just because I moved in with him doesn't mean I go on holidays *en famille*."

Aimée hadn't been too surprised when, after almost a year helming the right-wing daily *Le Figaro*, Martine had jumped to the women's magazine. And she'd moved in with Jérôme, the publicity director, a divorcé with a child. Joint custody was something Jérôme's ex pursued with vigor, insisting on shared vacations. Martine walked on shards of glass until they returned. A boyfriend vacationing with his ex would bother Aimée, too.

"Mind if I pick your brain?"

"Do you ever do anything else?" said Martine, her voice husky. "Just take me to Alain Ducasse's new restaurant, then I'll be putty in your hands."

That would cost next month's rent. Martine sounded bored, and edgy.

"*Madame Figaro* having problems?"

"The Madame and I might soon agree to disagree," Martine said. "*Tiens*, don't get me started. What do you need?"

"A lot of things. Info on the connections between Haader-Rofmein and Action-Réaction gangs."

"Time traveling? Blast from the past?"

"My mother. Kind of like that."

"Let me look." Aimée heard tapping as Martine's long nails

sped over the keyboard. The phone line clicked. "Hold on," she said.

"Any man in your life?" Martine asked, sighing as she returned. "But then you're different from me. I'd be crawling the ceiling."

"Well, I met this suit," Aimée said hesitantly. "A golden boy from the Bourse, but I doubt he's interested in me." She felt too embarrassed to even mention that his uncle was also a possibility.

"Aren't you, what do they call it . . . evolved?" Martine breathed into the phone. "Call him."

"Seems too 'nice,' but he has got a Harley."

"Impressive," Martine said. "You know capitalists have some good points."

"We met under adverse conditions," Aimée said.

"Doesn't matter . . . you met!"

Another click on the line.

"It's Jérôme, I have to get off," Martine said. "About your mother, I'll dig around."

AIMÉE'S CELL phone rang.

"*Allô?*"

"Christian Figeac called," René said. "His financial advisor sprang him from the Commissariat. He felt contrite, says his father used to keep tapes in some panel."

"Panel . . . where?"

Why hadn't Christian mentioned this before?

Irritated, she paused in front of a busy *tabac*, taking in the late afternoon paper's headlines: WORLD TRADE ORGANIZATION PROTEST and TERRORIST THREATS OF POISON GAS with photos of demonstrators being hauled away from the Palais des Congrès. When she saw the photo of a man captioned "Spokesman for Action-Réaction," she slipped four francs into the vendor's hand and folded it under her arm.

"The tapes are behind the desk in his father's study. But he's gone, he'll return later," René was saying. "He said he'd forgotten about them since his father kept most things at the bank or with his publisher."

These tapes might contain information about her mother . . . why hadn't Christian remembered sooner?

"I'll stop at Romain Figeac's, then come to the office."

"I'm driving to Media 9," he said. "A negotiation question and since you weren't there . . ."

She heard the complaint in his voice.

"Hold out for the exclusives," she interrupted. "We wouldn't want to design and implement a security system with our blood, sweat, and tears, only to see them hire a cheap-upkeep server to continue our work . . . and watch it crash."

"True," René said. "But I could use some help."

"*Bien sûr*, don't worry, I'll tackle my desk soon," she said. "But be careful, René, not like last time with Euroworld, eh? We've learned our lesson."

SHE NEEDED to get into Christian Figeac's atelier and she didn't want to wait for him.

In her apartment, she opened the worm-holed armoire and pulled out her kit. She'd find the hiding place for the tapes without anyone's being the wiser. It was her father's favorite tactic. She hoped Christian wouldn't mind.

She hung up her linen jacket and put on a blue service jacket and a cap with *L'eau de France's* logo of the Seine snaking across it. She struggled into the blue twill pants. Maybe she should try Morbier's pills. Every time she quit smoking she felt it in her hips!

"*OUI?*" ANSWERED a reedlike man wearing an apron double-tied around his waist who stood at the concierge's door. A burnt vanilla aroma wafted from the interior.

"*Bonsoir*, Monsieur, sorry to interrupt your dinner," she said, setting down her tool bag. She handed him a card reading PLOMBERIE DELINCOURT 24/7 SERVICE.

From inside his hallway a television blared *Questions pour un Champion*, the quiz show on France3.

"Monsieur Figeac called about a blockage. He's concerned about a compliance complaint." She gave him a big smile, pushed the cap to the back of her head, and pulled a clipboard from her bag. "*Tiens*, he's not home."

"You're the second one tonight."

"Eh, do you mean the cleaners?"

"People coming and going like this is the Gare de Lyon!" The man untied his apron. He stared at her clipboard as if it were dirty. "Come tomorrow morning."

"Sorry, Monsieur," she said, "but if you could unlock the apartment, I can lock up after."

Irritation clouded the man's face.

Aimée shrugged. "Just doing my job, Monsieur. Don't mind me, eh, a quick plumbing adjustment, then I'll be gone."

All she wanted was to get into Romain Figeac's writing room and search the back wall panels for the tapes. Why hadn't she noticed before?

She wished he'd hurry up.

He stood, not budging.

From the hall the pitch of the contestants' shouts mounted to a frenzy. The concierge was torn between the finale of his game show and escorting her upstairs.

"Make it quick," he said, glancing at his watch.

He wouldn't let her forget it, she could tell.

"Is something cooking on the stove?"

He reached for a big key ring. "I burned the sugar instead of caramelizing it." He shook his head. "A catastrophe with *crème brûlée!*"

Aimée hefted her *plomberie* bag and followed him into the

hallway to the staircase for the Figeac apartment. The concierge hit the light switch.

And then she saw the black smoke pouring down.

"Call the *pompiers*."

He stood paralyzed.

"Hurry—there's a fire!" she said, keeping the panic from her voice with effort. "Give me the keys. *Vite*, get help!"

He clattered over the parquet to his flat.

She climbed to the next floor, then crouched down in the hallway. From her bag, she pulled out her scarf, sprayed it with Evian aerosol, and, covering her nose and mouth, knotted it at the back of her head.

Praying it wasn't too late to find the panels, she unlocked the door to the Figeacs' apartment and crawled inside. But she didn't get far.

An inferno of heat, flames, and smoke enveloped her, fast and furious, blinding her, as searing pain shot through her hands.

She jerked back, her foot caught on a burning chair, and she stumbled. Embers fell from the burning ceiling, showering her clothing. Her work shirt ignited. Flames licked her ears, singed her hair. Ripping her shirt off, she grabbed her *plomberie* bag and rolled on the floor, smothering the flames.

She had to get out. Crawling forward, she reached the door, struggled to her feet, turned, then heaved herself backward. Hard.

She landed in the hallway, her shoulder ramming the grill-work. No time to deal with it. Heat and smoke choked her.

She crawled, trying to ignore her burns, through scorching heat. Red-orange flames leaped, dense black smoke poured across the foyer. Her lungs hurt but she took as deep a breath as she could. She had to get out of the building.

Coughing, eyes smarting, blindly she made her way down the stairs, bumping into the concierge, who was crumpled against the banister.

Startled, she grabbed him. Had he been attacked? Quickly, she scanned the stairs but couldn't see anything through the smoke.

She sat him up, bracing her wrists under his shoulder. Good thing he was thin. Her lungs burned. She had to pause on the cracked marble stairs to breathe even though each inhalation hurt. She heard the sound of glass popping and shattering as yellow-white flames shot from the windows.

Arson, she thought, as her mind grew foggy. Someone had set the apartment on fire ... Christian Figeac? No, she reasoned. He'd make more if he sold the place.

Beside her, the concierge stirred. Aimée heard sirens outside. Who'd called the *pompiers*? The concierge? She heard hatchets chopping, saw the streams of water arcing against night darkness, and felt the spray mist from the window cover her. Then a sharp blow struck her on the head.

And then, darkness.

Monday Evening

EX-POLICE COMMISSAIRE Marius Teynard, a snowy white-haired man in his late sixties, watched the streetlight pool in circles upon his desk blotter. Outside his window on rue de Turbigo, buses thrummed and the reflection of the spotlighted dome of the Conservatoire des Arts et Métiers glinted on his window.

Sighing, he balled up the offending faxes. "Coding cowboys, throbbing e-mail, Jews for Java" . . . *Zut alors!* What kind of language was this?

In disgust, he pushed back his burgundy leather armchair and stood. Cyber crime, encrypted e-mail . . . they called this detecting? Things traveled through the air like so many radio waves. Through the ether. He didn't understand the Web.

Didn't want to.

His nephew insisted he "get up to speed." Let his nephew handle the new computers, the intricate log-on procedures. When Teynard had been a commissaire, all he'd had to do was type. And two fingers had sufficed for police headquarters at Quai des Orfèvres, as Teynard often pointed out to him. His nephew smiled. But he'd seen him rolling his eyes.

The fax machine spat out more. He groaned. Just what he needed, more cyber gibberish!

But after Marius Teynard tore off the fax, he sat down in surprise. A tingle ran down the outside of his thick arms, all the way to his fingertips. He hadn't felt the once familiar rush in a long time. Like in the old days when his force could take care of vermin the way they should be dealt with, quickly and permanently.

How long had it been . . . five or six years since the last report? More? Now he remembered: It was when the Wall had crumbled and the Stasi files on the Haader-Rofmein and Action-Réaction gangs had come to light.

But now he saw that the terrorist Jules Bourdon was still alive. In Africa. Thriving.

Marius Teynard read further as the fax machine spewed out more sheets.

Correction, Marius Teynard realized. Jules Bourdon had left Africa . . . the embarkation reports from the Dakar airport were tallied once a week.

Teynard wanted to kick the fax machine to bits. And stomp on them. What did all this technological efficiency amount to when Jules Bourdon, that vermin, might already have been in Paris a week.

AIMÉE CAME TO IN THE parked ambulance outside Christian Figeac's apartment.

"Treatment for smoke inhalation, burns on the palms," a stocky blue-suited man with a crew cut was saying at her side.

She felt something hard over her mouth and looked about her. It took her a minute to realize she was in an ambulance, inhaling oxygen. Aimée watched as the bag filled, then collapsed, as if it were breathing lungfuls of air. She remembered doing this in an ambulance before, after her father's death in the terrorist explosion.

She tore off the mask, then clutched at her throat, unable to inhale. The *pompier* slipped the mask back over her mouth and nose and mimed taking several deep breaths.

"Back with us?" he said, not unkindly. "Bet you never thought being a plumber would be hazardous, eh?"

She looked down. She still wore the Plomberie Delincourt uniform.

She pulled the mask aside. "I'm fine," she gasped, still short of breath.

"*Voilà*, take it easy," he said. "To dissipate the carbon monoxide, you need hi-flow oxygen."

She let him slip the mask back on and greedily inhaled.

"That's the way," he said. He nodded encouragement until she'd inhaled the oxygen for a full five minutes.

"*Ça va?*"

She nodded and he took the mask off. Her head ached. The last thing she remembered was a whack on it from behind.

"Where's the concierge?" she asked. The *pompier*, who wore a badge that read HERVÉ PICARD pointed across the van. The concierge, a butterfly bandage over his brow, waved at her. He chewed on a baguette sandwich.

"Hungry?"

Tightness gripped her chest, but she nodded.

"We had extras from the canteen," the *pompier* said, handing her one wrapped in white waxy paper. "Just take it slow."

"*Merci,*" she said. She was now able to breathe without much pain, and she was grateful for something to eat.

"We'll watch you two tonight," he said. "Just a precaution."

"Not necessary," she said, raising herself up on her elbow. Her shoulder tingled with pain and she winced. But it wasn't dislocated. She knew the difference. It was her new tattoo, feeling as if it had been ripped raw. But she had no intention of spending the night in the hospital like the concierge. "What's that?" she asked, looking at the graphite-colored box on the end of her finger.

"This pulsoximeter tells us your red blood cell levels," he said, checking a ticker-tape type readout. "Your carboxy hemoglobin level was sixty-five percent. You were close to checking out. Permanently."

Her breath caught in her throat.

"Just that apartment was affected," he said.

"Only that apartment?" She sat up more slowly, rewrapped her sandwich, and stuck it in her jacket pocket.

Her chest tightened again.

But something bothered her more. She'd been hit from behind. A big welt on her head throbbed.

"Go slow," Hervé said. "You can claim workman's comp and disability from your union. I'll give you some forms. Patients always forget down the road."

She didn't want to disregard his advice; his warm blue eyes and wide smile were sincere. But she wanted to run inside the building and check to see if there was anything left.

"*Merci.* But I need my bag," she said. "And I've got to get home."

Hervé wrapped a blood pressure cuff around her arm, inserted a cold stethoscope against it, and pumped. "Can you tell me who you are, what day it is, where we are, and what happened?"

"Aimée Leduc, it's Monday night in an ambulance in the Sentier, and I was trying to fix a plumbing problem inside the apartment."

"A and O looks good," he said. "Awake and *orientée* but the captain wanted to talk to you when you came round. See how you feel after that."

She shrugged.

"Meanwhile, let's get your address."

Uh oh. If she admitted she was trying to gain entry to the apartment under false pretenses she'd be in trouble. Big trouble.

From outside, she heard raised voices. One was familiar. She recognized Christian Figeac.

"Of course, but I need to speak with the owner, he's my friend."

"*Bien sûr*, but let's get the paperwork out of the way," Hervé said with gentle insistence.

By the time Aimée made it out of the ambulance she'd accepted an ice pack for her head, given an address, signed a release form, and agreed to meet Hervé later for coffee. Too bad she had no intention of honoring that commitment.

Only when she reached the courtyard did she appreciate the irony. She'd have given anything to have found documents regarding her mother in the apartment, but doing so would have cost her life.

Uniformed *pompiers* rushed past her with more hoses, dampening the smoldering walls. A group with hatchets followed. Christian Figeac stood talking with a man who took notes and wore jeans. Either a reporter or an insurance adjuster.

White-faced, with soot smudges on his cheeks and hands,

Christian seemed shell-shocked. He wore the same silver synthetic leather jacket, his hair more stringy than before. She couldn't tell if he recognized her. The man handed him a card.

"Arson?" Aimée asked, joining them.

"Mademoiselle, after investigation the arson squad will inform us," the man said, snapping his notebook shut. "It's not what we'd call a typical Sentier fire. Contact me tomorrow, Monsieur Figeac."

And he was gone.

"You see," Christian said, turning to her, his gaze hollow. "A curse."

"Curse?"

"Like the ghosts," he said.

Stark halogen searchlights set by the fire crew illumined the dripping building foyer. *Pompiers* ran back and forth, shouting directions and releasing hose pressure.

Ghosts didn't set fires.

She took him by the elbow to a corner of the wet, dark courtyard. Black puddles reflected the crescent fingernail of a moon.

"Tell me one thing and the answer goes no further," Aimée whispered, pulling him closer. "Did you set that fire?"

Christian Figeac's expression didn't change. "You think I need the money?"

She figured that was a rhetorical question and stayed quiet.

"Money . . . there's a lot," he said, as if talking to himself, twisting his hands together. His dry skin made a raspy sound. "Accounts I never knew about."

It wouldn't make sense to burn the place down for the insurance if he had money.

"What did he mean by the typical Sentier fire?"

"In the rag trade," Christian said, "say the merchant can't sell last season's overstock, he has a fire and collects insurance, probably makes a profit, too."

Of course, this was different. But who could have done it?

"Would Idrissa set the fire?"

"Idrissa? She's afraid of the spirits, I told you." He shook her off. Anger sparked in his large eyes.

"I met her," Aimée said. "She admitted she had worked for your father. But she was hiding something."

Christian Figeac, clad in his thin jacket, the sleeves damp, shivered in the scant moonlight. He must have come home from jail only to find his father's apartment burning.

She felt sorry for him. After her mother left, Aimée's father had done his best to make up for it. Her grandparents had, too. But had Romain Figeac done the same for Christian?

"I've got an extra couch," she said. "You're welcome to it."

He blinked, shook his head as if coming to. "What kind of an outfit . . . a plumber?"

"I tried to break into your place and find that panel concealing the tapes," she said. "Are there any more?"

"In the bank maybe," he said.

"First thing tomorrow you need to get them. Listen, this is about your father. We need to talk."

He followed her out of the courtyard.

They skirted the ambulance, passed the parked fire trucks. On rue Réaumur, she raised her arm to hail a taxi.

"No, we'll take my car," he said, pointing to an olive Jaguar XKE, dented, with scratched paint. A battered classic.

Christian Figeac sank into the leather ribbed seat, switched on the engine.

"What do we need to talk about?"

He seemed calmer. She hoped he could handle what she had to say. Late-night strollers crossed in front of them, pale and caught, like frightened deer, in the Jaguar's headlights.

"Where to?" Christian asked.

"Ile St. Louis, Quai d'Anjou," she said. "My apartment."

He gunned the engine and shot toward Boulevard de Sébastopol.

She didn't know how else to say it. "I'm sorry, but your father was shot with a large-caliber gun, not the one you said he'd used."

"How do you know?" he asked, surprised.

"From the residue on the wall. It's not consistent with . . ." She hesitated. "A .25 has a nice recoil but it's not a blaster. I took a sample from the wall to the lab yesterday." Good thing she'd followed her instinct since everything had now gone up in smoke. And it struck her. "You know, that's what the murderer wanted . . . all the evidence gone."

He slowed down. "*Murderer* . . . why?" he asked.

"You tell me," she said. "Did your father have enemies, someone who didn't . . . ?"

Her phrase was lost in a blare of honking klaxons. Christian floored the pedal. He cornered rue de Palestro. The Jaguar responded, roaring bulletlike down the narrow medieval street.

"But he left a suicide note," Christian said. "How could he have been murdered?"

"Think back to when you found him. Tell me what you saw."

Christian's shoulders heaved. "It was dark, he was slumped over on the desk . . . like when he'd been drinking."

"I'm sorry," she said. "But really he was killed."

"Papa's writing played the most important role in his life," he said. "Everything else ranked below it."

"You're proving it yourself," she said. "He wouldn't have committed suicide."

They sped through the empty Sentier streets. Dark buildings encrusted with grime illumined by globular street lamps peaked above them. Alleys and passages jutted like capillaries from a veinous hub, calcified by old coaching inns.

"Christian—if I may call you that—with a suicide, the gun stays there. The .25 wouldn't . . ." She paused, trying to say it tactfully.

"I didn't pay much attention but it was his," he said. "The *flics* took it."

"Check the coroner's office, ask where it is," she said. "The coroner's making a report, they'll open an inquiry."

"Non," he shouted. "Papa's dead. I had enough of those reporters after Maman's suicide. They printed those awful photos, the ones of her remains in the car. They'll just hound me and want to rake up dirt."

"It's painful for you, I'm sorry," she said. Of course, he was right and how sad. But, she thought grimly, it didn't change the fact that his father had been murdered.

Aimée wished the bucket seat had a working seat belt. Christian Figeac seemed intent on crossing Paris in ten minutes.

"Why can't the past leave me alone?" he said. He combed his hair back with his fingers, stubby and bitten to the quick.

"Don't you see?" she said. "Someone murdered your father. Now they're after you."

He screeched his brakes on the quai before her apartment. They stopped with a jerk. "But I thought it was my fault." He slumped over the wooden steering wheel, pounded the leather dashboard.

"Christian, why did you think it was your fault?"

"Below his standard, never reached his expectations . . . ," he mumbled. Shadows curtained Christian Figeac's face.

All his life he had been haunted by high-profile parents; a renowned father and mother and a string of public tragedies. Sad to think of the pain stamped on his psyche.

"You didn't kill him. Someone else did," she said. Then she told him how Jutta Hald had appeared in her life.

"That's why I contacted you. Think again," she said. "Maybe she came to your door?"

He shook his head.

Again, he combed his stringy hair behind his ears with his fingers. It was as if he'd numbed out, refusing to deal with what she said. Who would want to know his father had been murdered?

She hadn't.

She got out of the car, slammed the dented door. But she stood on the cobblestones, unable to move her feet. She had to make him understand.

"What if it had been you in the apartment when it caught fire? You must realize you're in danger. And I am, too. Someone knocked out your concierge and whacked me from behind."

She turned and let him see the throbbing welt on her head in the quayside light.

Now he looked scared. And lost.

"What can I do?" He shook his head. "Even if you're right, everything went up in smoke."

True.

"You said he kept things at the bank or with his publisher," she said. "Idrissa transcribed your father's work. I need to talk with her again. Perhaps something can still be found."

"Go ahead, she won't talk to me."

"What's her number?"

"01 75 98 72 02."

She pulled out the first thing that came to hand from her bag, a lip-liner pencil, and wrote it down on the back of her hand.

"You asked me to help you, remember?" she said. "If I were you, Christian, I'd be afraid."

"Did I say I wasn't?" he asked. "So, girl detective, you think you will find out who killed my father?"

She nodded. And she would find Jutta's killer, too.

He wrote another check, thrust it through the window at her. Surprised, she stared at him.

"Not enough?" he shouted, reaching over to add more zeros.

"Throwing money at me?" But René would shoot her if she didn't take it.

She took it. Michel's loan hadn't covered it all.

A crow flew past, swooped, then perched on the quayside wall. His black silhouette was outlined against the lighted Seine.

"Let's look at the things he kept in the bank," she said. "My mother's trail led me to your father."

"Always your mother," he said. "I hardly knew mine."

"Neither did I. And mine was American, too."

Christian looked away. He flipped the key in the ignition and the engine sputtered to life. "I'll stay with Etienne," he said abruptly. "Meet me tomorrow at two at the Crédit Industriel et Commercial in Place des Victoires." And with that he roared off down the darkened quai.

Surprised by his continual changes of mood, she climbed up the stairs. Miles Davis sniffed her with his wet nose as she entered the apartment. She pulled out the half-eaten baguette sandwich Hervé the fireman had given her and set it in his bowl on the kitchen floor. Then she stumbled down the hallway to her bedroom and collapsed on her feather duvet.

Hours later, she woke up, her face wet, still in her sooty plumber's uniform. Her thirties Bakelite bedside clock showed green fizzy numbers. She rubbed her eyes.

3:04 A.M.

She remembered. Everything had gone up in smoke.

And she realized she'd been crying in her sleep, something she hadn't done in years. Her pillow was damp with tears.

Fragments of an old dream came back to her . . . running, trying to hand her mother something. Playing catch-up as always. But her mother was so far ahead . . . so distant. Aimée could only see her sleeve flapping in the wind. And then she was gone.

Why had her mother left them?

But she knew the answer. Deep down she knew she'd been a burden. She remembered her mother's irritated glances. How she had stuck her paintbrush in the jam jar of cloudy turpentine, annoyed by the annual teacher conference. *"Amy, such institutional parrots, they don't teach you creative expression!"*

Aimée had felt confused. Did that mean she was boring and

slow or that her teacher was? Or both? She only knew she didn't measure up to what her mother wanted. Just the way Christian felt.

Her strict teacher was fair despite her funny little chignon and severe curvature of the spine. "Scoliosis," her father had called it, her mother adding, "Never stare at others' deformities. Focus on the eyes."

The pain seared her as always. No differently than when she was eight years old. She undid the pants and shirt, kicked them onto the floor, and curled up in one of her father's old shirts. Soft and worn.

She stared up at the milky chandelier, many of its icicle drops missing, that hung from the plasterwork oval-inlaid ceiling. An occasional glint of light from the passing night barges was reflected in the crystals. Beside her, Miles Davis stirred in his sleep and nuzzled her. A cool breeze scented of the Seine drifted in through her open window.

No way could she fall asleep. Only one remedy for that.

She sat up in bed, pulled her laptop over, and went online. She searched deeper than she had the other night, finding more sites about the Haader-Rofmein gang. They'd existed until 1992, when some of the first-generation members had given themselves up. There was even a punk rock band named after Haader-Rofmein, noted for its song "Grandpa Was a Nazi, Papa Was a Commie, Oh My!"

Since Germany had undergone denazification and the integration of a communist state in less than two generations, the Haader-Rofmein background and identity had complex implications.

She realized the terrorists symbolized another era in which youths rebelled against postwar conformity, abhorring their government, which was filled with former Nazis, and the industrialists and financiers who had been members of the Wehrmacht.

They took violent political action. They wanted to overthrow what the Allies had created: a Germany divided between communism and strident capitalism.

She found the old Interpol WANTED posters. So many fugitives had been on the run across Europe.

Haader-Rofmein had kidnapped a wealthy French industrialist, Paul Laborde, near the German border. He'd died from injuries suffered during a shoot-out. After that, the gang members escaped or were imprisoned.

She scrutinized the photos: radicals caught in a bank heist by the security camera, bombed-out houses, BMWs riddled with bullet holes spun out on the Autobahn, figures in dark glasses with their hands up being frisked by police, the blood-smeared cells of Kernheim prison where emaciated RAD leaders lay dead on the concrete, eyes open.

No one resembled her mother. She was flooded with relief.

She found Action-Réaction, which proclaimed itself the French counterpart of the German struggle.

Apart from slogans inciting members to *Eat the state* and *Join class warfare*, Action-Réaction boasted its revolutionary ideas were in line with the 1789 French Revolution, blended with strains of Maoism and anarchism.

She searched for its headquarters or an address. Aside from an article on sweatshop worker rights in the Sentier and the listing of an address for an information office at 7, rue Beauregard, there was nothing. She finally fell asleep.

TUESDAY

BE RESPONSIBLE, SHE TOLD herself when she woke up. She had to act more responsibly. Not let this obsession take control.

She called Action-Réaction, got an answering machine, and left a message, using the name Marie, saying she'd like an appointment as soon as possible.

After walking Miles Davis on the quai, she dropped him at the groomer's for a much-needed trim, then stopped at the *charcuterie* for his favorite steak tartare. By eleven, she'd finished tests on the Media 9 security fire wall and e-mailed them to René.

Time for her to visit the person who'd know more about Romain Figeac's work than his own son—Alain Vigot, his editor.

Below her apartment's marble staircase, she wheeled René's battered Vespa over the old *losange*-patterned tiles. He'd loaned it to her since her moped had been stolen last year. Riding across deserted Pont Marie, a low glare reflecting from the Seine in the absence of pollution haze, she realized most Parisians had begun their annual vacations.

Over on the Left Bank, Aimée shoved the Vespa in the rack outside Tallimard Presse. Once a cloister, this medieval stone building with baroque and Empire additions still projected a meditative aura.

"Alain Vigot, please," Aimée said to the middle-aged receptionist.

"He's in conference," she replied after consulting an appointment book.

A yellow light spiraled from the turreted windows, softening the framed photos of Tallimard's authors and illuminating the arched recesses in the thick wall. The small reception lobby teemed with couriers delivering packages and an exodus of secretaries going out for lunch.

"I'll wait."

The receptionist tilted her tortoiseshell-framed glasses down her nose. "Better make an appointment."

"*D'accord*," Aimée agreed. "This afternoon?"

"Nothing until . . . let's see, after Milan . . ." She looked up. "Laure, this goes to Monsieur Vigot."

A young woman wearing a gray miniskirt and tunic top thrust a file onto the receptionist's desk and picked up a large envelope with "Alain Vigot, *éditeur de fiction*" written on it.

"Laure, when does Monsieur Vigot return from Milan?"

"Late September," Laure said, turning toward the door, obviously in a hurry.

"Any way you could squeeze me in today?" Aimée handed Laure a business card.

"Monsieur Vigot's in a lunch meeting."

"Christian Figeac suggested I speak with him."

"I'll give him your card," Laure said, her mouth pursed in a tight line.

"*Merci*, it's important."

"Like I said, I'll pass it along."

Not much of a guarantee, Aimée thought.

She left, then waited outside the Tallimard entrance until Laure emerged. Aimée followed her, at a distance, two blocks to Brasserie Lipp on Saint Germain des Près. Laure nodded to several publishing types, smoking and drinking at the sidewalk tables. The fashionable crowd, wanting to see and be seen, preened under the awning.

She was surprised when Laure continued several blocks down Saint Germain to a small covered passage, Cours du Commerce St. André, then turned left. Didn't Alain Vigot lunch with the trendy world of French publishing?

Laure entered a small café in the middle of the glass-roofed passage next door to a *crêperie* stall. Aimée's mouth watered at the smell of Nutella *crêpes*. Her favorite. She'd only had a brioche with her coffee this morning.

Aimée ducked into the *tabac* opposite, thumbed a copy of *L'événement*, and prepared for a long wait. The painted wood shop fronts showed the passage's gentrification. But Laure emerged empty-handed only a few minutes later.

Aimée hesitated, then opened the café door. The door's lace curtains swayed and the hanging bells tinkled. A few heads, all of them male, looked up from the zinc counter.

The clientele stood drinking, watching a motorcycle rally on television. The revving of engines and shouting voices of announcers, raised to a fevered pitch, filled the air.

Only one round table at the rear of the dark café was occupied. A man with thin graying hair and round, black-framed glasses sat at it, reading, oblivious to the noise. A white linen coat was draped over the back of his chair, his shirt was unbuttoned. Blue ink marks stained his shirt cuffs. He nursed a large *bière* and a copy of *Le Figaro*.

She checked to see if someone else was expected. But there was only one setting, a basket of bread, and a very full ashtray.

It seemed he had his own version of a lunch meeting.

"Monsieur Vigot?" she asked.

His eyes, behind his owl-like glasses, looked small and tired.

"*Oui.*" He gave a curt nod. "And you are?"

"Aimée Leduc. Pardon me for disturbing your lunch."

He said nothing.

"May I take a few minutes of your time?"

"Concerning?" He looked up, leaned back, and crossed his legs.

"Romain Figeac."

"No interviews about Monsieur Figeac," Vigot said. "I've made that clear. . . ."

"That's understood. I'm a detective," she said. "Christian Figeac hired me."

Now maybe Vigot would listen to her.

"Why?" he asked, reaching for his glass. He eyed her more closely this time.

"Could I sit down, please?" she asked with a big smile. "Maybe you can help me, I can't figure Christian out."

Amusement crossed Vigot's face. "Have a *bière brûlée* with me. I guarantee it will help." He waved to the waiter, who had a mobile charge machine stuck in his waistband. *"Encore . . . deux bières brûlées."*

The waiter nodded.

Aimée sat down. She moved the mustard pot and bread basket to the side. She didn't like the way Vigot's eyes swept up her legs.

Almost immediately, the glasses of *bière* flambéed with gin arrived. Little of the alcohol had burned off.

"Salut," Vigot said, clicking glasses.

Fruity fumes and acidic hops tore down her throat. If drinks could signal a color, she figured this would flash fuchsia.

"Christian still raving about ghosts?" Vigot asked.

Aimée watched him as she sipped. He seemed relaxed, his eyes calm. Not glazed. Like she would be if she kept drinking this stuff.

"Monsieur Vigot, what was Romain Figeac working on when he died?"

Alain Vigot's white puffy hands remained steady on his glass. "Christian still got that on his mind?"

"Actually, Monsieur," she said, "it's personal."

If Vigot was surprised, he didn't show it.

"You knew him a long time, didn't you?"

"Forty years of friendship, a working relationship," Vigot said, taking a long sip. "From the rocky to the sublime."

Aimée traced the condensation on her glass with her finger.

"Figeac's prose was velvet smooth, like a baby's cheek, but his mind was more barbed than a hacksaw. In literature that's called the hallmark of a civilized mind."

"And what about at the end?"

"Mademoiselle Leduc," he said. "I'm sorry to tell you but he hadn't written in years. Dried up."

She didn't believe him or like his condescending manner. Voices rose from the bar. A close smoky haze reigned over the tables.

"Christian said he was writing again," she said. "Furiously, as if possessed."

Vigot shook his head. "All I saw was a scared old man." He sighed. "I should have paid attention, seen it sooner."

"But you were his friend."

"A good friend!" Vigot's eyes sparked. "I carried him for years." His brow creased. "Compiled the anthologies, reissued works to keep his name alive. That American *pute* . . . she killed him."

Did he mean Christian's mother, the actress?

"But she committed suicide ten years ago," Aimée said.

"He never got over her," he said. "Never wrote the same. Something had died."

Aimée wished she was outside instead of in this dark masculine sports bar with this sad-looking man.

"Why don't you lunch at Brasserie Lipp?"

He grinned. "With all the literary sophisticates?" He surveyed her legs again, took another swig, and finished the glass. "Romain and I had an inside table; we lunched there for years. It bothers me to go there."

He nodded to the waiter again and pointed to his glass.

He turned to her with a restrained smile. "Now if you'll excuse me . . ."

"But I haven't gotten to why I came here," she said.

"What's that?"

"Figeac's apartment burned down last night," she said.

Vigot's eyes narrowed. "Is Christian all right?"

She nodded. "I'm sure that among the other left-wing radicals he befriended, Romain Figeac knew my mother. That's my personal interest. I want to find her, or at least find out about her."

"Don't tell me the old radical chic's back in style?

"As Figeac's friend and editor, you were close to him," she said. "Years ago he was involved with Action-Réaction, wasn't he?" She didn't wait for his answer. "Where are the tapes and boxes containing his work?"

Vigot recoiled as if she'd slapped him. "They're none of your business."

"Everything belongs to Christian Figeac as literary executor," she said.

"Leave him out of it."

"You're not very helpful." She shook her head.

"It's for his own good," said Vigot.

"My mother's name was Sydney Leduc. She was an American."

"You say that like it's supposed to mean something to me."

"I won't leave until you explain this." She took the sheet of paper she'd filched from Figeac's desk on her first unofficial visit to the atelier, the sheet that had been tucked under the typewriter, with the Tallimard logo, Alain Vigot's name at the top, the typographical symbols, and agit888 written on it and placed it in front of him.

Vigot studied her. He seemed to weigh his options. "I don't know much. There was an American who spoke excellent French and German, I don't remember her name," he said. "She helped Jean-Paul Sartre interview Haader in prison because he spoke no French."

Aimée sat back. Her breath was short. "The translator may have been my mother!"

"I'm not sure." Vigot shrugged. "Some of them used code names. But she was at Romain's apartment one day. Romain wanted to publish Sartre's interview in a left-wing magazine he was starting. But nothing came of the magazine, it never got off the ground."

"Tell me more about this American." She leaned closer to him.

"You're asking me about an afternoon more than twenty years ago with a woman whom I remember vaguely." He moved away.

"But you remembered she was an American." She gave him space, afraid of looking too desperate.

"The reason I remembered that much is that right afterward Ulrike Rofmein helped Haader escape from prison. They weren't caught until years later." He'd relaxed again.

"Why did Figeac write the words agit888?"

Vigot shook his head. "That's all I know. Romain always said if he'd published the article the magazine would have taken off."

"What happened to the article?"

"Sartre published it. That took courage, given the climate then. He looked like a toad, did you know that? Don't think me cruel, Sartre said it himself," Vigot said. "Just leave Christian alone, he's had a rough time." He gestured to the waiter for another drink and stood up. "I'm going to the rest room. When I return, you'll be gone, won't you?"

His gait was unsteady as he moved past the table. He turned and looked at her, his eyes unfocused and very tired. "Leave me alone. I like to get drunk in peace."

SHE LEFT the café to the chorus of invitations to join the men at the bar for more *bière brulée*. What did it mean if her mother had helped translate an interview with Haader? But she felt there was more to what Vigot had said. And that there were boxes of Figeac's work unaccounted for.

Still at sea, she hurried along Boulevard Saint Germain. Back at Tallimard, she hit the kickstart on the scooter and gunned the engine. She'd counted on Vigot enlightening her as to how Figeac was connected to her mother.

But she thought he knew more than he was telling.

She called René on her cell phone.

"*Allô?*" She heard René's fingers striking keys on the keyboard in the background. Then an insistent low buzz.

"Etienne Mabry wants you to call him."

A brief *frisson* of excitement hit her, then faded. Of course, it must concern Christian Figeac.

Aimée held the phone between her ear and neck as she rode across Pont Royal. The Seine breeze whipped up her skirt, scattered the perched pigeons from the large letter *N* incised on the bridge by Napoleon's orders.

"He needs your help with"—low static, clicks—"before we go."

Something sounded odd. The phone line was tapped.

"Hold on, René, I'll be there soon." She hung up. The office was five minutes away but she didn't want to tell him and the others who were listening that she was meeting Christian at the bank. She stuck her phone in her pocket.

She sped along the Quai des Tuileries, turned left under the Louvre's arcade, and veered by the Carousel roundabout past the Pyramide.

It bothered her that their phone line was tapped. A lot.

She squeezed her brakes before the Number 39 bus threaded the narrow grime-blackened arches to cross rue de Rivoli, almost flattening her against the Louvre's portal. She inhaled a big breath of exhaust.

ALAIN VIGOT LOCKED his office door and set the silver
flask on his polished cherry-wood desk. He lifted it up quickly.
The flask had left an oval of spilled Scotch and he wiped it up
with his sleeve.

Beside the window overlooking the publishing house courtyard near Saint Germain, framed book jackets filled Vigot's wall.
In the place of honor stood the photo of Figeac receiving the
Prix Goncourt. Figeac, oblivious of his own talent, had taken it
for granted.

But for Alain, as his editor, it had been the ultimate tri-
umph—the writer he'd discovered and nurtured, baby-sat
through drinking bouts, the birth of a son, disastrous political
choices, a failed marriage and bitter divorce—to see him
so honored.

He stared at the box of Romain Figeac's work. Inside lay partial manuscripts and dog-eared photos from Tallimard's banquets
honoring Figeac. The last one had been an affair to remember.
Jana, Figeac's movie star wife, once the darling of Godard and
the New Wave cinema, was there with her entourage of radicals.
Jana had gone from being his muse to orchestrating his downfall.
And her own.

Bored and restless when not working, Jana treated her son as
if he were an untrained puppy when she even noticed him. Her
cocaine-and-champagne lifestyle took a toll on her looks, yet she
remained a temptress who drove Figeac crazy. Crazy in love with
her. The miscarriage and her suicide five years later on its ghoulish anniversary had ended Figeac's writing, as far as he was concerned.

Alain conceded he'd been jealous of her . . . the self-absorbed bitch. Figeac had even banked her terrorist lover's loot for her, the loot of the supposed father of the child he'd always claimed was his.

Earlier that day Alain had submitted his resignation to Tallimard. He knew the time had come to withdraw from the world of publishing, which was being transformed by electronic books and on-demand publishing. Who knew what else they'd dream up? It was not Figeac's or his world anymore . . . the bottom line was what counted. Not literacy or literature. Who even used pen and ink anymore?

He'd burn the contents of this box personally. Let Figeac be remembered as the great writer he'd been, not the alcoholic hack who'd become obsessed with his wife's terrorist lover. But first he'd read what was inside the manila envelope Figeac had sent him before he killed himself.

RENÉ LOOKED UP as Aimée walked into the office.

"Christian Figeac cancelled your meeting," he said.

Disappointed, she walked toward her desk. Christian had given her big checks yet reneged on their deal. Was he in more trouble?

René wore a headset while working at his terminal. He pointed to the phone on her desk. The red light blinked; she picked it up.

"*Oui?*" she said.

"Frésnes Prison visiting hours start at two P.M.," Morbier said. "Prisoner number 3978. Today."

Aimée looked at her watch. "But it's . . ."

"Up to you," Morbier interrupted. "The prisoner's scheduled for transit and my contact's retiring tomorrow."

"Give me that number again," she said, snatching a pen and writing the numbers on her palm.

"I'm taking Marc," he said. "We're leaving for Brittany *en vacances.*"

"*Merci,*" she said, but Morbier had already hung up.

Apprehensive, she looked past the paperwork on her desk at René. "The phone's buzzing worries me, René."

"Maybe it's time to check for bugs, the wireless kind," he said, his fingers pausing on the keyboard. "Exterminator is my middle name."

She grabbed her jacket, tried it on, then threw it on the chair.

René's eyes narrowed to green slits.

"Problems?"

"What do you wear to prison?"

"Depends how long you're staying," René said. "Short-term, the linen works. Long-term, a jumpsuit with stripes. Why?"

"I'm visiting Jutta Hald's former cell mate," she said, scanning the faxes. "I'll knock this out later."

René gestured toward her linen jacket. "You mean we're postponing the sushi?"

"Désolée!" She slapped her cheek. Sometimes she forgot to eat. Or that other people did.

"Here's Christian's check for fifty thousand francs," she said. "Should tide us over."

René whistled.

That should mollify him and take care of some bills. "Don't forget to deposit it."

"I suppose you'll be eternally grateful to me," René said, pulling off his headset.

"And treat you to sushi every week."

AIMÉE BOARDED the dark pink Metro line for Porte d'Orleans. She hadn't had time to ask Morbier who this prisoner was and what she was in for.

She exited on the *péripherique* side and found bus number 187, the only public transport to Frésnes Prison.

Most of the bus passengers were African or of Arab descent, and female. An older French woman, haggard and bleary-eyed, pounded on the folding bus doors as they closed. With a shrug, the driver let her on. Women clutched babies and prisoners' laundry bags, as they tried to get past the folding strollers.

The ride wound past turn-of-the-century bungalows interspersed with "affordable" housing. Drab and uniform. A close commute to Paris was the only redeeming feature Aimée could see.

On the way she wondered why her mother had grown enamored of the radicals' cause and joined them? Had she been on the run for all the years since? She shuddered, wondering if her mother had bombed and murdered innocent people.

Frésnes finally appeared. The grimy hundred-year-old brick structure was forbidding, and encased in multiple walls. As she stepped off the bus, birds twittered in the hedgerows. The leaves of tomato plants and pastel tulips waved in the breeze by the warden's house.

She walked past the guarded gates in tandem with women lugging toddlers and pushing strollers laden with shopping bags. She felt sorry for those with children who were making this long journey. And she could imagine doing it in the rain.

Miniature vegetable gardens lined the walks of the guards' accommodations. Prison food was notorious for starch and carbohydrates; most inmates puffed out due to the diet and lack of exercise.

Frésnes was an all-purpose prison that handled mostly inmates serving sentences of under five years as well as those awaiting sentencing. She'd heard it said that seventy to eighty percent of the prisoners were nonwhite.

The visitors shuffled into the central *salle d'attente*, a large room with gray floor tiles and light yellow walls, lined with lockers that could be rented for one franc each. She filled out her visiting application and sat on one of the hard benches.

Posted on the wall was the list of items forbidden to the prisoners: hardcover books, caps, scarves, ties, work outfits, and blue clothing, since the guards wore blue. No leather gloves. She imagined this was to discourage escape attempts over barbed-wire fences. No ski masks, military fatigues, bathrobes, towels, or *peignoirs*. She wondered about that. No *djellabas, kumaros,* or *boubous,* the colorful African dress. No parkas, ski clothes, or shoes since the prison factory made shoes.

Under the allowed list she read: bags with handles, clothing, and plastic bags.

And then her group lined up to receive their visiting permits. Since this was a weekday, only a forty-five–minute visit was permitted. Each visitor furnished a photo ID to the guard.

One by one they walked through a metal detector. After everyone passed they went through another yellow door and sat down to wait in a dirty banana-colored room, this time for about twenty minutes until guards summoned them to an underground tunnel. The air in it reminded her of her grandmother's cellar, drafty and laced with mold.

The tunnel, partly painted with a mural by prisoners, was cold and peeling from the damp.

Aimée shivered and not just from the cold. She wondered how she would talk to number 3978, a woman who'd shared Jutta Hald's cell before her release.

She'd been lucky that Morbier had acted quickly. The permit said number 3978 was still in Centre National d'Observation but due for transfer back to the Clairvaux facility that night. Aimée had no knowledge of her crime. All she knew was that Clairvaux held those serving long-term sentences and lifers.

She was directed toward the CNO section and entered a dim visiting booth. Behind her, the fluorescent strips in the hallway provided the only source of light. She sat on a stool at a small wooden table, the surface of which was gouged and carved by the feel of it. The door closed, leaving her in a space about three feet wide and ten feet long. Her breath caught as the key turned in the lock, a sound that was hard and ominous.

This, she'd been informed, was a "contact" visit, with no screen or barrier between visitor and prisoner, the usual thing since the rules changed in 1980.

A row of women in everyday clothes, escorted by blue-uniformed guards, passed by in single file, silhouetted in the doorway ahead of her. A large-boned woman with short cropped hair paused and looked inside.

Aimée took a deep breath. Her spine tingled.

The woman was an amazon.

"*Non*, West Coast, next door," said a guard.

"Too bad," the woman said, "A visit with her would be worth the *mitard*, the solitary hole."

The guard moved the amazon on.

A wave of relief passed over Aimée. But not for long. The stool cut into her thighs and she hadn't sat on it for more than two minutes.

More figures walked past. From a neighboring booth came muffled laughter, in the distance she heard weeping. What seemed like a dark eternity went by before a lithe figure in worn sweats entered.

The woman, shorter than Aimée, peered at her in the dim light then shoved a creased folder onto the table. "*Tiens*, if you keep insisting about my mother's grave, I'll show you proof I paid."

Surprised, Aimée rose. Her foot caught the stool, which crashed to the concrete floor. "*Pardon*, my name is Aimée Leduc," she said. She extended her hand. "What's yours?"

"Liane Barolet," the woman said. Aimée felt a curious grip. "Like I said, the money was paid. Here are the papers."

What did this woman mean?

"You must think I'm someone else, Madame Barolet. I'm not sure . . ."

"Mademoiselle would be technically correct," the woman said.

She remained standing as Aimée righted the stool. "Let me explain why I've come, Mademoiselle Barolet," Aimée said. "It's nothing to do with your mother. It's to do with mine."

"I don't know you," the prisoner said, withdrawing toward the locked door. "And my socialist group meeting starts soon."

"Sorry, but we might as well talk," Aimée said. "They won't open the door until visiting time's over."

It was hard to tell if Liane Barolet shrugged; her clothes were too big for her.

"I don't get many visitors," she said, moving closer and sitting down.

Now Aimée could see more of Liane's face. Once she'd been very pretty, Aimée imagined. The cheekbones were still prominent, the lips full, but deep lines webbed the cornflower blue eyes, etched the forehead. She had that look Jutta Hald had—wan, doughy skin on a bony frame.

Prison life.

"Jutta Hald told me . . ."

"That pseudo Marxist?" Liane snorted.

"Wasn't she in the Haader-Rofmein gang?"

"You came here to ask me that?" Liane pounded her hand on the table.

"Jutta Hald was murdered." Aimée looked down. She realized Liane Barolet's hand consisted of a thumb, index finger, and pinkie. The middle and ring fingers were stubs.

"When?" Liane asked, as she leaned back in the shadows.

"The day she got out."

Aimée couldn't see her reaction. She decided to get to the point.

Her eyes had grown accustomed to the dimness. "Right before her death, Jutta showed up at my apartment. She said she'd shared a cell with my mother," Aimée said. "She wanted money to tell me more, then she was shot." She hoped the trembling of her lips didn't show. "My mother's name was Sydney Leduc. Did you know her?"

Liane Barolet's eyes crinkled in amusement. "*Mon petit*, guess what? Life is hard. Then you die."

"Jutta said the same thing."

"But it's true."

"I'm not asking for sympathy," Aimée said.

"So what do you want?"

This wasn't going well.

"Look, I'm sorry this is confusing," Aimée said. She drummed her fingers under the wooden table. They came back sticky. "All I want to know is if Jutta talked about my mother in prison."

"Why ask me?"

"You shared a cell with Jutta, she was excited about getting out. She might have told you something. You're in the system, you might have heard things. Or whether someone else knows. Then I can lay it to rest."

"I doubt that," Liane said.

Startled, Aimée looked up. "What do you mean?"

"If you wanted to forget about your mother, you'd have ignored Jutta."

Her astute observation rankled. Maybe because it felt true.

"Is it wrong to want to know what's happened to her?"

Liane Barolet shook her head. "The only wrong part might be the answer," she said. "What's that saying . . . let sleeping dogs lie?"

"Look, I'll make it worth your while," Aimée said. That struck home, she could tell.

"How could you do that . . . sleep with the warden at Clairvaux?" Liane gave a sneer, then shook her head. "*Non, mon petit,* I wish that on no one."

The way she said it gave Aimée a chill.

"But you *could* help me, they threatened to dig her up," Liane continued. "Even though I only just found out. I paid right away!"

Aimée realized she was talking about a cemetery. When the grave fees were not paid, the bodies were dug up. No wonder she was upset.

"*Parloir terminé!*" shouted one of the guards, signaling that visiting time was over.

Aimée stood. "Help me and I'll help you." If Liane was desperate enough she'd talk. "Did you know my mother, did you ever hear of her?"

"There was a lightweight, an American woman." Liane waved her hand dismissively.

Aimée's hopes soared. Then her fear grew.

"What was this American's name?"

"Who knows? I just remember her saying things like 'If I can't dance, it's not my revolution.' "

Her mother? "Can you find out her name . . . what happened?"

"She wasn't in long," Liane said. "Well, compared to me, eh?"

"How long?"

"The system moves prisoners around," Liane said. "I didn't keep track."

"You can do better than that," Aimée said. "What was she in for?"

"That's the thing." Liane leaned forward. "She'd been in on some heist with Jutta. But only Jutta was charged."

"But everyone gets charged who comes . . ."

Liane shook her head. "They hold people for months, sometimes years, before arraignment. At least they used to. She was one of those."

"So they use Frésnes like a jail?"

"Only for the special ones," Liane said. "That pissed Jutta off."

"Did she write to Jutta in prison?"

Pause. The bell sounded the second and final warning. Chairs and stools scraped over the concrete floor.

"The letters are in my cell," Liane said.

"Letters from my mother?"

"Reading material's scarce here," Liane said. "Jutta left me her books. She used to keep her letters in them."

Aimée's hope rekindled. She tried to keep her voice even. "What do these letters say?"

The cubicle door opened.

"Barolet! Visiting time's over," said the guard.

"Help me to keep my mother's bones beside my father's," Liane said. "My lawyer's in contact with me. I'll give the letters to him if you get me a receipt from the cemetery for the money they say is overdue."

"*D'accord,* here's my address," Aimée said, glancing at the paperwork she had been handed. "Matter of fact, I'll go there now. Your deadline's passed. But I'll take care of it and send you the receipt."

Liane stood up slowly. "Do you know what I'm in for?"

Aimée shook her head. "Whatever you've done, you're being punished for it."

"You should know," Liane said. "So you don't think I withheld anything."

"As I said . . ."

"Blowing up banks. Terrorism," Liane said, her eyes gleaming in the light. "I'm proud of that. No one ever called revolution a dainty proposition. My ideology hasn't changed. It never will." She stared at Aimée. "We regard these as acts of war. But I'm not proud about the little children who happened to be too near."

Aimée shuddered. She wondered if explosives had claimed Liane's fingers. Or had prison?

Aimée said, "Keep your end of the deal and I'll keep mine."

HER THOUGHTS roamed helter-skelter on the way back to Paris. Did Liane have letters to Jutta from her mother? Was her mother alive? During the long journey, Aimée made several calls.

When she reached Montmartre cemetery on rue Rachel, she remembered her schoolteacher saying that corpses had been thrown into an old plaster quarry—which was now the cemetery—during the French Revolution. And how the vineyards of Montmartre had produced an astringent wine with such diuretic properties that a seventeenth-century ditty went: "This is the wine of Montmartre, drink a pint, piss a quart."

The grave digger she finally located tapped his shovel. "The old bird was heavy," he said. "That's for sure."

Aimée groaned inwardly. She'd have to give him a big tip.

He looked pointedly at his watch, sighed, then said, "It's too late to put her back but you can see her for yourself."

They wound over the gravel and dirt, past the graves of Zola and Degas. Midway, the grave digger paused and wiped his brow. "Over there."

The marble mausoleum's gate hung open. Dead flies, fossilized bees, and dusty plastic flower bouquets were strewn within.

"Doesn't the Barolet family own this?"

"Leased for a hundred years," he said, his tone matter-of-fact.

"Surely, it's more trouble to dispose . . ."

"Mademoiselle, there's a long waiting list of people eager for this space." For the second time he looked at his watch.

"Her daughter paid," Aimée said. "Here are the receipts."

"Then she's been notified. According to my *patron*, she wasn't up to date with payments," he said. "If she disputes this, let her talk to him on Saturday when he returns."

A lot of good that would do, with Liane in prison.

"Meanwhile what happens?"

"We take what's left to the boneyard."

"Boneyard!"

The grave digger shrugged. "That's standard procedure." His blue overalls were stained and muddy.

What if this man was lying, trying to make more money.

"Let me see the coffin."

He gestured to the right. "Over there, behind François Truffaut."

Aimée walked behind the mausoleum. She saw two coffins, one newer and with tarnished brass handles, the other wooden and water-stained.

"Which one?"

"The fancy model," he said. "Think of this like an eviction, I tell people."

"Evicting the dead?"

"What do you want me to do, eh?" he sneered. "Someday you'll be here too, Mademoiselle high and mighty!"

Burn me first, she almost said. *Scatter my ashes from my balcony over the Seine, before a dirty old coot like you can rattle my bones.*

Of course it all came down to money.

"How much?"

"Take that up with administration," he said. "All I do is shovel up the leftovers and leave them for the bone men."

Aimée hoped he didn't see her shudder.

The cemetery office was closed. Shadows lengthened over the stone houses of the dead.

"Can't you put her inside the mausoleum until I straighten this out?" she said, placing a hundred francs in his palm.

He rubbed his arms. "She's heavy, that one!"

"I'll make it worth your while," she said, hating to have to smile and to try to coax the favor from him.

In answer, he wheeled a hydraulic lift from a nearby shed. She stared at the coffin, faded sepia images of her mother crowding her mind. Was her mother crumbling in one of these somewhere?

"If there's no payment in three days, she's out. Permanently," he said. "I don't do this twice." The grave digger pumped the lift and pushed the coffin toward the mausoleum.

Aimée watched him. She stood perspiring in the heat, and he hadn't even broken a sweat. "I thought you said she was heavy."

"*Mais* she was!"

"Don't tell me she lost weight since you moved her."

He leered. "The other day she was heavy . . . you think I'm lying?"

"But, look, aren't coffins supposed to be sealed?"

She pointed to the cracked white chips along the coffin lid ledge.

"I didn't do that."

"Why so defensive all of a sudden?"

"Freaks," he said, shrugging his shoulders. "Satan worshippers." He looked over his shoulder, lowered his voice. "We don't tell the families but cults break in here some nights. I find candles melted on the stones, even a dead chicken once!"

"Do they rob the coffins?"

He wouldn't meet her eye, but he swiped his dirty finger across his lips. She took it to mean that he wouldn't say.

"Open it," she said. "I'm not paying otherwise and I'll make a big stink with your boss."

It was the last thing she wanted to see but Liane Barolet should know if she was being ripped off for an already desecrated coffin.

He handed her the crowbar. "Not my job."

And he shuffled away over the gravel.

The lid moved easily. Too easily.

As the late afternoon sun slanted through the leaves, a bird swooped up into the hard blue sky. She steeled herself to look in the dark, earthy-smelling interior. Instead of a shrouded, decaying corpse she found an empty coffin.

She pushed the lid up further. The only things inside were a crumpled brown plastic bag with Neufarama written across it and dried leaves that crackled as she touched them. She remembered buying a sweater from a Neufarama store but they'd gone out of business in the seventies.

Tuesday Afternoon

OUSMANE SADA, THE KORA PLAYER, wanted to help Idrissa, but first he had to get direction. And only the marabout, the fortune-teller, could point the way.

Ousmane mounted the worn wooden steps of the Sentier hotel. Too bad Idrissa hadn't come with him, but at least she was safe staying at his place. He knocked twice on the hotel door with the number 5 stenciled on it. From inside he heard a muffled *"Entrez."*

He removed his embroidered skullcap, took a deep breath, then opened the door.

"Bonjour," he said. "I seek guidance."

The marabout nodded.

In the cheap hotel room on rue Beauregard, maps of star constellations were strewn over the ragged chenille-covered bed. He set an envelope in the marabout's hollowed-out gourd bowl. The marabout, a bland-faced foreseer of the future, ignored his action. A marabout never acknowledged *hadiya*, gifts from his *taalibe*, his followers. In Ousmane's village outside Dakar in Senegal, the price had been chickens.

The marabout's *taalibe* would rebuild their wealth on the path to salvation. Hard work and many *hadiyas* improved one's chances of going to Paradise. A spiritual economy, his father had called it.

But Ousmane's father's marabout, whose photo he wore in the talisman around his neck, would frown on this visit. Loyalty to one's marabout was important. Even though Senegal was thousands of miles away, his pulse beat rapidly.

Ousmane inhaled the familiar willow bark and cinnamon

scent from the burning cones. He saw the day's fortune in Arabic letters tacked on the gouged plaster wall. He twitched. He'd felt out of sorts for days now. Must have *la grippe*—the flu. Sweating and feverish, he felt thirsty.

The marabout would throw the shells, arrange the beads, and interpret the signs. Tell him if his woman, Cheike, still waited to marry him. So he would return home, which was what his heart told him. And the signs would show him how to keep Idrissa safe.

He'd borrow the fare from his cousin Khalifa, a sanitation engineer, to keep him from drinking it away. Khalifa was different, he liked it here. The food clotted with cow's excrement they called butter, the raw horse meat eaten only by jaguars and tigers in his country, the painted women who preened and sold themselves on the street like pheasants in the market.

Since his childhood, Ousmane had strung fishing lines, patched and woven the nets, to face another day in the tepid ocean. He remembered gripping the flapping fins and shining scales of the fish his family caught in the turquoise waters. At first, his work in the Sentier sewing factory had seemed bearable. He slept alongside other workers on mattresses on the factory floor, like he'd done at home on mats with his siblings. Yet the cold damp from the stone floor seeped into his bones. Stayed there. No crusty vanilla sand caked on his calves. There were no warm orange sunsets laced by the smell of roasting peanuts.

Idrissa had noticed. His music suffered. Some nights he felt so tired after pressing and ironing the clothes in the factory, too tired to pluck the strings of his *kora* to accompany Idrissa's songs.

"Ask your question," said the marabout.

A stained yellow floral drapery flapped in the breeze from the open window. Hesitant at first, Ousmane wiped his brow, then gathered his courage and spoke.

The marabout threw the shells. The sound as the cowries clicked competed with the shouts of cart pullers below in the street. The marabout frowned. "Your question was not framed with a pure heart," he intoned. He pointed to the shells' configuration. "Don't be stingy with the truth." The marabout's long brown fingers snaked over the shells. He waited, lost in thought.

"Tell me what the shells say." Ousmane trembled, asking in their language, Wolof.

"Tiens!" said the marabout, refusing to speak their native tongue. "Your request rebounds on you. Where is your respect?"

"I'm confused."

The marabout reached over and flipped Ousmane's shirt collar down. He pointed to the talisman around Ousmane's neck. "The shells confirm, you belong in another's following."

Ousmane cringed.

"It's forbidden, you know that," the marabout said. "Now a curse will bite at your heels, as wild dogs guard a village."

Guilt filled Ousmane. Would the marabout's curse doom him, or Idrissa?

WEDNESDAY

AIMÉE RAN INTO the office of Leduc Detective and threw her leather bag on the settee. "I need to go to Frésnes tomorrow. May I borrow your car, René?"

"What happened?"

"Something bizarre." She told him about visiting Liane Barolet in Frésnes and the empty coffin in Montmartre cemetery.

"For more than twenty years, Liane's been paying?" he asked.

Aimée waved the plastic Neufarama bag.

"Pretty expensive just to store a plastic bag," he said. "I'd demand a refund."

Now it came back to her. She recalled Jutta's comment that her mother must have returned to Aimée's apartment or to the cemetery. At the time, she thought Jutta had been talking in riddles. Now it made sense.

"Wouldn't Liane have asked Jutta to pay instead of you?" René asked.

"But she'd just found out after Jutta left," Aimée said. "What if Jutta was looking for something kept inside the coffin!"

René blinked. His fingers paused on the keyboard. "That's a big jump."

She perched on her desk. "Not really when you think about it. It's accessible to anyone who can hop over the walls at night and jimmy the coffin open. No need for storage keys or to evade guards at night. And it could hold something big. The possibilities are endless," she said. "Did Jutta find the coffin empty . . . is that why she came to me? Or did she find something, take it away, and hide it?"

"That doesn't make sense, unless Jutta was hiding it from someone else," René said. "But you said she insinuated that your mother had sent you something, or hidden it, for you to find, while you were away as an exchange student."

The old frustration returned. And the hurt of not knowing.

"Papa destroyed everything of hers," she said. "Nothing's left. But Liane Barolet hinted that Jutta received a letter from my mother," she said. "She must be alive!"

"How do you know? The woman could be desperate, lying just to get you to take care of the fees for coffin." René shook his head. "Face it, Aimée, you're chasing a trail that's been cooling for more than twenty years." He edged himself off the chair with effort and stood. "Your mother left, she never came back, and she's not going to."

"She's alive, René," she said. "She has to be. I'll find her."

René crossed to the coatrack, took his cane, and lifted his linen jacket off its hook with it. She couldn't see his face.

"Say it, René."

Instead of sympathizing, René seemed bitter.

"I'm going to my tae kwon do workout," he said. He picked up his bag with the Yuan Dojo label and paused at the door. "Have you ever thought, Aimée," he said from the door, "that if she is alive maybe she doesn't want to be found?"

RENÉ'S WORDS sliced her to the quick. She couldn't work. It seemed like the very walls mocked her. She walked to the mail pile, rifled through the bills, and found a fat brown envelope addressed to "A. Leduc—Personal."

She slit open the bulky envelope. Stuffed inside, she found one folio of her mother's small bound notebook. On it, in thick block letters, were written six words: "Cooperate and the rest is yours."

For a moment, joy rushed over her. Then came the awful realization that Jutta's killer had sent her this as a bargaining chip. She slipped on gloves, took the kit from her bottom desk drawer, and dusted for prints. Just in case.

Aimée looked at the postmark: Hôtel des Postes on rue Etienne Marcel. Two blocks from where Jutta was killed.

She swept papers off her desk, then gingerly set down the notebook pages. These pages were different from those Jutta had shown her. The book had been halved, or quartered, the binding ripped and split. Below a drawing of Emil with red suspenders was what looked like a diagram for a mouse house with tiny platforms, running wheels, and a spiral staircase, a tiny box, an arrow.

Aimée looked closer. Under the Emil drawing, was another, with a sketch of horizontal lines, banked. Slanted. She stood back. Was it some kind of pattern?

She walked over to the window. Faint warm breezes from the Seine brushed over her, then dissipated. Yet even at this distance, she couldn't make out the pattern.

With care she scanned all eight pages into her computer. Then lifted the prints. Blurry and indistinct . . . the fingers of hundreds who'd handled the envelope. Not a print came from the notebook, it had been wiped clean.

Of course.

Darting a furtive look around her office, she lifted the notebook pages, pressed them to her lips. Inhaled the old paper scent. Silly. No one could see her. Then she sat at her terminal, and tried to make sense of the lines.

She ran Viva-1, an industrial art program. She played with the lines. Stretching, bending, and looping them. All she got was psychedelic-colored bands when she enlarged them.

Of course, she thought. Enhance, then reduce them.

i n a i l g i d o m

An anagram?

She played around, trying to form the letters into words, substituting letters.

Nothing.

Then she simply reversed the letters.

m o d i g l i a n i

Amedeo Modigliani was a sculptor, painter, and friend of Picasso. An Italian, from a Jewish ghetto, who came to Paris and dissipated—or enhanced—his talents, depending on whom one read.

Had her mother admired Modigliani? She looked closer and saw elongated figures in the lines . . . an odd complementary fit. On each roof corner of the diagrammed mouse house were elongated gargoyles.

Aimée went online and did a search on Modigliani. His pieces were in museums, though a majority were in private collections. She dug further. An auction at Sotheby's a few years ago had netted hundreds of thousands. But some paintings had been missing since the war . . . several from the Laborde collection.

Something clicked in her head.

Laborde . . . Laborde . . . where had she heard that name?

Of course, he'd been kidnapped by Haader-Rofmein. She found a bottle of Badoit, poured the sparkling water into her espresso cup, and got to work.

She searched newspaper databases for information about the industrialist Paul Laborde. Born in Mulhouse, on the French-German border, of a French father and a German mother, he'd amassed great wealth after the war, rebuilding steel foundries along the Rhine. He'd made gobs of money. Smelled dirty, as her papa used to say.

Haader-Rofmein took a particular dislike to him and his business, especially after his firm acquired several steel foundries, then mines in Africa. They targeted his company, pointing out that his steel, reworked, of course, ended up as bayonets in Vietnam.

Laborde wasn't the only target, of course. The Krupp and Thyssen families suffered extortion and kidnap attempts. But

Haader-Rofmein discovered the address of one of Laborde's homes and burgled it as well as kidnapping Laborde. News coverage dried up after a shoot-out in the forest and Laborde's death.

A light went on in her head. Her mother, the Modigliani paintings, Laborde, and the radicals who'd kidnapped him were all connected. Somehow.

Here was Laborde's tie-in to Haader-Rofmein. From what Jutta had said, the Action-Réaction and Haader-Rofmein gangs had melded together. But how did, or could, Romain Figeac's manuscript fit in with Sartre's old interview with Haader about agit888, perhaps with her mother as interpreter?

She called Martine. Told her what she found and the connection she suspected.

"Laborde didn't get in bed with terrorists, Aimée," Martine said. "Quite the oppposite. His shady past included Vichy collaboration and using mercenaries for his African investments."

"Right, but they took over his house—"

"Whoa," Martine said. "You're right. They kidnapped him, then he went Stockholm Syndrome."

"Stockholm Syndrome?"

"Lots of hostages come to identify with their captors after a while. It was named after the Stockholm embassy incident."

"He couldn't have identified too long," Aimée said. "The gang killed him, didn't they?"

"Never proved, and no one was charged," Martine said.

Strange, Aimée thought.

"What about Laborde's art collection?"

"Give me some time," Martine said and hung up.

While Aimée downloaded more information, she turned the notebook pages. Her heart caught. Only one more drawing of Emil, his whiskers running off the page.

She wished the book hadn't been torn apart and ruined. She clutched her knees and rocked back and forth, lost in old thoughts. Here she was, an adult with a successful business and a partner, yet she was still obsessed with her mother. She had to admit it, she had no life beyond René, Miles Davis, her computer, and this obsession.

René was probably right. Liane Barolet might be leading her on. But that wouldn't stop her from finding out the truth, from finding her mother.

And what had Jutta wanted . . . what did her killer want . . . what had her mother left or hidden?

The phone rang.

"*Allô?*"

"So glad I caught you, Mademoiselle Leduc."

That dense, creamy voice. "Anything new with Christian, Monsieur Mabry?"

"Some issues came up," he said. "Can you meet me tonight?"

"Would this be a consultation?"

"You could call it that."

"What time?"

"Eight P.M."

She let a pause hang in the air, long enough, she hoped, to seem busy. "I'll fit you in."

"Let's meet opposite the Bourse in the Yabon art squat. He'll join us."

"So Christian's all right?" she asked. "I've been worried."

"No more of a crisis than usual," Etienne Mabry said. "Third floor, Hubert's salon."

Pleased and immediately panicked about what to wear, Aimée hung up.

SHE NEEDED to get back on good terms with René and to get up to speed with Michel's computer system. After tackling the pile of papers on her desk, she checked Michel's database and was struck by the volume of his supply orders, many dating from early spring, that showed up as unpaid.

How could Michel, a struggling new designer, obtain that kind of credit? She searched and discovered one of his uncle Nessim's companies, Kookie Mode, had guaranteed his line of credit and received the invoices for his supplies; leather, fabric, and sewing needs.

She dug further. The scary thing was, Kookie Mode had sought protection from its creditors. Wasn't that the first step on the road to bankruptcy? She made a note to check further.

Wednesday Afternoon

STEFAN UNSCREWED THE license plates of an old Renault parked near the cemetery. Once burgundy colored, the car now looked like a faded wine stain. He'd chosen Paris district plates ending in 75, figuring he'd fade into the scuffed woodwork of a teeming *quartier* like the Sentier. Blend in with the blue-collar crowd, the immigrants and the traffic of the sex and garment trades.

He'd worry about sending money to his old *maman* later. Poor *Maman* with her bad leg. He told himself to remain invisible, like he always did. Not to panic. First things first.

He drove with caution through Place de Clichy, past Café Wepler's outdoor tables. Jules, he remembered, had delighted in playing the tour guide. He'd pointed out to Stefan that in the thirties Henry Miller had nursed an espresso there for hours and during the Occupation it had been a *Kantine* and *Soldatenheim* for the Wehrmacht.

He followed the bus route past Gare Saint-Lazare, down the once grand Boulevard Haussmann, built on the old ramparts of Paris, behind the gold dome of the Opéra Garnier toward the Sentier. Stefan parked on rue de Cléry, behind a wide blue van with broken rear lights.

He loosened his raincoat, feeling conspicuous. So many wore only tank tops in this heat. The one-way street was crammed with parked cars packed tighter than herrings in a barrel. A delicious coolness came from the leaning stone buildings that lined the sloping street.

He passed the *ancien* Hôtel de Noisy, elegant despite cheap wholesale clothing stores taking up the ground floor. His goal, the building on rue de Cléry, was almost the same as Stefan remembered it, except for the blackened windows and smoky smell. He wondered what had happened. Stefan walked past.

He waited until dusk painted the tops of the stone buildings. Until early evening shoppers returned, climbing the narrow Sentier stairways. Until he smelled garlic frying in olive oil emanating from open windows and heard the clatter of plates at dinner tables.

Snatches of Hebrew came from the storefront on rue d'Aboukir as a man in a yarmulke carried out the trash. On the narrow street the *putes* clustered in the doorways, just as he remembered. Only now they carried cell phones and more were of African and Arab origin. Still the rag and shag trade carried on much the same as before.

Stefan stood until the street lamps furred with a dense glow, then he shoved open the tall dark green door of Romain Figeac's building. In the cobbled courtyard, dark shapes contoured the walls. The glass-paned door to the main staircase stood ajar. By the time he reached the third floor, the burnt smell alerted him. Blackened wood and yellow tape forbade him to cross the charred entrance of Figeac's apartment.

Too late . . . why was he always too late?

Whether because twenty years of being on the lam made him more aware or it had become second nature at the hint of danger, Stefan's hair rose on the back of his neck, his nerves tingled. The metallic sound, like the snick of a cartridge being loaded, echoed off the the stone.

Or he could have sworn it did.

He knew he had to run. And run he did. Without looking back or pausing to see if his instincts were right.

If he had, he would have heard the bullet whiz. Seen a large hole blown in the plaster where he'd just stood, bleeding chunks of grit and mortar over the parquet.

AIMÉE PUNCHED in René's door code at the house on the rue de la Reynie. She mounted his creaking stairs, which smelled of wax polish and stepped softly, mindful of his neighbor's sleep. He was a female impersonator who worked in Les Halles.

"Damn cyber squatters!" René greeted Aimée as she walked inside his apartment. His eyes raced up and down the screen almost as fast as his fingers did. "We registered *click.mango.fr* as a domain name before they did."

"Going to boot them out?" she said.

He nodded, tugging his goatee. "It won't be pretty."

"Talking about squats," she said, "we're invited to the *collectif* Yabon d'Arts." She wanted René to come and meet Christian.

René hit *Save*. His head turned.

"Looks like I got your attention. Now get dressed."

ALIGHTING FROM René's bullet gray Citroën, customized for his four-foot height, Aimée looked around. "Any fashionistas here?" she asked.

"You'll fit right in," René grinned, buttoning his black frock coat, then pointing to the artists' squat. "Tomboys in lace are *en vogue*."

She tucked her ruffled cuffs inside her leather biker jacket sleeves, pinched her cheeks for color, and tried for an appearance of *sang-froid*.

Before them, the Haussmann-era building stood out. Throbbing lime, violet, and silver graffiti mocked the staid financial district, home to the Bourse. Caricatures spread a floor high; filigreed iron balcony railings held signs emblazoned TURN

EMPTY SPACE INTO ART and FIGHT POLITICAL CORRECTNESS—
A NEW FORM OF TERRORISM TO THE ART WORLD.

"Talk about visual aggression!" René said. "The whole six floors are tagged."

Aimée hid her smile. "This *collectif* even occupied space across from the Musée Picasso," she said. "They claimed 'free space for artists in Paris' and baptized it Galerie Socapi, Picasso in *verlan*," she said. "No one can afford ateliers today, like those Picasso and the Cubists found at the Bateau-Lavoir in Montmartre. They take over buildings abandoned by banks and insurance companies that have deserted Paris for the cheaper suburbs."

René expelled a burst of air in disgust. "Arrogant artists."

"You can tell them how you feel at dinner."

This was the Paris Aimée had grown up in . . . grimy and full of *caractère*. Where stalls of white summer Montreuil peaches perfumed blackened stone facades, where concierges sat fanning themselves in the doorways, exchanging gossip while cats slunk around their legs. And everyone said *Bonjour* on the street. Where the tang of *pissoirs* and Gauloises hit her on the corner coming home from school, café patrons argued *philosophie*, and the only phones were the ones in the café that took *jetons*. Where individuals made statements. Statements that were heard.

She and René stepped over crunching brick to a hole punched in the flat end of the building. Above them, the flat *pignon*, the wall, sliced Parisian style, held peeling wallpaper and traces of chimney flues's snaking to the roof. Alongside grinned a three-story Barbarella caricature.

Inside, the worn marble staircase crawled with razor-thin men and young blondes. DEMYSTIFY ART was spelled out in multicolored floor tiles.

Renée's eyes widened. "Junkies and debutantes by the look of it," he whispered in her ear.

"Like the old days," she grinned, "when the Sorbonne was interesting."

"You liked those parties," René said.

"But you were the one who got lucky." Aimée leaned forward and saw a smile struggle across René's mouth.

A few golden boys, day traders from the Bourse, stood looking embarrassed, holding their briefcases, loosening their ties.

They saw the birdcage lift was stranded between floors. Aimée groaned. Why had she worn leopard-print high-heeled mules instead of her red high-tops?

René jerked his thumb upward. In the corners of the steps were syringes and dead pigeons. "I'm not hungry," he said.

By the time they had trudged up to the third floor, the crowd had grown more eclectic. Room after room held paintings, metal sculptures, and installations. The thrum of an electric generator powered the dim lights and pounding techno-beat. From the cavernous hallway came the sizzling crackle of cooking and the aroma of garlic.

A group of skinny models, working proletariat, and *aristos* sat drinking wine together at a long candlelit table. Conversation buzzed amid the clink of wineglasses. A man in tight black denim pants and a black shirt appeared. A slit-eyed iguana was draped over his arm.

"We're Etienne's friends," Aimée said, unable to pull her gaze from the candlelight flickering on the iguana's iridescent scales.

"Welcome, I'm Hubert," he said, planting *bisous* on both her cheeks and René's. "*Ça va?*" Hubert's thin shoulders twitched. She hoped he was keeping time with the music and not in need of a fix.

She dropped her scarf and bent to pick it up. Her shirt rode up, revealing the lizard design on her back.

"Nice tattoo! Nico?" Hubert asked.

Aimée nodded, and saw René's mouth drop open.

"Take that place, just in time," he said, sweeping them forward to a bench. She had the feeling she'd risen several notches in Hubert's estimation.

A man with thick black hair wearing a corduroy jacket with leather-patched elbows made space for them. He gestured, his mouth full, toward a wineglass and poured from a carafe of red wine. He raised his glass. *"Salut, mes amis,"* he managed, then attacked a *salade frisée* pomaded with glistening avocado vinaigrette.

Etienne appeared in the doorway. He wore a skinny black T-shirt and frayed jeans, and swiped his shock of reddish brown hair across his forehead. In nonwork clothes, he looked more like Aimée's bad-boy type. She didn't see Christian.

"Bonsoir," she said as Etienne joined them. "Meet René, my partner."

"A pleasure." He shook René's hand. Then hers. His long fingers enveloped hers with soft, warm pressure, his lips forming a smile.

That wonderful smile. Her fingers retained his warmth after he let go.

Most likely Etienne enjoyed a steady income and visited his parents in the countryside on major holidays and weekends.

But he didn't look boring now.

Opposite, their dinner partner was arguing with the woman seated next to him. "Five thousand francs . . . do I look loaded, Madame? Ask me when I win Thursday night at keno."

"Didn't Christian come with you?" Aimée asked.

Etienne shrugged. "I hoped he'd be here, waiting." He sat next to Aimée. "He's notorious for being late."

She was aware of Etienne's vaguely citrus scent, his long lashes, his muscular arms.

"I'm worried," she said. "Christian's been through so much. Did he stay with you last night?"

Etienne shook his head. "Never showed up. I'm worried, too. He's in financial trouble."

"Financial trouble?"

René reached for a carafe and poured a glass for Etienne.

"*Merci,*" Etienne said. "Frankly, it's beyond my scope. I just manage investments. But the back taxes and liens on his father's estate have mounted up. It's horrific."

Strange, Aimée thought. Christian told her there was money. Lots of it.

"Maybe he is being held at the Commissariat again?" René asked.

"Doubtful, but he's got to furnish them statements by Monday." As Etienne turned his wine goblet, licks of candlelight danced over its surface. "I'm concerned. His father must have kept records. Christian was supposed to meet me at the bank. Then he called, said for me to meet him here."

She was about to say Christian had pulled the same thing on them. She looked over at René. But René's eyes were on the women dancing in the hallway. Their shadows, distorted on the water-stained wall, twitched and jumped to the techno music.

"Didn't the Figeacs have an accountant?" She felt the pressure of Etienne's leg, not unwelcome, as more people joined them at the table.

"Excuse me," René said, getting up. He winked at Aimée and nodded toward the hallway.

"Our transactions were simple," Etienne said. "He wrote checks."

"But Christian called you his financial advisor." Had this been one of Christian's big ideas, as Idrissa termed them?

"A loose phrase." Etienne's smoke gray eyes probed hers, as if plumbing her psyche. Few men she'd met were so direct. It felt disturbing but nice. "I'm sorry, I don't know what he told you."

"Where could he be?"

Etienne looked down. "With Christian, well . . . it's typical. He makes plans and doesn't show up."

Then her phone rang.

"*Allô?*" But the music swallowed the response.

It was impossible to hear. She checked the caller ID, but didn't recognize the number. Then it hit her.

"*Pardonnez-moi*, I have to take this call," she said, tearing herself away from Etienne.

In the next room, Hubert was holding court near large cubes of pastel Plexiglas. She hit the call-back button and got a gruff "*Oui!*"

"Who's this?" she asked.

"What is this? Marie called. Georges here."

A call from Action-Réaction . . . finally!

"What do you want?" Georges didn't wait for her reply. "We're leaving for Strasbourg tonight."

"I have to speak with you," she said. "Give me fifteen minutes. I'm on my way."

Either Christian was a flake or in trouble. Right now she couldn't solve that. Back at the table, René's vacant place had been taken up by newcomers.

"René ran into his friend," Etienne said. "He said you'd understand."

Aimée felt awkward. Had he left on purpose so that she could be alone with Etienne? The music's pitch and the DJ's voice escalated so it was hard to hear.

"*Désolée*, but I've got to go. Something just came up," she said.

Etienne glanced at his watch. "I was hoping we could go somewhere together."

Torn, she figured Christian would come late or not show. Martine would call her nuts to leave but she had to meet this Georges and find out about her mother.

"It's business, *je le regrette*," she said.

Surprise crossed Etienne's face. This didn't happen to him often, she figured. Few women would walk away from him. Not if they were smart. Wrong place, wrong time.

"Why don't we meet later?" he asked. "At Rouge. I'll bring Christian if he shows up."

Did he think she was playing hard to get?

"Sounds good," she said, trying to sound casual.

"How will I reach you?"

She pulled out her lip liner and wrote her cell phone number on his arm.

"A *bientôt*." Etienne pulled her close and gave her a *bisou*. His warm breath seared her cheek. She almost sat back down.

Instead, she made her way through the packed crowd dancing in the hallway. Keep going, she told herself; she had no time for Etienne. No sign of René. Out on rue Feydeau she saw his car. Maybe he'd gotten lucky with one of the women.

Hurrying through the quiet Sentier streets, she reached Action-Réaction ten minutes later. The building on rue Beauregard, a squat survivor from the sixteenth century, had suffered a face-lift in the fifties. Unsuccessful by the look of it. Rusted neon signs advertised TEXTILE VASSEUR on the wall behind it. On both sides, seventeenth- and eighteenth-century buildings leaned over it, their clay chimney pots askew on their slanted roofs.

At the corner, several Pakistani men stood gambling on cardboard boxes. Beyond them, Aimée heard the gurgle of the drains as fresh water washed the gutters. Garbage containers, tall and green, peculiar to the Sentier, lined the street entrance.

In the courtyard, a man pushed a wire clothes rack, full of swinging wool- and fur-collared jackets, jiggling over the cobbled way. An office window stenciled with EAT THE STATE fronted the grime-blackened courtyard facing a wall of bricked-up windows.

A chill penetrated the dark courtyard recesses. She knocked on the door that read AR in faded letters.

Aimée expected to find a lair of old radicals or a seething den of subversives mobilizing for the World Trade demonstrations in Place de la Concorde.

But she had to knock several times on the thick wooden door.

Only the narrow crescent of the July moon illumined the dark courtyard. Finally, the door scraped open. A man with graying corkscrew curls tight to his head and a broken nose peered out.

"Georges?" she asked.

"We're in a hurry, *entrez*," he said, looking around behind her.

She stepped inside Action-Réaction's squalid office. Posters and old Maoist leaflets covered the ceiling and walls like wallpaper. A sagging sofa was draped with threadbare African cloth, Che Guevara's image smiled from behind the single pasteboard desk. The only concession to the present was a shiny new fax machine.

A damp mildew smell came from the corners. Typical in these buildings, the rot and mold of centuries. But Che stayed forever the gorgeous revolutionary martyred in Bolivia, while the movement declined. Chunks of plaster were missing, revealing laths, and a fine powdery sprinkle covered the floor.

Some men were passing around a bottle of Pernod, the licorice liquor.

"Look, I'm sorry, maybe you can help me. I need to ask you about . . ."

Georges did a double take. "Don't I know you?" He took a long, hard look at Aimée.

"I can't believe it!" he said, moving closer to her. "Frédo, look. Look!"

A thin man with paper white hair turned to look at her. *"Nom de Dieu,"* he said.

In the glare of a naked bulb, she saw furled banners piled against the dank wall. She felt Georges's face close to hers. Saw his bruised purple-red nose.

"You look so much like her . . . the resemblance is amazing!"

A cold shiver ran through Aimée.

"What do you mean?"

Frédo joined them. "You're her daughter, *non?*"

"Who?" Her hand shook, she couldn't help it.

"*Tiens!* You're Sydney's daughter!" Surprised, she noticed that their looks were welcoming instead of accusing. Finally, she'd found a connection to her mother. A positive one!

"Amazing!" Frédo stood, beaming at her. "That look. So innocent and wild . . . you have it. But of course, I should know, eh? We were intimate."

Wednesday Night

AIMÉE TOOK A LONG swallow, then passed the green bottle of Pernod to Frédo beside her on the couch. The licorice smell didn't even bother her anymore. Normally, it shriveled her taste buds.

Had she arrived on another planet? Finally she sat with people who'd known her mother, loved her, and talked about her.

"What luck our paths crossed, Marie!" Frédo said. "So you coordinate magazine photo shoots, eh?"

Aimée hoped her wince didn't show. "Crazy job. These art directors . . . so fickle, they changed their mind. Found another site on Boulevard de Sébastopol."

"But we found you!" Georges said, leaning forward from his perch on the cheap desk. He had a plastic bag of ice on his swollen nose. "Uncanny! Such a resemblance to your mother!"

Why had no one ever told her that?

Aimée put her hand out for another swig. Her trembling was controlled now. She took several deep gulps. On the wall was a framed yellowed notice from December 1981 titled "Our Sentier Initiative":

'Action-Réaction will organize the occupation of numerous secret ateliers or sweatshops in addition to helping rehouse a hundred or more foreigners: Turkish families, Senegalese, and refugees fleeing U.S. imperialism.

"Such an inspiration, you know," Georges said. "She surprised us. We thought she was soft, but she took action. So dedicated to the cause in her own way."

Cary ...
1606 Three Oaks
Cary, Il 60

Dying to find out more, she figured she'd better not appear too eager.

"We've been out of contact," she said. "I'm trying to find her."

"Let's see, she went to Spain. . . ."

"No, Greece with Jules," Georges interrupted. "But that was in the seventies."

Aimée's heart slowed. These men were out of date. Years out of date.

"Jules?"

"Jules Bourdon."

In the background, a radio played a plaintive Mozart aria Aimée recognized from *The Magic Flute*. Pamina's mother's voice trilled and vibrated, mourning the disappearance of her daughter, the daughter whom she'd tried to coerce to kill the rival king.

Aimée's grandfather had played the vinyl record on Saturday mornings. She'd heard the strains when she returned from her piano lesson and waited on the steps with the bag of warm *brioches* in her arms, until the aria had ended. As she didn't understand German, she'd only learned the story years later. And figured out why her grandfather changed the record when she returned. The evil mother sacrifices her daughter . . . maybe that came too close to home.

"You're off there, Georges," Frédo said. "She did time in Frésnes." His mouth tapered into a thin line. "We all did. Wasn't she involved in the squats we organized in the eighties?"

"You're asking me?" Georges didn't wait for an answer. "We were in Frésnes together in the eighties, Frédo!"

Bickering like an old married couple, she thought.

"Sydney flitted like a butterfly . . . from thing to thing," Frédo said. "Charming and elusive. One never knew her reality."

"But I heard she was involved with Haader-Rofmein," Aimée said.

"Didn't you know, Marie?"

"Know what?" Had Liane lied to her?

Silence. Georges took a big drink.

Frédo looked down. "What difference does it make now?"

Her heart hammered at his ominous tone.

"Tell me . . . she died?"

"Rumor had it she went to find Jules. He became a mercenary *en Afrique*."

"*Afrique?*"

"Old revolutionaries never die," Frédo said. "They just fade away. Though some change colors."

The room's atmosphere, close and stale, the glare from the hanging bulb, the tang of the Pernod and the whining violin made her claustrophobic.

She got off the sagging sofa. People changed, moved on, evolved. Most of the former radicals probably had mortgages paid off and grandchildren. Not these men. They seemed stuck in a time warp.

"Look at the former Maoists and anarchists in the Green Party or even in ministry positions," Aimée said. "Even Daniel Cohn-Bendit, Danny the Red, he's a European Parliament minister!"

Frédo stood up. "We've got to get these ready for the *congrès* in Strasbourg," he said, piling lists of signed petitions inside boxes.

"When did you last see my mother?"

Instead of answering, Georges motioned her outside. The dark courtyard held a welcome coolness. Water plopped from a mossy tap into a grooved marble urn. Probably the original water source, Aimée thought.

"He was more than a little in love with her," Georges said. "We all were."

Jealousy stabbed her. What right had these old radicals, these losers, to say that . . . had they ever really known her? Aimée's words caught in her throat. Pangs of bitterness hit her. Even though she was Sydney's daughter, she didn't know her.

"I'm sorry, Georges, I just want to learn everything I can," Aimée said. "She left us when I was young."

"Some women have the equipment but they're not made to mother," he said. He turned away.

She couldn't see his face.

"You're better off if you realize that."

Aimée tried to catch his expression.

"Was she a drug mule?"

"We're talking about the seventies. Who wasn't into drugs, eh?" Georges said, throwing up his arms. "People were politicized in prison, their awareness heightened. Focused on the movement's issues. Right now, two Action-Réaction members have been kept in solitary since 1987. They got married last year. *Alors*, the governor gave them a whole half hour!"

Georges snorted, then squinted as he moved the ice pack up his nose. "It's a blatant violation of the most basic human rights. We're protesting outside Strasbourg prison, presenting a petition to the World Court in The Hague."

Maybe they weren't the losers she'd thought. They'd stayed committed and dedicated to social change for more than twenty years.

"What about the protests against the World Trade Organization at the Palais des Congrès?"

"Tell me about it, eh!" Georges pointed to his nose. "This shiner's courtesy of the CRS* riot squad," he said readjusting the ice. "I'm getting too old for this."

She remembered the newspaper headline about the nerve gas Sarin. "What about that rumor of a copycat attack on the Metro, like that Japanese cult."

"Not Action-Réaction," Georges said. "We're for political change, not terrorism; that faction split off in the eighties."

*Compagnies Républicaines de Sécurité

Georges pointed to the buildings surrounding the courtyard. "But it's a tradition in my family. Socialists for generations. Even an anarchist or two. During the Occupation, the Resistance had a stronghold here, courtesy of my uncle's printing press. Funny thing is, a German headquarters was at the other end of the courtyard."

He stood straighter and grinned. "Before the war, the Sentier was home to newspapers and honeycombed with small presses, my uncle once told me. During power cutoffs, they'd print *Combat*, the clandestine Resistance newspaper, and counterfeit identification papers, by pedaling bicycles hooked up to the presses. In the eighties we squatted in the derelict buildings peppering the Sentier, agitating to rehouse the *sans-papiers*."

Aimée touched the cold, worn stone and wondered why her mother had gotten involved.

"Some of the old machines were left in the basement," Georges said. He rubbed his tired eyes. "We still use them. Same struggle against tyranny and oppression."

He made a *pfft* sound, shrugged. "*Alors*, it's a tradition in this blue-collar *quartier*. Revolution has been fomented here since the Bastille. In central Paris one works hard to stay afloat: shop owners, printing presses, the rag and shag trade, right next to couture houses and the Bourse. But now that the dot-coms have moved in, things may change."

She'd seen the nonstop activity in the streets, felt the pulse. The people who lived here worked here, a remnant of old Paris.

All true but none of this got her closer to her mother or her ties to Jutta. Then a thought occurred to her. Romain Figeac was an old radical, he'd lived a few blocks away, and his wife was rumored to have been pregnant with a terrorist's child.

"But you must have known Romain Figeac . . . wasn't he involved in Action-Réaction?"

Georges frowned. "Figeac held a grudge against us after his

wife left him. Blamed us. Never got over it," he said. "Like me, he's a grown-up *titi* from the *quartier*. He supported the movement at first. When it was fashionable, he housed us all."

Now she was getting somewhere.

"Did Figeac know my mother? I heard she helped Sartre with Haader's interview about agit888. Do you know about it?"

"An article?" He shrugged. "There were parties at Figeac's apartment. Everyone went. But your mother and Jana, Figeac's wife, never got along."

"What do you mean?"

"She thought Jana was too hard-core, too irrational, and took too many drugs," he said. "But that's all I remember."

"Georges, did you know Jutta Hald?"

Sadness crossed his face. "Radicals pass through here all the time. But I'm not into violence. Our group never was . . . like I said, we split from the terrorists."

"Jutta just got out of prison, did you see her?"

"My grandson said she came by, but I was at the *manif* demonstration."

"Did she leave you a message?"

Georges shook his head. "Why would someone kill her?"

Before she could say she'd found Jutta, he spoke.

"Why don't you help us?" he asked. "Like your mother."

Startled, she leaned against the dank wall for support. "What do you mean?"

"Provide places to stay for those who've gone underground," he said. "In the seventies we had a goal. We still do."

"But I don't . . ."

"There's someone now. If you want to know about Jules, he's the one to ask," Georges interrupted.

"Who?"

"No names."

He was right. It was better not to know.

"And my mother . . . ?" She felt Georges had deliberately left things out, withheld information.

"Her life was revolution and art," he said. "So you'll help?"

She looked down and nodded. She had to find out about Jules. "Call me," she said and gave him her cell phone number.

"Is your name Marie?"

"*Non.*"

"I didn't think so," he said, his mouth in a lopsided grin. "Like mother, like daughter."

SHE CHECKED her messages. Only one from Etienne, to meet at Rouge.

The bouncer, a massive, bald, ebony-skinned man with an earring and leather vest, stood guard at the door. A line of fashionable people waiting to enter the members-only club trailed around the corner.

"Your name?" The bouncer gripped her by the shoulder.

"Aimée, Etienne Mabry's guest."

"Let me check," he said. He spoke into a walkie-talkie.

Outside the club, the faded blue letters of an old hotel sign trailed across lichen-covered stone.

"Just left on his 'arley," he said in a broad Guadeloupe accent.

"Alone?"

His eyes shuttered.

"Masculine or feminine, that's all I want to know," Aimée said, wondering if he'd met up with Christian. "Several of us were meeting."

"Very feminine."

"For your help, *merci.*" Aimée smiled. Of course, he'd attract women like Velcro. She'd had her chance, sort of, but the timing had been off.

The bouncer winked, then turned to open the door of a Mercedes limo that had just pulled up.

*   *   *

AIMÉE WANTED to go home and research Jules but something nagged at her. On her way back, she stopped at Romain Figeac's apartment on rue de Cléry. Despite the darkness, she'd try once more to discover tapes, or anything she might have overlooked.

She stepped over the police tape. Using her penlight and the one remaining lamp that shone, she pulled latex gloves from her bag and shuffled through the charred debris. Wet ash, muck, and smokiness pervaded the gutted rooms. Romain Figeac's leather chair was turned upside down. She pulled out her Swiss Army knife, righted the chair, and checked the seams. But someone else had beaten her to it. A clean slice round the leather. She reached in, felt only soggy ticking and wire springs.

What a waste, she thought. Figeac's work, gone or destroyed. Everything floated midair, aloft. Out of her reach. She wasn't even sure of what she searched for.

This fire made no sense to her ... if someone was seeking valuables in the apartment, why burn it up?

She turned the chair upside down again, leaned against its wooden legs, and thought over what Georges had said. His conversation reinforced feelings she'd kept buried. Or tried to.

Her mother had risen above a mundane life of domestic worries and child care, devoting her time to fighting injustice. Imbibing new-found excitement in the heady seventies radical existence. Taking lovers, living in a commune, making art.

Her mother was no innocent. She'd been a drug mule, according to Jutta. A terrorist.

An addict?

Jutta had probably touched only the tip of the iceberg. Too bad her brains had been splattered on the stones of the Tour Jean-Sans-Peur before Aimée could find out what she'd known.

No answers. Only thoughts of a skinny woman with a faint, lingering scent of *muguets*, who at this moment could be roaming the backstreets of Africa.

She found a broom in a closet. With slow strokes, she swept the muck into a pile, then sifted it through her gloved hands.

All she found were blackened rattan and burnt jacquard drapery pieces. Mildewed, and home to a mouse nest.

But what if the arsonist hadn't found Romain Figeac's work either?

She tried to think as if she were Figeac . . . tried to relate to a washed-up writer, once a radical, who'd nursed thoughts of revenge upon those who ruined his wife. For the next hour, she raked through every crackled drawer, charred closet, and blistered wallpaper seam, even climbing on piled-up chairs to unscrew the faux ceiling plate from which the blackened and dust-covered chandelier hung.

Nothing.

In the kitchen, she checked the bottom of every dish, behind the cupboards, behind the old refrigerator, and in the flour bin in the pantry.

All she came up with was a white coating on her greasy, blackened latex gloves.

The *pompiers* had broken the glass to Christian's mother's room; her seventies jumpsuits and Afro wigs were smoke-and water-damaged. Little remained in the musty room besides stained and faded peach satin sheets on the four-poster bed. Despite the years, Aimée felt a disturbing sense of intimacy with this woman.

Smelling of soot and with blackened bits under her broken nails, Aimée left. Tired and discouraged, she went to the familiar marble stairs. She'd been here three times and grown no wiser.

She was convinced she'd missed something. Christian had paid her to find his father's killer and his work and it looked like the fire had been set by an arsonist who couldn't find the work either.

And she'd come no closer to her mother. Most of her life she'd been haunted by this woman who, it seemed more and more obvious, wanted nothing to do with her. Otherwise, why wouldn't she have come back?

Better to get rid of the smoky smell, soak in a long, hot bath, and warm her bones.

At the foot of the staircase, by the cellar door, a shrunken woman struggled with a case of empty champagne bottles. Whether she was bent over from its weight or osteoporosis, Aimée couldn't tell.

"*Tant pis!*" the old woman mumbled under her breath.

"Let me get the door for you," Aimée said.

"*Commes vous-êtes gentille,*" the woman said, glad of assistance. Her hair, pulled back in a tight chignon, was bone white and a scarf draped her caved-in shoulders despite the heat. "If you'd be so kind as to unlock it."

Aimée turned the big key, shoved the door open, and reached for the light switch.

"Madame, please let me help you get them downstairs."

"I won't protest, Mademoiselle. My great-grandson's baptism party," she said, as if the bottles needed an explanation. "I have to get them downstairs, can't stand them in my apartment anymore!"

Aimée hefted the crate and edged down the shadowy, steep steps. She wondered how the frail, elderly woman would have negotiated them. The jiggling bottles and the damp odor of mildew and rat traps on the beaten dirt floor made her regret her impulse. Then she spotted the gated tenant lock-ups with numbers on the rotting wood doors.

Of course . . . why hadn't she thought of this?

"*Voilà.*" She set down the full crate. A low-watt bulb illumined one end of the cellar, casting shadows over the vaulted stone.

"*Merci,*" the woman said.

"Do these numbers correspond to the apartments?" Aimée asked, looking around and dusting off her hands.

"Let me see, it's been so long since I came down here." The woman took the glasses hanging from a chain around her neck and peered up.

Aimée pulled out her penlight and shone the thin beam about her. Stone arches supported an aqueductlike array of storage alcoves. A wonderful chill traveled up her legs.

"That's better," the old woman said, shuffling forward. A faint fragrance of violets trailed her. "My key ring has my storage key."

Cobwebs, sticky and heavy with dead insects, caught on Aimée's sleeve. They clung like skin when she tried to brush them off.

"Which one's Romain Figeac's?" she asked.

"Number 311, that's his," the old woman said, turning the corner of the dank tunnel. "Right here."

Aimée pointed her penlight.

The busted lock shone, hanging by a hinge.

Beaten to it. Again! Her hopes sank.

She touched the door, which sagged open. Inside lay balled-up newpapers on the packed dirt. A water-stained plywood piece closed off the old stone wall.

Beaten at every turn.

"My storage stall sits over there." The old woman pointed. "By the old exit. Mind helping me?"

"The old exit?"

"*Bien sûr,*" said the old woman, clutching her scarf around her. "Paris sits on a big Swiss cheese, that's what my papa used to say."

Aimée grinned. She'd never heard it referred to like that before. "Like the catacombs in the Marais?"

"Older. Underneath here, it's limestone laced with holes. Much of the *quartier*'s built on limestone, like Montmartre."

Maybe that's why so much of Paris had stayed the same for centuries—the foundation wouldn't support new construction. Fascinating, but Aimée didn't understand the connection.

"How does that make for another exit?"

The old woman rubbed her arms in the dank chill. "They all connected at one time. Probably some still do. There was a colony of underground people, rumor had it." She shrugged. "Stories, eh? But during the war, people came down during air raids when they were too lazy to go to the Metro."

Aimée looked at the faded writing on the wood. "Looks unsafe." She peered closer. "Does this go to Place du Caire?"

"Wouldn't surprise me," the woman said. Stacked plastic boxes stood inside the woman's coved storage space. "What's that?" she said. "I haven't put anything down here in years."

Curious, Aimée stepped closer. Papers filled the clouded plastic. Had Figeac hidden his work here?

"How about we open one, just to check?" Aimée asked.

Before the woman could say no, she stepped in a puddle, rank and brown, then knelt down. The plastic cover stuck. Keeping her hand steady, she pulled, using so much force that when the top came off she fell back in the dirt.

Eager, she shone the penlight. Scraps of a browned discharge certificate and war medals attached to crumbling blue, white, and red ribbons.

"What does it say?"

"Yvon Edelman, distinguished service," Aimée said.

"My uncle," the old woman said. "I forgot, of course, I asked my grandson to bring these down. He carries the light things, always forgets the heavy ones."

Disappointed, Aimée put them back.

"Madame, did you know Romain Figeac?"

Aimée was surprised to see the old woman's mouth purse in disapproval.

"Of course! The great Monsieur 'Figeac,' as he called himself. *Alors*, try Monsieur Finkelstein—his real name! Maybe that didn't fit on those book covers. His father was a tailor like mine. From the same street in Lodz even!" She rolled her eyes. "Yet the way he acted, who'd know it. But the old poseur's gone. I shouldn't speak ill of the dead . . ." Her voice trailed off.

That's why Figeac lived in the Sentier—he'd been born here.

"Dabbled in politics, didn't he?" Aimée asked. "Wasn't he married to an actress?"

"That's him," the old woman nodded. She'd become reenergized. She stood up straighter in the thin flashlight beam. "He played at life. Never read his books so I don't know about them. But he still could run up a fine inseam, like his papa taught him. The young one, his son, seems so hapless!" She shook her head. "When he was little he was a sweet lost lamb. He's never gotten his life together."

Poor Christian. She could see what the old woman meant.

Ahead of them hung a rope ladder. Aimée grasped the rope, damp and frayed at the edges, and climbed. But her head hit something hard. She peered up to see a wooden hatch. It didn't budge.

She climbed down, dusted her legs off, and escorted the old lady upstairs.

"Have you noticed anyone hanging around . . . any strangers," Aimée asked.

"Like you, you mean?" The woman shook her head.

"I work with the arson investigators," Aimée said, stretching the truth. "If something comes to mind, here's my card. Please, give me a call."

The old woman trundled off to her apartment.

And then Aimée saw it. A bullet hole in the wall. Like a splattered graphite flower. She sniffed. Gunpowder . . . fresh or at least recent.

If a silencer had been used, as with Jutta, would the old woman have heard it?

She wished she had a fireman's hatchet with which to chop out the piece of the wall. She knew a .25 didn't blast a crater like this.

She found her metal nail file, Swiss Army knife, and clippers in her backpack and got to work. Finally the plaster gave way. By gouging, poking, and levering she managed to scrape down to something metallic. Five minutes later, she'd hooked the curved nail file edge under the bullet and pried it out.

The slug of a .357. She dropped it in a Baggie, put it in her backpack, and left.

TIRED, NO taxi in sight, and only few francs in her second-hand Vuitton wallet, Aimée caught the Metro, changed at Chatelet, and exited at Pont Marie. The soft summer night's wind lofted from the dark Seine. Blue lights of the *bateau-mouches* glided under her.

What a night, she thought, crossing the bridge—meeting Etienne at the squat but not Christian; Georges and Frédo's reminiscing about her mother; discovering the ancient underground vaults in Romain Figeac's building and then the fresh bullet hole in the wall. More questions and she was still no closer to her mother.

She strode along the edge of the walkway, kicking a pebble against the low stone wall, when she noticed lights shining in her apartment. And for a moment, time was suspended . . . someone was home waiting for her . . . like her papa . . . or Yves once . . . but her papa lay in the cemetery and Yves had returned his key. . . . René? *Non*, he always called first.

"*Maman?*" escaped her lips.

A woman walking her dog on the quai turned to look at her as she ran, crossing the cobbles at breakneck speed. She hit the numbers on the digicode and barreled inside her building. She bounded up the marble stairs, grooved and worn from centuries.

In the black-and-white-diamond-tiled hallway her apartment door lay open, the drone of conversation and static from a police radio coming from the foyer.

Nom de Dieu!

Of course, her mother wasn't here . . . what had got into her?

She went to the door. Someone caught her elbow. Gripped and held it. She turned to see a middle-aged blue-uniformed *flic* with a radio to his ear.

"Where might you be going in such a hurry?"

She surveyed the foyer. "I live here."

"You can prove that?"

She pulled out her *carte d'identité*, flashed her detective badge.

"*Merci*, Mademoiselle Leduc," he said. "Seems you've had a break-in."

Her heart hammered.

"A break-in . . . who informed the police?"

"A concerned neighbor," he said. "But you're the best one to let us know what's missing."

"Commissaire Morbier's in charge?"

If the *flic* was surprised at her knowledge he didn't show it.

"Lieutenant Bellan's on robbery detail," he said. "We just got here, Mademoiselle. It was like this—the door wide open, but no lights on. Sorry for the shock."

She studied the man, saw his shoulder stripes. He was more informative than most, downright human.

"You look familiar, Sergeant."

"Helier. I worked under your father briefly, Mademoiselle," he said. "Before he retired. I was proud of the opportunity."

Now she remembered. "Of course, Sergeant, thank you for your kind words. Aren't you from Quimper in Brittany?"

He nodded, a big smile on his face.

Her father always said the best biscuits came from there. He'd buy them from Fauchon for a treat.

"Mademoiselle, this way, please!" beckoned another *flic* from her kitchen.

As she passed Sergeant Helier, he covered his mouth. "I didn't believe what they said," he said in a low undertone. "Never. He was a good man."

Before she could reply or ask what he meant, a *flic* holding a squirming and barking Miles Davis approached her. Miles Davis yelped and jumped to the parquet floor.

"*Merci*. Where was he?" she said, opening her arms and catching him.

The *flic* rolled his eyes. "Locked in the bathroom."

"*Tiens*, furball," she said, ruffling his ears and smoothing the hair from his eyes. His chin dripped. "Drinking from the W.C.?" Miles Davis whimpered. "Of course, you were thirsty and someone bad locked you inside."

"How did they get in?"

"Forced entry, front door."

She expected to see furniture turned over, papers strewn about, and linens ripped up. But apart from the *flics* dusting for fingerprints, nothing appeared disturbed. She checked the high-ceilinged dining room, the corner converted to her home office. Her computer, the zip disks, and floppies, appeared untouched. She did a quick scan of her bedroom, the guest room, bathrooms, the unused parlor piled with her grandfather's auction-find furniture, the morning room, and her father's old bedroom.

Even her Fendi tote bag hung from its hook in the hallway. The sheen of dust in the unused rooms lay undisturbed . . . for once her lack of housekeeping skills was useful.

Nothing seemed unusual except the sugar spilled from a canister in the kitchen. Clumps of brown sugar trailed over the blue tiles.

"A thief with a sweet tooth?" said a voice behind her. "Or scared off by the neighbors?"

She'd thought the same thing, and turned around to a grim-faced Lieutenant Bellan.

"We meet again, Lieutenant Bellan," she said. "Isn't the 2nd arrondissement your turf?"

"*Par l'habitude*," he said with a shrug. "Vacation schedule, we're consolidating services. Which means most of the robbery detail lies on the beachfront at Biarritz while we sweat in Paris."

She nodded.

"You know the drill," he said. "We make a report, you come down to the Commissariat tomorrow, sign it. And stay somewhere else tonight."

He seemed downright affable. And tired. Big bags under his eyes. He glanced at his watch. "My wife's gone into labor . . . number three, shouldn't take long. If you'll excuse me."

"One thing, Bellan," she said. "What's the case against Christian Figeac?"

"Confidentiality laws forbid me to talk about that inquiry, Mademoiselle Leduc," he said. The pager clipped to his wrinkled jacket pocket beeped.

"Confidentiality?" She shrugged. "Looked like harassment to me."

He consulted his beeper. "*Zut!* I better hurry," he said, passing her and going down the hall. "Baby's crowning." Bellan shut the door behind him.

She knew she was in danger and her hands shook. She'd been hit from behind at the fire, her office phone tapped, and now someone had violated and invaded her apartment.

After she gave her statement to the *flics*, she punched in Martine's number.

"*Allô*," came Martine's breathy voice after one ring.

"Got a couch Miles Davis and I could borrow tonight?"

"Sounds like a perfect ending to a horrible evening," Martine said. "Any reason why? Not that you need one."

She told Martine about the break-in.

"*Tiens*, you better stay here," Martine said. "Hop on your Vespa. Now."

Aimée navigated her way to Martine's apartment in the exclusive 16th arrondissement, overlooking the Bois de Boulogne.

She avoided the notorious transvestite traffic in the *bois*, which could be quite active on a summer night.

The concierge of Martine's Belle Epoque building yawned and pointed for her to park the scooter in the courtyard. Backlit stained-glass windows illumined the plush red runner that carpeted the apartment stairs. She carried Miles Davis in his straw basket over her shoulder, hoping Martine hadn't acquired a cat since her last visit.

"*Entrez.*" Martine greeted her in a form-fitting coral tube dress, walking awkwardly on her heels, blue foam separators wedged between her toes. "Giving myself a pedicure."

"Don't you usually get that done?"

"Not if I'm waging nuclear war with Jérôme and waiting for you," Martine said. She led Aimée into the high-ceilinged white-and-gold trimmed salon with carved wood *boiserie* and gilt cornices. "How's Miles Davis holding up?" She nuzzled his chin and palmed him a biscuit. "You two can stay with me as long as you like."

"*Merci*, but after I fix the locks at my place, we'll be fine."

This flat was big enough for an army but Aimée didn't think Jérôme would appreciate their visit. He'd inherited it from his *aristo* family who were long on name but short on cash. His ex-wife had supplied that, but liked modern skyscraper living in La Défense better.

"Don't be silly," Martine said. "In this museum, you can have your own wing."

She gestured to a drinks cart loaded with decanters and bottles, then handed a champagne flute to Aimée.

Martine popped the cork of a Pol Roget, then poured the golden bubbled mixture. They clinked glasses and Aimée hoped she hadn't spilled any on the jade, peach, and white Aubusson rug.

"Are we celebrating?" Aimée asked. "Come up with anything I should know?"

Martine gave a small shake of her head as she blew on her toes. "*Voilà*. Did they take anything?"

Aimée knew Martine too well not to notice her evasion.

"If they did, it's not obvious," she said. "Tomorrow, I'll check."

"You've been busy," Martine said as she poured them another drink. "What about the Bourse hunk you met?"

Leave it to Martine to zero in on men.

"He wanted to meet at Rouge but I missed him."

Martine looked up, horror on her face. "So exclusive . . . he invited you there?"

She said. "Anyway, he left with a woman, *c'est la vie*. So I checked out Romain Figeac's burned-out apartment."

"But he invited you!" Martine clinked her glass to Aimée's. "Why scour Romain Figeac's apartment?"

Aimée told her what had happened so far: Jutta's murder, Christian Figeac hiring her, and the lead provided by Georges, from Action-Réaction.

Martine listened. "But you're in danger, Aimée. I think you should leave it alone.

"First tell me what you found, Martine."

"Not much," she said, looking away. "It can wait until tomorrow."

"Bad?" Aimée stood up, grabbed the champagne. "Guess this will make the news go down better."

"It's all exaggerated. Nasty stuff. Sure you want to hear it?"

"Better hearing it this way than by hints and rumors."

"I delved pretty deep," Martine said. "The night desk faxed me the hard copy." Martine lit a cigarette, blew a smoke ring. She pulled the foam from between her toes, tapped her coral pink polish to see if it had dried. "It's not pretty."

"That my mother ran drugs, got involved with terrorists, and escaped to Africa?" She didn't know that for sure, but Georges had intimated as much. She figured it was a good guess.

Martine's eyes widened. Then she blinked.

"Worse? She's a mercenary?" Aimée asked.

"Drink your bubbly, we'll talk in the morning."

"What did she do?" Aimée reached for Martine's cigarette. She took a deep drag, exhaled, and gulped her champagne. "I can take it."

Martine sighed. "Nothing's conclusive, the article's full of conjecture."

"Like I said, I can take it."

"The article says things about your papa . . . I'm sorry."

Martine gestured toward the silk-upholstered Directoire chair by the long windows. Some faxes sat on the arm. Beyond the dark black of the woods shone the distant glow of Neuilly. Aimée grabbed a paper and skimmed the article.

"Some investigation with my father . . . I don't understand."

"Rumor was terrorists blew him up. Seems there was a *l'inspection de police*, internal affairs had put him under investigation."

"Makes no sense," Aimée said, her hand shaking. "The *police judiciare* contracted with us for surveillance in the Place Vendôme. Routine. We did it all the time."

"Some mistake . . . they made a mistake, the reports are exaggerated," Martine said, her eyes down. "It's late, let's find you a room."

And then Aimée understood.

"They thought Papa was dirty, a bent *flic*!"

Her father's half-smile floated before her. She imagined his patient eyes and the way he combed his thinning hair over his bald spot. How she'd find him asleep in his uniform in the hard chair by her bed after an all-night stakeout. How he called her his little princess.

"They said he was dirty, didn't they?" She stood up, knocking over the champagne, which fizzed over the rug. "Never!" she shouted. "Papa worked hard. His men respected him. Not Papa!"

"Of course," Martine said. She lit another cigarette, passed it to Aimée. "Look at how it's written. All hearsay. Nasty innuendo."

"Every department has *flics* who lie, who shave the truth, stick bribes in their pocket. But not Papa!"

AIMÉE READ the article standing by Martine's guest bedroom window overlooking the Bois de Boulogne. The year she'd been an exchange student in New York had been a busy one for her parents. According to the article entitled A COUPLE IN CAHOOTS? by Jacques Caillot in *Le Figaro*, her father had been under review in connection with art heists. Her mother was mentioned in the same sentence as two bank robberies, one of them involving Haader-Rofmein, one attributed to Action-Réaction.

She remembered the kidnapped Paul Laborde and his Modigliani collection. And that her mother had written Modigliani backwards in the notebook. But the *Figaro* article only hinted, and gave no proof.

She'd assumed her father had joined her grandfather at Leduc Detective because he'd had enough of bureaucracy. Maybe there had been more to it.

So that's why Morbier never talked about her father, his old colleague from the police academy. He suspected he was crooked.

Desolation swept over her.

She finally fell asleep, Miles Davis beside her.

Her dreams were filled with bright-hued iguanas, scales swollen and pulsating, trampling through the artists' squat. Then the nightmare again. This time . . . her father crawling over the cobblestones, his face melted, her hands bloody from the explosion, only this time the doors led to bricked-in walls . . . doors to nowhere. Some were blood-smeared, others covered with peeling WANTED posters.

THURSDAY

AIMÉE WOKE UP with a start in Martine's guest room. Dust motes danced in the slanting sunlight on her pillow. Why hadn't she thought of it before . . . the old Interpol wanted posters! She'd find this Jules!

But before that she had to ask the reporter, Jacques Caillot, about the article he'd written. Specifically, how he had obtained his information.

She gulped a bowl of café au lait. Her head was hazy so she followed it with an espresso to help her wake up.

She called the visiting office at Frésnes to find when she could see Liane Barolet again.

"Lockdown," the officer said. "No visitors or mail."

"For how long?"

"Depends on the warden's mood," he said. "Big riot last night. It could last a week."

A disappointment. But she'd become suspicious of Liane's having any letters from her mother. Liane was too good a liar. Still, she'd send the papers proving payment to Liane's lawyer, as she'd promised.

After several calls she discovered Jacques Caillot no longer worked at *Le Figaro* but ran the Agence France-Presse archives.

"Sorry," the switchboard operator said. "Monsieur Caillot only takes appointments with press staff. Our archive is limited to journalists, correspondents, and news wire organizations."

Saying she was a researcher, Aimée made an appointment. Martine handed over her laminated clip-on *Madame Figaro* ID and her *presse* card to Aimée, then offered to take Miles Davis and drop him off at the Leduc office later. Aimée borrowed Martine's black linen Chanel dress and a straw hat. Ten minutes later, she was speeding along the Seine on her scooter.

"Credentials, s'il vous plaît," the wiry security man said from the booth at Agence France-Presse's door. His partner watched the monitors fed by surveillance cameras panning the small glassed-in sixties lobby. Outside, the Bourse and the graffiti-covered squat opposite glimmered in the midmorning heat.

Aimée flashed him Martine's ID and a large smile.

"Archives, please," she said.

He studied the card, turned it over. She held her breath, hoping he didn't ask for another piece of ID.

"Through these doors, Mademoiselle, take the second staircase to the basement."

"*Merci,*" she said.

She rushed ahead.

"Mademoiselle!"

She stopped. Afraid.

"Sign in, please."

"*Bien sûr,*" she said, and wrote "Martine Sitbon" with a flourish.

She passed through the double-swing doors he buzzed open for her. Photographers gripped portfolios, assistants scurried, and the world of breaking news engulfed her.

To the left, narrow linoleum-tiled stairs led down two dank flights. The cisternlike bowels of the building seemed much older than the modernized floors above. Sixteenth century, or even older, she thought.

At the microfiche desk, a pale-faced woman in overalls took her request.

"*Attends*, he's on the phone," she said, her tone listless. Maybe she'd worked down here too long.

By the time she nodded permission to go in, Aimée had written down her questions.

"First door on the right."

Aimée held her breath as she entered an arched door. The vaulted rose brick walls and stone floor resembled a medieval abbey. Maybe, originally, it was.

Jacques Caillot sat at a stainless steel desk, halogen beams illuminating an old card file he was sorting. Aimée noticed the framed press clippings on the walls from Saigon, Lagos, and Kabul with his byline. There were even foreign press awards.

"Sorry to intrude, Monsieur Caillot," she said. "I appreciate your seeing me."

He looked up. "Sit down," he said. "One moment, and I'll be finished."

The dim room and his greenish blue eyes reminded her of peering into an aquarium. She realized one of Caillot's eyes focused in slow motion. He shut the card file, noticed her gaze.

"Venetian glass eye. Thanks to the IRA's Enskillen Rembrance Day bombing in 1987," he said with a lopsided smile. "And I was one of the lucky ones. How can I help?"

"I'm researching European terrorism in the seventies for a Montreal journal," she said. "I came across your article. It made me curious."

She thrust the copy across his desk.

Caillot scanned the article, nodding. "Of course, I remember," he said. "Does Lepic still man the *Figaro* night desk?" he asked without looking up.

He'd got her. She'd only known Martine and her assistant, Roxane, at *Le Figaro*. He'd tested her and he'd won.

"Tell you what," she said, gambling. "You can kick me out, but I borrowed this ID from my friend Martine, the former *Le Figaro* editor."

"And why, may I ask?"

"Because, Monsieur Caillot, there didn't seem to be any other way to see you. You see this 'couple in cahoots' you described in the article are my parents." She stood up. "No one will talk to me." She sat back down, put her elbows on his desk, and leaned forward. "The only files available have been sanitized. At least your article makes me think so. So far, your piece has been the only one to surface."

"You lied to get in here," Caillot said, returning her gaze. His glass eye was fixed on a spot below the mole on her neck.

"D'accord," she agreed. "But I didn't know what else to do. I need to know about Action-Réaction, Haader-Rofmein terrorists still wanted by Europol, Romain Figeac, and agit888."

"Impressive," he said. "You've been doing some homework."

Metal rods behind his back caught the light as he leaned forward. She realized he sat in a wheelchair.

"Not enough," she said. "Help me out, please."

"Why do you think I'm down here, Mademoiselle . . . what was your name?"

"Aimée Leduc." She pulled out her detective's badge and *carte d'identité* with the less than flattering photo. "I'm guessing, but after Enskillen you wanted to let it all settle. Write a book."

"It's being printed as we speak. You're quick." He gave her another lopsided smile. "Why should I help you, even if I could?"

"You didn't get into reporting to stay safe," she said. "It's all about risks. Finding something, trying out hunches until one pays off. Like a detective."

The lid over his glass eye quivered.

"What evidence did you find?" she said, leaning over his desk.

"Don't badger me," he said. "I'm a pro."

She wanted to say, *So am I*, but she didn't feel like one.

"Please tell me where you got your information," she said. "Then I'll leave you alone."

"Know anybody at the DST?"

Her mind raced. "No one who likes me."

He tented his fingers. Tapped his index fingers together.

"I'm curious what you'd do with the information," he said, leaning back in his wheelchair, "if I had any to give."

She had to make him understand. And there was only one way. Something she hated to do. Reveal herself to a stranger.

"Monsieur Caillot, one day, when I was eight, I came home from school and my mother was gone," she said. "Papa burned her things. Told me we'd closed a chapter in our life and started another. Wouldn't talk about her."

She rubbed her goose-pimpled arms. "Years later, during a routine surveillance contracted for with our detective agency by the police, our van blew up. Papa died. No one gave me any reasons or answers. For years I've tried to find out who these terrorists were. All I reached was dead ends. My last shot, an informer in Berlin, gave me zip. But when I returned a few days ago, a former terrorist, Jutta Hald, appeared at my door—straight from a twenty-year prison sentence—telling me she'd been my mother's cell mate in Frésnes."

Jacques Caillot's hands remained tented. His odd gaze never left her face.

"Somehow, searching for leads to my father's death triggered the arrival of this terrorist who knew my mother. Then Jutta Hald was murdered. But that's just the beginning, Monsieur Caillot," she said. "Now it's your turn. Tell me what you know and how you found it out."

"But you still haven't said what you'll do with the information."

"All I want to know is who was behind my father's death and if my mother's buried in some lime pit in a field or alive in Africa."

"Africa?"

"It's personal, Monsieur . . . I need to know if they're connected . . ."

"You mean . . . ?"

"If she caused my father to be killed." There. She'd said it, then she hung her head. When she looked up, he hadn't moved.

"Guess I'm stubbborn, but I have to know and I won't leave until you tell me."

"There are a few life lessons I've learned," he said. "Important ones: When you find the love of your life, never hesitate, grab her; brush and floss every night; and don't mess with the DST."

"Thanks for the warning," she said. "I thought Papa's files were at the *police judiciare*."

"You're not wearing a wire, eh?"

"Wired? Only on espresso," she said. She stood up, took off her hat, and opened her backpack. "But you can check."

He paused, then shook his head. "If you mention anything outside this thick-walled dungeon, I'll deny it all."

Dungeon was right.

"You have my word."

Caillot took a deep breath. "Don't think I'm proud of the afternoon I spent on rue Nélaton more than twenty years ago." He shrugged. "But I was starting out, a hungry reporter, ready to chew on anything. Sounds trite, but live and learn."

"Rue Nélaton," Aimée said, "you mean where the DST's housed in the former Elf Oil building?" Aimée had long since dropped off a request to see her father's files at the Ministry of Interior located in the unmarked building constructed over the Vel d'Hiver, the velodrome that held Jews before shipment to Drancy, then the long train ride to Auschwitz.

"*Exactement*," he said. "They refer to it as *politesse* or good manners. Very simple, very civilized. Upon invitation, a journalist gets access to files the *flics* or the DST wants them to see. But the real agenda is that the story the *flics* want published gets published."

"Selective leaks?"

"From selective files," he said. "Your papa, a *flic*, would've understood. Take the agit888 file. They trailed Sartre for years; tapped his phone, noted whom he met, where he went. On the surface it looks suspicious, eh? A thick surveillance log, reels of phone tapes, hidden photos . . . and what did it show? Basically, that he and Simone de Beauvoir had an unsatisfactory love life and he was in trouble with his publisher. Missed his deadlines."

That dovetailed with what Morbier had told her about Sartre and agit888. And it made sense.

"But my mother probably translated Sartre's interview in the jail with Haader, and that's part of the agit888 file, isn't it?"

"Another nail in Sartre's coffin, but she didn't figure in the file or I would have written that."

So the agit888 file led nowhere.

"What about my father?"

"Same analogy applies," Caillot said. "Fingers pointed at him after an art heist. They left me in a room with his file and some Action-Réaction articles mentioning your mother. I figured they were helping me and I knew I'd have to repay them someday."

"So they used you," Aimée said.

"That's clear now, but then . . ." His voice trailed off.

"Did you repay them?"

He rearranged a foam pad on the arm of his chair. "After my tour of duty in the world's hot spots I came home to a secure job. Or so I thought. But they had another assignment, "like old times," they said. It backfired and I'm in a chair for life."

She refrained from asking if that's why he hid down here. "Did you find proof my father assisted in robberies?"

"For that, Mademoiselle, you'd have to look at *police judiciare* files . . . all I saw were the allegations of culpability. And that's what I reported. Seems I did the damage they intended. Forgive me."

He wheeled himself out from behind the desk. "For years it haunted me. I'm a reporter first of all. Word came out the investigation was dropped. Whether your father was dirty . . ." Caillot shrugged. "I don't know. Sixty percent of the force is rumored to be. But I heard he landed on his feet, ran a detective agency. Again, I'm sorry."

Caillot must have had a lot of time to think about the past. Aimée stood up. *"Merci."*

"Last advice: Narrow Africa down . . . try Senegal."

She thought of Idrissa, who came from Senegal. "Why Senegal?"

"The economy's more stable for *intellos* who become mercenaries."

She tried questioning him further but that's all he would say.

"I understand why you wrote the story, I might have done the same thing," she said. "But I didn't, and they're my parents. Here's my card, in case you want to talk later."

It seemed as if all she'd been doing was giving her card to people. People who knew things but would tell her little.

She consulted the microfiche directory at the archive desk on the next floor, searching entries for mercenaries, Senegal, terrorists, and links between European terrorists.

What she found made her glad she'd looked. She'd never have found them otherwise. Few of these articles appeared in Internet archives. They only lived in dank vaults like this one. She copied the relevant ones.

A few hours later, copies in hand, she emerged, glad to feel the sun's rays again. She pulled the scooter off the kickstand. While she'd been inside, a purple fluorescent sticker had been placed on it, MESSY ART FOR THE MASSES!

René would love that!

At a café on rue des Colonnes, a shady colonnaded arcade like the rue de Rivoli, she ordered *a double café crème*.

"Why not a *grenade?*" asked the man behind the counter, flicking a none too clean towel at a fly.

"Grenade?"

"What we call a depth-charge espresso drink," he said.

"Parfait!" she said, as the man hit the slow, late-summer fly.

She wanted a quiet place to read the articles, digest Caillot's words, and look at Modigliani prints.

After laying twenty francs on the zinc counter, she drove three blocks, parked the scooter in Place Louvois, which bordered the Sentier, and stepped across the street to the seventeenth-century Bibliothéque Nationale.

She showed her yellow research card then sat down at number 32, her assigned place, a seat away from the tall wood-framed windows in the Occidental manuscript section.

Her favorite section.

She sat fourth from the aisle, overlooking the cobbled court-yard. Floor-to-ceiling books covered the walls.

She took a deep breath, inhaling the musky manuscript smells emanating from the old paper. The aura of the past, the stillness, reassured her in this changing world. During her École des Med-icines years she'd studied here on Thursday afternoons. Now the familiar beams of fading lemon light and oversized hard wooden chairs brought back a timeless feeling.

In front of her, the upright wood cradles for books and man-uscripts and the oak spindle place holders were covered with a honeylike patina. All nineteenth century. Aimée fingered the book spindle, the pointed tip worn and darkened, aware of the overall hush broken only by the turning of pages and occasional patron's cough.

Next to her a man studied a tea brown parchment, stiff and oily, with a cracked lump of red sealing wax below an intricate flourish of curlicue script dated 1424.

She sat back, took a deep breath, and began. The copies she'd made from the microfiche took all afternoon to read. Before the last call-up of the day, she'd finished taking notes and listing the possible remaining Action-Réaction and Haader-Rofmein mem-bers. Six, counting Jutta and Liane Barolet, had done prison time or gone underground. If Jules Bourdon, who she discovered came from a wealthy intellectual family, and her mother had fled to Senegal . . . why had Jutta been killed now? The timing was im-portant but she didn't know why.

She gathered her papers, recovered her card from the reference desk librarian, and trudged to the *estampes et photographie* room. She found a book of twentieth-century prints. Modigliani's fluid, elongated lines and curves radiated sensuousness. And a haunting love of his subjects. Mainly women.

An essay accompanying a 1987 exhibition guide to Modigliani's paintings gave her perspective. A thought crossed her mind. Had Laborde, an Alsatian, identified with Modigliani, also an outsider in France?

She wondered how it all meshed: Modigliani, Laborde's abduction and death and her father's subsequent police hearing.

Her father couldn't be called an art connoisseur though her grandfather qualified as a dilettante. Money had been tight, but her father saw to it her shoes had no holes, her books were new, and the *boulangerie* honored a standing Saturday morning order of *brioches* after her piano lesson, since he couldn't be there to buy them.

She rode back to her office and parked the scooter below. Aimée hurried along the pavement, past the dark green shopfront with PARIS-ROLLERBLADE on it. She climbed the stairs, opened the door of her dark office, switched on the light, then her laptop.

"Working up Michel's system," said the Post-It on René's screen. Out of guilt, she put in some time and made a sizable dent in the pile on her desk. A sweet lucrative Media 9 contract would keep the wolf from the door. But they had to nail it with safeguards for their security setup.

Security, like anything, had to be continually upgraded and maintained. Hackers, crackers, and script kiddies always found a way in . . . at least she and René did. That's how they tested their security. But script kiddies, so called because they lacked the finesse of crackers, would manage, sooner or later, to break into a system and wreak havoc. Frugality, shortcuts, and untrained staff cost firms more in the long run. A lot more.

She'd seen it too often. Corporations who wouldn't pay for a strong lock yet cried when the barn door opened and the horses escaped. She and René refused to do damage control and inserted nonculpability clauses in every contract.

After another hour, she'd written alternatives to the client's questionable clauses, made René a copy, and faxed the revisions to Media 9.

On the wall she tacked up copies of the old WANTED posters. More than a million of them, printed and distributed in the summer of 1972. The equal numbers of men and women pictured, she imagined, stiffened the patriarchal backbones of Germany and France.

She tried the DST, asking for a status report as to her request for her father's file. All she got was a recording saying that file series was sensitive and only available to those with high security clearance.

Courtesy of her high-level contract with Equifax, she pulled up a fairly granular, up-to-the-minute credit report. With the password she'd stolen last year on a bank consulting job, she got to work. After entering the number, she found the information she wanted.

She picked up the phone and punched in the number she'd stored in her memory. One she never wrote down. She'd avoided calling it until now. She'd never before had enough material with which to do a deal with the devil.

"*Oui?*"

"I want to find someone," Aimée said.

"Then you have to pay," Léo Frot said at the other end of the line. His nasal voice competed with an occasional metallic ting in the background.

"How much?"

"Price mounts when someone doesn't want to be found."

"How do you know that, Léo?"

"Why would you call me if you could find them?"

Léo hadn't changed. He'd squeeze the venom from a viper and charge the snake for it.

Too bad he was right.

She couldn't data mine the files at the *police judiciare* on Quai des Orfèvres. None of them were computerized. Everything before the nineties was handwritten, stored in folders and police blotters. Dossiers. Face it, everything sensitive was done with pen and ink . . . probably quill pens.

"Someone do a walkabout, eh?" Léo asked.

"Walkabout?" she asked.

"We just came back from Australia," he said. "That's what they call an aborigine's disappearance there."

Typical Léo. Must be desperate to brag about his trip to someone, she thought. She'd known him for years. They'd gone to the *lycée* together. His father was her dentist.

"What if I do a systems security scan for you in return."

Silence.

"Why do I feel that's unfair?" Léo scraped something in the background.

"Suit yourself," she said. "But that's worth more than cash, believe me. You can't imagine the stuff I find."

"Like what?"

She knew he'd bite. His credit history lay before her on her screen. "Like the amount overdue on your Visa card. A gold one. And they're about to pull it."

"But they said . . ."

"Forget it," she said. "The process started six hours ago. . . . I see bad credit in your future. Very bad."

"Change it and I'll help you," he said.

She thought he caved in too fast.

"Files on Action-Réaction and the Haader-Rofmein gang," she said. "From the seventies on." She paused, hesitating. "And my father's police review."

A pause.

"Can't *you* find them?" Léo asked.

"If they were in the system, I would," she said. He knew that, too. "But I don't feel inclined to break into the *préfecture* at Quai des Orfèvres. Makes me squeamish."

"So I have to?"

"*Tiens*, Léo," she said, "it's your department."

There was a long pause.

"Only if you adjust my credit report."

"I'll do what I can."

She hit several keys and his bank balance flashed in front of her. "You're overdrawn, Léo!"

"Fix that"—he took a deep breath—"and you've got my fingers at your disposal."

"My partner hasn't broken Banque de France's encryption algorithms yet," she said.

But she lied. René had done it two years ago. Even amped up their security system to a faster, better-tested algorithm called Blowfish. As he often said, better to be paranoid than sorry.

"Everything's automated," she said. "Programmed for glitches . . . too late. . . ."

She let that sink in.

"But if I shut down the billing department with a postage-meter problem, that gives you an extra day."

Pause.

"One day?"

Greedy *mec*!

"Figure the weekend," she said, struggling to sound patient. "On Monday you pay the Visa and prevent a lifetime of nasty credit ratings that could screw up your application to refinance your Neuilly house."

"It's Chantal," he said, expelling air in disgust.

Aimée had met his wife, Chantal. Bubbleheaded but she seemed kind.

"Her heart's set on a Corsican holiday bungalow," Léo said. "With a hot tub!"

"I'm sure it's difficult." Aimée found it hard to feign sympathy for this couple. A vast majority of Parisian families struggled with two jobs even with subsidized day care, to buy necessities and pay the skyrocketing rents for their small apartments.

"But you have to come here to see the records; I'm so busy," he said, his tone petulant. "When I find them, they go no farther than the lavatory."

She'd met him in the Art Nouveau men's lavatory in the Quai des Orfèvres once before.

"Some files might have traveled to the DST," she said. "Can you check?"

"DST!" Léo groaned. "The ninth-floor division on rue Néla-ton?"

"Good place to start."

"Talk about paranoia," Léo said. "Everything one says or does there gets classified. Papers must be locked in office safes and even when you take a piss you have to lock your office."

"I bet you know the combinations of some safes."

She heard his slow chuckle.

"Or you know someone who does," she said.

"What did you say you'd do about the Visa?" he asked.

"I'll see what I can do."

MARIUS TEYNARD WALKED past his receptionist, Madame Goroux, who was busy at the keyboard.

"Mark me out for this afternoon," he said.

"Monsieur Teynard, there's a late afternoon appointment. . . ."

"Tell the boy to take it," he said. The boy, as he referred to his nephew, was fifty-five. Teynard slipped on his oatmeal-colored linen jacket, ruffled his white hair back from his temples, and gave her a half-smile. "You know how to handle him."

He knew Madame Goroux would think he was visiting his mistress, who lived on the next block in the rue de Turbigo. She often covered for him. Let her think what she wanted.

Out on the haze-filled street where the heat hovered, hemmed in by the tall Haussmann buildings, he turned in the opposite direction. Teynard headed toward the *préfecture de police* on Quai des Orfèvres.

Along the broad part of rue de Turbigo that sliced the edge of the Sentier, he passed the Kookai boutique. Salesgirls smoked outside on the steps and the *tatouage* sign on rue Tiquetonne blinked orange-pink neon in the dusk. A dope haven if he ever saw it, but he knew the *flics* let it slide as long as their informants checked in with them. And, he reminded himself, that wasn't his business.

Not anymore.

In the distance he saw the Tour Jean-Sans-Peur nestled behind the sandstone-colored school. The scum had been right here . . . a stone's throw from his office. *Merde!*

He was getting slow, admit it. Not on top of it anymore. Yet no one said that but himself. Be your own harshest critic, he'd learned, then no one else could be.

But that would change. He'd entered the fray. Time to wipe out the degenerate lice once and for all, if it was the last thing he did.

The hunt, the chase—these were the only things keeping him alive. The shivery tingle on the back of his arms . . . it was what he lived for. Face it, had always lived for.

He'd deluded himself when he retired from the *préfecture*, started the agency, and kept half-time hours. Even the DST contract work hadn't filled the need. Keeping a young mistress had become difficult, and so time-consuming. His true mistress was his work.

He needed to get this information face-to-face, without risk of compromised phone lines, big-eared subordinates, or his former cronies from the Quai des Orfèvres. Time to mine his old-boy network.

Thursday Afternoon

OUSMANE SADA'S FEVERISH brow was beaded with sweat. He felt worse than before his visit to the marabout. Across from the sewing factory where he worked, he stopped in a Sentier café.

A few old men played backgammon at a Formica table. It took a while before the owner excused himself and asked Ousmane, in a brisk tone, what he wanted. Propping himself up at the zinc counter, parched and shaky, Ousmane allowed himself one small luxury. He ordered a steaming glass cup of sweet black tea, mint flavored. So soothing and such a comfort. Then he'd find his straw mattress and sleep his fever off. He'd promised himself he'd try what his *maman* had always advised . . . nothing sweats out a fever like hot, sweet mint tea, she'd always said.

Idrissa needed him in a few hours . . . already he was feeling better. Mandinkas never let the grass grow under a baobab tree, he remembered his father saying. He paid for the tea, and the owner acknowledged his tip with a nod of his head.

Ousmane made his way toward the sewing factory downstairs in the narrow Passage Ste-Foy. The dark passage's light source was the flickering fluorescent bulbs in an upstairs office. Ousmane saw the yellow feather fetish, an omen of evil, just before he stepped on it. Too late. It crunched under his scuffed shoe. In horror, he clutched the stone wall. No way to reverse it, he knew. He'd been cursed for the second time that week.

AIMÉE TOOK care of Léo's online account, giving him a three-day grace period, then pulled up the virus she and René had discovered and neutered in Media 9's site. She wrote new code, programming the virus to self-destruct in twenty-four hours and rescind all its commands and any further ones. After rechecking and running a test, she sent the virus into the Visa postage-metering system. Half of France would thank her if they found out she'd given them a grace period. But they wouldn't.

Knocks came from her glass-paned office door. She hit *Save*, then *Quit*, and closed her laptop.

She opened the door to a woman with slate gray eyes wearing black-framed glasses on a pale, sharp-angled face.

"Fräulein Leduc?" the woman asked. Her silk polka-dotted scarf fluttered in the hall window air, hot and exhaust-laden from the back alley.

"*Oui?*"

"I'm Gisela. We need to talk."

"Concerning?"

"My mother and yours."

Taken aback, Aimée kept her hand rigid on the knob.

"What do you mean . . . who's your mother?

"Past tense seems the operative word here," said the woman. "Ulrike Rofmein."

Aimée gripped the door handle. "You'd better come in."

"We're Hitler's grandchildren, you know," the woman said. "The lost generation."

Aimée flinched. *Speak for yourself*, she wanted to say—it had nothing to do with her.

"And it affects you," Gisela said, as if she read Aimée's thoughts."

The hair on Aimée's neck rose.

Gisela strode into the office, stopping at a chair. Her gaze traveled over the filigreed-iron balcony rail, the eighteenth century still life hung above digital scanners, old sepia maps, and Interpol posters.

"May I?"

"Sit down," Aimée said. She needed a drink. "Like an espresso?"

"*Grazie,*" Gisela said, smiling. "We were raised in Italy."

"We?" Aimée twisted the black metal arm off the Lavazza espresso machine.

"My twin, Marthe," Gisela said. "Papa changed our names. Later, when I was in *Universität,*" she leaned forward, "I came to the realization."

"Realization?"

Gisela lowered her voice, as if to highlight the importance of her words. "I don't need to hide, none of us do," she said. "We weren't the criminals. They were. We're the victims."

"What do you know about *my* mother?"

Gisela rubbed her long fingers over Aimée's desk.

"Who really and truly knows anyone? That's the point."

Aimée didn't know how to reply. Something about this Gisela didn't feel right.

Aimée slammed the used coffee grounds into the trash.

Gisela didn't flinch. She fixed Aimée with a long stare.

"The Revolution was their child," Gisela said. "Not us."

Maybe that was true.

Aimée pressed the black switch on her machine. A grumbling answered, then a slow measured hiss.

"I don't understand how you found me, Gisela, or why you're here," Aimée said.

"We've inherited the legacy," Gisela said. "A badge of shame that I overturned."

Aimée let the steaming espresso drip into a demitasse cup. As she passed Gisela the *faïence* sugar bowl, their fingers touched, quivered, and held. It felt both intimate and unnerving.

Aimée pulled her hand away. They sipped, quiet for a moment.

She wondered what Gisela's angle was and why she seemed strangely familiar.

"What do you mean 'overturned,' Gisela?"

"We're going to change Europe," she said, "for the better."

"How?"

"Do something to make people understand," Gisela said.

Her eye rested on Leduc Detective's client list tacked on a cork board. "Computer security, *ja*?" She didn't wait for a response. "When you go home and your boyfriend asks about your day, all you can say is 'I can't tell you,' right?"

If I had a boyfriend, Aimée almost said before she could stop herself.

"Gisela, why don't you answer my questions? Why have you come to me now?"

Gisela sat back, pushed her glasses up on her nose, and nodded as if she'd made a decision. "When I went to *Universität* in Wiesbaden, I lived with my aunt," she said, her voice flat. "Every week, I washed her car, waxed it, filled up the tank. The owner of the car wash watched me. I thought he was a dirty old man. After Italy, I was used to it. But one Saturday as I paid, he snickered, asked wasn't I going to stick him up? I asked him what he meant. He said he remembered my mother, how she liked fast BMWs and how he'd keep quiet if I bombed the late-night Turkish grocer."

"Papa never told us about our mother." Gisela took a long sip. "So I ignored the man."

She took a nonfiltered cigarette from her bag. Didn't light it, just played with the tobacco threads at the tip. Pulled them out with her thumb and ring finger.

"*Aber*, he was serious. A few days later, going to class, the tram conductor refused my *Bahn* pass, said I should go steal a car like my mother, Ulrike Rofmein, did. Another fascist! Then a passenger stood up, pointed to me, and said, 'My brother has glass in his hip from your bombing, he's never walked the same since.' I wanted to say I was a little girl—I didn't do anything—I wasn't even in the country. My mother was the outlaw on the run. But contempt glared in their eyes. And icy hate. I ran. For years."

"What about your sister?"

"Marthe married an Italian, buried herself in a slew of bambinos, and won't even speak German. Then I met someone," Gisela said, her gaze wistful. "Big mistake. Turns out he was a reporter writing about 'Terrorist children of Haader-Rofmein— where are they now? Inhabiting society's fringe like the parents who abandoned them? Will they stike again?' . . . same old *scheiss*. Live and learn, eh?"

Live and learn . . . Jacques Caillot had said the same thing.

"What was his name?"

"Martin."

A world-weary sigh escaped Gisela's lips. She played with the tobacco with her pinkie and offered a cigarette to Aimée.

With an effort, Aimée refused.

Gisela lit up and inhaled deeply.

Aimée wanted to suck in the smoky gray spiral mounting lazily to her high ceiling. Instead, she fingered her pocket for Nicorette gum but found only a crumpled wrapper.

"I met journalists, old colleagues of my mother," Gisela said. "They once respected her. Even now some believe mother was set up by the *Polizei* and a bungling *Bundeswehr* who killed her in prison, fabricated her suicide."

To Aimée, Gisela's matter-of-fact tone seemed at odds with her tragic tale.

"I guess I realized we had things in common. And she wasn't so bad."

Aimée wondered what she'd have in common with her mother. She had a vague memory of a rally in Boulevard Saint Michel, a candlelit vigil in the biting cold. Aimée wondered if her father had been stationed opposite the protestors, enforcing the other political stance? What kind of couple had they been? She could never remember them fighting. Had she blocked the memory out?

She studied her fingers. Drummed them on her desk. "But you hate your mother, right, Gisela? Hate all of them."

Gisela squashed her glowing cigarette in the grounds of her espresso. "Don't you?" Gisela asked.

Aimée finished her espresso in one gulp. "Gisela, don't you find it hard to hate someone you don't know?"

Gisela's eyes flashed. Her lips pursed. "My mother betrayed the cause, so did the others," she said.

Aimée grew aware of the espresso machine's escaping steam vapor and the low thrum of the fax machine. Below, on rue du Louvre, the insistent blare of a klaxon sounded.

"Tell me how *my* mother figures in this, Gisela," Aimée said. "If you want me to turn helpful."

"She joined Jean-Paul Sartre to interview Haader in prison. They hooked up there."

"Tell me something new," Aimée said. Alain Vigot, Romain Figeac's editor, had already intimated as much.

"Your mother stole Laborde's stash," Gisela said.

Wary, Aimée stood up. Laborde, the industrialist. Had the stash been placed in Liane Barolet's mother's coffin?

"Work with me," Gisela said, "I know people. People who move things, no questions asked."

"I don't know anything."

Gisela leaned forward, intense, confrontational. "But she's sent you something . . . something only you can understand."

Aimée's spine prickled. Modigliani, in her Emil book?

She noted dark hair growing in, jaggedly, at Gisela's roots, a bad dye job. Gisela seemed a mixture of chic and seedy, like the Sentier. Like this whole affair. She wanted Gisela gone.

"Just thank me for the coffee, since you know nothing about"—she hesitated, then continued—"my mother. I understand if you must be on your way. I've got work. . . ."

Gisela didn't move. "We'll share."

Jutta had said the same thing.

Aimée ruffled her spiky hair. Maybe she was tired and that's why they all sounded the same. She'd tried to be polite but it hadn't worked. This woman was getting to her. "Clue me in. Or leave."

"The tower," Gisela said.

Tour Jean-Sans-Peur in the Sentier?

An awful feeling hit her. Turned her stomach. Was that why Jutta had set their meeting there?

"You saw Jutta Hald," Aimée said, her breathing slowed.

"Not in this lifetime," Gisela said.

"Of course, you thought the Laborde cache was in the tower, but you couldn't find it. Jutta wouldn't talk, then you killed her."

"Not me," Gisela said. "Maybe it was your mother."

Her mother?

She couldn't breathe. Had her mother sent her the book?

The familiar hiss of the espresso machine, the whine of a passing bus below shifted to another plane. A layer where familiarity lied. She floated, adrift in a netherworld of disguised people. Like the old nightmare of her childhood . . . opening doors, people pulling off masks revealing another mask, then another. No persona real or tangible.

Sweat beaded her lip.

She saw a bulge in Gisela's open purse. Something glinted dully. How stupid she was . . . Gisela carried a gun despite tight French gun control. What if she had come ready to use it?

Aimée clutched her desk. Her compact 9 mm. Beretta was in the drawer. She hooked her fingers around the drawer handle.

Gisela reached into her purse.

"Start talking. Or I'll get upset," Aimée said, raising the Beretta slowly. "Quite upset. Put your piece down."

"Live by the gun," Gisela nodded. Her gaze held no fear. "Marcus Haader liked to spout that. It was his favorite saying."

Aimée held her hand steady.

"It's in our blood," Gisela said, her eyes gleaming. She laid a stun gun on Aimée's desk. "We deserve the spoils."

Only a stun gun! Stop it, Aimée told herself, gain control. This woman unnerved her.

Aimée lowered her Beretta, ignoring the shaking in her other hand.

"Do you have a license for that?"

Gisela grinned. "Do you?"

"I'm a detective," Aimée said. Too bad the Beretta wasn't registered. But Gisela wouldn't know that.

"What happened to your hand?" Gisela said.

"You mean the scar? Terrorists blew up my father, I got in the way."

"A real daughter of the Revolution." Gisela's eyes shone. "You see, we're meant to carry on. Your mother hid the contents of the industrialist's safe. Now we need that money to finance our movement."

So that's what this was all about.

"If that were true, after twenty years why do you think anything would be left?"

"We'll carry on. We deserve it. Not all the bonds were cashed. They show up every so often."

"Bonds?"

"And land and mine deeds, in Africa."

"Why come to me now?"

Silence.

"So that's what Jutta Hald was after," Aimée said. "She thought my mother hid them? So my mother's alive?"

Gisela said nothing.

Aimée laid the gun back in the drawer. Scooped the tobacco into a pile and into the trash can.

"How old are you, Gisela?"

Gisela hesitated for the first time, unprepared for this question.

"Did you forget when you were born?" Aimée asked.

"1962," Gisela said.

The woman was a fake. From the clippings, Aimée knew Ulrike Rofmein had twins in 1963. This woman lied.

"Too late . . . wrong." She gestured to the door. "Better luck with the next one on your list. Sorry, I'm not in sympathy with sisterhood and shared terrorist memories. I don't buy your story."

"Maybe you don't like what I have to say," Gisela shrugged. She stood and walked to the door. "Your mother wasn't a saint," she said. "Get used to it."

Aimée felt like hurling the espresso machine at Gisela.

"If you don't cooperate, things might get . . . how do you say it?" Gisela paused. "Sticky for you?"

"What do you mean?"

"Your health and your partner's, for one thing."

Aimée froze. "He's got nothing to do with this."

"Don't worry, I'll keep in touch," Gisela said with a small smile. "I'm good at that."

By the time Aimée could move again, Gisela had ducked around the door. Her footsteps clicked faintly in the distance.

Aimée backed into the espresso machine, knocking it over. Hot muddy grounds, broken shards of black plastic, and mangled metal mesh littered the wood parquet. A fine chocolate-hued spray arced over her poster of the Miles Davis concert at the Olympia. Like old blood.

Aimée sagged and slid down her desk leg to the floor, fighting tears. She sprawled there, in the damp mess.

Aimée knew *Renseignements Generaux indicateurs*—informers— were trained to react that way. First lesson in the underground vault near Place Beauvau: With a pistol cocked at your head, keep up the story line, persevere, show sincerity, give nothing away. Classic RG training that appeared in no textbook.

Yet doubt assailed her; it added up wrong. A German trained by the French, undercover? Aimée caught her breath.

But RG recruited from every stratum of society . . . why not a daughter of a notorious terrorist who hated the cause that her mother had embraced instead of her? In the late sixties, RG infiltrated left-wing groups, established files based on phone taps, mail interceptions, and informers in schools and universities. Maybe Gisela was Ulrike Rofmein's daughter and also an RG agent. But then how could she be mistaken about her own birth-day?

René found her like that. Dazed and wet, choking on her sobs.

"Cheap machine," he said, kicking its carcass with his toe. "Never liked it. We need a new one." He set down Miles Davis, who beelined for her lap. "Martine dropped him off on her way to work; she told me someone broke into your apartment last night."

Aimée nodded. She hugged Miles Davis, burying her head in his fur.

"The Bazar Hôtel de Ville department store has a sale on," René said. "We'll get a new one at BHV."

He switched on his computer, then pulled out the broom.

"You're my family, René," she said, wiping her face with her sleeve. "This woman threatened me . . . said you'd be in danger if I didn't cooperate."

"Bring them on, I'm ready, I work out at the dojo every day," he said. "Give me a chance to take names and kick ass."

"If anything happened to you . . ."

"I know," he said. "And vice versa, partner."

Then she told him about Gisela and what had happened. She ruffled Miles Davis's stomach fur, then slowly pulled herself up and grabbed the broom from him.

"No luck with Etienne the other night?" René asked.

She shook her head.

"Michel arrived and we met some performance artists with their own ateliers," he said. "We talked until dawn!"

She was happy for him.

"There were some disturbing things about his uncle Nessim's letters of credit," she said, "I meant to show you."

René nodded. "Always a 'deal.' Michel's father was like that, and *his* father. His great-grandfather carted a sewing machine from the Lodz ghetto. With six mouths to feed, he set up the machine in the doorway fronting the one room the family rented in a crumbling Sentier building."

"The same building where Michel is now?" Aimée asked.

René nodded. "His great-grandfather sewed for the cloth merchants who passed by. He branched into buying cloth, making garments. Later on, he sold clothes to the burgeoning department stores of Samartaine and Bon Marché. And then he bought the old *hôtel particulier*, cheap and falling apart, but with huge work spaces. He patched it up, put in more sewing machines, hired immigrants newer than himself.

"His family and other Ashkenazi Jews were rounded up during the Occupation," René continued. "After the Algerian exodus, refugee Sephardic Jews from North Africa moved in. But the family still owned the building and the business, one of the few who returned and remained. These 'new Jews' were foreign, uneducated, too 'Arabic.' And more devious. Michel's father sold out to his brother-in-law, Nessim."

"Why did he do that?" Aimée asked.

"Michel says his father likened Nessim to mafioso; lending and protecting, filing bankruptcies, setting fires for insurance. Michel's father hated their saying: *Une mauvaise saison qui temine bien*—a bad season that ends well."

But before Aimée could pull up information as to Nessim on her terminal, loud beeping came from René's screen. He shook his head and sat down. In the halogen light, his forehead shone with a fine sweat.

"Rogue programmers!" he said, his hands racing over the keyboard. "Concocting new viruses, corrupting data, breaking into private networks, leaving irritating messages on computer displays, posting porn on the Web site. The usual."

"Our bread and butter, René," she said.

"We need to work on Michel's system before the dress rehearsal in Palais Royal. We've got work to do, cyber goddess."

Biting back a smile, she said, "I prefer cyber diva." She prised off her heeled sandal with her toe and pulled up the cryptographic hashes of the system files. She checked them against their known good backup to determine if any files were changed.

A few hours and several espressos from the downstairs café later, they found a chink in the security fire wall. René plugged it.

Then the fun part: putting the puzzle back together. René loved reconstructing the crackers' route. Over a bottle of mineral water they identified vulnerabilities that a cracker would exploit and updated Michel's system.

She didn't tell him about Léo Frot. No reason for René to know.

Thursday Evening

STEFAN WOKE UP in his car parked by the cemetery, broke and hungry. He realized he'd overreacted the night before when he'd run. Why hadn't he asked the concierge what had happened to Romain Figeac?

Now, when he reached the concierge's *loge*, it lay dark. Hesitant, he debated going up the stairs again . . . would a neighbor notice?

There was only one way to find out.

At the charred door, Stefan saw the yellow police tape, limp and dragging on the wet floor. He hit the timed light switch and his heart skipped. Right where he'd been standing the night before was a gouged hole. And there was a dent in the pillar on his right at eye level. A distinctive graze, like the mark of a bullet's passing.

His second sense had been right. And all he knew was that he had to get out of there and not be stupid twice. Then he heard scraping from below in the stairwell.

And he ran. He headed up the stairs, onto the roof.

Stefan's lungs burned. His pulse raced as his legs pumped. As he ran, he shed the raincoat, throwing it over the rooftop. Sweat poured down his shoulder blades.

Why hadn't he found the exit, planned his escape route like he usually did when entering a new building? Careless, he'd grown too soft and careless. And look what had happened!

He was running for his life and hoping to God he could shinny up the slick roof tiles and climb down to that wrought-iron balcony filled with fat pink geraniums. With luck he could slip in through the balcony door, shoot through the apartment, then hotfoot it to the next street.

At least he'd kept in shape. Lifted those weights, did sit-ups at dawn every morning.

Damn geraniums . . . he landed, kicking dirt everywhere!

Stefan picked himself up and raced past the half-opened glass door. An old man in a hair net sat reading by dim green light. The cat in his lap hissed.

"Who are you? Get out!" the man sputtered, pushing his glasses up on his nose and trying to ward off the blow he anticipated.

But he spoke to Stefan's wind.

Stefan slowed, cursing, unable to see in the pitch blackness. He felt his way along the raised linocrust lining the wall. With luck it would be a typical Sentier apartment—bedroom branching from hall to foyer to the front door.

He reached a smooth doorknob. Tried twisting but it didn't budge.

Locked.

Bright light blinded him. The old man, bowlegged in too-tight long johns and with a rusty meat cleaver, stood in the foyer.

"I fought the *boches*, I can fight you," he said, taking a step closer.

Stefan tried to flip the brass knob, but it stuck.

"*Scheisser!*"

"You are a *boche*!" said the old man, startled.

"Get back, old man!"

Behind them, something thudded from the bedroom.

Stefan rotated the latch hard until his fingers hurt. It turned. Then he flipped the dead bolt, ran out, and slammed the door.

He grabbed the metal handrail, guiding himself down the steep serpentine stairs, careful to avoid the light switch. Keep moving, he told himself.

Once he got to the street he'd lose himself in the sidewalk

crowds or in the Metro. Then double back to the Mercedes, get his suitcase full of the disguises he'd kept for years, just in case, from the trunk.

Stefan swung open the heavy Art Nouveau–style door, its glass held by curved metal strips. Flashes of red light, reflected on the glass, came from the *flic* car, which sat parked in front of him.

Thursday Night

AS SHE LEFT THE OFFICE with René, Aimée carried Miles Davis in her straw bag.

"I've got shank bones in the fridge," René said.

Miles Davis's ears perked to attention.

"I'm happy to keep him tonight if you need to take care of the apartment." René grinned.

"Merci," she said. "I'll take you up on your offer."

A welcome breeze from the Seine sliced down rue du Louvre, rustling the plane trees. She waved goodbye as René, carrying Miles Davis in the bag, hopped the bus on Boulevard de Sébastopol that would drop him by his apartment near the Pompidou Center.

She called the police for information about the break-in but so far they had no news. Before returning home, she needed to think. She walked toward the Sentier.

She saw aging women displaying their wares on rue Saint Denis. When the pimps discarded them, the lucky ones shared a van with others, parked in Bois de Vincennes. Leaning in the shadows. Hiding their age.

A granite-hard life with no retirement benefits. No *sécurité sociale*.

Aimée remembered Huguette, or Madame Huguette, as her father insisted she call her. They'd lived across the hall from her until they moved in with her grandfather. Huguette had minded her after school after her mother left them.

Huguette had buttered thick *tartines* on her kitchen table, let Aimée brush her toffee-colored Pekinese, and strictly enforced homework. Slim, compact, and stylish, Huguette knew more jokes than her father and how to make apple cider *à la* Breton. "I make the best," she'd said, letting Aimée stir the mixture, "an old recipe from my *belle-mère* in Saint-Brieuc."

Every evening Huguette—who disguised her long ears with pixie wisps of hair—applied makeup, then poured herself into sparkly evening dresses. What glamorous work, thought eight-year-old Aimée, like going to a cocktail party!

"Bistro Gavroche . . . I'm a hostess seating customers," Huguette had said. "Near the Strasbourg Saint Denis Metro, by the big *porte.*"

Aimée's eyes had gleamed. She knew the huge arch, the old northern gateway of Paris since the fourteenth century.

One night Aimée overheard her father and grandfather talking after she'd gone to bed. "What kind of choice is that . . . leaving your little girl with Huguette or keeping her with you at the Commissariat?" her grandfather had said. "Put her into boarding school."

"Did it harm me, hanging around *putes* and *flics?*" she'd heard her father ask. "Huguette's good for her, she needs someone who can do things I can't." Her grandfather had stayed silent.

And her papa had kept her with him, mostly. Until she got older and was sent to boarding school.

Years later on a job, she'd found herself passing through her former neighborhood. She'd walked down the narrow street. In her old building the mailboxes looked new. She hadn't remembered Huguette's last name. Or if she'd even known it.

But now curiosity got the better of her, and she walked to the lane behind their old building. Overgrown bushes in a vacant lot shaded the dead end. Once, there had been an Art Nouveau chalet with curving wood supports and an iron-framed glass terrace on the site. She and Huguette had often speculated as to who'd lived there. They'd made up stories about the owner, a Monsieur Roulard who worked at Gare Saint-Lazare and had the officious title *chef d'opérations* painted on his gate.

Now plastic bags whipped over dust and rubble in the wind, spiraled strands of rusted wire coiled around the single tree that stood where a garden had once bloomed. At Huguette's window she saw an old woman stroking ceramic gnomes on her back window ledge.

Aimée stopped. Each gnome perched on a green base, wore a pointed red cap, and stood in a different pose. The woman patted them, rearranged their order, then noticed Aimée. A half-smile came over the ravaged face. The long ears were recognizable. Aimée gaped open-mouthed, then raised her hand in greeting. But the old woman had bent over the gnomes, rubbing them with a cloth. Time passed, shadows covered Aimée's boots, and the woman still polished away, not looking up once.

Aimée turned and walked away over the broken cobbles under the night sky encrusted with stars.

"MONSIEUR . . . ARE YOU WELL?" the *flic* asked Stefan.

His legs paralyzed, Stefan realized he was panting, his lungs about to burst.

"Fine, *merci*," he managed and tried to wave the *flic* off. And wave off his own terror.

But the *flic*, his eyebrows rising in the flashing red lights from the patrol car, stared at him.

Stefan wanted to control his breathing. He tried but he couldn't, and he clutched the door frame.

"No problem, please," Stefan said.

Another *flic* alighted from the driver's seat. His badge shone in the streetlight, his mouth was set in a thin line.

"This your place of residence, Monsieur?"

"Stopped for a nightcap at my friends', Officer," Stefan said, his breathing more under control now.

"*Aaaah*," the *flic* nodded. "So you live in the *quartier?*"

Stefan thought of his ID; he couldn't lie.

"Visiting friends who do, Officer," he said, shifting his leg and keeping his head down.

"*Bon*. You seem very social," the *flic* said. "We'd appreciate your help in our inquiries."

"Inquiries?" Stefan's heart thumped. He thought it would leap out of his chest. "Like I said, I don't live in Paris."

"Actually, you didn't say, Monsieur," said the *flic* with the hard mouth. "If you don't mind, we'd like you to accompany us to the Commissariat."

"But I'm a visitor here. . . ."

"And probably with a sharper eye than we who take the scenery for granted, eh?"

Stefan wondered if someone had been shot in the building.

"Has something happened?"

The *flic* took his arm as if concerned for his health.

"A homicide, Monsieur," he said, escorting him to the car.

Thursday Night

AIMÉE'S CELL PHONE VIBRATED on her hip.

"Allô?"

"Have you found Idrissa yet?" Christian asked.

Finally!

"Where have you been, Christian? You didn't show up at your appointment to meet Etienne or at the bank. I've been calling you," she said. "Your father's editor, Vigot, knows more than he's saying about—"

"I know," Christian interrupted, his voice slurred. "Forget that . . . Idrissa's in trouble."

"Forget it?" she asked, angered at being brushed off. "Do you know if Vigot's got your father's manuscript?"

"No, but Vigot said . . ."

She heard a muffled sound, as if Christian had put his hand over the phone.

And then he hung up.

Worried, she hit the call-back button but the line was busy. Was he doped up and in trouble himself?

She'd keep trying his number as she headed toward Mala's apartment to find Idrissa.

No one answered the doorbell. Club Exe was a block away, maybe she'd find Mala there.

The club's narrow entrance on rue Poissonnière smelled of disinfectant. A sure sign of a health inspection or the rumor of one, Aimée thought. Clubs also spiffed up when they were nervous about immigration authority visits.

"I'd like to speak with Mala," said Aimée.

"She's not working tonight."

Great!

"Seen Idrissa Diaffa?"

"Not here anymore," the voice said. Only a brown elongated neck was visible above the man's red, yellow, and green Rasta-style tank top. His face was hidden by the Club Exe's cracked ticket-booth shade. Pounding techno music sounded from within.

"But the advertisement says she's still here." Aimée pointed to the sign. Club Exe advertised Tuesdays through Thursdays as "acoustic nights with Idrissa, accompanied on the *kora* by Ous-mane."

"That's old . . . but there's music upstairs," the voice said. "Re-mix downstairs. Either way, thirty francs."

"Pas de problème," she said. Fine, she'd see if anyone knew Idrissa's whereabouts or whether Ousmane had any idea where she was.

She passed the francs over worn wood. A brown hand took hers and stamped her wrist with the image of a red skeleton key. Inside, the techno beat amped up, savaging Aimée's ears. Several men with dreadlocks leaned on the bar, an old converted zinc. They nodded at her while sipping orange *punch gingembre*, a Se-negalese drink packing a rum wallop.

She found the back stairs. By the rear kitchen, she smelled and heard the hiss of palm oil spattering in a pan. The cook, his back to her, stood tasting a pot of *tibouaiénne* fish and rice.

On the next landing, past the public telephone, was a room with a small stage at the end. Patrons sat on banquettes around tables below smoky mirrors lining the walls. Some ate, most drank. It was a mixed crowd: young and old, white and black, listening to the strains of griot-inspired music. An old man wear-ing a long striped orange robe and what looked like a red velvet pillbox hat played the *kora*. He bore no resemblance to Ousmane in the photo with Idrissa.

He sang and plucked at the smooth calabash gourd backed by

animal skin. Strings held in place by metal studs went up the long-necked instrument.

Aimée saw no sign of Idrissa. She walked down the side hall and peered backstage. A young woman, short braids poking from her curly hair, stacked rolls of napkins and paper goods over a bricked-in mantel.

"*Bonsoir*, I'm looking for Idrissa," she said.

The woman shrugged, then moved her hands in what Aimée figured was sign language.

"*Muette?*"

The woman nodded. She was mute.

"Ousmane Sada?"

The woman picked up a flyer and pointed to the name Mbouela, a *kora* player "direct from Côte d'Ivoire." "So, Ousmane's gone?" Aimée asked.

The young woman nodded.

"What about Idrissa?" Aimée asked, pointing toward a dressing room. Maybe there'd be someone in there who knew her.

The woman shrugged.

"*Merci.*" Aimée smiled. "I'll just have a quick look."

The young woman returned to stacking paper goods.

The rectangular dressing room lay empty except for the costume of a clown in black and white, a Pierrot. Large windows overlooked the peaks of a wrought-iron-and-glass roof. Beyond that lay the tiled rooftops of the Sentier.

"The bitch . . . ," Aimée heard someone mutter, "where is she?"

She heard a crash as something fell to the floor. She didn't feel like waiting around to see whom they were looking for. She ducked out the open window. Below her spread the long glass-covered roof of Passage du Caire, the oldest passage in Paris.

On her left was an outdoor spiral staircase, remnant of an old conduit to the quarters above the passage where shop owners lived. She stepped out of the window and reached across to the outdoor metal staircase, pulled herself up by the railing, and climbed over. By the time she'd descended the stairs and reached the passage, the shop owners had long since closed and locked their doors. She made it out to the small triangular square of Place Ste-Foy.

Aimée looked back but no one had followed her. She paused at the dead end of rue Saint Spire. Where had Idrissa gone? She'd found no answers at the club or when she tried phoning her friend's apartment. If Idrissa was in danger, Aimée didn't know how to help her or where to look next.

And what did Christian's comment about Vigot mean? She hit the call-back button. But the phone rang and rang. No answer.

Stumped, Aimée sat down on a green bench, the Passage du Caire behind her, and pulled out her notepad. Her mother remained a mystery. As did everything else.

The Place Ste-Foy lay quiet: the cafés and wholesale clothing shops shuttered, plastic bags filled to bursting with cloth remnants and overflowing green garbage bins propped under the trees. The only sign of life was a young boy kicking a soccer ball under the watchful eye of an old woman, who wore a babushka. Aimée wondered what the child was doing up so late. Had it been too hot for him to sleep?

"*Attention*, Vanya," the old woman said when his ball bounced against the stone walls of an occupied building. "Kick someplace else."

A moped rode by, the tinny-sounding motor echoing in the square. Aimée heard its putt-putting as it sped into the distance. Only an occasional prostitute with her client turned into the ancient Passage Ste-Foy under the Roseline clothing sign.

Above her, dim lights from the narrow medieval apartments dotted the night. She thought Atget, who photographed the place in the 1900s, would probably still recognize the square. In a *quartier* with no green spaces but these few skinny trees, this warm pocket, Aimée realized, comprised nature and park to a *titi* like Vanya.

On the graph-patterned notebook page, she wrote three names, Christian, Romain, and Idrissa, and put question marks next to them. After Christian's name she wrote "dope" and "guilt," then connected the arrows to Romain. Christian had assumed responsibility for his father's suicide but his father had been murdered.

She connected Jutta and her mother and wrote "Laborde cache—Modigliani paintings?" None of this made any sense. Tired, she figured she better sleep on it. Aimée shouldered her bag and stood. The babushka's tone rose in anger. The young boy had kicked the ball into a garbage bag, knocking it over. Scraps and garbage swirled in the breeze, littering the deserted square. Cloth bits blew by Aimée's sandals. She looked over. At first she thought she saw the torso of a dummy, a mannequin. She stared.

A black mannequin.

Something was wrong.

Aimée ran over as the babushka screamed, covering the boy's eyes with her hands. Aimée tried to shield their view.

The dreadlocks twined with cowrie shells and yellow and red beads were familiar. Very familiar. Idrissa!

Aimée gasped. The half-open eyes were visible. There was a band of *toche noire*, a reddish brown tissue, across the pupils. Not a pretty sight. But a drying effect she recalled from premed.

She must have been killed several hours ago. Her face was distorted, her neck cocked at an impossible angle. Poor Idrissa, what a waste.

She knelt down. Something looked peculiar.

Peeling the bag lower, she saw dried rivulets of blood. But it wasn't Idrissa.

It was a man. A man who'd been in the picture with Idrissa at Club Exe. Ousmane, the *kora* player.

Don't get involved, she told herself.

Ahead, on rue Ste-Foy, she heard the whine of the late night garbage truck. Before the truck hit the square, she took a good look at the man. The pink bra and garter belt he wore were too large. Like an afterthought, Aimée figured. To make him look the Saint Denis type, on the off chance this bag, destined for the garbage truck, might be opened and the body found.

"We have to get the *flics*," she said, still trying to shield the boy.

Fear shone in the old woman's eyes. She shook her head, clutching him. She didn't know or want to know. Maybe she had no papers.

"*S'il vous plaît*, before the trashmen come!"

Aimée didn't want to do this. Get involved with this.

But the woman backed up, pulling the boy. What could Aimée do? The woman hobbled toward Passage du Caire. No time to follow them.

She'd been looking for Idrissa and now she'd found her accompanist. Why had Idrissa's partner been killed? Had the killer made a mistake?

AIMÉE DRUMMED her heels on the 2nd arrondissement Commissariat floor. She sat inside a smudged glassed-in cubicle with scuffed walls, her hands on the wooden desk. Crumpled paper cups and memos filled the metal garbage can. On the duty binder was a stenciled memo, "Don't forget the ten fingers of procedure!"

"Where's Sergeant Mand?" Aimée asked. "I'd like to speak with him."

"*En vacances*," the on-duty *flic* answered.

Too bad. She'd made her first Communion with his daughter. Knew the family well. She'd lost a baby molar down their bathroom drain.

"Let me get this right," the *flic* from the *découvertes de cadavres* unit said, pausing with his two fingers on the typewriter. "You found the body and recognized her?"

He really meant how would she recognize an African, *un noir*.

"A him, it's a man." Aimée didn't want to admit she'd been looking for Idrissa. Didn't want to tell him why.

"*Voilà*, a man," the *flic* said. "Then how did you recognize him?"

"He's well known in *nouvelle* griot music," she said. "I've heard him with his partner at Club Exe." The stale air and cigarette smoke made her nose itch. Itch for a cigarette.

"Let's see, you give your address as 17, Quai d'Anjou on Ile St. Louis." He pecked at the keyboard, not looking up. "What were you doing in the Sentier?"

She wanted to say *None of your business*. But in reality it was. *Flics* could stop you any place, any time, demand your identification, and hold you on suspicion. Suspicion of anything.

"Going to get my nails done," she said. She thrust her chipped red fingernails at him. "A disaster, eh? My friend has a nail salon."

"Not much stays open this late in the Sentier."

True. She thought quickly.

"But on rue Saint Denis, the girls stay open day and night, right? Who's investigating the case?"

"Right now I am, Mademoiselle Leduc," he said, his tone bored. "As I'm sure you're aware, the *police judiciare* takes charge and will confer with *le proc*,* when she gets here."

"*Le proc*, here? But that's unusual," she said. Normally, the *flics* submitted the evidence *dossier* to him or her at the Palais de Justice. Rarely did one get involved in investigation legwork.

"Unusual . . . good word," said the *flic*, nodding in agreement. He scratched the back of his neck. "Life's unusual these days. Especially with everyone on vacation!"

"The victim's not a *pute*," she said. "Nor a transvestite. He's a musician!"

Procurer de la République—the state prosecutor.

"I'm glad we have your word for it," he said, even more bored.

After ten minutes the *flic* gave her a typed statement to read. There were plenty of spelling and grammar mistakes. But she thought better of bringing them to his attention.

She was about to sign when loud shuffling sounds came from the corridor. A middle-aged man was escorted to the other desk in the small cubicle.

He gripped the frayed plastic armrest, then sat down with measured slowness. His ashen pallor contrasted with his grease-stained black fingers.

"Now if you'll sign this," the *flic* said, irritation in his voice, "you'll have done your civic duty and I can end my shift, Mademoiselle Leduc."

Out of the corner of her eye, Aimée saw the man's body jerk. After she'd signed and looked up, she realized he was staring at her. Staring with disbelief.

Like Georges and Frédo at Action-Réaction.

Again a shiver went up her spine.

"Monsieur Pascal Ourdours, residing in Conflans, Cergy Préfecture," said the blue-uniformed *flic*, reading his ID. "Pretty late for you to drive so far to your home, eh?"

"Not really," the man said.

"Can you explain your reason for being on rue des Jeûners?"

He sat, rodlike. "Visiting friends, like I told the officer."

"Did you see anyone running in that vicinity?"

But Aimée never heard his answer. The *flic* tugged her arm, indicating she should give up her seat to a miniskirted, blue-eye-shadowed middle-aged woman tapping her worn sandals.

"*Vite, chérie,*" the woman said. "My feet hurt."

On her way out, Aimée searched for familiar faces. She heard the duty desk *flic* talking over a police radio: "Quiet night except for a homicide, two witnesses, plus the usual working ladies. That's all, *patron*."

So Pascal Ourdours was the other witness.

She recognized Edith Mésard, the new Procureteur de la République, striding into the Commissariat. As *"La" Proc*, Mésard had a lot to prove in the male-dominated system. Aimée wanted to renew their old acquaintance and get information.

"Madame Mésard," she said. "Congratulations on your appointment to your position."

Edith Mésard paused.

"Merci," she said. Her voice quavered.

Aimée knew she'd had throat surgery. The woman sounded weak but her conviction record was strong. Strongest in the court.

Her gaze took in Aimée's outfit. "Investigators are waiting, if you'll excuse me. . . ."

"Bien sûr," Aimée said. "Perhaps later, I'd like to talk with you."

"Will what you say interest me, Mademoiselle . . . Leduc, isn't it? I'm sorry but my days get filled by eight A.M. I reserve my time for victims, enforcement officers, and the court docket."

Underneath the Rodier suit, graceful manner, weak voice, and *aristo* manners was pure iron—*formidable*, in a word.

"The information I have concerns the homicide victim," Aimée said.

"Please give a statement," Edith Mésard said, pointing a manicured finger to the cubicle.

"But I already have. Let's say there's a sensitive background," Aimée said. A good *Proc* kept communication lines open for those who wanted to pass on information—hookers, the gay community, and illegal workers—but were intimidated by the *flics*.

"I don't barter information, Mademoiselle, if that's what you're implying. In my job I must reveal my sources if it impacts the criminal proceedings." She reached in her briefcase, then handed Aimée a card. "But you can access my direct line between seven and eight A.M. only."

And then Edith Mésard was gone.

Outside the Commissariat on Place Goldoni, Aimée pulled out her cell phone and called Christian's number again.

No answer.

No answer at Etienne Mabry's either. In the dark Paris street, Lieutenant Bellan arrived. Behind him, a police car pulled up in the Commissariat parking place.

Lieutenant Bellan eyed her up and down. His wine-laced breath hit her square in the face.

"You again?" he said. His eyes were bleary. "We have to stop meeting like this."

Save your tired clichés for the bar, she wanted to say. He must have been celebrating.

"Boy or girl?"

"What?"

"Are you the father of a boy or girl?" she said. "Your wife was giving birth when my apartment was broken into."

Something caved in his face. He stumbled on the cobblestones.

What happened? she wondered.

The other police had caught up with them. They exchanged looks.

"Lieutenant Bellan, you're off duty," one of them said. "We'll give you a ride home."

"Down's syndrome, the doctor called it," Bellan said, his speech slurred. "Where I come from they called them Mongoloids . . . half-wits."

Oh God, no wonder he was falling apart.

"Forgive me, so sorry," she said.

"Want the good news?" Bellan blinked back the tears. "It's going to live!" Several of the uniformed police shifted on the cobbles, looked away. One of the officers took Bellan's arm. Bellan shook him off, staggered toward Aimée.

Why wasn't he with his wife, why weren't they comforting each other?

"Please, sir, no need for you to report back to the Commissariat," the *flic* said.

"Someone's got to pay the bills," Bellan said, raising his voice. "Work overtime. That's me. Question this woman," Bellan roared. He pointed to Aimée.

His voice echoed off the cobblestones.

"*Tiens,* Bellan," one of the men said. "Give it a rest."

"Right now! She's caused all this . . . from the beginning."

A window opened above them. "Keep it down," yelled an old woman.

Aimée's hackles rose. "What do you mean?" she asked, staring at Bellan and the group.

None of them met her gaze. Bellan spat, fumbled with a lighter, and managed to light his cigarette.

"Like father, like daughter. On the take. Dirty!"

Good thing the *flics* grabbed Bellan and hustled him away before her fist cracked his cheekbone.

"My father wasn't dirty," she said. "Never! Do I have to prove it to the whole police force?"

Maybe she did. Caillot's article implied her father was corrupt. Only the police files would hold the truth. The files Léo Frot owed her.

"I knew your old man," said a middle-aged *flic,* coming up to her. He slid his blue hat off, revealing a gray crewcut, and rubbed his forehead. "Try to ignore Bellan, eh? He's losing it over the baby. Bellan idolized your father. It hit him hard when your father left the force."

Startled, Aimée stepped back. "But nothing was proved. Nothing. Only a slick article with allegations . . . that's all. No stain on him, he got the posthumous award when he died."

"Some things in the department, well, the powers that be just let them slide."

"What do you mean?"

"Nobody talks about it," he said. "You should know the code, you're a *flic*'s kid. We stand together, we don't rat on each other. And you're one of us."

So that's how they thought of her? "Let me enlighten you, I'm a private detective, not police," she said.

"But you're getting a lot of attention these days."

"So elect me mayor," she said, nervous but trying not to show it. "What do you mean?"

Several *flics* were walking toward them. "Lie low, it's for your own good." He joined the others and entered the Commissariat with them.

More confused than before, she leaned against the stonewall. Doubts assailed her. Had her mother left because she thought her husband was corrupt? Would that have spurred her to leave them?

But her father wasn't corrupt. Aimée knew that in her bones. She felt sorry for Bellan but she also wanted to kick him.

She tried to put it out of her mind. She gazed at the *salon de thé* nestled in the Passage Grand Cerf. But the restored wire-and-glass-roofed passage was locked for the night. She settled for a glass of red wine at the zinc bar on the corner, listening to the weather report: continued heat and humidity.

In the long café mirror, she reapplied Chanel red lipstick, pinched her cheeks for color, and ruffled her hair with her fingers.

In a few minutes, as Pascal Ourdours emerged from the Commissariat, she approached him from behind.

"Monsieur Ourdours, let's go talk."

He stiffened.

"Please, I'm not police," she said. "How about a drink? There's a taxi," she said, signaling to a passing cab. "Let's go somewhere so I can get to know you."

"*Non* . . . I have to get my car."

She heard the furring of his syllables. Still scared, she thought.

So shaken he couldn't hide the traces of an accent. In the flickering streetlight, she saw his hunted expression.

He gave off the smell of fear.

"Nearby, there's a quiet café," she said. "We'll converse and then you can leave. I promise . . . a quick drink, eh? You look like you could use one. I know I could."

He took a step, then paused. Uncertain.

"Come on," she said, fanning herself with her hand, "the humidity hasn't let up. I'm thirsty and I prefer not to drink alone."

She sensed that a bit of his wariness had dissipated.

"I work nearby," she said, thinking fast to make the event nonthreatening. "There's a lovely old tearoom—on Thursday nights they have a small late-night gallery opening. Let's try it."

"Since you put it that way," he said, "why not?" He looked surprised but kept walking. She sensed he wanted to talk. She steered him toward Ventilo, the clothes shop with an elegant *salon de thé* in a pie-wedge-shaped Haussmann building. Two narrow streets flanked the several-storied building, whose voluted iron balconies were filled with geraniums. Conversation and the tinkle of glasses came from the lighted third-floor windows.

He paused. Hesitated. His brow furrowed.

Before them, a couple, arms twined around each other, came down the stairs laughing and headed into the night.

Aimée pointed to the exhibition sign. "Super!" she grinned. "I've been dying to see this exhibition. Old black-and-white photos of Paris at night."

She noticed he watched her lips.

"And the good thing is, we don't have to buy art to get a drink."

His brow unfurrowed. "After you," he said.

Inside the high-ceilinged Art Deco tearoom people holding drinks clustered around photos. He and Aimée took the glasses of white wine offered them, and dutifully looked at the photos.

"Mind if we sit down?" she said, as soon as it seemed sufficiently polite to do so. They sat on a bench by arched windows overlooking the narrow street.

His tense shoulders relaxed as she discussed the photos. Slowly, she began to feed in questions. "Do I remind you of someone, Pascal?" she asked, putting her face closer to his. "From the way you looked at me, I wondered."

"I used to know a woman," he said. "Long ago. She looked like you."

He'd used the past tense. Her hope wavered.

"What was she like?"

He opened his mouth. Then closed it. "Twenty years is a long time. I just was shaken because the resemblance is strong."

"True. Life can take bizarre turns," Aimée said. "My mother left when I was eight. Apparently she joined some radical leftists . . . who knows?" Aimée let her words dangle.

"How old are you?"

She told him.

He leaned forward, tapped his right ear. "Bad ear, speak in this one."

"My mother was American, perhaps you ran across her."

It had become less strange to say "my mother."

He shook his head, looking down at the old floor tiles, but not before she'd seen his eyes flicker in recognition.

She remembered the Frésnes envelope with B. de Chambly on it that Jutta had shown her. "Sydney Leduc was her name but I think she used another one, starting with B."

She couldn't read his expression. He kept his head down.

The man knew something. She took a big sip of wine, praying that he'd open up.

"Those were pretty heady times in seventies Paris from what I hear," she said, aiming for his good ear. "Lots of romance surrounded the radicals, some veered to violence, others to protests." She kept trying to find the button that would get him to talk. "Our generation seems pretty tame, eh? Even with the World Trade Organization demonstrations."

Silence.

She wondered if part of his fear stemmed from hearing loss, or the noises around him.

"Talk about a small world," she said. "Action-Réaction still has a base here in the Sentier. I met some of them, they're your age."

He looked up, saw her empty glass. "More wine?" he asked.

"Merci bien," she smiled.

He didn't return the smile, just favored her with an intense stare.

He was a hard nut to crack. Harder than the old Nazi collaborator in the Marais! Had she misread the man completely?

Was he simply an older man from the suburbs in the wrong place at the wrong time? Picked up because a homicide happened a block away? After all, she thought, the *flics* had soon let him go.

He returned and handed her a glass. She'd try one more time.

"You're kind," she said, accepting the wine. "I don't want to burden you too much, but I've been thinking of going to therapy over this . . . to find a way to cope."

And he was bobbing his head in agreement. "I'm in therapy myself. You know it's wonderful to be able to talk to someone about things!"

His eyes brightened and he leaned forward. His words gushed forth, as if a peg in a dike had loosened, letting the water flow. She'd found the right button to push. He spoke of his village, his job, and then she guided him backward to his youth.

"My brother was the smart one. Me, I loved cars. My head was always under a hood. Still is. Mercedes, far as I'm concerned, makes the best engine in the world."

Aimée nodded. No wonder his hands were grime-stained.

The crowd emptied out of the gallery. Pointed looks were cast in their direction by the staff.

"We better go, Pascal," she said.

His brow lifted. "Call me Stefan."

The man was full of surprises.

Down in the street, he motioned her into a darkened apartment doorway. He stood, his face in partial shadows by the letter boxes on the wall. He worried his hands, as if something fought inside him. "I met your mother once," he said finally.

"What was she like?"

"Sweet, like you," he said. "She knew how to listen."

Aimée remembered that about her, too. A quiet attention.

"They told me she went to Africa with Jules," she said.

He shrugged his shoulders. But he knew, she could feel it.

"I wanted to ask Romain Figeac but he's dead," she said. "Murdered."

Stefan averted his eyes. "I don't know anything about that," he said. "Now I've got to go.

"Stefan, let's talk more." She pressed her card into his moist palm. "I appreciate it. No one ever talked to me about her. No one."

He nodded. Understanding showed in his deep-set eyes.

"It's not safe to nose around," he said. "Especially now. . . ." He hesitated. He hailed a passing taxi.

"What do you mean?" She held his arm.

The taxi stopped.

Stefan shook his head. "It means so much to talk with someone. Really talk. But I don't want you to get hurt."

He got in the taxi, shut the door, and it sped off.

GREAT! HE fed her a morsel, then he was gone. But not before she got the number, 2173, of the Taxi Bleu.

She walked down rue du Louvre toward her office. The name Stefan repeated in her brain. Where had she seen it? Think, she told herself. But nothing came.

Taxis passed, their blue lights signaling they were free, but she kept walking. Who had murdered Idrissa's *kora* player and why? Could Stefan have been involved? Think harder.

Christian said she was in danger. Had the musician been killed to warn Idrissa, or by mistake? And that got her thinking about how Idrissa had disappeared after she'd asked her about Romain Figeac. People hid or disappeared to avoid bills, spouses, jealous lovers, revenge. Or to keep secrets.

She mounted the stairs to her office, flicked on the light. She opened the window onto rue du Louvre and the night sounds: footsteps, the *hee-haw* of a distant siren, snatches of music from an open car window.

She called Taxi Bleu. But the dispatcher wouldn't give out the location the taxi had driven to until she'd given him the police number she sometimes used for occasions like this. Morbier's police number. Montmartre cemetery, the dispatcher finally told her.

She'd gone there to pay for Liane Barolet's mother's crypt. Coincidence or . . . ? Something fit here . . . but what was it? Think! It was as if something stared her in the face.

Cool breezes drifted in, carrying the scent of the Seine.

Her eye rested on the photo of her with her father, the one taken the day before she went to New York as an exchange student. He'd treated her at Angelina's on rue de Rivoli to the famous hot chocolate so thick one used a spoon.

Then Aimée saw the old Interpol posters fluttering on her wall. One of the black-and-white photos caught her eye. She peered closer. With a jerk, she sat up. She realized she was staring at Stefan.

A younger Stefan, without glasses and gray hair. Very seventies and quite cute.

It said, "Stefan Rohl: wanted for kidnapping and accomplice to murder of a policeman." There was no statute of limitations on murder: He was still wanted.

Thursday Night

STEFAN FELT RELEASED, as if the years had lifted and he was floating. It had all bubbled out of him, and it had felt so good. So liberating. He hadn't told her everything but he'd told her so much. And she'd wanted to hear, like her mother had. His years of living like a mole were over.

But Jutta's killer was trying to flush him out. He had to come up with a plan.

"Where to, Monsieur?" asked the taxi driver.

"Montmartre," he said.

The driver gave a knowing look. "The ladies, eh?"

"The cemetery."

"But it's closed this time of night."

Stefan rolled down the window. Lights from the late-night cafés in Les Halles, snatches of conversation flashed past.

"That's right."

The driver would log the destination as Montmartre cemetery but Stefan always parked a few blocks away.

The fountain spraying in front of hulking gothic St. Eustache church and the circus posters brought the memories back. Back to the afternoon twenty years ago, when they'd planned the heist and kidnapping.

The sun had blazed in a sky enameled blue. The gang had joined bourgeois families and older couples at the zoo on a typical Sunday in Vincennes Park. He often wondered how people would have reacted if they'd known wanted terrorists strolled in their midst, eating spun sugar *barbes à papas*, standing beside them in the run-down zoo. Marcus, his arms draped around Ingrid, had insisted on feeding the monkeys, who looked so sad. The braying of an elephant was carried on the wind with the animal smells: dense and musky.

They'd bought tickets for the bumper cars at the cheesy fun fair. Ulrike, he'd noticed, stood apart, watching children beg reluctant parents for one last ride. She thrust a roll of tickets into a startled mother's hand and walked away.

Mallard ducks rippled in V formation from the grasses toward the small man-made island, the Ile de Bercy. He remembered the island well. At the dock, Marcus paid and they commandeered two rowboats and rowed to the island. They found Jules and Beate with other Action-Réaction members, sitting under a spreading willow. The group greeted them with roasted chicken and bottles of wine on a red-and-white-checked tablecloth, picnic style.

"Welcome to a Sunday in the country," Jules grinned. The afternoon held a luminosity, a quivering glow, that he still remembered. Probably the one time they'd been happy together. No fights or rivalries. That surfaced later.

"Your idea inspired us, Stefan," Jules had said, to his amazement. "That wealthy man in your hometown, Laborde, the industrialist you told us about, he's our target. Not only is he a munitions-making shit, he's a wealthy one, too."

Alarmed, Stefan realized he'd once talked about his boyhood in Mulhouse after smoking too much hash. How the only swimming pool around after the war had been at the château. Granted, a modest manor house, but for Mulhouse a point of pride.

During a battle over the Rhine, the Allies had bombed the château, and left a crater in the yard. The count had made it into the pool. As a boy, Stefan had sneaked over the wall when the count was away and gone swimmming with his friends. But when Laborde bought the property, he'd wired the fence and brought in dogs. Rumor had it he owned mines in Africa.

After they'd eaten, Jules had given Jutta a notebook to write in. By the water, Beate and Ingrid fed a baguette to the ducks.

"Laborde has skeletons in his closet," Jules said. "He collaborated with the SS. Rumor has it he was part of the Milice, involved with the Vichy government. Not to mention he ships arms to Africa and gets paid in diamonds."

"The Revolution is coming!" Ulrike's eyes flashed. "Fascist capitalism must be overturned. The proletariat deserves the spoils, not the merchant of death."

"We'll turn the money into tools to finance our cause, to help our oppressed brothers and sisters in prison, in the tenements," Ingrid said. Beate, her long hair falling to her waist, joined her and nodded.

Jules diagrammed the house layout in the dirt.

"We kidnap him, open the safe, then rendezvous at the farm," said Jules. "Jutta's working on the new passports, IDs, and cars, and Action-Réaction is providing the escape network."

Marcus sat cross-legged and pulled out a map, outlining Laborde's movements.

"His wife and children stay in Nice for the summer," he said. "On the weekends, he drives to Mulhouse, where he keeps a minimal staff." Marcus looked up, grinned. "We ambush him here on the N66, the small road he takes."

Jutta took notes. Stefan wondered how they'd found out this information.

"Since you know the lay of the land, you can guide us inside the château, Stefan. Then you can take your swim, eh," said Jules, his eyes slitted in amusement.

Stefan's spine prickled. "But I've never been inside!"

Verrucht! They were crazy! He wanted nothing to do with this, yet an irrational part of him wanted to swim in that pool. That exotic turquoise green kidney shaped expanse of water under the imported palms, once the talk of Mulhouse.

"Laborde will show us in and open the safe," Jules said. "He'll have to. His life depends on it."

"Everyone has something to do," Jutta said. She lifted up a paper. On it was each person's name, arrows pointing to his or her assigned job.

Perfect in theory. Events had proved differently.

They'd ambushed Laborde's chauffeured Mercedes on the forested road outside Mulhouse. Laborde, a stocky man with a bad toupee, had been drinking. He'd proved belligerent, kicking Jules and biting his hand. Finally, with Stefan's help, Jules had handcuffed Laborde's wrists together behind his back. They gagged the driver, stowed him in the trunk, then Stefan donned his uniform. Ulrike, Marcus, Ingrid, Beate, and Jutta followed in the local *blanchisserie*'s truck they'd stolen.

At the château gate, Laborde, with Jules's gun in his ribs prompting him, told the man to open the gates and take the weekend off. The Mercedes and the laundry truck pulled up the crescent drive leading to the gray stone château and parked against a chestnut tree.

The service staff, a gray-haired housekeeper in an apron and a butler in slacks and cardigan, stood smiling on the steps.

"What do we do now?" Stefan asked, paralyzed.

He heard scuffling in the back, but all he could see was Jules's shoulders in the rearview mirror. He heard heaving and grunts.

"Jules, what now?"

The butler had started walking down the steps to the car. "What do I do?"

A red-faced Jules stuck his face up. "He's sick, tell them he's sick and will go right to his room."

He had to move. To do something. They would know he wasn't the usual chauffeur.

He stepped onto the drive. The gravel crunched and shifted under his feet. He took off his cap, but kept his eyes down. "I'm the new driver. Monsieur Laborde feels unwell, his colleague will escort him to his room."

Surprise painted their faces.

"Monsieur Laborde wants you to take the weekend off."

The butler came to the car door. "But Monsieur Laborde specifically requested us to stay, especially today. The rest of the staff will return for this evening's dinner party. The minister called, he's arriving at seven P.M."

Scheisser! They were sunk.

Whichever idiot planned this hadn't taken into account Laborde's social life.

Words tumbled from his mouth.

"Everything's on hold. Monsieur Laborde's health is the most important consideration. He'll decide later."

"But he sounded fine this morning. . . ."

"Stomach flu," Stefan had said, the first thing that came to him. "Suddenly. I had to stop several times on the road so he could throw up."

"This is highly unusual," the butler said, his eyes narrow with suspicion. "Monsieur Laborde likes to confirm the details with me."

The housekeeper shrugged her shoulders. "One good thing, thank the Lord, the laundry's brought the linens."

She walked over to the laundry truck. At that moment, Marcus burst from the truck. He grabbed the housekeeper, who screamed. Jules rushed from the car and wrestled the butler to the steps. Marcus put a gun to the housekeeper's head and told her not to move.

In the midst of the screaming and fighting, Ulrike and Jutta hauled Laborde into the house. They'd agreed no one was to get hurt, but drops of Laborde's blood trailed up the stone steps.

By the time they'd tied the servants up in the kitchen pantry, the sun had slumped midway behind the chestnut tree. Stefan noticed the pool, cracked and dry, had been emptied.

"Time to change plans," Jutta had said. They all gathered briefly inside the cavernous foyer. Originally, they'd planned to spend the weekend and carefully loot the house and its safe. "We do it now, take what we can and get out."

"She's right—more servants will be arriving at any time," Ulrike said. "We'll sort everything out later."

"I'll be the lookout," Beate said, and walked down the driveway.

But Laborde, his toupee dropped in the gravel, had been knocked unconscious. He lay bleeding in the study where they'd carried him. They'd counted on him to point out the safe and open it. Marcus had a tantrum over the stupidity of the plans, throwing furniture about and trashing the rooms. By the time Jutta found the safe under a floor panel in the library, Laborde had groggily come to.

"Open it," Marcus had said.

"You're kidding . . . for punks like you?" Laborde panted, his breathing growing more labored. "Under Vichy you wouldn't have lasted ten minutes! You don't know trouble . . . you're a bunch of spoiled—"

"Capitalist pig, shut up!" Marcus had interrupted. He glared and stuck his finger in Laborde's face. "Show us the safe and open it now!"

Was Laborde arrogant or just plain stupid? Terrorists pointed guns at him but he still wouldn't talk.

"You idiots, the police chief's coming for dinner this evening. . . ."

Marcus kicked Laborde in the stomach. Over and over.

"Stop it, Marcus . . . we've got to get out of here while we can." Stefan stood fumbling in the dining room by the draperies Marcus had torn down.

"Get the car ready, Stefan," Jules said, pulling him aside.

Stefan couldn't look at Laborde and left hurriedly.

Outside in the driveway he met Beate. She clutched her

patchwork Indian skirt, looking as lost and scared as he felt. "What's taking so long?" she asked.

"Laborde's not cooperating," he said. "We should leave, forget the safe."

He'd wanted fun and excitement but hadn't bargained on this. Neither had she, from what he could see. Sure, they all believed in the cause, especially Ulrike. But Beate seemed to be under the spell of Jules; maybe her weakness was powerful men.

"Stefan, you're not like the others," she said.

Stefan was surprised she'd even noticed him.

"You know—" She hesitated.

Loud shouts came from the foyer.

"I'll get the Mercedes," he told her.

What he wanted to say was, *If they're not out in five minutes, let's drive away.* Beate gave him a funny look, as if she'd read his thoughts, but just nodded. She mounted the stairs to the tall doors and went inside.

The laundry truck's door was open and waiting. He pulled the Mercedes ahead of it, checked the back seat. The metallic smell of Laborde's blood sickened him. What had Jules done?

He felt like throwing up, but the others would see. He opened the hood—anything to keep busy—adjusting a misfiring valve, when he heard gravel pop and looked up.

"*Salut!*" Two women hailed him as they walked up the drive, fanning themselves in the heat.

His heart jumped. Beate was supposed to be the lookout but she was inside!

Judging by their stiletto heels, miniskirts, teased hair, and made-up faces, they didn't appear to be the arriving crew of domestics. More like working girls reporting for duty.

"The butler told us to come early, your gate's open," the taller one said, grinning. "Freshen up, you know. I'm Lisette and this is Tina."

What should he do? The less these two knew, the better. If

he sent them inside, they'd become hostages, too. He pointed to what he guessed was the gardener's cottage. "Freshen up over there and wait until the butler calls you."

She looked him up and down. "Nice bonus, we do the help for free when they look like you."

Years later, he'd heard Lisette had written a book, *I Loved a Terrorist*, which hit the best-seller list. He always wondered what story she'd concocted.

He shut the car hood, ran up the steps, and careened into Beate and Jutta dragging full plastic bags across the black-and-white-tiled entrance. Ingrid skipped past them, an Uzi hanging from her shoulder, oil paintings under her arm. They reminded him of paintings he'd seen in a museum.

"*Schnell*, quickly," Jutta said, "open the trunk."

He heard Laborde begging Marcus to stop. Then the tinkling of breaking glass, heavy thuds of furniture falling.

"Marcus, Jules . . . forget it, let's go!"

"Later." Jutta pulled his arm. "They'll join us. Let's go. Now!"

He didn't need any more urging if they were going to get away before the servants found them looting.

By the time they'd loaded the trunk and he, Jutta and Beate had gotten in the car, the others were running for the laundry truck. Ingrid started the truck. He gunned the car's engine and they shot down the graveled driveway. He jumped out to open the unlocked gates. People alighted from a bus at the stop down the road and walked toward them. He looked back. The laundry truck still hadn't moved.

"What about the others?" He wasn't about to wait but felt he had to say it.

"After Paris, we'll meet at the safe house."

He tore down the forested road, hoping to hit the next village soon. Once there he'd pull behind a gas station, jump out, and change the license plates. He'd paint the Mercedes later, but for now that should get them to Paris.

"What happened?" he asked. "Did Laborde open the safe?"

Jutta shook her head. In the rearview mirror he'd seen the look that passed between her and Beate. A strange knowing look.

"What's in the bags?"

"We found another safe in his desk." Jutta grinned at Beate. Then they burst into laughter. "We couldn't open it, so we just took all the drawers!"

And for a split second his mind jumped to the present . . . was that why Jutta had been murdered . . . for the Laborde stash? Was that why someone had chased him from Romain Figeac's apartment?

Thursday Night

SHE'D LET STEFAN GET away but she'd given him her number. She doubted that would be the last she'd see of him. He seemed so lonely. And carried such a burden.

Idrissa Diaffa was the missing link. Aimée felt convinced of it now; Idrissa knew what Romain Figeac had been writing. And it had to do with her mother and Jutta and the Laborde cache. Idrissa had disappeared after Aimée had asked her about it. Then Ousmane, her partner, was murdered. Had Idrissa been the intended victim or was this a warning to her?

Either way Aimée had to find Idrissa and get answers.

If Aimée barged into Club Exe again, she'd get the same shrugs and evasions. Locating Idrissa in the Sentier would be like searching for a sequin on a female impersonator's costume.

But maybe the club could find her. Aimée punched Club Exe's number on her office phone.

"Club Exe . . ." The rest of the man's words were lost in a deep bass beat.

"Idrissa Diaffa, please!" Aimée shouted. "I must talk with her."

"She quit," the voice said.

She expected that.

"It's important," she said. "Her *kora* player's been murdered."

"Ousmane . . . Ousmane Sada from Dakar?"

That was his name. She wasn't sure where he was from. "He's her partner, plays the *kora*."

She heard a mumbled conversation. Their language, Wolof sounded like upside-down words to her.

Now she had an inspiration.

"I have to reach her. Idrissa's needed to identify his body."

"Who are you?" Now the background was quieter; the man must have moved to another room.

"I came there earlier tonight, looking for her," she said. "Please, someone has to reach her."

"How do you know?"

"*Tiens*, it affects me!" She let the anger show in her voice. "They hauled me in for questioning, I found his body in place Ste-Foy. Poor *mec*, they'd stuffed him in a garbage bag, the truck was about to scoop him up."

Silence.

"Someone said he worked at your place. They're coming to your club to look for her if she doesn't show. With the immigration squad."

She lied but that should spur them to find Idrissa. Most of the help, she remembered from her last visit—the kitchen crew, musicians, and the deaf-mute cleaner—she figured they were *sans-papiers*, illegal.

"Where should she go?"

She'd guessed right.

"Place Mazas, the morgue," she said. "Tell her to be there at ten A.M. tomorrow when it opens."

The man hung up.

Aimée would call Serge at the morgue and be out front waiting for Idrissa.

She pondered sleeping in the office, not ready to face her apartment after the break-in. But she needed to change clothes.

She stuffed her phone in her bag, swung the laptop case over her shoulder, and headed downstairs. Tonight was her night for walking. She made her way down the quai, past lovers sitting by the Seine. And on the way she wondered if she'd always be alone.

Thursday Night

MARIUS TEYNARD MET ALPHONSE DRAY, his old police colleague, over a bottle of chilled Sancerre. Even this late at night the *brasserie* was full. The floodlights illuminating the préfecture on the Quai des Orfèvres shone in the background.

"So how's Jules Bourdon?"

"The words 'cocky' and 'arrogant' come to mind," said Dray.

"So he hasn't changed," Marius Teynard said with a smile. "Good. I'll get him this time."

"Any other reason you want to know his progress after leaving Senegal?"

"Catching him isn't good enough?" Teynard poured more white wine into his companion's wineglass.

"Don't you wonder why he's left now?"

"Homesick, broke, or both," Teynard said. He took a long gulp. "Maybe the mercenary jobs dried up."

"He's not alone."

Teynard paused. He eyed the woman opposite from them, who'd crossed her legs. "She's with him?"

"Let's just say you can buy followers when you've got the money."

Friday

AIMÉE WOKE UP and made coffee. She'd cleaned up the spilled sugar in the kitchen last night. One of the blue tiles behind the faucet was loose. She'd have to caulk it later.

"*Bonjour*, Serge," she said, when she reached him in his lab.

"Nice fragment of occipital bone with internal beveling from a bullet you had the other day," he said.

Trust Serge to be gruesome, but that was the medical examiner in him.

"There's a detective who wants to discuss the Figeac evidence," he said.

Finally!

"In conjunction with Jutta's murder, I hope," she said.

"Officially, it's the detective's job to request it," Serge said. "But I faxed him my findings concerning Jutta's wound. An exact match on the beveling of bone. Now the ball's in his court."

"I'm calling to see a corpse, probably a Franck, if he's been cleaned up. A man in pink underwear."

A Franck was a male unidentified corpse; unidentified female corpses were Yvettes. On average they stayed in the morgue coolers sixteen months. Some were held for years. The staff was always eager for a possible identification.

She heard paper crumple. "The *noir* found in the Sentier last night?" Serge asked. "Does this have anything to do with Romain Figeac?"

"They're linked but I don't know how yet. For now, we need an ID, Serge, that's all," she said. "Otherwise he could lie unclaimed for a long time."

Finally, he agreed.

René called as she was leaving. "Michel's dress rehearsal starts in less than an hour but we've got a snag in the operating system. We need to get it up and running today."

"Give me the address in the Palais Royal."

"Enter on the Galerie de Beaujolais side. Number 38, near Colette's former apartment."

"Not too shabby," she said, not adding that she had an appointment at the morgue first.

Riding her scooter down the quai, she phoned Christian.

No answer.

"LOOK AT it yourself," Aimée said, passing the Baggie with the wallpaper sample and bone over the detective's desk. "Romain Figeac's .25 didn't do that."

Detective Tolbiac, a barrel-chested man in his forties, shook his head. A radio blared, advertising summer bargains, from across the square into the open Commissariat windows. "You say the son hired you to find ghosts. But you feel Romain Figeac was murdered? Isn't it up to his son?"

"Why don't you check with your report?" Aimée asked.

"If memory serves me right," Tolbiac said, leaning back in his chair, "I recall a suicide note, the guy being blotto—his usual condition—then a cremation. Kind of a done deal."

"Don't you think the fragmentation of the occipital bone looks atypical for a .25?" Aimée asked. "Couldn't you test it?"

"Well, first we'd need DNA for a match wouldn't we? To see if this was Romain Figeac's bone. You could have picked this fragment up in the garbage for all I know."

Aimée stood up. Tolbiac made it sound as if everything was too much trouble.

"His son caused the hurry up," Tolbiac said. "Let him come talk to me."

Great. She'd put the lead to the murders of a terrorist and a writer on this detective's plate but he wasn't hungry. Obviously, no one would assist in finding the connection to her mother.

Outside the morgue, a tall ebony-skinned man in a green street-cleaner's jumpsuit stood where she had expected to see Idrissa. Curious, she approached him.

"I'm Aimée Leduc."

"Khalifa, I'm Ousmane Sada's cousin," he said, a pained expression on his long face. "Blood relation on his mother's side. Why didn't you call me?"

"Believe me, Monsieur Khalifa, if I'd known you existed I would have," she said. "I'm sorry. Is Idrissa Diaffa coming?"

"Ousmane's employer called me."

"His employer, you mean from Club Exe?"

"Nessim Mamou, the clothing manufacturer, where he worked. Ousmane wanted to go home, you know," Khalifa said. "To his village outside Dakar, to his fiancée."

Nessim Mamou . . . Michel's uncle?

Inside the red-brick Institut Medico-Legal building, Serge met them. "The autopsy's just finished," he said. They followed him down to the green-tiled basement. Aimée hated the formaldehyde smell and the reek of pine disinfectant. It reminded her of the time she'd had to come and identify her father's remains after the explosion.

Serge signed in at the desk and took them to the waiting room, furnished with a Naugahyde couch and orange plastic chairs. A rectangular window was covered with plastic shower curtains.

"I'll bring the body to the window."

When the curtains parted, Serge knocked on the glass.

Khalifa went to the window. He was so tall he had to stoop to see. He nodded his head. "I never thought I'd see him like this."

Aimée looked. Ousmane Sada's eyes were closed, thank God,

but the first of a series of black thread stitches was visible in his sternum.

The curtains closed. Serge joined them in a few minutes with a plastic bag. "Please sign here that you identify him and down here for his personal effects."

Khalifa opened the bag. The bloodstained pink bra and garter belt spilled over the Naugahyde couch. His eyes widened. "What kind of mistake is this?"

But Aimée's eyes fastened on the bit of beaded yellow feather fluff stuck in the dried blood on the pink elastic.

"It's a talisman, isn't it?" She pointed. "What does it mean?"

"Mumbo jumbo superstition," he said in a disgusted tone. "I don't believe in that stuff, but he did. Ousmane liked women, not to dress like a woman . . . I don't understand."

"Monsieur, the autopsy shows he suffered from virulent tuberculosis," Serge said, consulting the autopsy report.

Khalifa nodded. "He was a presser in a garment factory. They get this disease."

"He was very sick. Lung disease from long exposure to machine dust or the toxic gas from the flat irons and pressing machines. I've seen this too often in the Sentier. Without treatment he wouldn't have lasted. I know that's not any consolation but . . ."

"Why did someone kill him?"

Serge's cheeks reddened. "I'm sorry."

Outside in Place Mazas where the Metro rumbled by, Aimée pulled Khalifa aside. "I think Idrissa was the target. She's gone into hiding, maybe they wanted Ousmane to tell them her whereabouts."

Khalifa's eyes sparked with anger. "None of this makes sense."

"I'll help you," said Aimée, handing him her card. "I'm a detective. First, I have to find Idrissa."

"No one will talk to you. You ask too many questions."

Of course, to them she was an outsider, a white woman barging into private places, bringing attention to those who preferred to stay hidden in the Sentier woodwork. Especially the *sanspapiers* who hid from authorities.

"So help me, Khalifa," she said. "Romain Figeac, the man Idrissa worked for, was killed. And now Ousmane."

"What's it to you?"

"Like it says on my card, I'm a detective," she said. Not adding that she thought Idrissa had information about her mother but didn't realize it.

Khalifa shook his head. "My cousin's shamed by such a death." He put his head down. "Ousmane's supposed to be under my wing, my uncle won't understand a killing like this."

Who would understand?

"I'm so sorry."

"He's dead." Khalifa started to walk away. "What does it matter?"

"Idrissa's next," Aimée said. "I want to warn her, that's all. Please take my number."

She thrust a card into his large work-worn hand. "I don't turn people in."

With long strides Khalifa walked away over the cobblestones.

Her cell phone vibrated on her hip.

"*Allô?*"

"Meet me on my lunch hour," said Léo Frot in his distinctive nasal tone. "Show your *carte d'identité* at 36, Quai des Orfèvres. They'll let you in. Then you know where to go."

AIMÉE PARKED the scooter in one of the dark stone passages behind the Palais Royal. Once home to kings, the Palais Royal was an arcade-lined square laid out by the duke of Chartres, now housing cafés, shops, apartments, and the Comédie-Française.

Aimée crossed the gravel, crunching past the beds of blue

delphiniums bordering the long oasis of a garden. Under the double rows of plane trees providing leafy shade, children napped in strollers while mothers spoke on cell phones or read.

The water spray from the fountain beaded a fine mist on her arm. Refreshing and cool. And then she saw the sandbox past the trees. Just as she remembered it. And the pain welled up.

She pulled out the creased ad Jutta had given her, stared at it. But her mother wasn't a smiling *bon chic bon genre* type in pearls with a sweater knotted around her shoulders. She'd been a terrorist, linked to the bombing that killed her father, a druggie on the run with another man, in Africa. Or she was dead.

And for the millionth time Aimée asked herself why. But all she knew was that in her bones, she felt her mother was alive. And she had to find her.

Entering the exclusive wing of apartments, she mounted the massive oak staircase surmounted by a balustrade of Doric columns. At number 38, a harried Michel opened a beveled-glass-paned door, a crystal chandelier in evidence behind it.

"*Nom de Dieu*, at last!" He scurried ahead down the herringbone-patterned wood floor, a pincushion tied on his wrist. "The laptop program has glitches, the musician's late, and the model's gained two pounds."

"Don't worry, Michel," she said with a small smile, "things will work out."

Aimée wished her apartment looked like this one. And with the expenditure of several million francs it could. Her seventeenth-century apartment had good bones with high ceilings, airy salons and parlors, and period detail. But all were original and had not been repainted since the last century. Or maybe the one before, she could never remember.

She stepped into a white-and-gilt-paneled salon with wood-work moldings, pilasters and carved garlands, and a large, veined-marble fireplace. Delicate gilt chairs were lined up in rows.

A partially made-up model in jeans, with her hair in rollers, slinked toward her, runway style. All bony hips and hollow cheekbones. The other designer, a man in black Goth attire with black fingernails and lipstick and white makeup, crawled on the parquet floor, sticking down tape demarcating the model's route.

Murals and painted coffered ceilings decorated the adjoining eighteenth-century-style salon. The *enfilade* suite of rooms were done up in a mix of styles evoking different periods. Breathtaking and luxurious.

The music room, hung with green silk damask, doubled as the dressing room. Outfits hung from aluminum racks like dead puppets with numbers pinned on them.

René stood in a reception room paneled with carved arabesques adjusting a silver titanium laptop strapped to a woman's chest. Above him hung an ornate Venetian glass chandelier. Chinoiserie vases and antique busts stood in niches in the walls. He nodded to Aimée, indicating the laptops on a circular Louis XV-style sofa, nicknamed *l'indiscret* for obvious reasons.

"I've read the system and application logs." He shrugged. "So far, so good. But . . ."

She looked at the last line of code on the screen and saw suspicious hash marks. "*Voilà*, there's the little bugger now." She perched cross-legged on the sofa and got to work on the program. In the adjoining onyx-and-tile bathroom, models stood applying makeup.

Michel, clutching scissors, with a tape measure streaming from his pocket, poked his head around a pillar.

Aimée hit *Save* and gave a thumbs-up. "Got rid of the last naughty script-kiddie tracks."

"It's a go," René said. "The network's established so each client's order and measurements feed into your database."

A flurry of activity erupted among the models.

"Show time! It's *haute couture contre couture*," the Goth designer said, pronouncing it "*ot cootur contra cootur*."

"But isn't this a dress rehearsal?"

"An hour ago," René said. She heard the disapproval in his voice. "You missed it."

She'd been at the morgue identifying Idrissa's *kora* player and receiving the brunt of his cousin's anger and suspicion. But her reaction would have been the same.

Better to let René vent. She edged toward the salon, past the models stepping into dresses and sliding on shoes.

"Aimée, help me." Michel grabbed her arm, his white eye-lashes fluttering. "I'm desperate."

"But your system is up and running."

"Not that. My model Annika passed out," he said, pushing Aimée into the onyx-and-tile bathroom.

With those hollow cheekbones, Annika had looked about to cave in.

"How can I help?"

"Raise your arms." He began lifting off her white T-shirt.

"Michel, what are you doing?"

"Don't worry about your weight, that's easy to disguise," he said with a mouthful of pins. At least that's what she thought he said. "Step out of your skirt, into this."

"Don't get ideas," she said, startled. She hadn't shaved her legs in two weeks!

"See, I drape the fabric, pin a dart here."

Sharp jabs poked her skin. "I'm a computer geek, not a model."

"You're a model now," René said, handing her a palette of pressed shadows and blushes. "Hair and makeup is new to me, too!"

"Do this and you save my life," Michel said. "My uncle predicts a failure. This is my chance to show them a Sentier *titi* can do a couture show. For years the fabric dealers have laughed at me, called me a freak, a dreamer, saying, 'No one ever goes from wholesale to couture!' "

She couldn't disappoint him.

"What do I do?"

"Attitude," Michel said, as he pinned and sewed the fabric. "Show attitude." Akiva, Michel's cousin, had appeared and was on his knees hemming the silk.

"And don't breathe."

"Don't breathe?"

"No deep breaths. The stitching's temporary."

So she was being sewn into a dress like Marilyn Monroe. Michel, his cap back on his head, white eyebrows lowered in concentration, stitched her into a symphony of gray: a gunmetal butter-smooth leather bustier with billowing strips of charcoal silk as a skirt. He completed the ensemble with crocodile pumps and thick strands of Tahitian black seed pearls around her neck. The effect, an avant-garde blend of classic and streetwise, was stunning.

"Follow the Goth model," he said. He gestured toward an alabaster-skinned woman with huge black-ringed eyes and lips, who was wearing a spiderweb confection of a gown. "Do what she does."

'arry, his other assistant, had two big makeup brushes in his hands and was powdering her face, hollowing her eyes with charcoal shadow.

"My hair?"

René stood on a spindly-legged chair and scattered silver sparkles over her hair. "Now comb it through with your hands. . . . Perfect, the windswept lunar look!"

Voices and the sound of opening and closing doors came from the other room.

"The musician, I hope." Michel rushed off.

"How many outfits do I wear?"

"We're hoping Annika comes to and we can give her fluids," Akiva grinned. "Then she can finish the show."

Another model ran in, stripped off her raincoat, and stepped into a waiting dress. "Sorry, I've done three shows today, I came from Zaza's as fast as I could."

At least there were three of them to model for Michel now and the other models' clothes had been designed for them.

The clients had begun to arrive. Aimée took a few steps and tried not to breathe deeply. She saw how easily she could pass out. Akiva led her to the curtained door.

"Thrust your hips forward, keep your knees together, stare straight ahead. Whatever you do, don't smile!"

"Go ahead of me, I trip easy," Aimée said to the pigtailed rollerblader with the laptop strapped on, who sucked a lollipop. This eclectic show was definitely couture contra couture.

"Remember, don't smile," said Akiva. "Pout!"

Michel planted a kiss on her cheek, then shoved her beyond the velvet curtain into a glaring spotlight. For a moment, she was blinded by the hot light. Strains of griot music came from her left. She took a step and tottered on the four-inch crocodile pumps. Gritting her teeth and trying to pout, she righted herself, slanted her hips, and prayed her knees weren't knocking together.

The small gold chairs had filled with a variety of people. Flash-bulbs were forbidden, but several men in the front row had sketch pads. The majority of the women were *bon chic bon genre* types who, in their designer suits, looked like they could afford couture. A few older women wore Yves Saint Laurent but the majority were under forty and their eyes lit up. Like jaded predators at a feast, they were always looking for what was fresh and unique. A ripple of applause greeted the Goth model.

When Aimée reached the first row of chairs, the rollerblader swooped beside her. The rollerblader made her way among them, pointing to the dress numbers on her laptop. The audience laughed and applauded loudly.

Aimée kept following the Goth model. Walking like a slant-board hurt her thighs. And she had to pee. Damn it, why hadn't she gone before?

Loud applause greeted them.

The hot light followed her. She hoped she wasn't sweating in the silk. That's when she realized the heavy curtains draped the windows that overlooked the Palais Royal garden. And heard the familiar sounds of a *kora* accompanying a plaintive song, a mixture of French and Wolof. Like a sad love song.

Somehow it all worked: the luxurious rooms, the mix of outrageous and ultrafeminine, and the weaving rollerblader with the high-tech ordering system.

The audience appeared transfixed. And then Aimée saw the honey-colored face of the musician behind the dried palm screen, reflected in the tall mirror.

Idrissa.

STEFAN ENTERED THE FLEABAG hotel, the kind rented by the hour. He hadn't stayed in a hotel for years, but doubted the police checked the registers here.

And it was in a perfect location, standing on the edge of the Sentier. Leaning seemed a more appropriate word. Little had changed from the fifteenth century, Stefan figured, except for the ocher-painted Sheetrock and inexplicable fluorescent pink trim inside the foyer. The closet-sized hotel reception, illuminated by only a dim blue light, held room keys hung on nails from the greasy back wall.

"Anyone here?" he asked.

In the background, a conversation in Turkish continued without stopping.

He leaned on the thin board that served as a counter. "Service, *s'il vous plaît!*" he said louder.

The conversation paused, a door opened, and a small mole of a man appeared. He held a bottle of vinegar in one hand and a flashlight under his arm. Stefan wondered what the vinegar was for.

"Sign here," he said without looking at Stefan, shining the flashlight on the ledger.

Stefan scribbled something illegible below all the other illegible signatures.

"How long?" the man asked.

"I'll pay for the night." Stefan shoveled one hundred francs into the waiting palm. "I'd like a room with a view. Street view."

The man pulled a key from a nail. "Number 49, top floor."

His small molelike eyes raked over Stefan for the first time. "En-joy your stay."

Stefan took his time mounting the creaking wood stairs. He paused and listened. No one followed so he kept going. On the top landing was a pile of stained sheets.

Stefan unlocked the door. The previous occupants hadn't left long before. He smelled cheap perfume and the mildew from the damp bathroom. He pulled the tattered lace curtain over the glass, then opened the window, hoping to avoid other pungent odors.

The faded rose chenille bedspread, rucked and torn on the bottom, barely covered the mattress. Tired, he sank down on the wooden chair.

Outside the sweltering room's windows, rue Beauregard re-sounded with the blare of a car alarm going off and a loud con-versation being held across the narrow street. Stefan dimmed the one bed lamp, draping a towel over the patched, yellowed shade. It cast a muted cocoa light over the room.

He pulled the wooden chair with uneven legs to the window and trained his eye on the lighted windows in Action-Réaction's headquarters. He'd been underground for so long he felt like the feral urban creature he'd become. Jumping at every noise his limited hearing registered, wary of every glance or comment.

Funny, twenty years later, he was back in almost the same spot. Again in the Sentier, near the cache. Or so he assumed.

His mind went back to the journey from the château with Jutta and Beate. It had taken them several hours to drive from Mulhouse, near the German border, to Paris.

In the rearview mirror Stefan had watched the two of them sorting and rooting through the papers. At least they'd driven out of Mulhouse without being followed. But Stefan kept check-ing.

"Figeac's sympathetic to the cause, his wife, too. We leave

him the papers and some of the money. Figeac puts it all in a safety deposit box," Jutta said. "Slowly, when we need it, he sends some to us. No one's the wiser."

"Look at all this stuff," Beate had said, pulling dossiers and bundles of papers from a garbage bag. Her eyes widened. "Property and mine ownership in Africa. He's a bigger rat than we thought."

The papers blew all over since the windows had been opened to get rid of the smell of Laborde's blood.

"We can't do anything with African land deeds," Beate said.

"Not now," Jutta said. "But down the road, who knows?"

Jutta lifted up several stacks of compact paper bundles. Her face cracked into a smile. "Bearer bonds. We can do a lot with these."

"Can't they trace them?" Stefan asked.

"Not bearer bonds like these." She threw a wad over the seat onto his lap. "My God, there's more. Another box! He must have intended to pay people in bonds. So no one could trace them."

And, looking back, Stefan realized that was the moment. The moment he sensed that for him, Beate, and Jutta, the Revolution had changed.

"How can all these fit into a safety deposit box?" Beate asked.

"We just need to find a safe place and dip in from time to time."

They were fugitives in a Mercedes speeding into Paris, with loads of untraceable bearer bonds and Pink Floyd blaring on the radio.

Stefan had never been more thrilled in his life.

Arriving in Paris, he'd parked in a garage around the corner from Romain Figeac's apartment. For all Figeac's liberal tendencies, once they arrived at his door, he seemed nervous and then point-blank refused to help them. Told them to leave.

But when his wife saw them she welcomed them with open

arms. She jumped into the fray, calling it the first real worthwhile thing Figeac could do with his life. The rest of the time she spent shaming him into hiding them, into participating in "the most exciting and life-changing event ever to happen to them."

Events, Stefan realized, proved her right.

Liane Barolet, an Action-Réaction groupie dressed in black, dropped by, en route to her mother's funeral. And that's when, sitting on the floor with a magnum of champagne on ice in Figeac's son's sand bucket, they came up with the idea.

"There are empty vaults in my family's mausoleum," Liane had said. "Who'd look there?"

Thinking back on it over the years, Stefan had figured Liane hadn't wanted to be the only one at her mother's funeral in her melancholy state. Nothing deeper or more revolutionary than that. And they drank champagne all afternoon, which probably helped.

Liane, Jutta, and Beate divvied up the contents of the plastic bags in Romain's son's bedroom. A holiday atmosphere reigned. They left the uncashable items in the little boy's toy chest for Romain to deposit in the bank.

He had erupted later, after he found the radicals playing with his son. Stefan felt sorry for the little boy with the big eyes who craved attention from his tipsy mother. She'd ignore him, then smother him with kisses after he'd become engrossed in a puzzle. Erratic, immature, but a breathtaking blonde.

She made a game of outfitting them in all the black clothing in her closets, then hiring a limo to ferry them to the funeral. Figeac had refused to attend.

Twenty years later, the funeral remained a haze to him. A wild haze. The simple ceremony consisted of the grave digger announcing, upon seeing the crowd, that he'd return later to seal the crypt.

Stefan had stayed outside in the sunlight with the little boy, who chased butterflies among the tombs. He never knew how it transpired that Liane's mother ended up in another vault while the bonds and most of the remaining contents of the plastic bags were entombed in the musty casket bearing her name, Emilie Barolet.

On the way back, the limo was stalled in traffic: a routine police check on drivers. But they'd panicked. Jutta jumped out of the car with Beate, tugging a bag between them. They ducked behind construction on the Metro. All he remembered was a medieval tower of sandstone.

Back at the apartment, Romain Figeac had greeted Stefan with an ultimatum.

Leave.

The police had identified the Mercedes in the garage around the corner. Not only that, they had rough composite sketches of them from descriptions by Laborde's staff. By the time Jutta and Beate turned up at the apartment, Figeac insisted on driving all of them to a suburb outside Paris to fend for themselves. They were to take a bus to the safe house and meet the other terrorists there.

His actress wife winked when they left, implying she could handle her husband and the safe deposit box. But en route, when Jutta told Figeac about the cache in his son's toy chest, he pulled over and pounded the steering wheel.

"If my wife acts crazy, that's one thing," he said. "Don't involve my son."

"Look, we've laid our life on the line for the Revolution," Jutta said. "Struck a blow for the proletariat against a scumbag Nazi collaborator who's stealing diamonds from our African brothers."

Stefan had never heard Jutta so political, so impassioned, or so drunk.

"The cause needs your help to continue!"

Later on, when Romain Figeac found out his wife was pregnant by one of them, Jules Bourdon, he cooperated.

But Stefan knew it was with hate in his heart. And, after his wife's suicide over the miscarriage, with revenge in his mind.

For the first five years, Stefan hid deep underground, moving all the time. He was terrified. But for the past fifteen years, he'd dipped into the coffin modestly, always leaving a pile of cash for Jutta or Liane or Beate. The wads of bonds had never varied, until now. Now they were all gone.

Friday Afternoon

SHOCKED AT FINALLY SEEING Idrissa, Aimée caught herself before she tripped. She surveyed the girl through the fringed palm leaves. Upon closer scrutiny, she saw that Idrissa wore a colorful African head scarf while, with quick strokes, she plucked the long-handled *kora*.

At least some luck shone on Aimée. Idrissa sat in the rear, behind a palm-leaf screen, adjusting a microphone and small amplifier. She wouldn't be going anywhere for awhile. Aimée slid in beside her.

"No more avoiding me, Idrissa," she said. "We're going to talk. I just helped Khalifa identify Ousmane at the morgue."

Fear registered in the girl's eyes. A wide gulf of panic.

"You were the target, not Ousmane, weren't you?"

"Not now, we can't talk now," Idrissa whispered.

"What was Romain Figeac working on? I must know."

Idrissa gasped, "He was crazy. I didn't understand what he wrote."

"Why don't I believe you?" Aimée pressed her face close to Idrissa's. "You're in danger, so am I."

Michel beckoned her frantically, pointing to a shimmering outfit. Frustrated, she wanted to handcuff Idrissa to the Doric column or eighteenth-century harpsichord behind her. Keep her here.

"Please, you must wait for me, Idrissa!"

Idrissa nodded.

If the girl fled again, she'd hunt her down with wolfhounds this time.

Aimée stepped into an urban chic black silk tunic decorated with embroidered white lilies and antique Lanvin buttons. The chalky face powder of the Goth designer and a cloying perfume made her sneeze.

Michel looked up in horror. "Don't sneeze again."

She pinched her nose. "I'll try not to. Any orders, Michel?"

His head bobbed, his hands and mouth too busy with pins and stitching her into the gown.

"You have a new career, Aimée," René grinned. "But if you're serious you have to stop eating and start smoking again."

Not a bad idea, she thought. Did chocolate count?

She kept her eye on Idrissa as she catwalked. The rollerblader seemed busy with clients, and she was glad for Michel.

Her last outfit was a miniskirt of fine silver metal mesh, reminiscent of a knight's chain mail, along with an off-the-shoulder gauze lace top. Michel draped the lace around her lizard tattoo.

"Parfait!" said the Goth designer, admiring her back. "The Marquesan lizard symbolizes change . . . the perfect accessory."

Was her life going to change, Aimée wondered, as she catwalked past the palm screen.

Annika, Michel's premier model, had revived and now appeared in his variation of the traditional last outfit, the wedding gown. An off-white creation of pearlescent beads embroidered an old-fashioned lace twenties style tunic with a train of tiny ivory ostrich feathers draping down her back. Michel's low bow met with resounding applause.

Aimée gestured to Idrissa, indicating a mirrored corridor outside the salon's door.

"Let's finish our conversation."

Idrissa's eyes were large with panic, but she set the kora in its case and stood up.

"Out here, away from the crowd," she said.

After the hot lights and buzz of the collection, Aimée welcomed the stale air and creaking wood floor. She leaned against the wall, about the same height as Idrissa, in the crocodile pumps. Their reflections, Idrissa in her bright African head scarf and Aimée in the chain-metal-mesh mini, kaleidoscoped in the grainy half-silvered mirrors.

"Talk to me, Idrissa, tell me why you're in danger. I won't hurt you."

Idrissa's eyes filled with tears. "You killed Ousmane!"

Aimée blinked in surprise. "What gives you that idea?"

"Because you wouldn't stop looking for me," Idrissa said.

Talk about guilt transference. "Listen, Idrissa, Christian hired me to find out about the 'ghosts,' but I discovered that his father didn't commit suicide," Aimée said, with effort keeping her voice patient. "His father was killed. You'd worked with Romain but you wouldn't talk with me. You ran away. I tried to call you but I couldn't find you. Then I went to Club Exe. No one had seen you. And in the square beyond, a *titi* kicked a soccer ball into a garbage bag by mistake and there was poor Ousmane."

Aimée looked down. The image welled up again, the ebony skin and dried blood on his neck.

"Ousmane was superstitious," Idrissa said. "He listened to the marabout."

From the salon, Aimée heard Michel's laughter. Voices congratulating him.

"*Tiens*, did something happen in Senegal? Something to do with Romain Figeac and terrorists?"

"I don't know what you mean," Idrissa said, but her involuntary shudder gave her away.

"You're a bad liar, Idrissa," Aimée said. "I should know, I'm a good one."

Idrissa scanned the mirrored corridor. Her lips worked but no sound came out.

"Of course, you're scared," Aimée said. "Stay at my place, I'll help you. Please trust me."

"My father's a doctor in Dakar." She motioned Aimée to move farther down the corridor, away from the voices. "He treated

Monsieur Figeac when they summered there." The words came
slowly, as if she weighed each one. "I knew he was moody, ob-
sessive. He asked me to help him. His memoirs, he said. But he
would ask me to go to the market and the docks with him, to
translate the gossip in Wolof. He was looking for someone, I
knew, but he never told me straight. Some Frenchman."

She took a deep breath. Then another. "When I transferred
here to the Sorbonne, my music wasn't enough. I needed more
work. So Monsieur Figeac hired me to transcribe his memoirs.
He'd written most of it, you see, in longhand. With Waterman's
sea blue ink. Like always. The last part he'd spoken on tape. I
hadn't yet finished everything."

Aimée thought back to the classic red Olivetti on his desk.

"But he had a typewriter."

"Never used it."

"Why?"

"It was some famous writer's—Hemingway's, I think. The
story I heard was that he'd found it at an auction, called it his
good-luck charm," Idrissa said. "But he wouldn't have the au-
dacity to use it, he said. And he hated computers."

That fit with the .25 he'd been given by Hemingway, kept
framed under glass.

"So, did he find this Frenchman?"

A pause. Idrissa looked around. "A woman came the day Figeac died." She hesitated. "Then a man. It was right before."

Jutta? But it couldn't be Jutta, she'd been released from prison
after Romain Figeac was killed.

"What did this woman look like?"

Silence.

Then, "She wore dark glasses," Idrissa said. "A scarf around
her head, a long coat. Seemed bizarre in such heat."

Her mother? Idrissa's words reverberated like a tuning fork in
Aimée's head. Her mother alive?

"What did she sound like?" Aimée was surprised at her own question. Of all the things she wanted to know, why had she asked this?

"Never spoke. At least I didn't hear her."

"How long did you see her?"

"A few minutes. I left. I never saw Figeac alive again."

Her mother Romain Figeac's killer? . . . But why? She didn't know whether to hope this stranger was her mother or to fear it.

"But . . . wait . . . you said there was a man."

"Outside, coming up the stairs," Idrissa said. "A Frenchman. He entered Figeac's apartment. I was rounding the stairs but he saw me."

"Saw you?" Aimée asked but didn't wait for an answer. Now she put it together. "So that's why you think he's trying to kill you?"

Idrissa gave a small nod. "He swore at me in Wolof." Fear pooled in her eyes.

It made sense. Idrissa was terrified.

"But why didn't you tell Christian?"

"I'd gone to Fontainebleau for my business seminar class," Idrissa said. "Four days later, when I returned, Christian told me he'd found his father dead. Suicide. Showed me the note. The *typewritten* note. He said it happened the afternoon I left. And I suspected. But Christian had cremated his father already. He had a horror of the Press after his mother's suicide. Then we heard the noises and I saw the death fetish."

"The yellow feathers?"

Idrissa nodded. "But Christian was taking uppers and downers, he made no sense. I kept trying to question him. But where his father was concerned, he saw nothing. Crazy as he was, his father loved him."

"Why was Ousmane killed?"

"He wasn't well but he was hiding me." She blinked back tears. "Maybe a warning . . . I don't know. Then one day, when I went back, the man was sitting in the café opposite. So I ran."

"Can you describe him?" asked Aimée, keeping her hand steady with effort.

Idrissa went rigid.

Behind them in the salon, people milled and conversed.

"What's wrong?"

Idrissa was backing away from her.

Aimée half turned and saw a crowd coming toward the door into the corridor. Idrissa began to run.

Who had she seen?

"Wait!"

Aimée ran, too, past the mirrors distorting their movements. But she was in heels and Idrissa wasn't. Idrissa cornered the hall and Aimée had just about grabbed her when her heel caught in a crack in the parquet. She flew, landing in the Goth designer's arms, which were full of his costumes.

"I'm sorry," she said, scrambling up.

Michel caught up with her, his face wreathed in smiles.

"Aimée, we're going to celebrate," he said, pulling her arm.

"I have to find Idrissa," she said, to his surprise. By the time she'd gotten up, kicked off the shoes, and run downstairs, the entrance lay empty.

Aimée pushed open the heavy glass doors, rushing over the cobbles down narrow Passage Montpensier.

No one.

She ran back the other way toward the Comédie-Française, listening for footfalls. But only slanted shadows, and the sounds of her feet slapping on the cobbles and the meow of a cat reached her. She ran past the restaurant Grand Vefour into the Palais Royal gardens, blinking in the sunlight and shading her eyes.

Mothers sat on the shaded benches minding their toddlers. A

dragonfly buzzed over the sandbox, swooping lazily in the afternoon sun with shimmering blue-green wings. Aimée sat down with her feet in the warm, coarse sand, as she had as a child.

And the strangest feeling came over her. As if someone watched her.

"Did you see a woman running?" she asked a mother who sat nursing her child.

"Just you," said the mother with a shake of her head. "What a great outfit!"

A few of the mothers had looked up, scrutinizing her bare feet and slinky look.

"*Alors*, if I ever get my figure back," she said. "I'd want that."

"A Michel Mamou design," Aimée said. "Remember his name, *couture contre couture*."

She stood up and backed away, wishing the years had evaporated and she was playing in the sand with her *maman* watching her.

Going back up the stairs, she ran into the crowd.

Michel stood surrounded by a group of admirers. She scanned the faces, but there were none she recognized. Who had frightened Idrissa?

She found René in the salon working on a laptop. "Twenty-two orders. Not bad for an unestablished kid—"

"Who won a prestigious award," she interrupted, "and has a surreal and magical design sense. Pretty impressive!"

"That's you," a creamy voice said from the tall double doors. "Dirty feet and all."

Startled, she looked down at her toes, then saw Etienne grinning in the doorway. Beside him stood an older man, tanned, with slicked-back salt-and-pepper hair, smoking a cigar. Familiar looking.

"I wish I could say it was made for me," she smiled, "but Michel stitched me into it."

Etienne had exchanged his pinstripes for an olive linen suit.

He looked like a model himself, she thought. And she'd like a private showing. But he probably had come with his girlfriend, or this man who could be his father-in-law.

And then an odd thought unnerved her. Had he been here when Idrissa ran away? Suspicion crossed her mind. This older man, where had she seen him? Now she remembered.

"So you're in the market for couture, Etienne?"

"Didn't René tell you I was coming?" he asked, surprised. "Your lip-liner number rubbed off, you know. I finally found René at your office, and he said you'd be here."

René shrugged with a grin.

"Let me introduce my uncle, Jean Buisson," Etienne said. "He's visiting on my birthday. Sort of a family tradition."

Why was she attracted to nice men now?

"But we've already met," Aimée said, shaking his hand, once again on the receiving end of this handsome man's laserlike smile. "At the Bourse reception room."

"Of course, but you never joined me for the good champagne across the hall." His uncle moved forward. "Let me make amends. Downstairs in the Grand Vefour. Both of you, my treat!"

A very seductive offer.

But she was late for her meeting with Léo Frot.

"*Désolée,*" she said. And she meant it. "I'd like to but I have an appointment at the Quai des Orfèvres."

René rolled his eyes in disgust.

Stupid. She was being stupid. But she couldn't get involved with this man. She had no time. She had to see the files on her father, and somehow find Idrissa again.

"Maybe later?" she asked.

"Feel like dinner at my place?" Etienne asked.

She nodded, wondering if he was for real. He even had a Harley.

"Take your chances with the chef," his uncle said, "but I'll bring the champagne."

And they left; only a whiff of the cigar aroma remained.

"Don't blow it, Aimée," René said. "Even I can see he's a catch. And he's interested."

"You've been talking with Martine."

"Sometimes she makes a lot of sense," René said. "This one's not flying all over the world and making pit stops like Yves."

Bad boys had always been her downfall, but this Etienne was different.

"I better change clothes." And retrieve my own shoes, Aimèe thought.

"Michel said it's yours," René said. "A gift."

"*Non*, I can't accept." It was too much.

"But you sold ten of them," René said. "Michel said it belongs on you."

SHE PUT the scooter in gear and headed down rue Saint Honoré for the Quai des Orfèvres. At the Pont Neuf she crossed the Seine, sparkling in the sun, and took a left on the Ile de la Cité.

She parked the scooter and showed her *carte d'identité* to the blue-uniformed *flics*. Once inside the cobbled courtyard she veered to the left, passed under the portal that bore the inscription DIRECTION DE LA POLICE JUDICIARE, and climbed the five hundred steps to reach the blue insignia of the Brigade Criminelle.

It had been a long time. But she remembered the way well.

After again showing her ID, she was buzzed in. She found the vaulted wooden doors marked *toilette*. Now it served both sexes since the former ladies' room had become part of the communication systems control room.

This was no classic hole in the floor or stinky urinal like many in the building but an elegant Art Nouveau lavatory: private wooden stalls with inset stained-glass panels and a glazed ceramic frieze accompanied by an elegant shoe-shine stand circa 1905.

The usual lavatory attendant was off duty, probably at lunch. A box with five franc tips sat on a ledge. A stall door opened a slit and Léo beckoned with a crooked finger.

"Timing is everything," he breathed, as she joined him.

She slipped his amended credit report, with proof of the postage-meter glitch and three-day grace period for his online account, into his freckled hands.

His small sharklike teeth, crooked nose, and full head of curly brown hair gave him an academic air. "Devious nerd" best described him. And that, she thought, was being generous. Given his proclivity to taunt and blackmail fellow students in the *lycée*, his skills were wasted in the *préfecture*'s Records Department.

"Twenty minutes," he whispered, handing her a manila envelope, "then I'll come back for them. DST files are shut tighter than a nun's legs."

"Léo, that's not the deal!" She pulled back her file.

He put his finger on his lips. "But I got this. My housecleaner sleeps with the adjutant's clerk. . . ."

"Look," she said, making a moue of distaste. "I don't want to know."

"No photos."

She nodded, and set her phone to Vibrate. "Call me when you're coming back."

He yanked the brass pull chain. A thunderous flushing noise filled the stall as he slid out the door.

Aimée shut the mahogany toilet lid and leaned on a shiny chrome knob. From her leather backpack, she lifted the portable scanner bar, then connected it to her wireless palm organizer revved up with extra memory by René. She punched in her office fax number. The organizer would simultaneously fax the scanned pages to her office. Scanning wasn't photographing, was it? Apprehensive, she took a deep breath. She had a terrible thought . . . what if René hadn't paid the France Télécom bill? Then she saw the familiar handshake logo indicating *Connect* on the tiny screen. Thank God!

With a studied calm she didn't feel, Aimée thumbed open the folder from the IGPN, the disciplinary branch within the police. Inside lay a lined yellow sheet with notes written in an angular hand.

With the bar, she began scanning the notes, which were dated 1976. The first page had a coffee stain and recounted surveillance on rue de Cléry. She recognized the address. Romain Figeac's apartment.

Her brow beaded with sweat. The air in the lavatory was stifling and the scanner's speed was only about five pages per minute.

The surveillance entailed the comings and goings from the apartment of a female suspect. The phone tap report stated she'd used Figeac's phone for calling and receiving calls from a Left Bank gallery owner, known by the police to fence stolen paintings. From what Aimée gathered, the gallery owner was feeding information to the police. There were several blurred black-and-white photos of a woman wearing what looked like a long blond wig, in sunglasses, carrying a shopping bag supposed to contain Modigliani paintings. The woman caught in the act was named—Sydney Leduc.

Her own mother caught (by her father?) in a police sting. Aimée sat in the small cubicle, and the world, as she knew it, crumbled.

Aimée's mother had been jailed and brought to trial, not for terrorism, but for the theft of Laborde's paintings. There was no proof of her participation in the kidnapping and murder of Laborde. So that's why she'd only been in prison a year.

But why hadn't Aimée known about any of this? She looked at the date . . . That year she had been sixteen, that was the time she'd been an exchange student at a high school in New York!

Aimée read further. Offered the chance to inform on the gang for a lighter sentence, Sydney had agreed to find out the location of terrorist gang members and their loot. But Aimée read between the lines. Her father had cut a deal for her mother.

Yet at the end of the report, her father had been brought up for disciplinary hearings. Why? That didn't make sense.

There was no explanation, unless he had been found in possession of the seized paintings on July 15th during the surveillance sting.

On another sheet, with "Surveillance Unit" written across the top, were several names:

Szlovak

Dray

Teynard

Leduc

She recognized Szlovak, a middle-aged man on her father's Commissariat team who'd retired early. Dray had been kicked upstairs to the préfecture at the Quai des Orfèvres ten years or so before. Teynard had been posted to the STUP, the narcotics branch of the Brigade Criminelle.

Her wrist ached. She managed to scan the Action-Réaction files before her cell phone vibrated. Within two minutes she'd finished, disconnected the scanner bar from her palm organizer, and stood reapplying Chanel red lipstick at the old silver-edged mirror.

The lavatory attendant, an older woman with her white hair in a bun, a copy of Telé-Journal under her arm, appeared as Léo returned. Aimée watched him enter the stall but not before she winked and dropped ten francs in the bowl.

A half hour later, back at her office, she found Szlovak's number on the Minitel, left a message, looked up Dray in the préfecture, and had no luck finding Teynard at the Brigade.

At the préfecture, the receptionist said Dray had left for vacances the day before. Aimée sat down to reread the pages she'd faxed and to read those she hadn't had time to.

Something felt off. Way off.

She didn't know what was bothering her but . . . and then she looked up. The dates were wrong. They had to be.

She reread the file. On her office wall was her favorite photo of herself with her father, taken the day after Bastille Day in 1976. They'd spent the whole day together before her flight to New York. She looked closer at the surveillance log dated July 15, 1976, containing her father's name. The day the paintings were recovered.

But Bastille Day was always July 14th.

So her father had been with her on July 15th. Not on stakeout.

He'd been set up. And she was the proof.

She took the photo from the wall and stuck it in her bag with the Modigliani data she'd copied from the Agence France Presse.

A further search showed Teynard had retired. He ran a detective firm with his nephew on rue de Turbigo.

Close. On the edge of the Sentier and a few blocks away.

Forget the scooter. She needed to walk. Work out some angry energy, so she wouldn't arrive at Teynard's swinging. At least not at first.

"*DESOLÉE*, MADEMOISELLE Leduc!" said the secretary, Madame Goroux. "Monsieur Teynard's evening seems totally booked."

"Please, can't you fit me in?" Aimée asked, letting the whine rise in her voice. "Something's come up, it's important."

"He handles cases jointly with his nephew," Madame Goroux said. "Let me see if he's available."

"*Merci*," Aimée said. The nephew might help her to get to see his uncle.

An express delivery man wheeled in a package on a dolly. "*Bonjour*, Madame Goroux, I need the *patron*'s signature."

"I can sign, Cédric," she said.

"Sorry, but the sender specifically required Monsieur Teynard's signature."

"Come back in a while," said Madame Goroux, consulting her schedule. "He marked himself out until his three o'clock appointment."

Aimée glanced at her Tintin watch.

Twenty minutes. If he was on time.

She left and descended the worn stairs. In the quiet mosaic-tiled lobby of Teynard's building, her mind raced. She chewed Nicorette furiously, dying for a cigarette. Within ten minutes, a dapper white-haired man in his sixties in a wheat-colored linen suit entered the lobby.

"Monsieur Teynard?" she asked, standing partially behind a pillar.

He removed his sunglasses and blinked, adjusting his eyes from the glare outside to the darkened lobby.

"Mademoiselle, are we acquainted?" he asked, a smile spreading over his face. A whiff of scented aftershave accompanied him. Perhaps he fancied himself a ladies' man.

"Indirectly," she said, walking toward him. "That's what I'd like to talk about."

He squinted.

Aimée hit the light switch, flooding the lobby with light.

Teynard's brow furrowed as he stared at her.

"If I didn't know better," he said in a low voice, "I'd say the past has come back . . ."

"To haunt you?" she finished for him. "Let's go talk."

Aimée pointed to the café in Passage du Bourg-l'Abbé directly opposite Teynard's office.

WITH A wary look, Teynard watched her set two espressos on the café table. She pushed the round aluminum sugar cube bowl toward him. The young owner, wearing a Lakers tank top and prayer beads around his wrist, sat behind the counter reading a Turkish newspaper.

Apart from Aimée and Teynard, the narrow café, with its

yellowed smoke-stained walls, hammered-tin counter, and brown leatherette chairs, was empty. From the corners came the musk-like smell of lingering genteel decay. Wood-framed windows fronted the passage under a glass-and-iron roof probably unchanged from Napoleon's time.

"Monsieur Teynard," she said, "you were part of the Galerie Arte surveillance on July 15, 1976, weren't you?"

"That's a long time ago," Teynard said, smoothing back his hair. His ice blue eyes darted over the café.

"I'm interested in your version."

"My version?"

"You were there along with my father, Dray, and Szlovak."

"I don't remember."

She nodded, unwrapping the sugar cube's paper. "Good point. Maybe you weren't there either. I know Papa wasn't."

"What's this all about?"

"Shouldn't you tell me, Monsieur Teynard?" She stirred her sugar.

"I have appointments. . . ." He smoothed his linen trousers and started to stand up.

"I told Madame Goroux your plans had changed."

For the first time he looked surprised.

"This might refresh your memory," she said, wiping the sticky table off with a napkin and spreading the file in front of him. "I'm a visual person. Seeing things in black and white brings it home to me. Maybe you are, too. See, there's your name."

Teynard's chin sagged.

She pointed. "Here's another visual." She pulled out the photo of her and her father. "There's a date. See *Le Figaro* on the *tabac* stand behind us—July 15, 1976. I even checked. The old noon edition came out at eleven A.M. Doesn't fit with the surveillance record, does it? My father was with me July 15, not on surveillance as this shows."

"You're talking about ancient history," Teynard said.

"My father was framed," she said, "for something he didn't do."

"The facts speak for themselves."

"*Pas du tout*—they lie," she said. "But the rumor he was dirty follows him and me, even now."

"That's old news," he said. "If you had more going on in your life you wouldn't be hung up on the past."

Rude man. Maybe that was true. But it was none of his business.

"Move on, young lady," he smiled. "Get a life. Isn't that how they say it?"

Teynard didn't like women. Or maybe just her. But something about his dapper persona didn't match his hard eyes.

"Good advice, Monsieur Teynard," she said. "I'll move on to the prosecutor, Edith Mésard."

She saw a flicker of interest in his eyes.

"And Monsieur Szlovak," she lied. "He has a better memory than you."

"Talk with Dray," he said. "Before you make more of a fool of yourself."

And then she knew. Dray and Teynard were thick. Pudding thick, like thieves.

"It was you two, wasn't it?"

Something caught in his throat. "What are you . . . ?"

"Don't lie again," she said. "For more than twenty years, you've been afraid someone would accuse you of that, haven't you? But my father took the fall. Maybe he was just convenient, having a terrorist wife and all."

Teynard shook his head. "You aren't making sense," he said in a quiet voice. "I need to get back to the office."

"But it makes perfect sense," she said. "Especially if he got my mother to inform, and cut a deal for a light prison sentence for her. He left the force with honors, too. Things don't often happen like that if a police officer has been under disciplinary review, do they?"

Teynard looked away. "Typical *flic*'s kid!"

"Matter of fact"—she leaned forward and downed her espresso—"in the Commissariat, you probably bounced me on your knee!"

That should make him feel old. And dried up, like he looked under the tan and his GQ fashion attempt.

"What do you want?"

"Papa's vindication," she said. "And what you know about my mother."

He shrugged. "I'm retired. What makes you think I know anything?"

She'd saved the best for last, hoping he'd nibble. Well, he'd sort of nibbled.

"But I know about the Modigliani paintings, you see," she said, pulling the *Figaro* article out. "They weren't lost at all. You signed for their consignment to the police repository. But here they are in a 1984 London exhibition."

He stood up. "I'm not the bad guy," Teynard said.

"Maybe from your perspective . . . what did you and Dray do with the money?"

"I don't have to listen to this."

"But the prosecutor will," she said. "Especially when I reopen the inquiry. You're in deep, Teynard. Deep and dirty."

"How? There's no proof," he said. But for the first time his eyes were unsure.

"Looks like proof to me," she said. "Laborde's stolen paintings confiscated from the Left Bank Gallery by you, then showing up in London . . . sold to willing buyers. One work was acquired for 379,000 FF* in a Paris sale in June 1985. The other was bought for 1,737,000 FF** in March 1991, again at auction."

Teynard's shoulders sagged.

---

*(US$ 54,930)
**(US$ 251,739)

"Chump change Teynard . . . they'd be worth so much more now," she said. "You should have held onto them."

He sat down. He looked much older.

"What have you done with the money?" she asked.

"I've been tracking Jules Bourdon for years," he said, his voice flat. "He's here and I get a bad feeling you'll try to screw it up."

"Screw what up?"

"None of your business."

Is that why Stefan had surfaced?

"My mother went to Africa with him, didn't she?"

"Fool!" Teynard said. He shoved the espresso away. "There's more. Much more."

"More?"

"Diamonds. Investment-quality diamonds from Africa."

Diamonds . . . is that what Jutta and Gisela were after? Was that what this had all been about? Were the diamonds what had been in Liane Barolet's mother's coffin?

"When the terrorists kidnapped Laborde he was fat with investment diamonds," Teynard said. "They had perfect planning or a stroke of dumb luck, who knows, but the minister and Laborde's old Milice comrades were coming for their cut. Laborde had bribed his friends in the government for concessions. They were happy to use the old colonial network and keep the spoils among friends."

But nothing for the Africans who lived there, Aimée thought.

"That's why Bourdon's here, risking his life," said Teynard.

And she saw it in his eyes, alive and predatory.

"Bourdon's what you want, isn't he?" she asked. "Some kind of vendetta?"

"Call it payback time." Teynard rolled his pant cuff up to midcalf. Above his sock, she saw a flesh-colored prosthesis. "He shot my kneecap to bits. They removed my leg to my thigh and called me lucky. Now it's my turn to make him lucky."

"I see," she said.

"Do you?" Teynard had warmed up. "They're lice. Punks who called it a political statement when they blew people up or threw bank-robbery money from the Metro windows. Calling it capitalism for the masses. But Jules Bourdon, he was a smart *arnaqueur*, a con who used the idiots. And he's never stopped."

"So Jules Bourdon fled to Senegal . . . why?"

"Not a lot of options when you're wanted on several continents," Teynard said. "He worked there as a mercenary."

"What does Romain Figeac have to do with it?"

"Figeac had a score to settle, too. Seems his wife's baby was Bourdon's. Not his. He wanted the world to know what a con man Bourdon really was."

"So Jules Bourdon killed Figeac before Figeac could expose him? And Ousmane was killed because he hid Idrissa?"

Teynard's eyes narrowed. "Something like that. I could have sworn time stood still when I saw you," Teynard said. His voice had changed. It was low and full of something. Some dark emotion riding near the surface.

"Why?" But she knew.

"She took my breath away," he said.

Aimée's hand shook. The way he said it made her sick. Like he had some claim on her.

He took in her reaction. "Has she been in contact with you?"

So he was looking for her mother, too.

Aimée shook her head.

"And you wouldn't tell me if she had," Teynard said.

STEFAN RUBBED HIS EYES. His back hurt from sleeping in the stiff chair. He'd ordered a meal from the café opposite, had it brought up. He'd spent the whole night and day watching. A woman had gone into the building. The only things visible now were silhouettes in the Action-Réaction window.

Stefan wished he had company. But he was alone as orange dusk painted the red tile rooftops. He wanted to talk; talk about the past, his feelings, the things he wanted to do. Outline his plan to own a garage specializing in Mercedes restoration.

He fingered the card she'd given him. Turned it over in his grease lined palm, remembered her engaging silence and how she was the spitting image of her mother.

He reached for the old-fashioned black phone.

"*OUI.*" AIMÉE ANSWERED her cell phone, turning away from Teynard. She winked, signaling the café owner for two more espressos.

Silence. Was it Etienne?

"*Allô?*"

"Have some time to talk?" asked Stefan.

"Tell me where and when." She stood and walked to the counter, away from Teynard.

A pause.

She repeated it; maybe he hadn't heard her.

"My therapist said I should talk it out."

Aimée bit back her surprise. "Please do, Stefan, I'm listening."

"For years I've wanted to talk with someone," he said. "I have to share the burden."

He sounded broken, older than he was. It dawned on her that she'd have to protect him.

"People are chasing me."

"Who?" She wondered who else besides Europol and the DST. Teynard?

"Talk to me, Stefan," she said. "Have you seen my mother?"

"Jules came back. Sooner or later he'll show at Action-Réaction," he said. "Chances are she's with him."

Aimée's heart sank. Didn't her mother want to see her? Or had she been watching Aimée, following her, even as Aimée was seeking her? But purposely not making contact as René had warned.

"Where are you? I'll help."

His voice sagged. "Help me? I doubt it once you hear what I've done."

"Weren't you a little fish caught swimming with the sharks?" she said. "Or did you become a shark, too?"

"The old hunter," he said, his voice jagged with regret. "I buried his things under a tree. His family should know what happened to him."

She nodded. "Making some amends will help you." She held back the questions about her mother, realizing Stefan had to unburden himself in his own way.

Then what sounded like a glass shattering.

"Ça va?"

"Later," he said and she heard the dial tone.

He'd wanted to talk but something had happened. She slapped the counter . . . so close, yet again out of her reach!

She hit the call-back key.

The phone rang and rang. She was worried. The steaming espressos were on the counter and she reached for them.

But Teynard had opened the door and was walking down the passage. Rude again.

She grabbed the first bill in her pocket, threw down a hundred-franc note, and rushed after him. Pedestrians crowded the busy corner of rue de Turbigo. She ran to catch up with him. He stood at the curb facing the zebra crossing stripes, his back to her, white hair glinting in the late afternoon sun.

"Look, Monsieur Teynard, you've got to stop . . . ," she called out.

He turned and the rest of her phrase was lost in the revving of a motor scooter.

She raised her hand to shield her eyes from the sun. "We didn't finish talking." They were still several feet apart.

"Quit following me," he said.

Teynard's annoyed look turned to surprise. His shoulders jerked. Then jerked and jerked again.

And she knew something was wrong.

He clutched his side, grimacing as if in pain.

Aimée pushed through the crowd of hot, tired Parisians. Several exclaimed in irritation. Teynard staggered toward her, then slumped to his knees, as the crowd parted around him. A woman screamed as he reached for the handle of her baby stroller. Three gaping red-black holes showed in his linen jacket. Teynard staggered and fell face down onto the hot pavement.

Startled, Aimée looked up to see the scooter with a black-helmeted driver pull away. A battered green scooter. The rest of her view was cut off as a bus pulled up and the pedestrian throng crossed the street.

Everything had happened in seconds.

"Call a doctor!" someone shouted.

And then it hit her. The green scooter was the one René had loaned her. Her spine tingled. Someone had stolen it. Teynard had been shot by someone riding her scooter. And if she wasn't mistaken, that someone was Jules Bourdon.

So he was watching her. Or Gisela was. Or her mother? Waiting for her to lead them to the diamonds?

Scared, she backed away. She heard murmurs in the crowd . . . "raised her arm" . . . "following him." Were they talking about her? The eyes of the couple standing next to her narrowed in suspicion.

An ambulance siren bleated, coming closer. She tried to melt into the crowd. Disappear. She had no wish to explain and no time to spend at the Commissariat. She was being hunted, too.

She'd almost made it to the passage when the woman with the stroller looked over and pointed at her. "Her . . . her . . . it was her . . . she shot him!"

As Aimée turned her heel broke.

She took off both shoes and ran.

"Stop . . . don't let her get away!" the woman yelled.

Aimée ran by the two sculptures of Commerce and Industry flanking the white stone of Passage du Bourg-l'Abbé.

The café owner came out, waving a fifty-franc bill at her. "Keep the change!" she yelled. Footsteps sounded behind her. There was a loud *ouff* as he knocked whoever was chasing her to the ground. She turned around to see the café owner wave and give a big grin.

She ran out of the passage and turned right onto rue Saint Denis. Sex shops and wholesale clothing stores lined the street. She entered the first one and plunked five hundred francs on the smudged glass counter, careful to avoid touching it.

"That one," she said, panting and pointing to the pink page-boy wig. "And this." The man handed her the leather choker-type bondage necklace. She looked around. Most of the outfits had too many holes to wear on the street. She chose the one that provided the most covering. "This one, too." He pushed the items over the counter. She heard the siren wail in the distance. She had to hurry.

"I need to change."

He jerked his head toward a back booth. She went straight there, not looking to either side, or at what was going on outside.

She tried to hold her breath for as long as it took her to shimmy out of Michel's miniskirt and into the tight black vinyl PVC cat suit. But she couldn't. She tied the choker, adjusted the wig, and pulled a snub-nosed pair of Manolo Blahnik's sexy version of Minnie Mouse heels onto her feet, then stuffed her clothes into her bag.

Now if she didn't have to run, she'd be okay. Black PVC in this humidity could become a steambath.

By the time she'd gone a few blocks, a middle-aged man had offered her five hundred francs, which she'd declined; she hadn't really planned on recouping the investment in her outfit. A police car cruised by but she blended in with street life. Perfectly. Prostitution was legal, though solicitation was not and since the Middle Ages, rue Saint Denis had been the working girls' beat.

She stopped at the corner of rue Blondel and rue Saint Denis.

Twilight descended over the street, the first rays of neon casting their glittering reflections on the rain-spattered car windshields. There was a bite to the wind on rue Blondel. An infamous bordello had flourished here before and during the war, referred to affectionately by some as *le trente deux*, the thirty-two. Even Picasso and Brassai had talked about "the flowers of rue Blondel."

"*Chérie*, you working or you buying?" asked a woman, her black shiny boots and straining halter top just visible from the dark passage entrance ahead of her. "You want to check with me first, eh? You're on my corner."

Oops. Bad move. She didn't want to get in trouble with this woman or her pimp. Where could she go? Jules probably knew all her friends' houses . . . even René's. But Etienne Mabry's apartment was near, in the back courtyard, or so his card said.

Aimée grinned. "*Pardon*, I'm looking for someone upstairs. My partner forgot to tell me which floor."

"Those computer *crétins?*" The woman's booted foot tapped on the cobbles, echoing in the passage.

Another working girl sauntered by, saw the boots, and kept walking.

"They like to play with themselves on the Internet. What kind of a world is this, eh, when a *mec* gets off on a computer?"

Business must be tough for these working women . . . especially if they were of a certain age.

Aimée nodded. "I remember coming here after school. My friend's mother had a zipper factory near here, but it's all different now."

Aimée could see the woman's highly made-up face now, and the sagging skin on her arms, goose-pimpled in the chill passage.

A shadow covered the woman's gloved hand, edged in red lace net. A client. And she led him upstairs.

Aimée stared through the quadruple courtyards to the shiny

lights of traffic on Boulevard de Sébastopol. Dirty grime-encrusted limestone balustrades didn't hide the charm of the historic Hôtel Saint Chaumond, the ornately carved sculptural details or delicate sloping mansard roof and dormer windows. Once elegant, the classical facade was neglected and now nearly hidden under plastic shop signs. Clothing carts were parked in the adjoining cobbled courtyard, piggybacked against the wall like so many tired toys.

Aimée paused, catching her breath. These pitted cobblestones were murder on heels. Before her, a mahogany-faced man, perched against a cart, spoke Hindi into a cell phone as he consulted an order sheet. She wanted to join him and take a break but she had to make some plans. And needed a safe place in which to do so.

Mustering her energy, she entered the old converted building. The wire-cage lift's door was padlocked shut, a stroller propped against the curved handrail. The sawing of the scales played on a violin reached her ears. By the time she arrived at the third *étage* her bag felt heavier than granite.

The cool expanse of hallway gave way to a series of double doors. Beyond them she saw a pair of carved wooden doors reaching from the tiled floor to the high ceiling.

She knocked. But the doors were so thick her knuckles made no sound. Then she saw a buzzer.

Etienne Mabry opened the door. His eyes widened. "*Entrez.*"

"Dinner ready yet?"

"Only if you're the dessert," he smiled, taking in her unusual outfit.

"I like to dress up."

Aiming for a casual entrance, she stepped inside and promptly skidded on the waxed wooden floor.

He caught her elbow and grinned. "Talk about elusive. I thought you wouldn't come and . . ."

". . . now I'm early."

He kissed her on both cheeks. His warm gaze lingered. He looked delicious in worn jeans and a faded Rolling Stones World Tour T-shirt.

Hooking his arm around her shoulder, he led her to a loft-like white room with high ceilings, sparse and clean. Antique black-and-gold lacquered Japonaise screens provided the only color. She pulled off the pink wig and fluffed up her hair. Her scalp felt damp.

"You look like you could use a drink. *Kir royal?*"

She nodded. *"Merci."*

Silver-framed photos of small children and an elegant blond woman lined the white marble fireplace.

Of course, his wife was away. Or, worse yet, she'd be returning soon and he'd beg off dinner.

He followed her gaze. "My ex-wife and children. They live in Rouen. I see them on weekends."

He handed her a flute of pinkish froth and sat beside her on the all-white couch.

"Salut." They clinked glasses.

"How about you?"

Did she want to tell him how scared she felt, how at sea she was after Teynard's murder, not to mention clueless about the alleged diamonds and her mother, who remained truly elusive?

"Me?" She felt nervous. Yet there was something so nice about him. Why couldn't she relax? She took another sip of the *kir.* What was wrong with her?

Here she was, in a tight vinyl PVC cat suit, throwing herself at him. Yet she was as afraid of intimacy as of Teynard's killer.

"Involved with anyone?"

"Too busy." Why did he have to sit so close? "You know me, work, sleep, and ride the Metro. I work too much. Like everybody else."

Of course, right now she didn't look like everybody else in her black vinyl and dog collar.

"How can I help you?" He touched her hair, ran his fingers down to her shoulder. "You're full of contradictions, but that's interesting. And I like you."

"Feels like a relationship minefield to me," she said. "At least right now."

Etienne removed his hand from her shoulder, leaving a warm remaining patch.

"You're like an alternating current," he said. "Switching from hot to cold."

So what if it was true . . . his words stung.

"What about your children and ex-wife? That's more emotional baggage than I can handle."

"Afraid of taking chances?" he asked. "Afraid of the work?" He shrugged, tracing his thumb down her cheekbone. His brownish red hair tumbled around his ears. A soft citrus smell came from his shirt. "What can I do? I'd like to try . . . but I guess you don't want to."

René and Martine would shoot her. Why wouldn't she let herself go? *Merde!* Why did it have to be so difficult?

Her head swam. All she knew was that she felt she was in way over her head.

"Look, Etienne, I'm a disaster with relationships. Like Latin in the *lycée*, those ancient intricate verb tenses elude me. So do relationships. It's some complicated thing I can watch but not duplicate." She shook her head. What a loser she was. "Sorry for whining."

"Making excuses is more like it," he said. His citrus scent had transferred itself to her skin. Bad. But she didn't want to rub it off.

And then she wondered if it mattered how she'd screw up this time . . . he certainly was walking in with his eyes open. *Tiens*, he was of age, a consenting adult.

"You're a funny woman . . . wild and innocent all at once!"

Georges had described her mother like that.

She pushed his hair behind his ears and knew she was headed for trouble.

"*Tempus fugit,*" he mumbled in her ear.

"What does that mean?"

"Time flies . . . your first Latin lesson," he breathed on her hair, pulling her close. "Not difficult, is it?"

Friday Evening

STEFAN STOOD IN THE shadowy courtyard outside Action-Réaction's window. He'd seen Jules Bourdon case the building an hour ago, then go inside. Even after all these years, his moves were classic. The same. Should he confront Jules? Ask Jules why he had killed Jutta and Romain Figeac and tried to shoot him?

Grow up, he told himself. For once. Stand up. After all these years of hiding, now he was being hunted by the con man who had recruited him. The big talker, the mastermind of the disaster-ridden Laborde kidnapping.

Strange to say, the Brigade Criminelle and the *gendarmes* had been the ones who'd actually killed Laborde. He'd seen it in the papers later. All the gunshot wounds resulted from the police rifle attacks on the farm before they firebombed it.

Was Jules ransacking the office, looking for twenty-year-old loot? He couldn't be that stupid. Especially if he'd survived as a mercenary in Africa. Jules had a cultivated nose for money. So he'd be sniffing after whatever he thought Beate and Jutta had hidden.

Silence. He peered in, his head up against the yellowed lace curtain. No one. A door was open. The door to the cellar.

Stefan crept inside the Action-Réaction office. Beams from a flashlight shone in the darkness below. He moved toward the cellar, then stopped. The wooden floor creaked behind him. A whiff of patchouli wafted in his direction. The scent from the commune. Ulrike's scent.

He turned, saw the gun, and stiffened, his baffled look replaced by fear.

SOMETHING CHIRPED NEAR AIMÉE'S ear. Groggy, she reached out. Warm skin. Crisp sheets. She blinked in the darkness. Now she remembered where she was. And the glow she'd felt afterward. Still felt.

She reached for her cell phone and Etienne's citrus scent rose from the skin of her hand. Too late. She'd missed the call but there was a voice message. Her Tintin watch said ten o'clock.

She rolled from the bed and tiptoed over the sisal rug, down the long hall, toward the kitchen. They'd never made it in here for dinner.

She was starving and thirsty. Where were her clothes? She found the cat suit in a heap on the floor, her bag and shoes under a chair. She'd check her messages, drink some water. Then get some for Etienne and crawl back in with him.

She couldn't find a glass in the dim kitchen or drinking water, but did find a bottle of champagne. A nice, frosty Veuve Cliquot. Leaving it on the counter, she searched for glasses. She stumbled through café-style louvered swinging doors into a pantry.

The pantry counter was loaded with stacks of dishes, a polished silver coffee set, and an answering machine. She found glasses in a cupboard. Beside her, the machine clicked on without ringing. Odd. But she knew you could bypass ringing if you just wanted to leave a message.

"You're late, Jules!" said a raspy voice.

She froze.

Jules? Jules Bourdon?

"The café off Place Ste-Foy. Bring Figeac's son. And hurry . . . Nessim's with me."

Click.

Footsteps came from the kitchen. Was Christian here?

"*Tonton?*" asked Etienne. "Are you back?"

She was about to answer.

And she went rigid with fear. With a sickening certainty she realized who Etienne's *tonton*, his uncle, was. *Jules.*

She crouched down in the dark pantry and put her finger on the erase button. A quick *whoosh* and the message was gone. She half-crouched below the swinging door.

She saw Etienne's rumpled hair silhouetted against the backlit stove, the gleaming of the champagne bottle in his hand.

Had she misunderstood. Was she wrong—all wrong?

Ready to rush into his arms, she saw the barrel of a .357 reflected in the silver surface of the coffee pot.

Through the slats in the shutters, she saw him staring at her bare feet, the gun aimed right at her as he shoved the door open.

She slammed the door closed on his hand. He yelped, the gun flew away, and the champagne bottle clattered to the floor.

She rushed out.

"*Salope!*" he yelled, grabbing for the gun with his other hand.

She clubbed him with the champagne. A loud crack and he slid to the floor. She heard a yelp, then he grabbed her ankle. Twisted it. Pulling her off balance and slamming her into the cabinet.

She righted herself and kicked him hard in the head.

Panting, and terrified that Jules would return before she could find Christian, she grabbed dish towels and bound Etienne's wrists and ankles with them. Then she stood back, wondering how she could have slept with him. But she had.

Another smart relationship choice! She pulled him to the laundry porch by the ankles, shoved him out there, and locked the door.

As she picked up the .357 she wondered if it had killed Jutta and Romain Figeac. She struggled into her PVC cat suit, and in the hallway found a red leather zip-up jacket. She pulled on the jacket, stuck the gun inside her leather backpack, and slipped into her shoes.

Then she went to look for Christian.

The long hallway led to a series of old offices, closed off by glass partitions.

A low moaning came from the fourth one.

She saw a needle in an aluminum kidney-shaped tray and Christian standing beside it. His eyes rolled up in his head and she was just in time to catch him before he fell to the floor.

Just her luck! They'd been giving him dope. Etienne had probably kept Christian here since she'd last seen him, the liar.

Christian was tall and heavy-boned for such a thin person.

"Don't check out on me, Christian. Move. You have to walk."

She hooked her arm under his and tried to help him. At the same time, she pulled out her cell phone and dialed 18 for the paramedic-trained *pompiers*. "My friend's OD'd, what do I do?" she asked.

"Keep him walking until we get there."

She gave them the address.

"We'll meet you on Boulevard de Sébastopol."

She prayed Christian could hold out and that they'd make it to the street before Jules came looking for him. She made him walk. He kept nodding out, his breathing stopping then slowly starting.

On the landing she paused and listened. She took the back stairs just in case. Narrow winding rusty ones. And all the while she kept talking to Christian, making him move his feet, and slapping him awake.

By the time the *pompiers* arrived, they'd made it to the boulevard and Christian's eyelids were fluttering. The blue-suited crew took over, tying him down in their ambulance van and giving him a shot of Narcan, the junkie jaws of life. He struggled to sit upright and almost gave one of the crew a black eye.

"Where am I?" he asked.

"Christian, you're safe," she said.

"We'll stabilize him at the *hospital*," the paramedic said, getting an IV going in Christian's arm. The emergency van took off.

IN THE café's tarnished wall mirrors, Aimée watched the two men, huddled in conversation. She didn't know which was Nessim, Michel's uncle. She remembered what she and René had found out about his laundering of profits and false bankruptcies.

Where was Jules?

Too bad she couldn't see their mouths well enough to read their lips. The heavyset one, wearing wire-framed glasses and with a tonsure of graying frizzy hair, drew with his finger on the table. The man across from him, completely bald, nodded his head from time to time.

A certain urgency permeated the late evening crowd, mostly *habitués* of the *quartier*. Conversation buzzed at the crowded zinc bar, while the miniskirted cashier with the beehive hairdo made change and shouted orders back to the kitchen through the dense haze of cigarette smoke.

A harried waiter leaned across her table. He whisked aside crumbs, wiped the marble top with a blue cloth.

"*Un café noir*," Aimée said.

He cocked his head and disappeared.

Outside, in the narrow street, Aimée saw droplets of water fall on carts parked on the broken pavement. A fitful July rain danced and skirted the façades, teasing Parisians anxious for the arrival of a tepid August that still seemed too far off. Trucks blocked access to the small square.

She surveyed the small Bar Tabac. An Asian man, his cell phone on the table, took orders from a fabric catalog; two shop girls picked at an Auvergnat salad; an older blond hooker she'd seen on Saint Denis ate *choucroute*, part of the day's Alsatian sausage special, and kept an eye on the racing results flashing on the *télé* perched above the bar.

Aimée realized the place stretched from one street to the other; the bar side fronted busy rue d'Aboukir while the restaurant tables opened to narrow rue Ste-Foy. The women, with their clients, disappeared into Passage Ste-Foy, a covered alleyway wedged between peeling buildings. And right across from her table. Perfect for a getaway, Aimée thought.

She watched the two men. Friar Tuck shook his head, pulled a notebook from his pocket, and wrote something. Aimée couldn't see the other man's reaction since the waiter had appeared with her *café noir* and blocked the mirror.

When she could see again, they'd stood up, their chairs scraping the linoleum, and were headed out the glass doors. Aimée took a gulp of espresso and threw some francs on the table.

They paused in front of the old stone portal of the passage by the Roseline sign. She couldn't see their faces, only their black suit jackets beaded with rain and the frizzy-haired man's fist pounding his palm. And then the other man violently shook his fist.

Aimée pulled the leather jacket's collar up for protection against the rain and turned to study the café window. Men clustered in doorways, leaning on their hand trucks and smoking. She tried to appear nonchalant as rain beat down, avoiding a tall African woman in blue leather hot pants sashaying into the passage.

And then they were gone. One man walked toward the square and the other disappeared into the passage.

Whom should she follow?

The heavyset man took off down the street in a waiting black Peugeot.

She slipped into the graffiti-covered sandstone passage. A blackened crust of grime coated the damp walls. Drainpipes leaned crookedly, loose electric wires trailed from the ceiling. The passage opened to an unroofed area lined with green garbage bins, then forked toward some stairs, mounting to vestiges of the ancient ramparts.

On her left was an entrance to the crumbling, flaking stairway. A musty coldness hit her. The stairs sagged and creaked as she mounted them. She heard moans from behind doors, and over the passage roof came the whine of sewing machines.

From a coved window on the small landing she saw the man's shiny bald dome in the apartment across the way. Instead of a light well where the buildings joined, there was open space. In medieval times, she imagined neighbors conversing with each other across the way or the king's men leaning out and throttling their enemies.

The bald man turned. And before she could duck, he saw her staring at him. She moved aside.

Opposite her, a door opened. Inside the room, a man combed his stringy hair with his fingers before a cracked mirror. His false teeth on the cheap dresser caught the light.

"*Adieu, chéri,*" the *pute* said, tucking franc notes into the tiny pocket of her blue leather hot pants. She shut the door, showing no surprise at seeing Aimée on the landing.

"My horoscope today said quick and easy." She rolled her eyes. "Not even slow and hard!"

Aimée controlled her shudder at the thought of the old man.

"Know him?" Aimée gestured across the window to the bald man. "Over there."

"Not as a client but . . . " the *pute* said, her voice trailing off.

Aimée hoped she invited a confidence. She folded a hundred-franc note and gingerly slipped it into the woman's already stuffed pocket.

"As my landlord," the woman continued, as if there'd been no pause. "The *salaud*'s raising our rent and won't even fix the hall lights. At night, with my johns, I have to use a flashlight."

"His name?"

"You a *flic?*"

It was Aimée's turn to roll her eyes. "Would I hunt small fry like this?"

"Didn't think so, but then you could be some new type of undercover," the woman said.

"People hire me," Aimée said. "Kind of like you. Every job isn't picture-perfect or smooth sailing but it keeps my interest." She smiled. "I get bored easily."

"You mounting a sting?"

He must be a bigger fish than she thought.

Aimée looked down to cover her surprise. The woman's turquoise platform heels were worn down on the sides. She pounded the cobbles, all right.

"*Mais* could I tell you even if I wanted to?" Aimée said.

The *pute* grinned. "Just get Nessim Mamou into hot water . . . maybe it will warm him up."

So that was Nessim, Michel's shady uncle. "I'm looking for Jules, his partner."

The prostitute shook her head.

"Distinguished, white-haired *mec*, nice tan."

The woman nodded. "He's around."

She saw Nessim scurry through the passage. Aimée walked down the stairs, and past the overflowing green bins of garbage marked PROPRIÉTÉ DE PARIS.

She strode over the pitted cobbles, toward the punch of machines coming from the rear courtyard, as if she knew where she was going. She didn't. Her teeth ached from clamping down so tightly. But attitude counted, especially in the Sentier.

She'd lost him.

Reaching the last courtyard, the one with a faded sign saying WASNARD, she veered to the left. She mounted the curved wooden stairs, the treads of which were grooved and worn. A cotton taste filled her mouth. Dry and bland. What if someone asked her why she was here? She had to think of something quickly. And she had to find out where Nessim Mamou had gone.

Above, the punching noise of machinery grew louder. Voices, in what sounded like Chinese, pattered from an open window. She peered closer. Across the well, open windows spiraled upward along the path of the stairs. Opposite her, one was cracked open. A dark-skinned man, his hair tied back, fed cloth into an industrial sewing machine. She could see mattresses behind him stacked against the walls.

Did these workers sleep here? Sprawl after work on the floor in buildings little changed from the fifteenth century?

The solid door opened in front of her and a muttered curse caught her before she could move. Several faces looked up from the pressing machines.

"What are you doing standing here, eh?" Nessim asked. With his long face and jowly cheeks, he resembled a basset hound. His brown suede jacket enhanced the effect, she thought.

"Monsieur, I'm looking for . . ."

"The showroom's downstairs," he interrupted, edging her toward the staircase.

"But you're the *patron*, of course," she said, managing a smile. Widening it and winking. "*C'est dur.* You're a hard one to catch up with."

"Like I said . . ." His eyes narrowed, looking her up and down. Sizing her up. Good thing she had the leather jacket on.

"I'm a location scout for Canalt + film," she said, improvising.

"The cinema?"

"A historical production, a made-for-TV drama," she said, injecting a world-weary tone into her voice. "You know, a sixteenth-century vehicle for Depardieu, his favorite kind. Good thing he plays the king, he's gotten immense."

In the dim light, she saw the man grin. Then frown. He had an olive complexion and wore gold chains around his neck.

"Why here?" he asked.

Good point, she thought, standing in this peeling arched hall-way, plaster crumbling onto the weather-beaten tiles and pigeon droppings coating the opaque glass. The sweatshop crew watched them.

"Cutting corners on a fast production schedule," she said, her voice lowered. "We plan to use parts of the Sentier, filming at night and on weekends when it's empty. Paris can be a cheap location with a local crew."

The man nodded. Cheap and quick, he understood.

She glanced around. "After all, the old wall of Paris ran through here, didn't it?"

She was making this up as she went along. But she remem-bered from her school days that Charles V had built battlements that crossed the present-day Sentier.

He liked that, she could tell. Maybe she'd just made a friend.

"Come with me to my office."

He locked the door with a slender long-handled key and ges-tured for her to go ahead. Now no one could see them.

She stuck Etienne's gun against his ribs. "Let's meet Jules in-stead." He tried to sprint past her but she stuck her foot out and tripped him. He crashed into the stone wall. She put the gun to his temple, rolled back the trigger.

"Where's Jules?"

He was breathing short and quick. "He didn't show up."

"Why?"

Nessim tried to twist away but she pinched a nerve in his neck and he went stiff with pain.

"That's just for appetizers." She pinched harder.

"I don't know," he gasped.

"You're Michel's uncle Nessim, aren't you?"

Surprise painted his face. He nodded.

"That's another reason I don't like you," she said. "But you're going legit soon. And all your little sweatshops, too. The ones with poisonous equipment that give people TB."

"What are you talking about?"

"I didn't like all those fake credit guarantees by the Kookie Mode company, which fronted for Michel's supplies, and the ordered merchandise that they never paid for, and then their filing for bankruptcy. You face seven years in Frésnes."

"I'll be a poor man . . ."

"But a happy one," she said. "Where's Jules?"

He shook his head.

"He was late. Before our appointment, he was meeting those old radicals."

"Action-Réaction?"

He nodded, his eyes fearful.

"Stay here for awhile." She shoved him into a dark alcove, and, grabbing pink plastic twine from boxes in the hall, twisted it around his wrists and ankles just as she had tied Etienne. Tight. She was getting good at doing this with a gun in her hand. "Think about how good you'll feel starting a new life after giving Michel that building with all new electric wiring."

She slipped Etienne's gun back into her backpack. Nessim's eyes popped. He started shouting. She pulled off his shoe, slipped off his dirty gray sock, and stuffed it into his mouth.

SHE WALKED quickly toward Action-Réaction, taking a shortcut through another passage.

From the far end of the dim, deserted passage came the sounds of the shops' closing up: the emptying of garbage, locks clicking. Suddenly a whizzing sliced by her ear and the half-silvered long mirror in front of her shattered.

A bullet . . . she ducked, fell over a trash bin and scrambled over the floor. A sharp pain sliced her calf then raced up her thigh as a glass shard cut her. Cloth and material scattered over the uneven tiles. Feathers and bits of fiberfill sprayed over her, like snow in July. She clawed her way over the damp material and leaned against the passage wall.

No time to catch her breath. Ahead of her the metal grate over the passage exit had been locked!

Footsteps pounded in the distance.

She pulled herself up on the protruding water pipe that snaked over the stone wall. As she dug her toes in where the pipes joined and gripped the rusted metal supports, she wished she was wearing high-tops instead of Manolo Blahnik heels. Every toe-hold hurt. But the only way out was over the passage's glass roof.

The tinted, metal-framed glass peaked above the locked passage. Grayish blue light dribbled over the dark storefronts, creating a webbed pattern on the tiled floor. The rusted fire escape at the far end was broken; she had no option.

She clutched the stonework, feeling the pipe sway dangerously below the oval mezzanine window that overlooked the passage like a balcony. Two floors rose above her. Below in the shadows, she heard the metallic click of a door.

She shimmied up the stone, reaching and pulling herself to the next window ledge, which was dusty and sharp. An ominous crack came from the pipe and she climbed faster, searching for toeholds, panting and praying. She tried not to look down but every few meters her grip slipped and her eyes locked on the dirty tile below.

Power tools, glass rectangles, and metal rods filled the walkway skirting the glass roof. She jumped onto the walkway, landing by a bucket of plaster, hammers, and saws. She stood and tried the window handle. Rusted shut. No way to get out.

Thuds and pounding shook the water-stained door on her right.

Whoever it was had made it up here by the stairway while she'd had to do it the hard way.

She reached into the pack for the .357 and used it as a hammer against one of the panes in the heavy glass roof. The several-meter-thick glass didn't even chip. She didn't want to waste bullets so she put back the .357 and picked up the nail gun at her feet, flicked the switch, and shot nails into the glass, which veined into rivers of tiny cracks, sparkling in the dim light. Panes quivered and then shattered.

Stooping, she was about to crawl through the hole she had made when an arm caught her and spun her around.

Gisela's face glistened.

"Like I said, I'm good at following up," she said, pointing a Beretta, like Aimée's, at her. "They belong to me. My mother died for them."

"The diamonds? Your mother committed suicide because her political convictions crumbled and she couldn't take prison anymore," Aimée said. "But wherever they are, you're welcome to them. Ask Jules."

"You're lying about my mother," she said. "Jules was supposed to be at Action-Réaction but he's not there.

Then were Gisela and Jules in this together?

"You killed Teynard," Aimée accused her. "Why?"

"Jules said he was in the way," Gisela told her.

So she had guessed right. Gisela and Jules were in league!

"Where's Stefan?" Aimée asked.

"That's where I'm taking you."

Was Stefan in on this too? "Gisela, you think outwitting two terrorists who've evaded capture for twenty years . . ."

"Stefan's gone soft," said Gisela.

Then there would be only two against her, instead of three.

Aimée knocked the Beretta from Gisela's hand into a sack of plaster.

Gisela grasped a long wrench, and Aimée followed its arc in slow motion as it sliced down toward her head. She ducked, pulled the nail gun up, and emptied it into Gisela's thigh. Gisela's screams resounded in her ears.

By the time Aimée could get sense from Gisela she knew she had to hurry or Stefan would be the next to die.

Tour-Jean-Sans-Peur . . . why hadn't she thought of it before . . .

Jutta and the renovation at Tour Jean-Sans-Peur! She made her-self run. Narrow rue Sentier lay deserted. She tried to ignore the pain in her leg and the sticky feel of her own blood accompa-nying her strides.

A crescent of moonlight reflected on the cobbles of the tower's courtyard. She climbed over the locked gate. The tower lay silent and dark, like a chess piece. Beyond the tower's entrance was the adjoining school construction site. As she went closer, dis-tant noises came from below the partially gutted tower—a mea-sured scraping, like digging. Moving behind a small cement mixer and pile of sand, she pushed aside a plywood barrier.

Inside, an incandescent work light, yellow cable and wire trail-ing from it, illuminated a stone floor. An arc welder, and forklifts were parked by a cordoned-off ventilation duct. Several holes in the floor were taped over and crossed by rebar scraps she'd barely noticed last time. Frigid air rose from the subterranean depths. She pulled the red leather jacket tighter over her cat suit and headed to the stone stairs. The smell of old stone and powdered plaster filled the stairwell. The stair treads were piled with big suction disks, the kind used by glaziers to move glass.

She pulled Etienne's .357 from her backpack and followed the scraping noise down the steps. Rusty-colored rebar of all different lengths poked out of the cement walls on the next floor. A gaping hole in the wall revealed a dimly lit tunnel. The scraping was louder now. She entered the curved, packed-earth tunnel.

Several bare bulbs lit the scene before her. Stacks of thick glass panes braced by a single two-by-four lined the vaulted stone walls. Ahead lay what looked like part of an abandoned Metro platform with an old cement control booth.

Suddenly, a deafening roar shook the walls. With the smell of burning rubber, a lighted train hurtled past. She jumped back as the squealing of brakes made her cover her ears. And that's when she saw Stefan, chipping with a shovel at the tiled wall.

A hand grabbed the .357 from her, pushed her face to the cold tile, held it there.

"Nice of you to return this," said Jules, Etienne's uncle, gripping her arms and putting the barrel to her temple. The smell of cigars clung to him. "Your mother was thoughtful, too."

"Showing off your mercenary technique?" Aimée asked, gritting her teeth, disgusted to think she'd found him mildly attractive when she'd met him in the Bourse. And then she'd slept with his nephew. The stupid things I do, she thought.

"Is my mother here?"

"You miss her, don't you?" Jules asked, pushing her toward Stefan. He felt in her pocket and took the Beretta. Gisela's Beretta.

Jules held both guns now.

Not only stupid, dead stupid.

Stefan's knuckles on the shovel handle were bleeding. He looked tired and beaten. "Aimée, why didn't you back off?" he asked.

Cold air rose from the dense earth. Crumpled Béghin Say sugar wrappers littered the cracked concrete. She thought back to the sugar spilled on her counter. A sweet tooth. "You broke into my apartment, but didn't find anything," she said.

Aimée looked at the curved arches, the platform, the small control booth, and saw how the lines intersected.

"If my mother was here with you, you'd know where to look for the diamonds," Aimée said. "She switched them on Jutta, didn't she?"

Aimée went on, not waiting for Jules to reply.

"But I know where they are now. You sent me the map."

Jules grinned. "So enlighten me."

"First, tell me where she is."

"If I knew that, I wouldn't have waited twenty years to come back," he said.

"That's not why ... Romain Figeac lured you to Paris. He

spread word in Dakar that he'd found you. That he'd expose you."

It was a good guess. Jules slapped her head, so hard she fell against a steel drum. Her whole body stung.

"Why do you think the diamonds are still here?" Aimée asked, gasping. "Wouldn't she have taken them long since?"

"Your mother cut a deal with the *flics* and turned our group in," Jules said. "Stefan and I got away. But when she got out of Frésnes, word was she never made it back here."

Jules's eyes shone with a calculating coldness.

"You're digging in the wrong place," she said, pointing to the area next to where the glass was stacked by the rusted metal lockers.

"Prove it," Jules said.

"Look in my backpack."

"Empty it, Stefan," Jules said, kicking Aimée against the tile wall. Jules pulled out the notebook. "Show me."

She turned the page to the one showing Emil and the platforms.

"See, the vaultlike lines are the same," she said. "And there's the treasure chest she drew. See what looks like an arrow? But it's pointing the other way."

Jules pushed her forward and threw down a pickax at her feet.

"Get to work," he said. He'd started the small cement mixer, which made a grinding noise.

And with horror she realized that Jules would make them do the dirty work, then take the diamonds and cement their bodies into some hole.

"After twenty years, do you think there are any diamonds left? It's crazy," she said.

"Tell her, Stefan," Jules said. He swatted Stefan with the gun.

"She told me . . . on the way to the safe house," Stefan said, his voice rasping. "We thought the *flics* were following us from the cemetery. There was a traffic jam, and all this Metro construction. Jutta and Beate jumped out of the car and hid the diamonds here, buried, by the tower, in the wall. They were going to come back and move them. But then there was a shoot-out."

"Why didn't they hide them in the coffin, too?" Aimée asked.

Stefan shook his head. "At the cemetery, Jana convinced them she had a connection who could fence the diamonds. So only the bonds were hidden there. Those were enough for me. But Jutta became greedy.

"After the shoot-out your mother was scared. I figure that she must have moved the diamonds. Jutta spent twenty years, plotting to find them when she got out of prison. When she saw the construction, she figured you would know where your mother had moved them."

Aimée's pickax hit something hard. And when the hole gaped open, she saw the metal box.

"You left the death fetish, the yellow feathers, to scare Idrissa, didn't you?" said Aimée.

"I learned a few things living in Senegal," Jules said.

"Etienne cultivated Christian . . . became his broker," she said. "But why?"

"Etienne's a good boy, my sister's boy," Jules grinned. "Smart. He sent me a new passport, has a deal for the diamonds already in place."

"Too bad he won't be joining us."

She took another swing and this time, the pick made a dull thud.

"Why?" Jules's eyes narrowed.

She wanted to stall him. "I tied him up," she said.

Jules turned and shot Stefan in the shoulder. He cried out and fell down.

"Pull the box out slowly," Jules ordered her.

She wedged it back and forth, easing it out of the hole, but it felt light.

He'd shoot her next.

Jules shot the lock off, stooped, and opened the box.

Empty.

Aimée rammed Jules with her shoulder and dove to the dirt. Her leg hit the two-by-four and it came loose. She scrabbled up on her elbows and tried to get behind the stack of thick three-meter-high panes of glass. Each must weigh several hundred kilos, she figured. They'd deflect the bullets.

But the stack of glass wobbled. One pane tipped and fell on top of Jules with a loud, shuddering thud.

"Get this off . . . me!" Jules gasped. The glass glinted, pinning him on his stomach in the dirt. He was caught under the glass up to his shoulders. Short of breath, he waved his arms. "Help!" And then the next glass sheet teetered and fell with a jarring crash. His chest was being compressed as the sheets of glass, like shimmering dominoes, fell on top of him, making the earth and the stacks of metal lockers jump.

Stefan tried to crawl away but fell bleeding onto the tiles.

Aimée kept her head down and curled up in the space where the stack of glass had leaned against the wall.

Then the metal lockers toppled over, blocking her way, jamming her behind them. All she could hear was moans, as Jules slowly suffocated to death.

She couldn't move, she was stuck.

Behind the old lockers was a hole in the crumbling cement wall, rebar sticking out. She tried to ease her way around them. And then Aimée knew. The backward arrow from the treasure chest pointed here.

Carefully, she reached in. She felt something damp and smooth. She pulled it out. The moldy smell from the Neufarama bag made her gasp, but not as much as what was inside.

SATURDAY

Saturday Early Morning

AFTER THE AMBULANCE picked up Stefan, and the *pompiers* of the emergency squad and the forklifts had cleared things away, Aimée hitched a ride to the Commissariat on Place Goldoni. Fueled on espresso from the nearby café, she asked the sleepy-eyed night clerk for Lieutenant Bellan.

"Not in yet," the clerk said.

"Hand these to him, will you?" she said, shoving several heavy, mildew-smelling Neufarama bags onto the desk.

The clerk's nose wrinkled.

"Please, make sure these go to the robbery detail and to Lieutenant Bellan right away," Aimée said. "But first I want them signed for and your stamped receipt."

She walked into the dawn, which spread like a golden yolk over the Seine. When her Tintin watch showed seven A.M. she punched in Edith Mésard's number on her cell phone.

"*Bonjour*, Madame Mésard," she said. "Refresh my memory, but does the state show leniency if a fugitive wanted for twenty years gives himself up?"

By the time Aimée made it to her apartment, Edith Mésard had struck a deal for Stefan.

"HOW COULD YOU TURN in all those diamonds?" René sat at his desk, shaking his head in wonder. "Our rent, the equipment we need, and the new insurance premium . . . !"

"I don't like *flics* remembering Papa as dirty," she said. "Or me. Sorry, but I had to show we weren't."

She tore the WANTED posters from the office wall, balled them into the trash. A breeze carried the Seine's scent through the open window. Lights twinkled on the distant quai.

"I understand." He nodded. "*Désolé*, Aimée, about your mother." He meant because he'd been right. She remained an enigma. And probably always would.

"Thanks, René," she said, not looking up. Keeping the pain from welling up again. "Seems I'm just not meant to know. But I owe you a new scooter."

"Don't worry, that beat-up thing . . ."

She reached into her pocket, then scattered a handful of unpolished rocks over his keyboard. "Think these will cover it?"

He picked one up, turned it between his stubby fingers. His eyes bulged.

"Have them polished before you get them weighed. Here's a ticket to Antwerp." She grinned, handing him a train ticket. "Belgians do world-class *moules-frites* and chocolate!"

THE SOFT evening air beckoned her and she walked slowly toward the Sentier, trying to ignore the three stitches in her leg. The life and bustle in this untamed part of Paris had grown curiously comfortable to her. Her steps carried her past the shadowy Bibliothéque Nationale. From a *crêperie* stand, she bought a Nutella *crêpe*. Then she wandered. Some time later she looked up and saw the old building where her family had once lived. Aimée mounted the worn stairs and stood on their old landing.

She knocked on the door. Silence. A peephole moved.

The wide wooden door opened. A small, stooped woman peered at her.

"*Bonsoir*, Huguette," she said. "It's Aimée. Do you remember? I lived across the hall?"

"*Mais oui!*" Huguette smiled and her face crinkled in fine lines. "Such a long time. Come in."

Aimée stepped through the foyer into the front room. Ceramic gnomes lined the shelves.

"Come to the kitchen, I was making some tea," she said, taking Aimée's arm. Her hand trembled and age spots covered her skin.

"I remember you taught me how to make apple cider," Aimée said, sitting down at the same table she'd sat at as an eight-year-old.

"Don't let anyone fool you," Huguette said, "we Bretons make the best, eh? I showed you."

They talked until the moon rose outside Huguette's window and traveled across the sky, only interrupted by Huguette's stroking of her gnomes every so often or her need to bring them in from the window ledge as it got late.

Aimée stood up, hoping it wouldn't be as long before she saw Huguette again. As Huguette made her painful way to the door, she leaned more heavily on Aimée's arm. She stopped.

"*Tiens,*" she said. "Something came for you. I almost forgot, but it was so long ago." She gave a small smile. "Sorry, but your papa wasn't good at keeping in touch."

Huguette opened the small hall desk, rummaged under some papers, and handed Aimée an envelope tied with a faded pink bow.

"See, I did that so I could find it when you came," Huguette smiled.

The envelope was addressed to:

Amy Leduc c/o Huguette Loisir

The faded postmark was illegible. All she could read was ". . . USA." The date was too smudged to decipher.

"*Merci*, Huguette," Aimée said, her eyes filling with tears, and kissed her on both cheeks.

She walked through the warren of streets, holding the envelope to her heart.

> Dear Amy,
>   I want you to know I think of you. All the time. You are my little girl. Always. But your life now is with Papa. Mine is somewhere else. You will grow big and strong and take care of yourself because I know you can . . . and you will.
>   Emil misses you, too.
> Love,
> Mommy

Under the luminous Paris moon, big hot tears dripped onto the ink, smudging it, but they were happy ones.

ACKNOWLEDGMENTS

Thanks and appreciation belong to so many: Jean Satzer, Dot Edwards, Grace Loh, always in my corner, merci, James N. Frey, the Tuesday gang, Mark Haddix, AIA, Dr. Terri Haddix, for her patience and humor, Isabelle and Marion, Tim Fewell and Joe Scannell of the San Francisco Fire Department, Mark Baenziger and Mark Miller on cyber patrol, and in Paris: Anne-François, for her generosity and spirit, Pierre-Olivier, the true *Sentier titi*, Elke, Martine, Jean-Jacques Cabioch and Stéphanie Pasquet, *agents de recherches privées*, Pierre Ottavioli, former Commissaire with the Préfecture, officer Cathy Etilé and Commandant Michel Bruno, of the Commissariat Central du 12ème Arrondissement, David, Hervé, Elise, Donna and Earl Evleth for the Frésnes visit, Bertrand, Linda Allen for her support, Melanie Fleishman for her encouragement, and deep thanks to Laura Hruska, to my son, Shuchan, who lets me, and, always, to Jun.